"A pure joy to read. . . . Medeiros combines humor and passion in her beautifully drawn characters, serving up a memorable story that will have you reading the last page with a sigh." —*The Oakland Press*

"Tartly spiced with bawdy references and sexy love scenes, laced with light humor and populated with a cast of fun characters, this latest not-so-Grimm tale should please Medeiros's sturdy fan base." —*Publishers Weekly*

"The irrepressible Medeiros pens another irresistible fairy-tale romance." —*Booklist*

"Plenty of fun." —*Kirkus Reviews*

"Sensuality and humor result in an entertaining reversal of the classic Sleeping Beauty fairy tale."
—*Library Journal*

"A delightful tale to remember and treasure."
—*BookPage*

"A perfect pool-side read." —*Cincinnati Enquirer*

"Medeiros has done it again. . . . The book is an un-qualified success. It has enough steam to satisfy any romance fan, but it also has humor, humanity and a message that lingers beyond the last page. It is a joy to read." —*The Lexington Herald-Leader*

"*A Kiss to Remember* is a story you will never forget. Medeiros cements her place in your hearts with another classic." —*Romantic Times*

"Delightfully funny and sometimes poignant . . . I found myself touched and smiling as I read this book. Teresa Medeiros has a smooth and polished writing style that was a sheer pleasure for me to read."
                                        —*All About Romance*

"Clever, funny, and touching . . . an absolute delight of a read that kept me thoroughly enthralled."
                                        —*Romance Reviews Today*

"A delightful romantic romp. . . . Readers will laugh aloud. . . . A very satisfying read from one of [America's] best-loved writers."—*Kentucky Monthly*

BANTAM BOOKS BY

Teresa Medeiros

A Kiss to Remember

Teresa Medeiros

BANTAM BOOKS

This edition contains the complete text
of the original hardcover edition.
NOT ONE WORD HAS BEEN OMITTED.

A KISS TO REMEMBER
A Bantam Book

PUBLISHING HISTORY
Bantam hardcover edition published July 2001
Bantam mass market edition / May 2002

Library of Congress Catalog Card Number: 2001025818

ISBN 0-553-58185-6

Published simultaneously in the United States and Canada

Bantam Books are published by Bantam Books, a division of Random
House, Inc. Its trademark, consisting of the words "Bantam Books"
and the portrayal of a rooster, is Registered in U.S. Patent and
Trademark Office and in other countries. Marca Registrada. Bantam
Books, 1540 Broadway, New York, New York 10036.

PRINTED IN THE UNITED STATES OF AMERICA

OPM   10 9 8 7 6 5 4 3 2 1

Dedication

To the memory of my precious Pumpkin—you were my miracle kitty who warmed my lap and my heart for thirteen years. I still leave your blanket out every night just in case you decide to pop in for a visit.

To the good Lord—I came to you every morning with a full heart and empty hands and you sent me away with more blessings than I could carry.

And for my Michael, whose every kiss is one to remember.

Acknowledgments

I would like to thank the entire staff of the Bantam Dell Publishing Group, including Anne Bohner, Amy Farley, Theresa Zoro, Betsy Hulsebosch, Susan Corcoran, Barb Burg, Yook Louie, and Irwyn Applebaum. I'd also like to thank Margaret Evans Porter, whose exquisite handouts on Regency courtship and marriage inspired my imagination to new heights. (So if I got anything wrong, don't blame her. Blame me!) I'd like to thank the writing pals who keep me sane—Jean Willett, Elizabeth Bevarly, and Rebecca Hagan Lee. And I'd especially like to thank Wendy McCurdy, Andrea Cirillo, and Nita Taublib. Cinderella only had one fairy godmother while I've been blessed with three.

A Kiss to

Remember

Prologue

Sterling Harlow had to draw up an ottoman and stand on tiptoe to peek out the drawing room window. He might have had an easier time of it if a plump yellow cat hadn't been draped bonelessly over his arm. His warm breath fogged a perfect circle on the chill glass. He rubbed it away with his sleeve just in time to see an elegant town coach draw to a halt in the curving drive of the whitewashed manor house. As a bewigged and liveried footman leapt down from the back of the coach and moved to swing the door open, Sterling leaned forward until his nose touched the glass.

"I've never met a real duke before, Nellie," he whispered, giving the long-suffering tabby who was his constant companion an excited squeeze.

Ever since his mama and papa had informed him that his great-uncle would be honoring them with a visit Sterling had spent every waking moment poring over his storybooks, searching for a picture of a duke. He'd finally settled for an image of his uncle as a cross between Odysseus and King Arthur—kind, brave, and noble with a red velvet mantle draped over his broad shoulders and perhaps even a shiny sword dangling from his waist.

Sterling held his breath as the coach door swung open, the sun glinting off the heraldic arms painted on its glossy canvas.

"Sterling!" His mother's voice crackled across his taut nerves, nearly sending him tumbling off the ottoman. Nellie sprang out of his arms, seeking refuge behind the curtains.

"Come down from there this instant! It wouldn't do for your uncle to find you gawking at him like one of the servants."

Deciding it would be ill-advised to remind his mother that they could afford only one servant, Sterling jumped down from the ottoman. "The duke is here, Mama! He's really here! And he's riding in a coach drawn by four white horses just like Zeus or Apollo!"

"Or the devil," she muttered, licking her fingers so she could smooth down the cowlick that always plagued his sunny hair.

As she brushed several cat hairs from his coat and retied his miniature cravat in a knot so tight it felt like it was choking the life from him, Sterling tried not to squirm. He wanted to look his best for the duke. Wanted to make his mama and papa proud. Perhaps if he did, his papa wouldn't spend so many nights in London and his mother wouldn't cry herself to sleep every night. Her muffled sobs had woken him more than once in the past week.

"There, now." She stepped back and tilted her head to study him. "You're quite the handsome little gentleman."

Without warning, her pretty face crumpled. She turned away, pressing a handkerchief to her lips.

Bewildered and alarmed, Sterling took a step toward her. "Mama? Are you crying?"

She waved him away. "Don't be silly. I've something in my eye. A cinder from the kitchen fire, I suppose, or one of Nellie's hairs."

For the first time in his young life, Sterling suspected his mother of lying. Before he could press, the drawing room door swung open.

Sterling turned, his mother forgotten as his heart began to pound in his ears.

Papa stood in the doorway, his blue-veined cheeks as ruddy as his nose. It usually took a winning night at the gaming tables or at least three bottles of port to put that feverish glitter in his eyes.

"Ellie. Sterling. It is my great honor to present my uncle—Granville Harlow, the sixth duke of Devonbrooke."

Impatiently jostling Sterling's father aside, the duke swept into the room, followed by a towering footman. To Sterling's keen disappointment, the duke didn't wear a dashing red mantle, but a severe black frock coat and knee breeches stripped of all ornamentation. His shoulders weren't broad but narrow and hunched, as if in imminent danger of caving in on themselves. A heavy brow shaded his pale eyes and a ragged tonsure of stringy white hair ringed the shiny crown of his head.

Sterling stared as the man's long, pinched nose began to twitch. He exploded in a violent sneeze, making them all flinch.

"There's a cat in here, isn't there?" His narrow gaze

raked the drawing room. "Remove it at once. I can't abide the nasty creatures."

"I'm ever so sorry, Your Grace. If I'd have known, I'd have shut her up in the barn with the other animals." Still murmuring clumsy apologies, his mother unlatched the window and dumped Nellie unceremoniously into the garden.

Sterling started to protest, but the duke shifted his icy glower from the cat to him, freezing his tongue to the roof of his mouth.

"How fortunate that you've arrived at teatime, Your Grace." A tremulous smile curved his mother's lips. "I've had my cook prepare an array of refreshments for your—"

"I've no time for pleasantries or dawdling," the duke said sharply, squelching his mother's smile. "I must get back to London as soon as possible. A man of my station has more important business than this to be about, you know."

As the duke advanced on him, Sterling's own nose began to twitch. The old man smelled even more unpleasant than he looked—like some moth-eaten undergarment that had been stored in the attic for centuries.

"Is this the lad?" he barked.

Sterling's father moved to stand beside his mother, slipping a bracing arm around her waist. "Aye. That's our young Sterling."

Sterling recoiled as the duke leaned down to peer into his face. The withering curl of his thin upper lip made it clear that he was none too pleased with what he saw. "A bit small for his age, isn't he?"

Papa's laugh was just a degree too hearty. "He's only

seven, my lord. And I was something of a late bloomer myself."

The duke gave one of Sterling's ears a tug, making Sterling thankful that he'd remembered to wash behind it. Before he could recover from that indignity, the man's bony fingers dug into his lower lip, stretching it forward so he could examine his teeth.

Sterling jerked away, glaring up at the duke in disbelief. He might have bitten the old man, but he was afraid he would taste even worse than he smelled.

Obeying a pointed nudge from his father, his mother stepped forward. "He's an obedient boy, my lord. And he has such a kind and generous heart. I've always called him my little angel."

The duke's snort warned them that he didn't place much value on those particular virtues.

She wrung her skirt in her hands. "But he's devilishly clever as well. I've never seen a lad so young with such a keen head for letters and sums."

The duke began to circle him, making Sterling feel like a succulent piece of carrion spotted by a hungry vulture. A moment of tense silence passed before the old man finally stopped and rocked back on his heels. "I've wasted enough of my precious time already. He'll have to do."

His mother's hand flew to her mouth. Relief washed over his father's face.

The heat of desperation finally thawed Sterling's tongue "Do? What will I do? I don't understand. What is he talking about? Papa? Mama?"

Papa beamed at him. "We've a marvelous surprise for you, son. Your uncle Granville has generously agreed to make you his heir. You're going to be *his* little boy now."

Sterling looked wildly from his father to his mother. "But I don't want to be *his* little boy. I want to be *your* little boy."

His uncle's yellow-toothed smile was more full of menace than any glower. "He won't be anybody's little boy for long. I've never believed in coddling a child. I'll make a man of him in no time."

Sterling's father shook his head sadly. "You see, Sterling, Lord Devonbrooke's wife went to heaven."

"To get away from him?" Sterling glared defiantly at his uncle.

His father's eyes narrowed in warning. "She went to heaven because she was ill. Unfortunately, she died before she could give him a son. He wasn't blessed with a little boy of his own as we were."

"The weak-willed ninny left me with a girl," the duke snapped. "A daughter. The chit's of little use to me, but she'll be company for you."

"Did you hear that, Sterling?" Mama clung to his father's hand, her knuckles white. "You're to have a sister. Isn't that wonderful! And you'll live in a grand mansion in London with lots of toys to play with and a pony to ride. You'll have the best education that money can buy and when you're old enough, your uncle will send you on a grand tour of Europe. You'll never again lack for anything." Tears began to spill down her cheeks. "And someday—many, many years from now, of course," she added, shooting the current duke a frightened look, "*you'll* be the duke of Devonbrooke."

"I don't want to be a duke," Sterling said fiercely as

his own shoulders began to shudder. "And I won't be. You can't make me!"

Thinking only of escape, Sterling darted around his uncle and sprinted for the door. But he'd forgotten about the footman. The man swept Sterling up and tucked him beneath his beefy arm as if Sterling weighed no more than a Christmas ham.

Sterling kicked and clawed in blind panic, deaf to everything but his own enraged howls.

Until he heard the clink of coins.

Lapsing into silence, Sterling blinked the tears from his eyes to discover that his father was clutching a fat purse that the duke had just tossed to him.

Malicious triumph glittered in the old man's eyes. "As we agreed, nephew, I've included the deed to Arden Manor. No matter what turn your luck at the tables takes from this day forward, you'll never again have to worry about being turned out in the street by your creditors."

Sterling went utterly still as understanding dawned.

They were selling him. His parents were selling him to this vile old man with his cold eyes and yellow teeth.

"Put me down."

His words echoed through the drawing room, stilling every motion. They were spoken with such authority that not even the hulking footman dared to defy him. Sterling slid stiffly to his feet, his eyes no longer wet, but dry and burning.

Granville Harlow's mouth twitched with reluctant admiration. "I'm not averse to a show of spirit in a lad. If you're all done with your histrionics, you may bid your parents farewell."

His mother and father came forward, as shyly as if they were strangers. His mother knelt by the door, his father's hand on her shoulder, and opened her arms to him.

Sterling knew it would be his last chance to wrap his arms around her waist and bury his face in the softness of her bosom. His last chance to close his eyes and breathe deeply of the orange blossom fragrance that scented the shimmering auburn wings of her hair. Her muffled cry cut him to the marrow, but he walked past her and out the door without a word, his small shoulders set as if he were already the duke of Devonbrooke.

"Someday you'll understand, son," his father called after him. "Someday you'll know that we only did what we thought best for you."

The sound of his mother's broken sobs faded as Sterling settled himself into a corner of the coach. As his uncle climbed in and the vehicle lurched into motion, the last thing he saw was Nellie sitting on the windowsill outside the drawing room, gazing forlornly after him.

Part One

The Devil hath not,

in all his quiver's choice,

An arrow for the heart

like a sweet voice.

—George Noel Gordon, Lord Byron

Chapter 1

*My darling son, my hands are
shaking as I pen this letter. . . .*

The devil had come to Devonbrooke Hall.

He hadn't come drawn by four white horses or in a
blast of brimstone but in the honey gold hair and angelic countenance of Sterling Harlow, the seventh duke
of Devonbrooke. He strode through the marble corridors of the palatial mansion he had called home for the
past twenty-one years, two brindle mastiffs padding at
his heels with a leonine grace that matched his own.

He stayed the dogs with a negligent flick of one
hand, then pushed open the study door and leaned
against the frame, wondering just how long his cousin
would pretend not to notice that he was there.

Her pen continued to scratch its way across the
ledger for several minutes until a particularly violent
t-crossing left an ugly splotch of ink on the page.
Sighing with defeat, she glared at him over the top of
her wire-rimmed spectacles. "I can see that Napoleon
failed to teach you any manners at all."

"On the contrary," Sterling replied with a lazy smile.

"I taught him a thing or two. They're saying that he abdicated after Waterloo just to get away from me."

"Now that you're back in London, I might consider joining him in exile."

As Sterling crossed the room, his cousin held herself as rigid as a dressmaker's dummy. Oddly enough, Diana was probably the only woman in London who did not seem out of place behind the leather-and-mahogany-appointed splendor of the desk. As always, she eschewed the pale pastels and virginal whites favored by the current crop of belles for the stately hues of forest green and wine. Her dark hair was drawn back in a simple chignon that accentuated the elegance of her widow's peak.

"Please don't sulk, cousin, dear," he murmured, leaning down to kiss her cheek. "I can bear the world's censure, but yours cuts me to the heart."

"It might if you had one." She tilted her face to receive his kiss, her stern mouth softening. "I heard you came back over a week ago. I suppose you've been staying with that rascal Thane again."

Ignoring the leather wing chair that sat in front of the desk, Sterling came around and propped one hip on the corner of the desk nearest her. "He's never quite forgiven you for swearing off your engagement, you know. He claims you broke his heart and cast cruel aspersions upon his character."

Although Diana took care to keep her voice carefully neutral, a hint of color rose in her cheeks. "My problem wasn't with your friend's character. It was with his lack of it."

"Yet in all these years, neither one of you has ever married. I've always found that rather . . . curious."

Diana drew off her spectacles, leveling a frosty gaze at him. "I'd rather live without a man than marry a boy." As if realizing she'd revealed too much, she slipped her spectacles back on and busied herself with wiping the excess ink from the nib of her pen. "I'm certain that even Thane's escapades must pale in comparison to your own. I hear you've been back in London long enough to have fought four duels, added the family fortunes of three unfortunate young bucks to your winnings, and broken an assortment of innocent hearts."

Sterling gave her a reproachful look. "When will you learn not to listen to unkind gossip? I only winged two fellows, won the ancestral home of another, and bruised a single heart, which turned out to be far less innocent than I'd been led to believe."

Diana shook her head. "Any woman foolish enough to trust her heart into your hands gets no more than she deserves."

"You may mock me if you like, but now that the war is over, I've every intention of beginning my search for a bride in earnest."

"That bit of news will warm the heart of every ambitious belle and matchmaking mama in the city. So tell me, what brought on this sudden yearning for home and hearth?"

"I'll soon be requiring an heir and unlike dear old Uncle Granville, God rest his black soul, I've no intention of purchasing one."

A bone-chilling growl swelled through the room, almost as if Sterling's mention of his uncle had invoked some unearthly presence. He peered over the top of the desk to find the mastiffs peering beneath it, their tails quivering at attention.

Diana slowly leaned back in her chair to reveal the dainty white cat curled up in her lap.

Sterling scowled. "Shouldn't that be in the barns? You know I can't abide the creatures."

Giving Sterling a feline smile of her own, Diana stroked the cat beneath its fluffy chin. "Yes, I know."

Sterling sighed. "Down, Caliban. Down, Cerberus." As the dogs slunk over to the hearth rug to pout, he said, "I don't know why I bothered going off to war to fight the French when I could have stayed here and fought with you."

In truth, they both knew why he'd gone.

It hadn't taken Sterling long to discover why his uncle wasn't averse to a show of spirit in a lad. It was because the old wretch took such brutal pleasure in caning it out of him. Sterling had stoically endured his uncle's attempts to mold him into the next duke until he'd reached the age of seventeen, and like his father before him, shot up eight inches in as many months.

Sterling would never forget the cold winter night he had turned and ripped the cane from his uncle's gnarled hands. The old man had quailed before him, waiting for the blows to begin falling.

Sterling still couldn't say whether it was contempt for his uncle or for himself that had driven him to snap the cane in two, hurl it at his uncle's feet, and walk away. The old man had never laid a hand on him again. A few short months later, Sterling had left Devonbrooke Hall, rejecting the grand tour his uncle had planned in favor of a ten-year tour of Napoleon's battlefields. His stellar military career was punctuated by frequent visits to London, during which he played as hard as he had fought.

"You might consider coming home to stay," Diana said. "My father's been dead for over six years now."

Sterling shook his head, his smile laced with regret. "Some ghosts can never be laid to rest."

"As well I know," she replied, her eyes distant.

His uncle had never once caned her. As a female, she wasn't worthy of even that much of his attention.

Sterling reached for her hand, but she was already drawing a folded, cream-colored piece of stationery from beneath the blotter. "This came in the post over five months ago. I would have had it forwarded to your regiment, but . . ." Her graceful shrug spoke volumes.

Proving her judgment sound, Sterling slid open a drawer and prepared to toss the missive onto a thick stack of identical letters—all addressed to Sterling Harlow, Lord Devonbrooke, and all unopened. But something stilled his hand. Although the fragrance of orange blossoms still clung to the stationery, the handwriting was not the gently looping script he had come to expect. A strange frisson, as subtle as a woman's breath, lifted the hairs at his nape.

"Open it," he commanded, pressing the letter back into Diana's hand.

Diana swallowed. "Are you certain?"

He nodded curtly.

Her hand trembled as she slid an ivory-handled letter opener beneath the wax seal and unfolded the missive. "'Dear Lord Devonbrooke,'" she read softly. "'I regret to inform you that your mother has passed from this world to a much kinder one.'" Diana hesitated, then continued with obvious reluctance. "'Although you chose to ignore her repeated pleas for reconciliation over the past few years, she died with your name on her lips.

I trust the news will not cause you any undue distress. Ever your humble servant, Miss Laura Fairleigh.'"

Diana slowly lowered the letter to the desk and drew off her spectacles. "Oh, Sterling, I'm so sorry."

A muscle in his jaw twitched once, then was still. Without a word, he took the letter from Diana's hands, dropped it in the drawer, and slid the drawer shut, leaving the fragrance of orange blossoms lingering in the air.

A smile curved his lips, deepening the dimple in his right cheek that always struck dread in his opponents, whether across the gaming tables or the battlefield. "This Miss Fairleigh sounds less than humble to me. Just who is this cheeky chit who dares to reproach the all-powerful duke of Devonbrooke?"

He waited while Diana consulted a leather-bound ledger. His cousin kept meticulous records on all the properties that had once belonged to her father, but now belonged to him.

"She's a rector's daughter. An orphan, I believe. Your mother took her in, along with her young brother and sister, seven years ago after their parents were killed in an unfortunate fire that destroyed the estate's rectory."

"How very charitable of her." Sterling shook his head wryly. "A rector's daughter. I should have known. There's nothing quite like the righteous indignation of some poor deluded fool who fancies she has God fighting on her side." He whipped a sheet of stationery from a teakwood tray and slid it in front of Diana. "Pen a missive at once. Inform this Miss Fairleigh that the duke of Devonbrooke will be arriving in Hertfordshire in a month's time to take full possession of his property."

Diana gaped at him, letting the ledger fall shut. "You can't be serious."

"And why not? Both my parents are dead now. That would make Arden Manor mine, would it not?"

"And just what do you plan to do with the orphans? Cast them into the street?"

He stroked his chin. "I'll have my solicitor seek out situations for them. They'll probably thank me for my largesse. After all, three children left too long to their own devices can only arrive at mischief."

"Miss Fairleigh is no longer a child," Diana reminded him. "She's a woman grown."

Sterling shrugged. "Then I'll find her a husband— some enlisted man or law clerk who won't mind taking a cheeky chit to bride to curry my favor."

Diana clapped a hand to her breast, glaring at him. "You're such a romantic. It warms my heart."

"And you're an incorrigible scold," Sterling retorted, tweaking her patrician nose.

He rose, the casual motion bringing the mastiffs to attention. Diana waited until he'd crossed to the door, the dogs at his heels, before saying softly, "I still don't understand, Sterling. Arden is nothing but a humble country manor, little more than a cottage. Why would you wish to claim it for your own when you have a dozen vast estates you've never even bothered to visit?"

He hesitated, his eyes touched by bleak humor. "My parents sold my soul to obtain the deed to it. Perhaps I just want to decide for myself if it was worth the cost."

After sketching her a flawless bow, he closed the door behind him, leaving her to stroke the cat in her lap, her brow furrowed in a pensive frown.

* * *

"Soulless devil! Odious toad! Truffle-snorting man-pig! Oh, the wretched nerve of him!"

George and Lottie watched Laura storm back and forth across the drawing room in slack-jawed amazement. They'd never before seen their even-tempered sister in such an impressive rage. Even the rich brown hair that had been gathered in a tidy knot at the crown of her head quivered with indignation.

Laura spun around, waving the letter in her hand. The expensive stationery was woefully crumpled from having been wadded up in her fist numerous times since it had arrived in the morning post. "He didn't even have the common decency to pen the letter himself. He had his cousin write it! I can just see the heartless ogre now. He's probably rubbing his fat little hands together in greedy glee as he contemplates snatching the very roof from over our heads. It's no wonder they call him the Devil of Devonbrooke!"

"But Lady Eleanor died over five months ago," George said. "Why did he wait so long to contact us?"

"According to this letter, he's been abroad for the last several months," Laura replied. "Probably off on some Continental tour, no doubt gorging himself on the shameless pleasures of any overindulged libertine."

"I'll bet he's a dwarf," Lottie ventured.

"Or a humpbacked troll with broken teeth and an insatiable appetite for ten-year-old brats." George curled his hands into claws and went lurching at Lottie, eliciting a squeal shrill enough to send the kittens napping beneath her petticoats scattering across the threadbare rug. Lottie never went anywhere without a herd of kittens trailing behind her. There were times when

Laura would have sworn her little sister was spawning them herself.

Laura was forced to make an awkward hop to keep from tripping over one of them. Rather than darting for safety, the yellow tabby plopped down on its hindquarters and began to lick one paw with disdain, as if their near collision was solely Laura's fault.

"You needn't look so smug," she informed the little cat. "If we get evicted, you'll soon be gobbling down barn mice instead of those nice, juicy kippers you fancy."

Sobering, George sank down beside Lottie on the settee. "Can he really evict us? And if he does, what's to become of us?"

Laura's laugh held little amusement. "Oh, we've nothing to worry about. Listen to this—'Lord Devonbrooke begs your forgiveness,'" she read with contempt. "'He sincerely regrets having been lax in his duties for so long. As the new master of Arden Manor, he will gladly shoulder the responsibility of finding new situations for you.'" She crumpled the letter again. "Situations indeed! He probably plans to cast us into the workhouse."

"I've never cared much for work. I do believe I'd prefer to be cast into the streets," Lottie said thoughtfully. "I'd make a rather fetching beggar, don't you think? Can't you just see me standing on a snowy street corner clutching a tin cup in my frostbitten fingers?" She heaved a sigh. "I'd grow paler and thinner with each passing day until I finally expired of consumption in the arms of some handsome, but aloof, stranger." She illustrated her words by swooning onto the settee and pressing the back of one plump little hand to her brow.

"The only thing you're likely to expire of," George muttered, "is eating too many of Cookie's teacakes."

Reviving herself, Lottie stuck her tongue out at him.

George sprang to his feet, raking his sandy hair out of his hazel eyes. "I know! I'll challenge the blackguard to a duel! He won't dare refuse me. Why, I'll be thirteen in December—nearly a man."

"Having no roof over my head *and* a dead brother isn't going to make me feel one whit better," Laura said grimly, shoving him back down.

"We could murder him," Lottie suggested cheerfully. A precocious reader of Gothic novels, she'd been dying to murder someone ever since she'd finished Mrs. Radcliffe's *The Mysteries of Udolpho*.

Laura snorted. "Given the unfeeling way he ignored his mother's letters for all these years, it would probably take a silver bullet or a stake through the heart."

"I don't understand," George said. "How can he toss us out on our arses"—catching Laura's warning glare, he cleared his throat—"on our *ears* when Lady Eleanor promised us that Arden Manor would always be our home?"

Laura moved to the window and drew back one of the lace curtains, avoiding her brother's shrewd gaze. "I never told you this before because I didn't want either of you to worry, but Lady Eleanor's promise possessed certain . . . *stipulations*."

George and Lottie exchanged an apprehensive glance before saying in unison, "Such as?"

Laura faced them, the truth tumbling out in a rush. "To inherit Arden Manor, I must marry before I reach my twenty-first birthday."

Lottie gasped while George groaned and buried his face in his hands.

"You needn't look so appalled," Laura said with a sniff. "It's rather insulting."

"But you've already turned down a dozen proposals from every unmarried man in the village," George pointed out. "You knew Lady Eleanor didn't approve of you being so persnickety. That's probably why she tried to force your hand."

"Tooley Grantham's given to gluttony," Lottie said, ticking off Laura's reservations about her potential suitors on her pudgy little fingers. "Wesley Trumble's too hairy. Huey Kleef slurps when he eats. And Tom Dillmore always has little creases of dirt in the folds of his neck and behind his ears."

Laura shuddered. "I suppose you want me to spend the rest of my life with some hulking bear of a man with no table manners and an abhorrence of bathing."

"It might be better than spending the rest of your life waiting for a man who doesn't exist," George said darkly.

"But you know I've always dreamed of marrying a man who could carry on Papa's work in the parish. Most of the men in the village can't even read. Nor do they care to learn."

Lottie twined one long golden curl around her finger. "It's a pity I'm not the older sister. 'Twould be a great sacrifice, of course, but I'd be perfectly willing to marry for money instead of love. Then I could take care of you and George forever. And I wouldn't have any trouble catching a rich husband. I'm going to be quite the Incomparable Beauty, you know. Everyone says so."

"You're already an Incomparable Bore," George muttered. He turned his accusing gaze on Laura. "You might have mentioned needing a husband sooner, you know. While there was still time to find you one who meets your exacting standards."

Laura plopped down on a creaky ottoman and rested her chin in her hand. "How was I to know that anyone but us would even want this run-down old place? I suppose I thought we could simply go on living here as long as we liked with no one ever the wiser."

Unshed tears stung her eyes. The sunlight pouring through the east windows only served to underscore the genteel shabbiness of the drawing room. The petit-point roses embroidered on the settee cushions had long ago faded to a watery pink. An unsightly mildew stain marred the plaster frieze over the door, while a moldy stack of leather-bound books was being used to prop up one of the broken legs of the rosewood pianoforte. Arden Manor might be a humble country house that reflected only a shadow of its former glory, but to them it was home.

The only home any of them had known since they'd lost their parents over seven years ago.

Slowly becoming aware that her brother and sister's dejected faces mirrored her own, Laura rose, forcing a smile. "There's no need for such long faces. We've an entire month before this Lord Devil arrives."

"But we've only a little over three weeks before your birthday," George reminded her.

Laura nodded. "I realize the situation seems hopeless, but we must always remember what Papa taught us—through prayer and persistence, the good Lord will provide."

"What should we tell Him to send us?" Lottie asked eagerly, bouncing to her feet.

Laura pondered her answer for a long moment, her pious demeanor at odds with the determined gleam in her eye. "A man."

Chapter 2

*It seems an eternity since I last
laid eyes on your sweet face. . . .*

Sterling Harlow was going home.

When he had summoned Thane's groom and ordered his mount to be readied that morning, he would have sworn he was simply going for a ride in Hyde Park. He truly believed he had no more pressing expectations for his day than to flash a lazy smile and tip his hat as he engaged in a series of mild flirtations with any lady who happened to catch his eye. That was to have been followed, as it invariably was, by a hearty lunch, an afternoon nap, and a night of gaming with Thane at the tables of White's or Watier's.

Which didn't explain why he had driven his horse into a feverish canter and was already leaving the congested alleys of London behind for the open country lanes.

The hedgerows and stone fences flew past, framed by the ripe green of the rolling meadows beyond. The summer sky was a dazzling blue with clouds grazing like fluffy lambs across a field of azure. Fresh air flooded his lungs, driving out the city soot, and making him feel drunk and more than a little dangerous.

He rode hard for nearly an hour before he recognized the emotion seething through him.

He was angry. Angry as hell.

Shocked by the discovery, he slowed the mare to a trot. He'd had twenty-one years to perfect the chill detachment suitable for a man of his station. And it had taken one sanctimonious country miss two minutes to destroy it.

He had tucked her letter away in the drawer of Diana's desk three days ago, never to be seen or read again. But her voice still echoed through his head—prim and waspish in its attempt to prick a conscience deliberately dulled by years of indifference.

Although you chose to ignore her repeated pleas for reconciliation over the past few years, she died with your name on her lips. I trust the news will not cause you any undue distress.

Sterling snorted. How difficult was it for Miss Laura Fairleigh to appoint herself his mother's champion? After all, his mother had given her a home.

She had cast him out of one.

It was only too easy to imagine the self-righteous little prig ensconced in the cozy drawing room of Arden Manor. She had probably sat at the rosewood secretaire to write the missive, tucking the pen between her pursed lips while she searched for a scathing turn of phrase with which to damn him. He could even see her smug siblings hovering at her elbow, begging her to read the letter aloud so they could make sport of him.

Perhaps after she'd sealed the letter with a tidy wafer of wax, they had all gathered around his mother's beloved pianoforte in the gentle glow of the lamplight to sing hymns and thank God for making them so morally superior to an unforgiving wretch like him.

The image brought him yet another astonishing realization.

He was jealous. Ridiculously, pathetically, ragingly jealous.

The emotion was utterly foreign to him. While he might covet a beautiful woman or a fine piece of horseflesh that belonged to another man, he had never suffered any particular hardship on those rare occasions when he was denied what he admired.

But he was jealous of the children who lived in the house that had once been his home. He hadn't even allowed himself to think of Arden Manor for years, but suddenly he could almost feel the prick of the thorns on the tangle of roses climbing up the whitewashed bricks. He could smell the piquant tang of his mother's herb garden and see a fat yellow cat drowsing on the back stoop in the noonday sun.

He felt a pang in his chest, uncomfortably close to his heart.

Sterling dug his heels into his mount's flanks, urging her into a gallop. They traveled several leagues at that grueling pace before he slowed the horse to a sedate canter. It wouldn't do to kill a loyal horse over a woman. His mouth tightened.

Especially a woman like Laura Fairleigh.

Sterling paused at a ramshackle inn to rest and water the horse before continuing on his way. The sun had peaked in the sky and began its lazy slide toward the horizon before the landmarks began to look vaguely familiar to him. He drew the horse to a halt at a lonely crossroads. If his memory served him correctly, the village of Arden lay just over the next hill, the manor less than a league beyond.

He would rather not endure the curious stares of the villagers if he rode through their isolated village on a sleepy Thursday afternoon. He also didn't want one of them rushing ahead to warn Miss Fairleigh of his approach. She wasn't expecting him for another month and if his years of sparring with Napoleon and his minions had taught him one thing, it was to take full advantage of the element of surprise.

Sterling guided the mare off the road and down a sun-dappled path. To reach the manor without being spotted, he would simply have to cut through the oak wood that bordered the western corner of the property.

As he neared the ancient copse, a smile quirked his mouth. As a boy, he'd fancied that the wood was haunted, home to any number of hobgoblins and sprites seeking to do him mischief. His mother had done little to dispel the notion, obviously hoping his fear of the forest would keep him from falling into a fast-running stream or tumbling down some stony gorge. His smile faded. She'd ended up giving him to a monster worse than any he could have imagined.

The wood was even darker than he remembered.

A thick canopy of branches tangled overhead, forbidding the sunlight, but welcoming the shadows. Sterling's eyes struggled to adjust to the primeval gloom. No matter how hard he tried to focus on the path ahead, he kept catching odd flickers of movement from the corner of his eye. But when he would turn his head, everything would go eerily still, like the air before a storm.

Without warning, a bird took wing from a twisted hawthorn. Sterling's horse shied nervously, nearly unseating him.

"Steady, girl," he murmured, leaning forward to stroke the animal's neck.

He'd spent the last ten years staring down the mouths of a madman's cannons. It was ridiculous that a deserted forest should so unsettle him. He should never have returned to this accursed place, he thought bitterly. He should have instructed Diana to give the manor to the sanctimonious Miss Fairleigh with his blessing.

He brought the trembling mare to a halt, struggling to rein in his own treacherous emotions. He might be traveling back to his boyhood home, but he was no longer a boy. He was Sterling Harlow, the seventh duke of Devonbrooke, and soon to be master of Arden Manor.

Sterling flexed his thighs and gave the reins a sprightly snap. The mare responded to his cue, setting an exhilarating pace as Sterling guided her through the maze of trees.

He leaned low over her neck to avoid the dangling branches, determined to leave the forest and all of his fears behind once and for all. Before long, he caught a glimpse of thinning trees ahead of them. Sunlight poured through the lacy canopy of leaves, gilding the air with the promise of freedom.

A promise broken by the ragged gorge that loomed up out of the earth, threatening to swallow him whole.

Sterling refused to panic. The mare had made jumps twice as long and three times as deep during foxhunts at Thane's country house. He had faith in her.

Until she planted her front hooves and let out a shrill whinny, informing him that he would be making this particular jump on his own. He went hurtling over the horse's head, the reins torn from his fingers. He had approximately a quarter of a second to be thankful the ground was padded with fallen leaves before he spotted the towering oak in his path. The last sound he heard was the dull thud of his head striking the trunk.

Laura had always loved the old oak wood.

She loved its wildness, its gloom, its bold promise of pagan delights. Although she'd known every rock and cranny of the forest since she was a little girl, pretending that she might still get lost within its shadowy maze gave her staid life the delicious thrill of danger it so badly needed.

As a child, she'd actually believed she might someday top a rise in the land and encounter a wizened elf sitting on a toadstool or find a fairy flitting amongst the glossy bracken. As a young girl, she had imagined hearing the ghostly thunder of hoofbeats and turning to see a bold knight on a pure white charger come galloping through the trees.

The wood was a magical place where even an orphaned rector's daughter was allowed to dream.

Laura sank to her knees in the soft loam beneath the spreading boughs of her favorite tree. Today she hadn't come to the wood to dream. She'd come to beg a favor of an old friend.

She closed her eyes, bowed her head, and clasped her hands in front of her, just as her mama and papa had taught her. "Um, God? I'm terribly sorry to trouble you, Sir, especially after having all of those uncharitable thoughts about Lord Devil"—she winced—"I mean, Lord Devonbrooke. But it seems the children and I are in something of a pickle."

Even when George and Lottie were tottering about with bad knees and wooden teeth, Laura would still think of them as "the children." She couldn't help wanting to shield them from realizing just how grave their situation was. Especially for her.

"I hate to be such a bother when I know I haven't been as faithful as I should," she continued. "Why, only last week I neglected my psalms two mornings in a row, drifted off to sleep before I'd finished my prayers, gobbled up the last scone when I knew Lottie wanted it, and snapped at Cookie for burning the porridge. Then when I scalded my cheek with the hair tongs, I said"— she peeked through her lashes to make sure there was no one around to witness her shocking confession—"a *very* wicked word."

The wind ruffled the leaves, sighing its disappointment. Perhaps a recitation of her shortcomings wasn't the best way to begin, Laura thought, nibbling her bottom lip.

"I wouldn't have troubled you at all, but if I am to thwart this Lord Devil"—she winced again—"Lord Devonbrooke . . . and keep a roof over the children's heads, it seems I must wed before my birthday. Which leaves me lacking in only one thing—a gentleman that I might marry."

Laura ducked her head deeper, her words spilling out in a rush. "So that's what I'm asking you to send me, Sir. A gentle man, a decent man, a man who will cherish me for all the years we shall live as man and wife. I'd like for him to have a warm heart, a faithful soul, and a fondness for regular bathing. He doesn't have to be terribly handsome, but it would be nice if he wasn't abominably hairy and had a reasonably straight nose and all his teeth." She grimaced. "Or at least most of them. I'd rather he not beat me, even when I deserve it, and I'd like for him to come to love George and Lottie as I do. Oh, and a tolerance for kittens might ease things considerably."

Deciding that it couldn't hurt to make a few promises of her own, Laura added, "And if you'll send me a man who can read, I'll see to it that he takes up where Papa left off." It only made sense that if God was generous enough to bless her with a husband, she should be generous enough to share him with God. Fearing she had already asked too much, she blurted out the rest. "Thank you for all of our blessings. Give Papa and Mama and dear Lady Eleanor all our love, and amen."

She slowly opened her eyes, gripped by a tingling sense of anticipation. She couldn't have said what she expected from the Almighty in that moment. Rolling thunder? A majestic blast of trumpets? Incredulous laughter?

She scanned the dazzling swath of blue visible through the branches of the towering oak, but the heavens seemed as far removed as the elegant ballrooms of London.

Climbing to her feet, she brushed bits of dried leaves from her skirt. She was already beginning to regret her hasty prayer. Perhaps she should have been more specific. After all, hadn't God already sent her several prospective husbands? Kind, decent village lads who would be proud to make her their wife and Arden

Manor their home. Men with loyal hearts and sturdy backs willing to work from dawn to dusk to keep a roof over all their heads.

Even tenderhearted Lady Eleanor, fearing the future could be nothing but bleak for an unmarried woman with a brother and sister to provide for, had chided her for spurning their clumsy but earnest proposals.

What if God now sought to punish her for her pride? What better way to teach her humility than to have her spend the rest of her days shaving Wesley Trumble's back or scrubbing behind Tom Dillmore's ears? Laura shuddered as a choking wave of panic rose in her throat. If God didn't send her a gentleman before her birthday, she would have no choice but to swallow her pride and marry one of the village men.

Half fearing that His answer to her prayers might be lurking in the meadow beyond in the lumbering form of Tooley Grantham, she turned away from the manor and plunged deeper into the wood. Between caring for Lady Eleanor in her last days and managing the manor since her death, there had been little time in the past few months to wander. Or dream.

The sun-dusted shadows seemed to beckon her forward. Even though Laura was old enough to know she was unlikely to encounter anything more dangerous than a cranky hedgehog or a patch of poisonous toadstools, she still found the wood's illusion of mystery irresistible. As she ventured deeper into the forest, the web of branches overhead grew more tangled, filtering the sunlight and lacing the air with a delicious chill.

As she wandered, her thoughts strayed back to her dilemma. How could she bear to wed a Huey or a Tom or a Tooley when she'd always dreamed of marrying a

Gabriel or an Etienne or a Nicholas? If she married a Nicholas, she could call him Nick when they had a lovers' spat and Nicky in moments of great passion. Of course, she'd never had a moment of great passion, but she remained optimistic. And he would call her by some pet name like . . . well, Pet. She was so busy pondering the charms of the imaginary gentleman she was going to marry that she nearly walked right into the rock-strewn gorge that bisected her path.

She was turning to go in search of a fallen log to use for a bridge when she saw him.

She froze, blinking rapidly. It wasn't the first time she'd had to blink away her fancies in this wood. As a child, she'd often had to pause and blink madly, turning a forbidding face into the gnarled trunk of an elder or a grizzled dwarf back into the squat rock he'd been all along.

But this time her frantic blinking was to no avail. She closed her eyes, counted to ten, then opened them.

He was still there, sleeping on a bed of moss at the edge of the gorge beneath the broad boughs of the oldest oak in the wood.

Laura drifted toward him, mesmerized. She might not have seen him at all if a stray sunbeam hadn't pierced the gloom, bathing him in its golden glow.

She knelt beside him, her dismay growing as she noted how still and pale he was. Her fingers trembled as she unbuttoned the top two buttons of his waistcoat and slipped her hand inside. The crisp lawn of his shirt molded itself to her hand with each steady rise and fall of his chest.

Laura didn't realize she had been holding her own breath until she sagged against him, going dizzy with relief. His heartbeat was strong and true beneath her palm. He was alive.

But how had he come to this place? Laura anxiously scanned the underbrush. There was no sign of a horse, no telltale hints of a skirmish. Had he been the victim of foul play? An attempted abduction perhaps or a highwayman's attack? Such crimes were almost unheard-of in the sleepy little village of Arden and the surrounding countryside, but then again, so were handsome strangers dressed in elegant finery. Laura rummaged through the pockets of his riding coat. His purse was still as intact as the mystery of his appearance.

It was as if he'd dropped right out of the sky.

She sat back on her heels, her eyes widening.

There could be no denying that he had the face of an angel. Not the plump, rosy cherubs Lottie was so fond of sketching in her primer, but the towering seraphim who guarded the gates of heaven with their flaming swords. His was a purely masculine beauty, strong of brow and rugged of jaw. His regal cheekbones and the hollows beneath them gave his face a faintly Slavic cast, but the ghost of a dimple in his right cheek dispelled any notion that he might be given to brooding.

Laura tilted her head to study him with a critical eye. Although there was a faint dusting of gold along the backs of his hands, most of his wavy, fair hair seemed to be growing on his head instead of out of his ears or nose. She leaned toward him, sniffing warily. The scent of some masculine soap—crisp, yet rich—emanated from his skin. She closed her eyes, breathing deeper. Even the earthy musk of his sweat was oddly compelling.

She opened her eyes to find herself level with his

nose. A nearly imperceptible bump marred its aquiline perfection, giving his face a winsome charm.

Laura sat back, shaking her head at her own folly. She was being as silly as Lottie. For a moment there, she'd actually allowed herself to entertain the ridiculous notion that he might be the answer to her prayers. But you couldn't just find a man in the woods and keep him for yourself. It simply wasn't done. She sighed wistfully, taking in the flawless cut of his buckskin trousers and the beguiling curl of his hair around his starched collar. Especially a man like him. A man like him would be sorely missed by whoever had been unfortunate enough to lose him.

Her gaze flew to his hands. He wore no wedding ring that might indicate there was an anxious wife waiting at home for him. Nor was there an ornate signet ring to provide a clue to his identity. She reached to touch his long, tapered fingers without realizing it, then jerked back her hand.

He needed a soft bed and a warm poultice for his head far more than he needed her mooning over him. She didn't relish having to explain to the local authorities how he'd perished while she wasted precious seconds admiring the chiseled curve of his smooth, firm lips.

Laura started to rise, then hesitated. She'd already lingered this long. Surely it wouldn't do any harm to steal a quick peek at his teeth. At least that's what she told herself she was going to do as she leaned over him once more.

With the sun streaming over his noble features, he looked as timeless as a prince who had waited a thousand years for someone to come along and stir him from his enchanted slumber. Gilded dust motes drifted all around the two of them like a sprinkling of faerie glamour.

Later, she would swear that she must have fallen beneath the spell of the wood, for that was the only explanation for the shocking impulse that led her, Laura Fairleigh, a pious rector's daughter who had never so much as allowed any of her suitors to hold her hand, to lean down and touch her lips to his.

They were even smoother and firmer than they appeared, giving her an alluring taste of strength and softness. Her breath escaped in a dizzying rush, mingling with his. Since she had never kissed a man before, it took her several dazed seconds to realize that he was kissing her back. His lips had parted ever so slightly beneath hers, matching the subtle pressure of her own. As the tip of his tongue brushed her bottom lip, a wicked thrill sizzled through her, warning her that she had finally found the danger she had been seeking all of her life.

His hoarse groan shocked her to her senses. She slowly lifted her head, even more shocked to realize he had been groaning not with pain but pleasure.

"Who? . . ." he whispered, gazing up at her with amber eyes fogged by confusion.

Laura couldn't have been any more mortified had she just awakened from one of those dreams where she was strolling down the streets of Arden wearing nothing but her stockings and her Sunday bonnet.

She shoved herself away from him, her words tumbling out in a nervous rush. "My name is Laura Fairleigh, sir, and I can assure you that regardless of how this appears, I am most definitely not in the habit of kissing strangers." She smoothed her hair away from her flaming cheeks. "You must think me the most shameless of hoydens. I can't imagine what came over me that would cause me to behave in such an outrageous manner, but I can assure you it will *never* happen again."

Before she could leap to her feet, he seized her by the arm. "Who? . . ." he repeated, his voice emerging in a desperate croak. His eyes narrowed as they struggled to focus on her face. "Who? . . . Who . . . am I?"

There could be no mistaking the pleading expression in his eyes. His fingers bit into her arm, demanding an answer she could not provide.

Even though she knew she was about to commit the most damning sin of her life, Laura could not stop the tender smile from spreading across her face. "You're mine."

Chapter 3

Sometimes I feel as if
you are a stranger to me. . . .

Over the years, Laura had entertained more than one fantasy of her betrothed arriving at Arden Manor to claim her hand. Sometimes he rode a glossy black steed with a white star emblazoned on its forehead; other times he emerged from a handsome carriage decorated with the ancient coat of arms of a renowned and noble family. But never once had she pictured him draped facedown over the back of a donkey led by an ill-tempered Cockney who had been blistering her ears with curses ever since she'd dragged him away from his flocks. Fortunately, even after nearly forty years in the country, the last twenty of which had been spent serving as Lady Eleanor's devoted man-of-all-work, Dower's accent was still so thick Laura couldn't make out most of them.

As the donkey plodded into the yard, Cookie came running out of the kitchen door to greet her husband, wringing her apron in her hands. "Oh, my heavens! What on earth happened to the poor lad?"

"Poor lad indeed!" Dower snorted. " 'E's probably some fugitive just escaped from the London gallows. 'E'll murder us all in our beds tonight, see if he don't."

"He's not a fugitive," Laura attempted to explain for the tenth time. "He's a gentleman."

Dower nodded sagely. "I knew just such a gent once— Gentleman 'Arry, they called 'im. Charmed all the fine folk with 'is pretty manners an' sweet talk—till they woke up with their nostrils slit an' their purses gone."

Looking doubtful, Cookie grabbed a handful of the stranger's sun-streaked hair and twisted his head to the side. "He has an honest enough face, I s'pose. For a gent."

The man groaned, no doubt protesting the indignities he was being forced to endure. Laura gently wrested his hair from Cookie's grip and smoothed it back down around his collar. "If we don't get him inside and tend to that lump on his head, I doubt he'll live long enough to slit anyone's nostrils."

She wanted to groan herself when Lottie and George came running out of the barn, trailed by a wobbling line of kittens. She had hoped to prepare them for the new arrival before they could fire a barrage of questions at her.

"Who's that?"

"What's his name?"

"Did he fall off a horse?"

"Did he tumble out of a tree?"

"Was he set upon by robbers?"

"Has he fainted?"

"Is he dead?" Lottie asked, gingerly poking at one buckskin-clad hip.

"You're not going to be able to tell from that angle,"

George pointed out, fingering the fine kerseymere of the man's riding coat.

"He's a gent," Cookie announced with no small amount of proprietary pride.

Dower shook his head. " 'E's a fugitive from the law, 'e is. Goin' to murder us all in our beds soon as we close our eyes tonight."

Lottie's round blue eyes brightened. "A murderer, you say? How delicious!"

Laura gritted her teeth, wondering what the good Lord hoped to teach her by cursing her with a family of Bedlamites. "He's not a fugitive or a murderer. He's simply an unfortunate traveler in need of some Christian charity." She snatched the hem of the man's jacket out of George's hand, her voice rising. "And I'll tell you what we're going to do. We're going to give it to him. And we're going to do it, by God, before he expires from neglect!"

They all stared at her, their mouths hanging open. Even Dower, who spoke profanity more fluently than he spoke the King's English, looked taken aback.

Recovering her aplomb, Laura gave her hair a prim pat. "Now I'd appreciate it very much, Dower, if you would remove our guest to the house without further delay."

Still grumbling beneath his breath about escapees from the gallows and having his nostrils slit while he slept, Dower obeyed, heaving the stranger over his shoulder. Although the old man was bandy-legged and his face was as grizzled and brown as a strip of dried beef, his shoulders, chest, and arms were thick with muscle earned from years of wrestling with Hertfordshire sheep even more cantankerous than he was.

The nearer Dower drew to the manor door, the bolder his tongue became. "Don't say I didn't warn you, missie. Mark me words, this divil'll be the ruin of us all, 'e will."

All Laura could do was trail behind them and pray the old man was wrong.

Moonlight bathed the stranger's face.

Laura sat in a chair beside the bed, wondering if he was ever going to wake up again. Although he seemed to be in no distress, he had barely stirred since Dower had dumped him on top of the chintz coverlet over seven hours ago. She checked the warm poultice Cookie had applied to the nasty lump at the crown of his head, then touched his brow, searching for any sign of fever. She was beginning to fear that whatever trial he had suffered had damaged more of his faculties than just his memory.

She had shocked everyone by insisting he be taken to Lady Eleanor's chamber. Although Cookie kept the room dusted and the linens aired, neither Laura nor the children had dared to breach its sanctuary since Lady Eleanor had died. There were simply too many memories of her last days with them hanging in the orange blossom–scented air—both bitter and sweet.

But the graceful half-tester was the most comfortable bed in the house and Laura was determined that their guest should have it.

She owed him at least that much.

At first Cookie had refused to leave her alone with him, claiming that " 'tweren't seemly" for an unmarried girl to tend to a gentleman in his bedchamber. Only when Laura had agreed to let Dower sleep in a chair outside the door, an ancient musket laid across his lap, had Cookie relented, although she had *tsk*ed beneath her breath all the way back to the kitchen. The old man's snores were already rattling the closed door.

The stranger lay sprawled across the coverlet, the feather quilt from Laura's own bed drawn up to his waist. Although Dower had removed the man's jacket at Laura's command, it had fallen to her to untie his cravat and loosen his collar. With his sun-gilded hair tousled on the pillow and lashes a shade darker resting flush against his cheeks, he looked to be more boy than man. But the haze of gold that was just beginning to lay claim to his jaw warned her that his innocent mien was only an illusion.

Laura desperately searched his face for any sign of animation. Had his flesh not been so warm beneath her hand, she would have sworn he was fashioned of marble—an effigy on the tomb of a hero who had died too young. She had yet to breathe a word of her plan to the children or the servants. If he never woke up, they would never have to know what a foolish dream she had dared to entertain. Now that she could no longer blame the wood's enchantment for her madness, practical considerations had begun to crowd in. How was she to convince him that he was betrothed to her? And how could she prove to herself that he wasn't already bound to another woman?

She leaned forward. His breathing was deep and even, his lips parted ever so slightly.

Her kiss had roused him once. Did she dare? . . .

He looked vulnerable in the way that only a very strong man can look when at the mercy of a woman.

He might very well have died in the oak wood if she hadn't found him, yet she felt as guilty as if she'd been the one to strike him this terrible blow.

Drawing the quilt to his chest, she leaned over and pressed a tender kiss to his brow.

He must be dreaming.

How else to explain the scent of orange blossoms, the gentle brush of a woman's lips against his brow? Something stirred deep within him, some hazy ghost woven from a mist of memories and dreams. But before he could grasp it, it drifted out of his reach, calling out what he thought might be his name in a voice that was too faint and far off for him to recognize.

He longed to pursue it, but there was a tremendous weight pressing down on his heart. He opened his eyes to find a fat yellow tabby cat sitting on his chest, peering at him with wise golden eyes.

"Nellie," he whispered, thinking how peculiar it was that he could remember her name but not his own.

He reached to touch her, expecting her to melt into the mist along with that other elusive shade. But her fur felt soft and clean beneath his trembling hand. As he stroked her, her purr rumbled through him, producing an echoing wave of contentment. His eyes drifted shut.

If he was dreaming, he never wanted to wake up.

Cookie bustled into Lady Eleanor's chamber the next morning with a washbasin loaded with rags tucked under her arm and a cheery whistle on her lips. As her gaze fell on the bed, the whistle died on an off-key note.

"Well, I'll be . . ." she whispered, shaking her head.

Sometime during the night, Laura had relaxed her vigil long enough to slump forward in the chair and rest her head on the stranger's chest. She slept the sleep of the utterly exhausted, her back curved at an awkward angle and one arm hanging limp off the side of the bed. The lad still slept as well, but with a hand cupping Laura's head, his fingers tangled possessively in what was left of her once neat topknot.

Cookie scowled. If the rascal had dared to compromise her young mistress in any way, Cookie wouldn't hesitate to bash him over the head with the washbasin and send him to sleep for good.

But as she crept nearer, her fears subsided. With their eyes closed and their mouths open, the two of them looked as innocent as a pair of toothless babes.

Cookie gave Laura's shoulder a gentle shake. The girl sat straight up, an unruly lock of hair flopping over one eye. "Oh, Lord, I shouldn't have gone to sleep. He's dead, isn't he?"

"Don't be silly. Of course he ain't dead! Why, your nursin' has even put a spot of color in the lad's cheeks."

Laura stole a look at her patient. Cookie had spoken the truth. His breathing was smooth and even, and his cheeks had lost their haunted pallor.

Cookie nodded knowingly. "All the lad needs now is a good scrubbin'."

"I'll do it," Laura said automatically, reaching for the basin.

Cookie held it out of her reach, her expression scandalized. "I think not, girl. It's bad enough I let you tend to him durin' the night. If I was to let you bathe him, Lady Eleanor would roll right out of her grave." She stabbed a finger at the bed. "I been married to that randy old goat of mine for nearly forty years now and I can promise you this young buck ain't got nothin' an old woman like me ain't seen a hundred times before."

As if to prove her point, she lifted the quilt, blocking Laura's view, and peered beneath it. Since he was still wearing those flank-hugging buckskin trousers, Laura couldn't imagine what made the maid's crinkled cheeks turn bright pink.

Cookie dropped the quilt, swallowing hard. "Old Cookie might have spoken in haste, but never you mind, child." Catching Laura by the arm, she steered her toward the door, sloshing water out of the basin with each step. "I've drawn a hot bath for you in the kitchen. You just go and get yourself all tidied up while I tend to your gent."

Before Laura's bleary brain could even form a protest, Cookie had closed the door, gently but firmly, in her face.

He must be dead.

How else to explain the brisk, impersonal feel of female hands against his body? He might not remember his name, but he did remember that female hands were designed to provide only pleasure: to trail across his skin with tantalizing grace; to envelop his engorged flesh in a vise of delight; to dig their flawlessly painted fingernails into his back as the expert rhythm of his hips drove the woman beneath him into a frenzy of ecstasy.

He had been touched in innumerably inventive ways by countless women during the course of his lifetime, but never with such perfunctory disregard. As these hands stripped and bathed him, they were neither rough nor gentle. They were simply intent upon the job they had set out to do.

He was left to draw only one conclusion. They must be preparing him for burial.

He longed to cry out, but his tongue had turned to stone along with his limbs. The final humiliation came when those indifferent hands peeled down his trousers and their owner let out an admiring whistle more suited to a cattle drover.

"Me mum always told me the rich was blessed, but I thought she was talkin' about gold." She leaned over to cackle in his ear, then actually patted him on the head as if he was some slavering lapdog. "You might have escaped the gallows, lad, but you was already well hung."

Several interminable minutes later, the bathing was finished and something soft and warm was drawn over him. He shuddered inwardly, believing it to be a shroud. His tormentor whistled a tuneless dirge as she bustled about the bed, gathering her supplies. A door clicked shut. The whistle faded.

For what seemed like an eternity, he was alone.

Until the door creaked open again, ever so slowly, sending an icy chill down his spine.

The devil had come for him.

Although their appointment was long overdue, he had always expected to meet the devil face-to-face on some smoke-hazed battlefield, not while he was lying dead on his back in a stranger's bed. And he hadn't even had the decency to come alone. Instead, the old rogue had invited along a legion of demons that bounded up on the bed and began to swarm all over his helpless form.

One of them seized his big toe and began to worry the joint between its teeth while another scampered up and down his legs in a gleeful frenzy. He might have been able to endure that torture if a third demon hadn't pounced between his legs, jabbing its needle-sharp claws into his most vulnerable flesh.

His eyes flew open. He struggled to lift his throbbing head, squinting through a chalky fog. It seemed the bed wasn't swarming with demons after all, but with rats. The jolt that gave his raw nerves was nothing compared to the shock of discovering that the devil wasn't a red-faced gentleman with horns and a pointed tail but a golden-haired, blue-eyed imp who hung upside down from the half-tester, peering intently into his face.

Without even considering the price his poor aching head would pay later, he shot straight up in the bed, bellowing at the top of his lungs.

Laura was basking in a tub of warm water behind a curtain in the corner of the kitchen when all hell was unleashed.

One minute she was half dozing with her head resting on the rim of the tub and her eyes closed; the next she was standing stark naked and streaming water in the middle of the tub, her every muscle tensed with shock.

The masculine roaring that filled the air was foreign to her ears, but she would have recognized the earsplitting shrieks anywhere.

"Lottie!" she breathed, her eyes widening.

Perhaps Dower had been right and the stranger *was* murdering them all. Surely having her pert nostrils slit was the only fate dire enough to justify Lottie's frightful squealing. Another voice joined the fray. Laura poked her head out of the curtain just in time to see Dower go charging past, pitchfork in hand and a steady stream of curses flowing from his lips.

Laura's panic swelled. If she didn't get upstairs, their guest might not be the one doing the murdering.

There was no time to towel off, no time to don the neat pile of underclothes she had laid out on a bench beside the tub. She jumped out of the water, wincing with pain when she hit her forehead on a copper kettle hanging from the rafters, then snatched up her clean dress and jerked it over her head. The pink muslin clung to her wet skin. Squandering only enough time to make sure the gown was covering everything pertinent, she untangled herself from the curtain and went flying, barefoot and dripping, through the hallway and up the stairs.

Laura was halfway to the second floor when the hellish cacophony ceased as abruptly as it had begun. She froze, gripping the banister.

Good heavens, she thought, Lottie must be dead! How else to account for the terrible silence that had fallen over the manor? Dread slowed her footsteps to a near crawl as she approached the yawning door of Lady Eleanor's chamber. She peeked around the doorframe, half expecting to find the faded carpet strewn with golden curls and bloody limbs.

A very different sight greeted her.

Lottie stood in the middle of the bed, clutching a squirming armful of kittens to her chest. Her bottom lip was trembling, her big blue eyes brimming with tears. Lottie's tears did not alarm Laura. The child had been known to work herself into hysterics because George ate the last crumpet at teatime.

But she *was* alarmed by the feral snarl on Dower's lips as he thrust his pitchfork toward the heaving chest of the man plastered against the wall between the windows.

Her heart leapt in her throat. It seemed Sleeping Beauty had awakened.

Although he was the one cornered and unarmed, he managed to look even more dangerous than Dower. His tawny hair was tousled, his eyes wild. Except for the quilt wrapped around his midsection and secured with a white-knuckled grip, he was as naked as Laura had been only minutes before. She stared without realizing it, distracted by his broad chest with its dusting of gold that arrowed downward to the tightly knit muscles of his belly.

He was forced to suck in that belly as Dower made another nasty swipe with the pitchfork. As the deadly tines passed just an inch from his flesh, he bared his teeth and growled low in his throat. Despite that primal warning, his helplessness tugged at Laura's heart.

"Put down the pitchfork and step away from him, Dower," she commanded.

"And give the bloody divil a chance to rip m' throat out? I think not, missie."

Since it appeared there was to be no reasoning with Dower, Laura fixed her hopes on the stranger. She sidled toward him, praying that he wouldn't interpret her outstretched hand as a threat.

"You don't have to be afraid," she said softly, her lips curving into what she hoped was a heartening smile. "No one here is going to hurt you."

Her words might have been more convincing if Cookie hadn't chosen that moment to come careening into the chamber, clutching a bloody hatchet. George was fast on her heels.

George rested his hands on his knees, struggling to catch his breath. "We heard the hullabaloo all the way down in the yard! It sounded like a piglet was being slaughtered."

"What in the name of Mary, Joseph, and Jesus is goin' on up here?" Cookie demanded, frantically scanning the chamber.

"Perhaps you should ask my sister," Laura suggested, shooting Lottie a frigid look.

"I didn't mean any harm," Lottie wailed. "I just wanted to steal a peek at him. Then he started roaring like a lion and frightened me half to death and I fell down into the bed and started screaming and—"

"The little imp put rats in my bed."

They swung around as one to gape at the stranger, surprised by the deep, cultured tones that had emerged from his mouth. Dower slowly lowered the pitchfork as the man shifted his glare to Laura's sister.

Lottie was the first to regain her composure. She nuzzled one of the beasts in question beneath her pointy little chin. "They weren't rats, sir. They were cats."

He snorted. "There's not much difference, as far as I'm concerned."

Lottie gasped.

Cookie came bustling over to draw Dower out of the man's reach. "There, there, you poor dear. I'm sure our little Lottie didn't mean to give you such a fright." Her motherly clucking might have been more soothing if she hadn't still been gripping the bloody hatchet. Following the stranger's wary look, she tucked the weapon behind her back. "Don't you mind old Cookie, now. I was just slaughterin' a nice plump hen for your lunch."

"Perhaps he'd prefer kitten stew," Lottie suggested icily, her snub nose tilted at its most haughty angle.

"I was rather hoping for broth of brat," the stranger shot back.

Laura didn't know whether to laugh or cry. "Please don't tax your strength so, sir. You've suffered a terrible shock. You're not yourself right now."

Everyone else in the room seemed to disappear as he turned that fierce gaze on her. "Then why don't you tell me who the bloody hell I am?"

Chapter 4

*But at other times, I feel as if
you must still be my precious little boy. . . .*

The emotion in the man's golden gaze was part
fury and part plea, underscored by a panic that was almost palpable. If she didn't act, and act quickly, someone in that room was going to blurt out something that
would make her plan impossible.

"Oh, you poor darling." Favoring him with her most
sympathetic smile, she stepped forward and took his
arm. "I can't blame you for waking up in such a
wretched temper after all you've been through."

His eyes narrowed as he stared down at her. "Why
did you call me darling?"

"Why'd you call him darlin'?" Cookie repeated sus-
piciously, drawing the bloody hatchet out from behind
her back.

Ignoring both of them, Laura turned, planting herself firmly between her guest and everyone else in the
room. "What he needs right now more than our fussing
and coddling is some peace and quiet."

The man snorted. "I hardly consider being accosted

by a pack of rabid cats and a hatchet-wielding harpy 'fussing and coddling.'"

Breaking free of Cookie's grip, Dower lunged forward. "I'll coddle you with this pitchfork, I will, if you speak ill o' me missus again."

Ducking beneath the tines of the makeshift weapon, Laura placed a soothing hand on Dower's chest. "He doesn't mean to be unkind. He's just exhausted and confused. Which is why I'm going to have to ask the rest of you to leave us alone."

Dower began sputtering anew. "You've gone plumb balmy in the 'ead if you think I'm leavin' you all alone with that savage."

"And a half-naked savage at that." Cookie gave the quilt shielding the lower half of the man's body a nervous look.

"Don't be ridiculous. You know as well as I do that he would never hurt me." Laura stole a glance over her shoulder at the large, glowering stranger, hoping she was right. He'd looked much shorter and less menacing while unconscious.

"If he lays so much as a finger on you, gel, all you got to do is scream and I'll come a-runnin'," Dower promised, brandishing the pitchfork in the man's direction.

"If she screams anything like her sister, I'll be the one doing the running," the man stiffly assured him.

Still grumbling, Dower and Cookie reluctantly filed out of the chamber, leaving Laura to retrieve Lottie and her armful of kittens from the bed. Lottie dragged her feet, sniveling most piteously until Laura leaned down and hissed, "March, young lady, or I'll give you something to cry about."

While she shooed Lottie into the hall, George continued to lean against the doorframe, a thoughtful glint in his eye. Her brother had always known her better than anyone else and he obviously suspected that she was up to some mischief. When she turned her glare on him, he ducked out the door, but his smirk promised her that his cooperation wouldn't come without a price.

"Sweet dreams," he called to their guest just before Laura closed the door in his face.

She took her time twisting the brass key in the lock, then slowly turned to face her companion. She was already wondering if she had made a terrible miscalculation. Even garbed in nothing but a quilt and a scowl, he looked about as helpless as a hungry lion.

"Why did you call me darling?" he demanded again, as if the answer to that question was of more import than how he had ended up naked in Lady Eleanor's bed.

"Just a habit, I suppose," Laura replied, her expression one of studied innocence. "Would you prefer I call you something else?"

"You might try my name." His steely tone suggested that she was already trying his patience.

"Your name?" She choked out a rusty laugh. "Well, we've never before had to stand on such ceremony, but if you insist . . ." Laura had always prided herself on her honesty. It was only by picturing herself trying to dig the dirt out from under Tom Dillmore's fingernails on their wedding night that she was able to softly add, ". . . Nicholas."

His bewildered scowl deepened. "Nicholas? My name is Nicholas?"

"Why, of course it is! Mr. Nicholas . . . Radcliffe,"

she added firmly, borrowing a suitably dashing surname from Lottie's favorite author.

"Nicholas Radcliffe. Nicholas Radcliffe," he muttered. "Damn it all! I can't seem to make sense of any of this." Slumping against the wall, he cradled his brow in his hand. "If I could only stop this infernal ringing in my head . . ."

Laura started toward him, drawn by genuine sympathy.

"Don't!" He flung out a hand, glaring at her from between the strands of hair tumbled across his brow. It was almost as if she posed more of a threat to him than a crazed Cockney wielding a pitchfork.

Catching a glimpse of her reflection in the mirror that sat atop Lady Eleanor's dressing table, Laura realized what a sight she must be. Her feet were bare, her cheeks flushed, her hair piled carelessly atop her head with dark tendrils tumbling this way and that around her face. The damp muslin bodice of her high-waisted gown clung to the gentle slope of her breasts. Torn between smoothing her hair and tugging her skirt down to cover the pale expanse of her ankles, she settled for awkwardly folding her arms over her bosom.

"We seem to have determined who I am. But that still doesn't explain who *you* might be." He cocked his head to study her, making her even more aware of her state of dishabille. "Or why you feel compelled to address me with endearments."

He obviously didn't recall their first meeting in the wood. Or their first kiss.

Since her folded arms no longer seemed adequate protection against his penetrating gaze, she tried to distract him by plucking one of Lady Eleanor's shawls from the armoire and wrapping it around her shoulders. "There's a bit of a chill in the air, don't you think?"

"On the contrary. I'm finding it rather warm in here. As a matter of fact, I'm not sure I'll be needing this quilt any longer."

As his fingers threatened to relax their grip, Laura's eyes widened. "You most certainly will! At least until Cookie launders your trousers."

The dimple in his right cheek made a brief appearance, informing her that he had only been toying with her. "Cookie? By any chance, would that be the harridan wielding the bloody hatchet?"

"Oh, you needn't be frightened of Cookie. She wouldn't hurt a fly." Laura frowned. "A chicken, perhaps, or any other animal that can be baked into a pie . . . but not a fly."

"I daresay you can't say the same for the man who tried to skewer me with the pitchfork."

Laura waved away his concerns. "You shouldn't pay any mind to him, either. He was just being Dower."

"He most certainly was."

Laura laughed. "Not *dour*. *Do-wer*. Jeremiah Dower, to be precise. He's Cookie's husband and sort of a man-of-all-work about the manor. Cookie has always claimed that his disposition is so sour because his mother nursed him on lemon juice. I'm sure he didn't intend you any harm. He probably believed you to be in the grip of some sort of violent fit. You've been drifting in and out of consciousness ever since they returned you to us."

"Returned me from where?"

"You really don't remember, do you?" Sighing dolefully, Laura plucked at the row of silk rosettes adorning her bodice to avoid looking him in the eye. "The doctor warned us that it might be this way."

"And what doctor would that be?"

"Why, Dr. . . . Dr. Drayton from London. You see, Arden doesn't have a physician of its own, although Tooley Grantham, the blacksmith, has been known to lance a boil or pull an abscessed tooth if the occasion demands it. So it was this Dr. Drayton who told us that it wasn't uncommon for a man to experience some degree of memory loss after suffering such a traumatic injury in the woo—" She barely stopped herself from saying "wood"—"in the *war*."

"The war?" he repeated softly. "I remember the war."

"You do?" Laura forgot to hide her surprise.

He had slumped against the wall again, his eyes clouding as if with the smoke from a distant battlefield. "I remember the smell of the gunpowder, the shouting . . . the thunder of the cannons."

"You . . . you were with the infantry. You were quite the hero, we've been told. Which is why you stormed up that hill at Waterloo and tried to capture one of the French cannons after its fuse had already been lit."

He straightened. "Are you sure I was a hero? That sounds more like the action of an addlepated lackwit."

"Oh, it was very brave! Had the impact occurred another foot to the left, you would have been blown to bits instead of being thrown clear of the worst of it. Of course, you might have escaped injury altogether if you hadn't . . . hadn't . . . landed on your head," she finished quickly, pained to discover that she possessed a talent for lying that might actually exceed Lottie's.

He massaged his brow with those long, elegant fingers of his. "I suppose that would explain this devil of a headache."

Laura nodded cheerfully. "It certainly would. We were beginning to wonder if you'd ever regain full consciousness."

"But now I have." He lowered his hand.

"Yes," she agreed, unnerved by the contrast between the silk of his voice and the predatory glint in his eye.

"With you."

"With me," Laura echoed, backing into a three-legged occasional table. How on earth was he managing to stalk her without taking a single step in her direction?

"Whoever the hell *you* are!" he suddenly thundered, making her flinch.

The table behind her teetered dangerously. She turned to steady it, stalling for time. It had taken negligible effort to lie about *his* name. So why was she finding it nearly impossible to tell the truth about hers? She toyed with the items on the table, trailing her fingers over a satin pincushion and a pewter thimble. When her hand absently came to rest against the worn leather cover of Lady Eleanor's Bible, she nearly snatched it back in shame. But a surge of defiance stopped her. She had asked God to send her a man and He had. How could it be a sin to keep him?

Swallowing the last of her misgivings, Laura turned and met his burning gaze with a cool aplomb that surprised even her. "Don't you remember me, darling? I'm Laura Fairleigh. Your betrothed."

His rugged jaw and regal cheekbones could have been cast in granite. He didn't even blink. "We're engaged?"

Laura nodded.

"To be married?"

She nodded again, this time with a doting smile.

He closed his eyes and began to slide down the wall.

Laura made a small sound of dismay. She hadn't expected her lie to strike him a fatal blow. All the gold drained from his skin, revealing just how much the effort of staying on his feet that long had already cost him. This time he didn't protest when she came rushing to his aid, although he did muster enough strength to pry open his eyes and glare at her through his lashes.

Laura caught him before he hit the floor, no easy task considering he must have outweighed her by at least five stone. It was only by wrapping one arm around his waist and bracing his shoulder with her own that she was able to keep him on his feet. Locked in that awkward embrace, they staggered toward the bed in a graceless waltz. She tried to ease him to the mattress, but the slick chintz of the coverlet gave her no choice but to half tumble into the bed with him.

She lay there in a gasping heap, her arm still trapped beneath his weight. She couldn't have said whether her shortness of breath was due to exertion or the heated press of all of that smooth, bare male flesh against her side.

"It's fortunate that we're already engaged," he said dryly, his warm breath tickling her ear. "If that manservant of yours caught us in this predicament, I suspect I'd be marrying you at the point of a pitchfork."

Wrenching her arm free, Laura shoved herself to a

sitting position on the bed. She tucked a wayward curl back into her topknot, her cheeks burning. "Don't be silly. Dower knows as well as I do that you're not the sort of man who would compromise his fiancée's virtue."

"I'm not?" He frowned up at her. "Are you absolutely certain about that?"

"Of course I am," she assured him. "You've always behaved with perfect decorum."

Groaning, he flung an arm over his brow. "No wonder I was trying to throw myself in front of that cannon. I had no reason to live."

With those piercing eyes of his hidden, Laura was free to study the beguiling curve of his lips. Free to remember the tantalizing kiss they'd shared in the wood.

"You had the best reason of all," she said softly. "So you could return to me."

He lowered his arm. An emotion even more disquieting than suspicion glimmered in the depths of his eyes. "Just how long have we been apart?"

"Almost a year, I suppose." Laura ducked her head, beset by both shyness and shame. "Although it feels more like a lifetime."

"Yet you waited for me."

She met his eyes. "I would have waited forever for you."

A spasm of bewilderment crossed his face. It was almost as if that tiny kernel of truth was more unkind than all of her lies. As he moved to cup her cheek in his hand, she realized it had been a mistake not to escape his reach when she'd had the chance. She doubted she could move now if the bedclothes beneath them burst into flames.

His fingers were only an inch from her cheek when he let out a startled yelp.

A yellow tabby kitten, all ears and gangly paws, was scrambling up his right thigh, its claws digging into the quilt with each exuberant bounce. Relieved by the distraction, Laura scooped up the tiny cat, cradling its fat, furry belly in her palm. "This one's so small my sister must have missed it."

"Get it out of here, please," he said through gritted teeth. "I can't abide the beasts."

Rubbing the kitten's downy fur against her cheek, Laura beamed at him. "I'm afraid your memory is failing you again. You adore kittens."

His eyes widened. "I do?"

She nodded. He watched with visible horror as she deposited the wriggling kitten on his chest. Man and cat eyed each other with equal mistrust for a tense moment before the kitten finally yawned, stretched, then curled itself into a purring heap, making a cozy nest of his breastbone.

He shook his head. "I suppose next you'll be telling me I adore that insufferable little brat who set the cats upon me in the first place."

Laura chose her words with care. "Despite your occasional clash of wills, you and Lottie have always been quite fond of each other."

Closing his eyes, he turned his face away from her as if that last revelation was more than any man could be expected to endure. Laura gently drew the quilt up over his chest, stopping just short of where the kitten napped. "You've had more than enough excitement for one day. You need to conserve your strength."

She was turning to go when he caught her wrist in

his hand. His thumb brushed the sensitive skin at its inner curve in a motion dangerously near a caress. "Laura?"

She drew in a shaky breath. "Sir?"

"Do I adore you as well?"

Her only defense against the rush of wistfulness his words invoked was to make light of them. Wrinkling her nose in a mischievous smile, she said, "Of course you adore me. How could you resist?"

Laura slipped free of his grip and made her escape, hoping it wasn't too soon to begin congratulating herself on her own cleverness.

"She's lying through her pretty white teeth."

Since there was no one else in attendance, the man on the bed was forced to address his cynical observation to the ball of golden fluff nesting on his chest. The kitten stirred itself from its nap, eyeing him with drowsy interest.

He reached to stroke the velvety triangle between the creature's ears. Despite his initial reluctance, the motion felt oddly familiar, as if he'd done it a hundred times in the past. "I know she's lying, but how am I to prove it when I can't remember the truth?"

The kitten's eyes began to droop. Its mouth opened in a gaping pink yawn.

"You haven't the least bit of interest in what I'm saying, have you? You're just indulging me by pretending to listen." Ignoring the cat's affronted mew, he lifted it over his head and peered beneath its belly. "Female," he pronounced, shaking his head in disgust. "I should have known."

He sent the kitten trundling toward the footboard with a pat on the rump, then sat up and eased his legs over the side of the bed. A fresh wave of vertigo washed over him, making the room spin. He dropped his throbbing brow into his hands. It would have hurt less had the blasted cannonball taken his head clean off.

When the throbbing began to subside, he cautiously peered around the bedchamber. Overall, its air was one of faded gentility—shabby, but not unwelcoming. The walls weren't hung with silk but papered in a pattern of pale roses he suspected had once been pink. A threadbare rug covered most of the wooden floor. The room's furniture consisted of a chair, a mahogany tallboy fitted with drawers, a dressing table, a washstand crowned by a porcelain bowl and pitcher, and an occasional table that was probably a castoff from some refitted drawing room. Not even a fresh coat of beeswax, lovingly applied, could disguise the fact that most of the color had been leached out of the wood by time and repeated polishings.

As he breathed deeply of the orange blossom fragrance that scented the air, another wave of dizziness enveloped him. He closed his eyes and waited for it to pass. He couldn't accuse Laura of lying about one thing—he knew this place. He knew the white-and-gold fluted columns that supported the half-tester and the chipped stone of the hearth. He knew the shadows that gathered beneath the corner gables and the slant of the morning sun through the glass of the tall windows. There was a sense of rightness here that even he couldn't deny. Everything about the room was familiar.

Everything but him.

He slowly rose, taking care to secure the quilt

around his waist. The dressing table with its brocaded stool and oval mirror seemed a hundred leagues away and he didn't want to be caught off guard by any more surprise visitors. Each shuffling step sent a thunderbolt of pain through his skull. By the time he arrived at the table and sank gratefully down on the stool, his skin was clammy with sweat and his hands were trembling.

He gripped the edge of the table, waiting for them to steady. Not quite ready to face the mirror, he studied the surface of the dressing table instead. There was an air of charming disarray about it, making it appear that a lady had just finished her toilette and might wander back into the room at any time. A paper of pins lay open, their pearl heads spilling across a thin dusting of rice powder. A silver-backed hairbrush still held several threads of auburn hair interwoven with gray. He lifted the stopper from a bottle of scent. The heady scent of orange blossoms filled him with an ineffable sense of loss.

Spilling out of a lacquered box was a gold locket inlaid with mother-of-pearl. He drew it into his hands, fumbling with the delicate hasp. A lock of blond, baby-fine hair had been tenderly tucked inside the graceful oval. He wondered if anyone had ever cherished him enough to preserve such a memento of his innocence. Snapping the locket shut, he dropped it back in the box.

He couldn't avoid the man in the mirror forever. Drawing in a shaky breath, he leaned forward, desperate for any glimmer of recognition.

A stranger gazed back at him.

He wanted to recoil, but couldn't. He was too fascinated by the wild-haired, wary-eyed satyr who inhabited the mirror. He possessed a face most of society would call irresistibly handsome if they didn't mind the hint of arrogance in his brow or the sardonic slashes framing his mouth. It was the face of a man accustomed to getting what he wanted, the sort of face that would wield power in this world, not by virtue of its goodness or character but because of the sheer physical force of its fluid planes and angles. He had to admit that it was a remarkably compelling face.

He just wasn't sure it was one he cared to wear.

Regardless of what Laura claimed, it did not appear to be the face of a man who behaved with perfect decorum toward his betrothed.

"How do you do," he said to the man in the mirror. "My name is Nicholas. Nicholas . . . Radcliffe." He frowned. The name felt as strange and thick to his tongue as a foreign language. "I'm Mr. Nicholas Radcliffe," he repeated forcefully, "and this is my fiancée, Miss Laura Fairleigh."

There. That felt a bit more natural. Her name rolled off his tongue with the familiarity of a well-loved song.

He ran a hand over the golden whiskers stubbling his jaw. What on earth had those two dim-witted servants been thinking to leave an innocent girl at the mercy of a man who looked like him?

If she *was* innocent, that is.

With that faintly snubbed nose that crinkled when she smiled and the smattering of freckles across her sun-kissed cheeks, she certainly looked the part. The thick brown hair piled atop her head had held just a hint of curl while her sable eyebrows arched over eyes as rich and sweet as a vat of melted chocolate.

She was no beauty, but she was the prettiest woman he had ever seen. "Bloody hell," he muttered, glaring at his reflection, "for all you can remember, she's the *only* woman you've ever seen." Unless you counted the harpy with the hatchet and the faint shadow of a mustache on her upper lip—something he most certainly wasn't inclined to do.

The glint in the eye of the stranger in the mirror was unmistakably cynical. He would advise a woman to lie to such a man only at her own peril.

So why was Laura Fairleigh willing to take the risk? He couldn't even say why he was so sure she was lying to him. Some instinct deeper than memory seemed to be warning him. Perhaps she wasn't lying so much as not revealing the whole truth. Was their betrothal an arranged one, lacking in true affection? Or had they had a nasty quarrel before he last went off to battle? His next thought left him feeling strangely cold.

Perhaps she had been unfaithful to him in his absence. Perhaps she'd grown weary of waiting for him to return and sought solace in the arms of another man.

Guilt would explain her stammering, her reluctance to meet his eyes, the way her pulse had raced beneath his fingertips when he had caressed the silky skin of her wrist.

But so would shyness. If they'd been apart for as long as she'd implied, it would only be natural for his physical nearness to intimidate her. Perhaps, like any maiden, she was simply waiting for him to woo her back into his arms with pretty words and chaste kisses.

Remembering the way the rosy pink muslin of her gown had clung to her rosy pink skin, he was forced to admit that he just might enjoy devoting himself to such a task. His fiancée might be as slender and long limbed as a colt, but her curves possessed a woman's alluring grace. He'd learned that in the moment they'd tumbled into the bed together and her high, firm breasts had come to press against his side. He adjusted the quilt, discovering that it wasn't as much of a relief as he'd hoped to have something other than his head throbbing.

"Well, Nicholas, my man," he said to his rueful reflection. "Until your memory returns, I suppose you've no choice but to bide your time and get to know both yourself and your young bride-to-be."

His fiancée might be hoping to trap him in a web of lies, but one undeniable gem of truth hung in its glistening threads—Laura Fairleigh would not be a difficult woman to adore.

Chapter 5

Missing you has driven me
nearly mad with grief. . . .

Have you lost your wits, child?" Cookie wailed, plopping down on a bale of hay. "You can't just up and marry a stranger."

George pounded his fist on the splintered bench he was straddling. "She certainly can't! Because I'm the man of this family and I damn well won't allow it!"

"Don't swear, George," Laura said automatically.

Dower reached down and gave George's ears a gentle box. "You 'eard your sister, lad. Don't swear. It ain't Christian. And besides, if anyone round 'ere is to stop 'er from marryin' the swivin' bastard, it'll be me."

Laura sighed. Taking into account George's tendency to be overprotective, Lottie's inability to whisper, and Dower's colorful vocabulary, she had decided to call a family meeting in the barn, well out of earshot of the object of their discussion. After she'd outlined her plan with what she believed was the perfect mix of brilliant ingenuity and irrefutable logic, they had all erupted with varying degrees of disbelief and outrage, proving her instincts sound. Even the aged milk cow hanging her head over the stall Dower was leaning against blinked her liquid brown eyes and let out a reproachful moo.

From the nest she'd made for herself and her kittens in the hayloft, Lottie began to sniffle, the usual precursor to noisy sobs. "What will happen to us if he finds out we've lied to him? Suppose he summons the authorities and has us hung?"

"Hanged," Laura corrected gently.

Dower snorted. "And 'ow's 'e to bring the hauthorities down on our 'eads when 'e's prob'ly a fugitive from the law 'isself? A clever gent loik 'im ain't goin' to risk gettin' 'isself 'anged."

"He'll never believe us," George predicted glumly.

"Of course he will," Laura insisted. "You just have to get into the spirit of the thing. It won't be one whit different from the theatricals Lady Eleanor helped us put on for the village children every Christmas. Why, everyone has always said that Lottie's portrayal of the Baby Jesus was wrenching enough to bring a tear to the eye of even the staunchest heathen."

"It brung a tear to my eye," Dower said. "'Specially when I 'ad to tote a babe wot weighed over five stone to the manger." He rubbed at his lower back. "Me lumbago's been plaguin' me ever since."

"At least you didn't have to try to convince them village brats you was a virgin," Cookie said. "When I gave that fancy speech 'bout never havin' known a man, Abel Grantham laughed so hard he fell off his donkey into the manger and nearly crushed poor Baby Jesus."

Laura remembered the incident only too well. She had been the one who had rushed forward to drag a sputtering Abel off a howling Lottie. No amount of frankincense and myrrh could have covered up the stench of whiskey on the Wise Man's breath.

Reluctant to remind them of the other disasters that had occurred during their amateur theatricals, such as the time Dower's smoldering pipe had set George's turban afire or the night the flocks had escaped their shepherds and wandered bleating through the aisles of the village church, Laura pasted on a cheerful smile. "That's exactly how you should see our latest endeavor. As naught but a harmless bit of playacting."

Cookie shook her head sorrowfully. "What you're proposin' ain't playactin', child. It's lyin'. And no good ever come from lyin' to a man." She shot the barn door an uneasy look. "Especially a man such as that one."

Laura's cheery smile vanished. "That may be true, Cookie. But I'm fully convinced that even less good can come from telling the truth."

They all stared at her, taken aback by the steely edge in her voice.

As Laura began to pace between the stalls, the only sound that accompanied her was the fluttering of the swallows that roosted in the eaves. "As I see it, we're running out of choices. Since I have no intention of marrying one of the men from the village and being miserable for the rest of my life, our only other option is to entrust our future to the hands of Sterling Harlow. And I doubt they call him the Devil of Devonbrooke for naught. The last thing I wanted to do was frighten you, but have any of you really stopped to ponder what manner of *situations* a man like that might arrange for us?"

Resting her hand on a splintery post, Laura peered up into the loft. Her sister's eyes glistened down at her from the shadows. "Lottie, I don't think it's uncommon for girls of your age to be banished to the workhouses. To labor from dawn to midnight until their spirits are as broken as their backs."

"I shouldn't mind," Lottie said fiercely. "As long as you didn't have to marry that ill-tempered troglodyte."

"But what would become of your fine, soft hands? And your hair?"

Lottie touched a trembling hand to her curls. They all knew that the only thing she remembered of their papa was that he used to call her his little Goldilocks. "I could wear it in braids, I suppose."

Laura shook her head, hating herself in that moment nearly as much as she hated Sterling Harlow. "I'm afraid that wouldn't be possible. Once the lice got hold of it, they would have no choice but to crop it all off."

George surged to his feet. "He wouldn't dare put me in such a place! I'm old enough to run away and join the navy!"

Laura turned to him, her expression as regretful as her tone. "As much as you like to fancy yourself a man, George, you're not one yet."

Her brother flung himself back down on the bench, refusing to look at her.

Laura moved to kneel before Cookie, peering up into the old woman's stricken face. "And what about you and Dower? How long do you think this duke will keep you in his employ at your age? If Lady Eleanor hadn't considered you members of her own family, she would have put you both out to pasture years ago."

"This old ram's still got a bit o' fire left in 'is 'orn, 'e does," Dower proclaimed.

Laura reached up to cradle one of the old man's knobby hands in her own. "During the summer months, perhaps. But what about those cold winter nights when your knuckles swell and crack and bleed until you can hardly bend them? You know what I'm talking about, don't you, Cookie? You've heard him pacing the floor at all hours of the night because he was in too much pain to sleep."

As Cookie looked away, avoiding her gaze, Dower pulled Laura to her feet. "It don't matter if we all end up in the work'ouse with broken backs and bleedin' knuckles. We still think too 'ighly o' you to let you sell yourself to a stranger on our account."

Laura snatched her hand from his, her desperation growing. "That's precisely what I'm asking you to do— think of me! Have any of you stopped and asked yourselves what will become of me if this duke claims Arden Manor for his own?"

Dower scratched his grizzled head. "You're an educated gel, ain't you? You could become one o' them there gov'nusses wot teaches the gents' brats."

Laura sighed. "I know this is going to come as a shock to you all, especially to Lottie, who has always fancied herself the Incomparable Beauty of the family, but there's a reason all the men in the village want to marry me."

They stared at her blankly.

"I'm pretty." Laura spoke as if it were the gravest of shortcomings. "Far too pretty to be a governess. Even if a lady would welcome me into her home, which I doubt, it would only be a matter of time before one of the males of her household—her brother, her son, or perhaps even her own husband—cornered me on the back stairs. Then I would lose not only my situation but my reputation as well. And in this world, once a woman's reputation is lost, she becomes prey for all manner of scoundrels and rogues."

She swept a somber look over them all. "And that's not even the worst of it. There's one other possibility we must consider. Suppose the duke himself takes a fancy to me and decides to make me his mistress?"

Dower bit off a blasphemy and Cookie made the sign to ward off the evil eye as if Laura had suggested becoming a concubine to the devil himself.

"Who's to stop a man with his wealth, power, and social connections from forcing his attentions upon a penniless country girl? Why, there are even those in the village who would claim that I should be grateful for his protection." Despite the blush warming her cheeks, Laura lifted her chin defiantly. "I might be selling myself to a stranger with this scheme, but at least it will be to a stranger of my own choosing."

Her proud words hung in the air, shaming them all.

Dower ran a hand over his throat. "If it's that young ram you mean to 'ave, then I s'pose I've no choice but to 'elp you 'erd 'im into the shearin' pen."

Laura threw her arms around the old man, pressing a kiss to his prickly cheek. "Bless you, Dower! I couldn't do it without you. First thing in the morning, you must set off for London to consult with some of your old cronies. I want you to try to find out if there's been any word of a missing gentleman in the past few days."

"Or an escaped convict," Dower muttered beneath his breath.

"I'm rather hoping he'll turn out to be the orphaned second son of a second son with no inheritance and even fewer prospects." Laura began to pace again, her steps much lighter than before. "If we're to marry before my birthday, the banns must be published in the church on three successive Sundays, beginning day after tomorrow. That means I have less than three weeks to make sure he doesn't already have a wife tucked away somewhere." Given the brief duration and nature of their acquaintance, Laura was surprised by how much that thought pained her.

"I'm relieved to learn your scruples won't let you stoop to bigamy," George drawled. "But just what do you mean to do if Dower finds this man's family . . . or his wife?"

Laura sighed. "Then I suppose we'll have no choice but to return him to his rightful owner."

"Loik a stray sheep," Dower provided.

"Or a lost pig," Lottie added spitefully.

"What if you marry this fellow," George asked, "and then someone from London comes to Arden and recognizes him for who he truly is? What then?"

"And when's the last time our humble village received a visitor from London?" Laura's question silenced even George. In truth, none of them could remember.

But her brother seemed determined to prove he could be as ruthless as she could. "What if he signs the marriage register under a false name? Will you truly be married in the eyes of the Crown?"

Laura paused in her pacing, having not considered that fact. Swallowing back a lifetime of spiritual instruction, she faced her brother, head held high. "We'll be married in the eyes of God, and as far as I'm concerned, His are the only eyes that matter."

Without a word, Cookie rose from the bale of hay and started toward the door.

Laura had managed to hold on to her composure through Dower's grumbling and George's skepticism, but if good-hearted Cookie denounced her again, she feared she might just burst into tears. "Where are you going?"

Cookie turned, her broad face wreathed in a tender smile. "If I'm to stitch you up a weddin' dress before your birthday, I can't be dawdlin' in the barn all day with the cows and the chicks. I do believe Lady Eleanor left some white crepe stashed away in the attic for just this day." The maidservant dabbed at her damp eyes with the hem of her apron. "I wish our dear lady was goin' to be here to see you stand up at the altar with that handsome young buck. It was one of her fondest dreams, you know."

Laura blinked back her own tears. There was only one dream Lady Eleanor would have held more dear— the dream that someday her son would come striding down the lane and into her arms.

Laura linked her arm in Cookie's. "Do you think she would mind if we filched a bit of Brussels lace off the curtains in the drawing room to trim the sleeves?"

As she and Cookie drifted out of the barn, chattering about posies and bride cakes, Dower trailed after them, shaking his head in disgust. "They should a' stayed in the barn where they belonged. There's nothin' loik a weddin' to make a perfectly sensible gel go all calf eyed."

A long, silent moment passed after the others had left. Then George exploded into motion, springing to his feet and lashing out to kick a tin feed bucket. Grain sprayed through the air in a golden arc. The bucket landed with a metallic clang that echoed like a lightning strike in the taut stillness of the barn.

"She says she's doing it for herself, but she's not!" he shouted. "She's doing it for us. She's doing it because I'm too damn young to provide for my own family." He collapsed against a post, his hands clenched into impotent fists. "God in heaven, if I were only half a man . . ."

Above him, Lottie sat cross-legged in the hay with no sign of the histrionics he had expected. Her little round face was pale and still, her voice oddly calm. "We simply can't allow her to do it. We can't allow her to sacrifice her virtue on our behalf. She deserves better than to endure a fate worse than death at some scoundrel's hands."

"You didn't notice the way she was looking at him," George said darkly. "It was almost as if she might welcome the sort of death those hands could bring."

"That's easy for you to say. You're not a woman."

"Neither are you," he reminded her.

Lottie rested her chin on one hand. "If Laura marries before her twenty-first birthday, she inherits the manor."

"That does seem to be the point of all this lunacy," George agreed, wary of his sister's calculating expression.

"But there was nothing in Lady Eleanor's will that said she has to *stay* married."

"You know as well as I do that Laura would never survive the disgrace of a divorce."

"Who said anything about a divorce?" Lottie stroked the puff of gray fur in her lap. "In Miss Radcliffe's novels, the villain who seeks to compromise the heroine's virtue always meets with an untimely demise before he can succeed."

Planting his hands on his hips, George glared up at her. "Why, Carlotta Anne Fairleigh, you're not thinking of murdering that poor wretch, are you? Regardless of what you read in those silly books of yours, you can't just go around killing people because they don't fancy cats. Or you."

"And why not?" Lottie retorted. "Just consider the advantages. As a widow, Laura would reap all the benefits of marriage, but suffer none of the constraints. And if her groom should happen to meet with just such an untimely accident *after* the wedding, but *before* the wedding night, then she would never even have to endure the shame of having him put his rotten, stinking hands all over her."

George could not help but be swayed by the last. He moved to the barn door, hoping the breeze would sweep the haze of anger from his brain. The burned-out rubble of the rectory they'd once shared with their parents was tucked in a distant corner of the property, but on warm, windy days such as this one, he would have sworn he could still smell the acrid scent of smoke, still taste the bitter tang of ashes on his tongue.

"If Papa and Mama were here, they'd know what was best for Laura," he said, turning his face to the morning sunshine. "They'd know what was best for all of us."

"But they're not here. We are."

He sighed. "The three of us have gotten along so well for so long. I suppose I thought we could just go on that way forever."

"We can," Lottie said softly. "If you'll agree to help me."

George closed his eyes, but could not blot out the sight of his sister in a stranger's arms. For a timeless moment, even the wind seemed to be holding its breath, awaiting his answer.

When he finally turned back to the shadows of the barn, his lips were twisted in a grim smile. "Black has always been very becoming on Laura."

Lottie's teeth gleamed down at him from the loft. "Precisely my point."

Chapter 6

*You were always such
a perfect angel. . . .*

Nicholas Radcliffe had a temper.

He learned that about himself around teatime of the following afternoon when the bedchamber door creaked open for what seemed like the hundredth time in that endless day only to reveal someone else who wasn't his fiancée.

It seemed that the elusive Miss Fairleigh had decided he was best left to the ministrations of whoever happened to wander past his room at any given hour. Dower had even paid him a brief visit that morning, smelling of sheep and glowering like a death mask. The man had informed Nicholas that he was on his way to London to visit the livestock market. He had crumpled his broad-brimmed hat in his hands and bitten off a curt apology for nearly impaling Nicholas with his pitchfork, all the while assessing him with beady black eyes that made Nicholas feel as if he were being measured for a coffin.

Laura's brother had appeared next, bearing a tray of

kippers and eggs and wearing a sullen scowl. When Nicholas had inquired as to the whereabouts of the lad's sister, George had mumbled something noncommittal and fled the room.

When the door had swung open a short while later, Nicholas had sat up eagerly in the bed, ignoring his lingering dizziness. He had a thousand questions, most of which only Laura could answer. But to his keen disappointment, the white mobcap sitting askew on grizzled curls had belonged to Cookie. He had wrested the basin, soap, rags, and razor from the maidservant's chapped hands and insisted upon bathing and shaving himself, having no desire to repeat yesterday's performance.

As she was taking her leave, he had not been able to resist blinking innocently, and saying, "You needn't hurry away, Cookie. I doubt I've anything under here that a woman like you hasn't seen a hundred times before." Arching a mocking eyebrow, he had peeked beneath the blanket. "Or at least once."

Cookie had flushed scarlet, then buried a girlish giggle in her apron. "Go on with you, sir. You're a right naughty gent, you are."

"That's not what your mistress tells me," he had murmured after she was gone, his grin fading to a pensive frown. The yellow kitten nestled in the crook of his knee had given him a quizzical look. Despite his repeated efforts to shoo the bothersome creature away, the little cat refused to leave his side for more than a few minutes at a time.

As the hours lengthened and his temper shortened, he began to feel less like a patient and more like a prisoner. If he had his trousers, he could at least get up and pace the room. The throbbing in his head had subsided to a dull ache that was annoying, but not unbearable.

Shortly before teatime, just when he was settling into a fitful nap, the door began to inch open again. When Laura failed to materialize, his first instinct was to hurl something breakable at it. All he could see from his reclining position was a mass of golden curls bound by a lopsided pink ribbon. It seemed his latest visitor was crawling on hands and knees.

A small hand with plump fingers and blunt fingernails crept over the side of the bed and began to grope about in the bedclothes dangerously near to his hips. When it failed to locate what it sought, the curls began to rise like a gilded fountain. As Lottie Fairleigh peeped over the side of the bed, Nicholas narrowed his eyes to mere slits, watching her through his lashes.

"There you are, you naughty beast," she hissed, reaching for the cat that was napping at his side.

"That's not a very nice way to address the man your sister is about to marry," Nicholas drawled, propping himself up on one elbow.

Lottie tumbled to her backside on the faded carpet, her mouth a pink 0 of surprise.

"I should warn you that if you start screaming again, so will I, and then we'll be right back where we started."

She snapped her mouth shut.

"There, now. That's better," he said. "You're almost tolerable when you're not shrieking like a banshee."

"I wish I could say the same for you," she retorted, making him smile in spite of himself. Rising, she dusted off the rumpled white dimity of her pinafore, striking just the right note of offended dignity. "Forgive me for disturbing your rest, sir, but I came to fetch my kitten."

"And to think I'd unfairly assumed you'd come to smother me with a pillow."

Lottie's head flew up, curls bouncing. Her blue eyes looked so guilt-stricken that he almost felt ashamed of himself for teasing her. But she recovered quickly, smiling sweetly at him. "A rather crude, if effective, method of dispatching an unwanted guest perhaps, but I much prefer poison. There are so many different varieties from which to choose. Why, in the old oak wood alone, I've catalogued seventeen different varieties of deadly toadstools."

Nicholas sat up in the bed, eyeing the remnants of his lunch tray askance.

"Now, if you'll excuse us." She reached for the kitten.

The animal lashed out at her with its sharp little claws, drawing blood.

"Ow! What have you done to her?" Lottie sucked her wounded knuckle as the kitten butted its head against Nicholas's bare chest, purring with rapture.

Running a hand over the cat's silky fur, Nicholas shrugged. "Despite what you seem so eager to believe, I'm not without my charms."

"Neither is Napoleon. Or so I've read." She waved a haughty hand as if it had been her idea to banish the animal from her company. "You may keep the little traitor if you'd like. There's plenty more where she came from." Tilting her nose in the air, Lottie sailed toward the door, obviously hoping to leave with more aplomb than she'd entered.

"Carlotta?" When she turned without hesitation, Nicholas knew he'd guessed correctly at her Christian name. He studied her guarded little face, hoping for some glimmer of recognition. But she remained as alien to him as his own reflection. "Despite the fact that we're obviously both strong-willed individuals, your sister assured me that we were quite fond of each other."

The child met his gaze without blinking. "Then it would seem we are."

She dismissed him with a regal curtsy, leaving an exasperated Nicholas to throw himself back on the pillows.

By the time the copper glow of the rising moon began to seep into the chamber, Nicholas was beginning to long for Lottie's querulous company. He didn't think he could bear another minute of being confined to bed like some feeble invalid. Even the kitten had deserted him, scampering out the open window to hunt crickets on the starlit roof.

He threw himself to his stomach, pummeling his pillow into submission. Perhaps being confined to bed wouldn't be so wearying if he had someone to share it. It was no great stretch of his imagination to envision the rich spill of Laura Fairleigh's hair across his pillow, to see himself kissing each freckle that dusted her cheeks as he pressed her into the softness of the feather mattress with his weight.

He took pleasure in the wicked thought, even though it ill befit the staunch moral character his fiancée had assured him he possessed.

The old house finally settled itself into the creaking rhythms of sleep, magnifying his restlessness. He sat up, tossing the blankets away, and flung his legs over the side of the bed. To his surprise, the room held steady, not tilting or swaying as he'd feared.

That was when he saw his ticket to freedom folded neatly on the brocaded cushion of the chair.

A pair of trousers.

Someone must have returned them while he was drowsing.

Shaking off the last traces of vertigo, he crossed the room with confident strides and drew on the trousers, savoring their familiar fit. He was delighted to discover a shirt draped with equal tidiness over the back of the chair. He fingered the crisp lawn, thinking it a rather extravagant fabric to be purchased on the stipend of a mere foot soldier. As he shrugged the shirt over his shoulders, he noted that several rips in the cloth had been mended with such care as to be almost undetectable. Perhaps the shirt had been the castoff of some benevolent officer.

Once he was fully garbed, he stood with hands on hips, feeling more like himself.

Whoever the hell he was.

Nicholas raked a hand through his untidy mane, wincing when his fingers made contact with the tender goose egg at the crown of his head. He'd learned something else about himself that interminable day. He didn't fancy being held hostage to the whims of a woman. Laura had no right to inform him that she was his betrothed, then abandon him to make what he would of that shocking revelation.

Gaining resolve along with his strength, he slipped

into the darkened hallway, unable to say whether he was going in search of his fiancée or himself.

Laura haunted the drawing room like a beleaguered ghost. She hadn't bothered to light a lamp or a candle, preferring the moon-dappled gloom for her fitful pacing. She feared she was only moments away from wringing her pale hands together like an overwrought heroine from one of Lottie's beloved Gothics.

It was one thing to imagine sharing her life with a stranger in the bright sunshine of day, but quite another to contemplate sharing his bed in the shadows of night. She'd dreamed of marrying just such a man since she was a little girl, but those dreams had always ended with a tender declaration of love and a chaste kiss, not with six feet two inches of undomesticated male in her bed.

A panicked little whimper escaped her. Her betrothed might have lost his memory, but she had surely lost her mind to have concocted such a harebrained scheme.

She'd spent the entire day avoiding his company and rehearsing the history she'd invented for the two of them. She didn't dare commit a word of it to the pages of her journal for fear he might discover it later.

Be sure your sins will find you out.

It had been one of her father's favorite homilies and Laura could almost hear his gentle voice chiding her. Of course, her papa never would have believed his innocent little girl capable of committing any sin more damning than failing to learn her daily epistle or snitching a lump from the sugar bowl when her mama's back was turned. It had probably never occurred to either of her parents that she might snitch an entire man.

Laura's shoulders slumped. It was too late to confess what she'd done and beg his forgiveness. Too late to whack him over the head with a candlestick and carry him back to the wood where she'd found him. He was hers now—for better or for worse.

"We were introduced by a cousin," she mumbled, veering to the right to avoid stumbling over the ottoman. "A second cousin thrice removed. Or was that a third cousin twice removed?" She rubbed her aching temples with her fingertips, thinking she might have done just as well to stay in bed and listen to Lottie snore.

The old rosewood secretaire loomed over her in the moonlight. A piece of crumpled stationery lay abandoned, but not forgotten, among the desk's clutter. It was the letter penned by Sterling Harlow's loyal minion. Laura despised the arrogant duke more now than ever before. After all, he was the one who had set her on this path to certain destruction.

Fumbling in a darkened cubbyhole, she drew out a tinderbox. She struck a match, then touched its flame to the edge of the letter, feeling a surge of triumph when it began to crinkle and blacken.

"Take that, you miserable devil," she murmured, holding it aloft. "May you roast in hell where you belong."

"'But heaven has no rage like love to hatred turned,'" someone quoted from behind her, "'nor hell a fury like a woman scorned.'"

Chapter 7

Although I let them take you away from me,
I have always kept you close to my heart. . . .

As those deep, silken tones emerged from the shadows, Laura whirled around, fearing irrationally that she'd summoned the devil himself with her blasphemy. It wasn't the Prince of Darkness but her betrothed who leaned against the doorframe, the flames reflected in his golden eyes warning her that she might be playing with something even more dangerous than fire.

Wrapped in nothing but a quilt, he had resembled some sort of magnificent savage fresh from the jungles of Madagascar. He looked no less uncivilized in trousers and a shirt. Without a coat and cravat to bind his masculine vitality, it seemed to spill from him in restless waves. The tawny gold of his hair, worn slightly longer than was the current fashion, brushed his broad shoulders while his shirt lay open at the throat. Laura glanced down, then wished she hadn't. The clinging buckskin of his trousers perfectly defined the elegantly chiseled muscles of his calves and thighs. He was certainly no spidershanks who had to use sawdust to pad his limbs.

Or anything else.

Pain seared her fingertips. Yelping, she dropped the smoldering remains of the letter and began to stomp on them with her slippers. "It was the latest bill from the butcher," she explained breathlessly, lifting the hem of her nightdress to avoid the scattering sparks. "He can be rather intractable if he doesn't receive his money by the first of the month."

Her fiancé watched her graceless dance with keen interest. "So tell me, do you consign all of your creditors to hell or only the ones who insist on being paid?"

To avoid answering, Laura tucked her singed fingertips in her mouth.

"Let me have a look at that hand." As he crossed the room, shadows veiled his face, making him look even larger and more menacing than he had in Lady Eleanor's chamber.

Laura's heart skipped a beat. What if Dower was right? What if she had brought a murderer or thief into their midst? Suppose he hadn't been set upon by a band of highwaymen but was a highwayman himself? Surely any highwayman worth his salt could afford the outward trappings of a gentleman. Perhaps he had even discovered her subterfuge and had come downstairs to strangle her.

Without realizing it, she began to back away from him.

He stopped abruptly. "If you're my fiancée, then why do you behave as if you're afraid of me?" He drew nearer, looking so genuinely aggrieved that it was almost as if she were the one who had wounded him. "Have I ever hurt you or led you to believe that I would?"

"Not yet." Her shoulders came up against the mantel, setting a porcelain vase to swaying. He reached around her to steady it, effectively cutting off her means of escape. "I mean, no."

Her stinging fingertips were forgotten as he cupped her cheek, the callused pad of his thumb playing softly over her downy skin. Instead of shrinking from his touch, she found herself wanting to turn into it.

His husky voice was mesmerizing. "If I'm the sort of bullying churl who would lift a hand to a woman, then I'd just as soon you'd have left me to the mercy of the French. It would have been no crueler a fate than I deserved."

Laura ducked beneath his arm, seeking shelter in the moonlit bay of the window seat. She sank down among the cushions, folding her hands in her lap. "I'm not afraid of you," she lied. "I just thought it best to avoid any appearance of impropriety."

"It's a bit late to worry about that, isn't it, considering that we've yet to have a conversation while fully clothed." His eyes sparkled with dark humor. "At least not in my memory."

Laura glanced down at her nightclothes. The modest nightdress with its ruffled bodice and high lace collar was far less revealing than her damp gown had been. Oddly enough, it was the unbound hair rippling around her shoulders that made her feel the most exposed. Surely only a husband should see it in such disarray.

"Despite your condition," she said, "there are still certain niceties that should be honored."

His smile faded. "Is that why you kept yourself from my bedside all day? To honor the *niceties*?"

"You'd suffered a terrible ordeal. I assumed that you needed your rest."

"Just how much rest can a body stand? According to

you, I've already been drifting in and out of consciousness for . . ." He stretched his arm along the length of the mantel and drummed his fingertips on its polished surface. "Exactly how long was it?"

Even as he stood there, looking perfectly at ease with his tousled hair and bare feet, he was watching her face intently. Searching for the truth? she wondered. Or for any hint of deceit?

She forced herself to meet his eyes. "Two of your commanding officers delivered you to our doorstep nearly a week ago. Given the nature of your injury, they weren't sure you'd ever regain full consciousness."

"Now that I have, I suppose I'll be expected back at my post."

"Oh, no," she said hastily. "Since Napoleon has abdicated and Louis is back on the French throne, they assured me that they would have no further need of you."

"Well, at least I'm not to be hanged as a deserter." He frowned. "What of my family? Have they been informed of my return?"

Laura gave all of her attention to arranging the skirt of her nightdress into tidy pleats. "I'm afraid you've never spoken of your family to me. I gathered that you'd been estranged from them for quite some time before we met. You seemed more than content to make your own way in the world."

A shadow that had nothing to do with the moonlight passed over his face, ever so briefly. "How very odd," he murmured.

"What is it?" Laura asked, fearing that she'd inadvertently said something to jog his memory.

A melancholy smile quirked one corner of his mouth.

"That's the first thing you've said that's made perfect sense to me."

"Not having parents is something we have in common, you see. My mother and father perished in a fire when I was thirteen. Which is precisely why dear cousin Ebenezer thought we'd get along so well. He's the one who introduced us when you came home with him on a Christmas furlough two years ago. Dear, dear Ebenezer Flockhart . . . my second cousin thrice removed," she added, wincing when she realized how awkward it sounded.

"Remind me to thank him the next time I see him."

"I'm afraid that won't be possible. Why, he . . . he . . ."

"Was killed in the war?" her fiancé ventured.

Laura had been tempted to give dear fictional Ebenezer a noble death in the service of his country and king, but the tattered shreds of her conscience prevailed. "He sailed to America. It was always a dream of his and now that the war there is over as well, he was finally free to make it come true."

"Perhaps we can visit him someday. Since he's the one who introduced us, I'm sure he would like nothing more than to see the shining faces of our children."

"Children?" Laura echoed, not quite able to keep the squeak out of her voice. "Just how many children will there be?"

He shrugged. "I couldn't say. I suppose a half dozen should suffice." He ducked his head and gave her a bashful glance that was completely at odds with the wicked glint in his eye. "To begin with."

Laura's own head was beginning to reel. In just two days, she'd gone from stealing a chaste kiss from a stranger to bearing him half a dozen babes.

To begin with.

He laughed aloud, startling her. "There's no need to go so pale, my dear. I'm only teasing you. Or did you neglect to inform me that I don't have a sense of humor?"

"I knew you were teasing," she assured him with a nervous hiccup of laughter. "You always told me that you wanted only two children—a boy and a girl."

"How very tidy of me." He slid into the window seat next to her, flexing his long legs. Laura scooted as far away from him as the cozy half-circle of cushions would allow. He captured her icy hands in his warm ones before she could tumble onto the floor. "I'm a bit puzzled by your demeanor, my dear. You tell me we've been apart for a very long time, yet you seem less than eager to become . . . *reacquainted*."

"You'll have to forgive my shyness, sir. We've been engaged for nearly two years, but due to your military career, your visits here were quite infrequent. Much of our courtship was conducted through correspondence."

He drew her closer, genuine excitement replacing the mocking light in his eyes. "Do you have my letters? They might prod my memory or at least give me some insight into what manner of man I am."

Laura had not anticipated this request. "I'm afraid I don't have them. They've been disposed of."

He freed her hands, plainly taken aback by her words. "Well, at least no one can accuse you of trite sentimentality."

"Oh, no, you misunderstand me!" She put her hand on his arm without realizing it. "I cherished each and every word you wrote. I slept with the letters beneath my pillow . . . which is how Cookie came to boil them in lye on laundry day. I'm dreadfully sorry."

"So am I." Sinking back on the cushions, he raked a hand through his hair, frustration spilling over into his voice. "How is it that I can remember every dusty corner of this house, but not a moment of the time I spent here?"

"I don't know," Laura replied, more puzzled than he was.

"It maddens me that I can't recall anything about you. Or us." He leaned forward again, peering into her face. "Have we kissed?"

She might have thought he was teasing her again if not for the challenge in his gaze. She averted her face, thinking it terribly ironic that she could lie to him without flinching, but blush while telling the truth. "Once."

He captured her chin and gently tilted her face toward his. "That's most odd. I would have sworn I wasn't the sort of man who would be content with only one kiss from lips as sweet as yours." A wicked shiver of anticipation ran through her as his thumb played tenderly over those lips. "There's no need to be frightened, Laura. Weren't you the one who assured me that I would never compromise my fiancée's virtue? I can promise you that it's not unheard-of for even the most respectful of bridegrooms to steal a kiss or two from his bride before the wedding."

A scudding cloud veiled the moon. All the artifice between them melted away, leaving them two strangers in the dark. Laura was keenly aware of the clean, soapy smell of his freshly shaven jaw, the warm whisper of his breath against her mouth in that fragment of time before he touched his lips to hers.

Laura had kissed, but she had never *been* kissed. The difference was subtle, yet profound. At first he seemed content to simply brush his mouth back and forth across hers in a tingling caress, as if to savor the satiny plumpness of her lips. Before she even realized it, they had bloomed beneath the tantalizing pressure, parting just enough to invite him inside. He didn't require much coaxing.

Laura gasped as the warm, rough sweetness of his tongue invaded her mouth. He cupped the back of her head in his hand, slanting his mouth over hers to deepen the kiss.

She had been wrong. He *was* teasing her. Not with witty retorts or gentle mockery but with an unspoken promise of forbidden delights. As shocking as that intimacy was, she could not stop her own tongue from responding in kind, from dancing out to lick at his with a shy boldness that astonished her. He nibbled and tasted and stroked, lingering over each new sensation as if he had the rest of the night to devote to pleasuring her mouth.

In the wood, her kiss had awakened him from a brief sleep. Here in this darkened drawing room, he was awakening her from a lifetime of slumber, sending blood thrumming from her heart to the most secret recesses of her body, where it settled into a steady, insistent beat.

Just when she thought she might faint from the dizzying wonder of it all, his mouth left her lips. She quickly discovered that it was no less persuasive on the curve of her jaw, the hollow of her throat, the lamb-soft skin just beneath her ear.

"Call me darling," he whispered, catching her earlobe between his teeth.

"Hmmmm?" She gasped as his tongue flicked out to ravish the shell of her ear.

"Call me darling. You haven't called me darling all day. I've missed it."

Her head fell back as his mouth caressed its way back to her greedy lips. She twined her fingers in his hair, searching for something to cling to in a world that was shifting dangerously beneath her feet.

"Oh . . . darling," she sighed.

Her capitulation earned her another kiss, this one even sweeter and deeper than the last.

But he was not to be so easily satisfied. "Call me by my name," he urged.

Laura suffered an instant of paralyzing blankness. She was so addled she wasn't sure she could remember her own name, much less the one she had given him. "Um . . . uh . . . Nicholas."

"Again," he murmured against her lips.

"Nicholas . . . Nicholas . . . Nicholas . . ." It became a breathless chant between each kiss. If this didn't qualify as a moment of great passion, Laura wasn't sure what would. "Oh, Nicky . . ."

That throaty purr of surrender was nearly Nicholas's undoing. If Laura wasn't already a liar, he was about to make one of her. About to prove that he was precisely the sort of man who would compromise his fiancée's virtue. The sort of man who would drag her into his lap and soothe away her maidenly protests with deep, drugging kisses and murmured promises he had no intention of keeping.

Except this time he would be bound to keep those promises for a lifetime.

That realization made Nicholas do the impossible. He stopped kissing her.

Somehow she had ended up in his arms with his hand splayed over her ribs, his thumb poised only inches from the tantalizing swell of her breast. Her heart hammered against those ribs in a thundering echo of his own. When she realized he was no longer kissing her, her lashes slowly fluttered upward.

Her eyes were misty, her baby pink lips still plump and glistening from his kisses. She had tasted of passion and innocence, an intoxicating brew he would swear he'd never sampled before.

"Did that happen the first time we kissed?"

The accusing note in his voice seemed to snap her out of her daze. She stiffened in his embrace. "I should say not, sir. You were the very model of restraint."

"Then perhaps I've lost my scruples as well as my memory." He smoothed her tousled hair away from her cheek, surprised to note that his hands were shaking. "Why don't you take yourself off to bed before you lose something even more valuable?"

His words might have been a plea, but she wisely decided to take them as a warning. She extracted herself from his embrace with all the dignity she could muster. "Very well, sir. I bid you a good night."

She maintained that dignity until she was out of his sight. Then she went pounding up the stairs as if the devil himself were fast on her heels.

Nicholas ran a hand over his jaw. Perhaps he was.

He had intended to woo his betrothed with chaste kisses and pretty words, not ravish her within moaning distance of her family. That thought summoned up a powerful image of Laura reclining on the cushions of the window seat, the skirts of her nightdress ruched up to her waist while he muffled her sobs of pleasure with his kisses.

"Bloody hell," he swore, coming to his feet.

There could be no denying that his response to the innocent brush of her lips had been fierce, primal, possessive. According to her, they had been separated for almost a year. Had it been that long or longer since he'd kissed a woman? A peculiar thought struck him. Here he was, obsessing about her fidelity, when he had no way of knowing if he'd been faithful to her during the time they'd been apart. Perhaps he, like so many other soldiers before him, had sought the baser comforts in the arms of some lusty camp follower while dreaming of the woman he was to wed.

He shook his head, still marveling at the passion that had flared between them. The kiss they had shared had proved Laura true in yet another thing—she belonged to him. Of that, there could no longer be any doubt.

He was on the verge of seeking the cold, lonely comfort of his bed when he remembered the charred remnants of the paper he had caught Laura burning. He knelt down, sifting through the ash.

His fingers stumbled over a lump of melted wax—still warm and as soft and malleable to his touch as Laura had been. He slowly straightened, flattening the wax between forefinger and thumb. He might not recall anything about his life before yesterday morning, but he did remember that village butchers rarely, if ever, sealed their bills with expensive wax.

Chapter 8

I pray for you every night
without fail. . . .

When Nicholas awoke the next morning, the ringing in his skull had returned with a vengeance. Groaning, he dragged the pillow over his head, muffling the sound to a bearable drone.

That was when it occurred to him that the ringing wasn't coming from inside his head but from outside the window. Rescuing his trousers from the foot of the bed, he slipped them on, then stumbled to the window.

Shoving it open, he leaned out over the gabled roof, drawing a breath of cool, crisp air into his lungs. The night had left a veil of dew on the grass that shimmered beneath the caress of the morning sun. And still the bells rang on, echoing over the rolling hills and meadows in a chiming carillon, both wistful and lovely. It was the sort of song that might force a man to swallow past a curious catch in his throat, the sort of song that might call a man home.

If he had one.

Nicholas gently, but firmly, drew the window shut,

but not even latching it and drawing the curtains could completely mute those compelling strains.

When the door behind him creaked open, he swung around, thankful he had donned his trousers. "Doesn't anyone in this infernal household ever knock?"

Although her arms were piled with garments, Laura still managed to offer him a mocking curtsy and a cheery smile. "And a pleasant morn to you, too, sir."

His fiancée looked most fetching in a white muslin gown dotted with blue floral sprigs. A matching blue sash gathered the fabric beneath her high, round breasts. The scalloped hemline revealed trim ankles swathed in white stockings and a pair of silk pumps. She even wore a straw bonnet trimmed with a rosette of ribbons and secured beneath her chin by a jaunty bow. All she lacked was a lamb on a ribbon and she might have posed for a portrait of a shepherd maiden painted by one of the masters.

Nicholas scowled. After last night, he had no intention of letting her make a lamb of him. Especially a sacrificial one.

She set the pile of garments on the dressing table stool. "I've brought you some church clothes. Cookie found these in the attic. They may be a bit out of fashion, but I doubt that anyone in Arden will notice."

He folded his arms over his chest, deepening his suspicious glower. "Why would I have need of church clothes? We're not to be married this morning, are we?"

She laughed. "I should say not."

"Then why are we going to church?"

"Because it's Sunday morning."

He continued to glare at her blankly.

"And we *always* attend church on Sunday morning."

"We do?"

"Well, *I* do, anyway, and from what I gathered from your letters, you try never to miss a service." Her eyes shone with admiration. "You're extremely devout."

Nicholas scratched at his whisker-stubbled throat. "Well, I'll be damned. Who would have thought the Almighty and I were even on speaking terms?" He gave her a defiant look. "You might as well know that I have no intention of begging His pardon for kissing you last night. I'm not the least bit sorry."

Although color rose to her cheeks, she met his gaze boldly. "Perhaps it's not forgiveness we should pray for but restraint."

"And perhaps you're being overcautious. A kiss can be an innocent enough expression of affection, can it not?"

Laura might be unversed in the arts of love, but she wasn't so unversed as to believe there was anything innocent about the kisses they had shared. "It *can* be, I suppose," she reluctantly agreed.

"And weren't you the one who assured me that I was the very model of restraint the first time we kissed?"

She had been afraid those words would come back to haunt her. She was already regretting her decision to lie to him no more than was necessary. "There's something about that kiss I neglected to tell you."

He waited in expectant silence.

She took a deep breath. "You were unconscious at the time."

His eyebrows shot up.

"It was just after you were returned to us, and I suppose I was trying to convince myself that you weren't hurt but only sleeping. You looked so tragic and vulnerable lying there—like a prince in some fairy tale who had suffered a cruel curse. I know it was only a childish fancy, but I honestly believed that if I kissed you, I might be able to stir you from your slumber."

"Why, Miss Fairleigh, I'm shocked! I can't believe such a model of decorum as yourself would take advantage of a man's helpless state to force your attentions upon him."

Without thinking, she crossed to him and placed one hand on his arm. "Oh, please don't think ill of me! I'd never done such a wicked thing before. I can't imagine what came over me. Why, I . . ."

Her protests died as she realized he was laughing out loud, the dimple in his cheek making him look more George's age than his own.

Stiffening, she stepped away from him. "You needn't make sport of me, sir. It was only a brief lapse in judgment and moral character. I can assure you that it won't happen again."

His laughter died to a warm chuckle. "More's the pity."

She sniffed primly. "Given the lack of gravity with which you view our betrothal, I can see that it will have to be my responsibility to make sure our lips don't meet again until we stand before the altar of St. Michael's to take our vows. Until that day, I shall simply have to ensure that we are never alone."

"We're alone now," he pointed out, a smile still playing around his lips.

Laura glanced around the shadowy bedchamber, keenly aware of the cozy half-tester with its rumpled bedclothes that still bore the imprint of his big, warm body. "We are, I suppose. But you wouldn't dare kiss me with Lottie right down the hall and Cookie down-stairs."

He arched one golden eyebrow. "Oh, wouldn't I?"

As he slid his hands beneath her elbows and drew her into his arms, she realized that, heaven help her, she half hoped he would.

But as he gazed down into her face, the sparkle fled his eyes, leaving them oddly somber. "Was I kind to you, Laura? Was I considerate of your feelings? Did I make you happy?"

She drew in an uneven breath, finding his intensity even more disarming than his charm. "You were most considerate. You wrote every single week without fail and twice on the week of my birthday. Since you weren't here to bring me flowers, you would sketch clever little bouquets in the margins of your letters. When you did visit, you always brought back some small gift for Lottie and George."

As the lies came tumbling effortlessly from her lips, Laura realized she was describing the man of her dreams. A dream made flesh right before her eyes.

"In your letters, you always spoke of how happy we'd be once we were wed. How we'd sip chocolate in bed every morning and take long walks as twilight fell. At night, we'd gather in the drawing room with the rest of the family to play cards and sing songs around the pianoforte. You would read to us in front of the fire un-til we all grew drowsy." She lowered her eyes, beset by sudden shyness. "Then we'd retire to our bedchamber."

Nicholas's eyes had clouded as if that idyllic image was somehow painful to him. "And I never gave you cause to regret your pledge to me?"

Laura shook her head. "No. Never."

Urging her closer, he leaned down and touched his lips to hers. The melting sweetness of his kiss caught her off guard. But before she could fully surrender to it, he had drawn away, his expression unreadable. "Then I can only pray I never will."

As Nicholas slid into the family pew after Laura and her siblings, he decided that the entire population of Arden would have had to be born blind not to notice how out of fashion he was. Despite the fact that he couldn't remember anything of his former life, he was reasonably sure he'd never felt so ridiculous. The knee breeches should have been humiliation enough, but Laura had compounded his misery by providing him with striped silk stockings, buckled shoes, an embroidered waistcoat, and a scarlet coat with shiny brass buttons. He would have been perfectly at home in any drawing room—of a generation ago. If he'd had a powdered wig to complete his ensemble, he could have applied for a position as the king's footman.

He pinched his twitching nose, comforted by the fact that the old stone church smelled slightly mustier than he did.

George slouched at the end of the row, putting as much distance between himself and his family as the long, narrow pew would allow. Lottie perched on the other side of Laura, the cherubic innocence of her countenance spoiled by the fact that her squirming reticule kept trying to leap out of her lap.

Nicholas stole a glance at Laura's serene profile. She

appeared to be as oblivious to his discomfort as she was to the warm press of his thigh against hers. Her white-gloved hands were folded demurely around her prayer book, her face tilted attentively toward the mahogany pulpit set high in the chancel from which the rector was deigning to offer them his blessing. As the opening strains of "Come, Thou Fount of Every Blessing" flooded the nave, she nudged him to stand. Her voice wasn't the airy soprano he expected but a throaty alto that sent a shiver of raw desire through him. He cast a rueful glance heavenward, half expecting the Lord to strike him dead with a thunderbolt for entertaining such lascivious thoughts in His house.

While they were standing, he became aware of a strange prickling at the nape of his neck. He batted at his collar, fearing some unfortunate moth had become trapped there, but the prickling persisted. Glancing behind him, he discovered a man with a single bushy black eyebrow draped across his forehead glaring daggers at him. As he turned back, he caught sight of another glower, this one directed at him from across the aisle by a pockmarked fellow whose face looked as if it could use a good scrubbing. The man returned his cool stare for less than a minute before sheepishly lowering his eyes.

Baffled, Nicholas returned his attention to the altar. Given his ludicrous attire, perhaps he was just being overly sensitive, misinterpreting curiosity as hostility.

As the congregation sank into their seats, the white-haired rector launched into a droning sermon that soon had Nicholas fearing he was going to lapse back into his stupor.

He was just beginning to doze off when the rector's

ringing voice jolted him awake. ". . . my privilege to publish the banns of marriage between Mr. Nicholas Radcliffe and Miss Laura Jane Fairleigh. If any of you know cause or just impediment why these two persons should not be joined together in holy matrimony, ye are to declare it. This is the first time of asking."

Nicholas wasn't the only one caught off guard by the rector's words. Instead of the expectant silence that traditionally greeted the reading of the banns, an unmistakable rumble swept through the church. Nicholas stole a look to the left, then right. Several men were glaring at him now, making no attempt to hide their resentment. Nicholas could not help but wonder if one of them might be educated enough to have penned the note he had caught his fiancée burning, and eloquent enough to stir her passions to such a fever pitch.

Laura continued to stare straight ahead, the color high in her cheeks. Her body had gone rigid, drained of the melting softness she had offered in his arms last night.

As the rector launched into the offertory, Nicholas took her gloved hand in his, and whispered, "You might have warned me this was coming."

Her nose crinkled in a nervous ghost of a smile as she whispered back, "It's only the first reading of the banns. You still have two more Sundays to declare your opposition to our union."

He ran his thumb over her knuckles in a possessive caress. "And why would I want to do that when I'm obviously the envy of every man in the village? From the looks I'm getting, I gather that mine wasn't the only proposal you received."

"But it was the only one I accepted," she reminded him.

"So was our engagement a secret one or have all your other suitors lost their memory as well?"

"Sshhh," she said, drawing her hand from his. "The time has come to ask God for forgiveness of our transgressions."

As they stood along with the rest of the congregation, he leaned close to her, deepening his voice to a husky murmur. "And what sin could an innocent like you possibly have to confess?"

There it was again. That flash of fear in eyes that should never have to know even a shadow of distress. "Perhaps you've forgotten your Scripture as well, sir. There is no one among us who is without sin. Not even one." As Laura slipped to her knees, the curved brim of her bonnet shielded her face from him.

He gazed down at her creamy nape for a long moment before awkwardly kneeling beside her. He would have sworn that he wasn't a man accustomed to kneeling in front of anyone—not even God. Although he dutifully closed his eyes, he could only pretend to pray. The words that seemed to come so effortlessly to Laura's soft, pink lips were denied him, along with the conviction that anyone who cared might be listening.

"They make a pretty pair, don't they?" George grumbled, swatting a speckled butterfly away from his face.

"I don't think they suit at all." Lottie dragged her nose out of the well-worn copy of *The Murderous Monk* she had smuggled inside of her prayer book. "He's much too tall and disagreeable for her."

Brother and sister perched on the stone steps of St.

Michael's, glumly watching throngs of well-wishers cluster around Laura and Nicholas in the sunny churchyard. Although many of the men who had once courted Laura themselves hung back, the rest of the villagers surged forward to bask in the excitement of the upcoming nuptials and the novelty of having a mannerly stranger in their ranks. The charm Nicholas had boasted of to Lottie was well in evidence as he accepted hearty slaps on the back from the married men and fawning smiles from their wives. Even sour old Widow Witherspoon was reduced to simpering like a schoolgirl when he brought her bony hand to his lips.

"So did you ask God to forgive you for the murder you were planning to commit?" George asked.

Lottie snapped the book shut. "I prefer not to think of it as a murder but as a rather well-timed mishap."

"A mishap is misplacing your spectacles or forgetting to button your boots, not falling down dead an hour after your own wedding. Have you given any real thought as to how you might carry out the dastardly deed?" George watched Laura smile up at Nicholas, her face radiant. "I was rather hoping for the pleasure of shoving his smug face into the bride cake and smothering him."

Lottie shook her head, stroking the fuzzy, bewhiskered face that had emerged from her reticule. "Too obvious, I fear. In Mr. Walpole's *The Castle of Otranto,* Conrad was found crushed to death by a giant plumed helmet. But I'm rather partial to poison myself."

"That's fortunate since I doubt there are many giant plumed helmets floating around the parish."

"Of course, I haven't completely ruled out accidental

gunshot or drowning. I plan to conduct several experiments in the next two weeks to seek out the most plausible method of ridding oneself of an unwanted bridegroom."

"And what will you do if none of these *experiments* yield the results you had hoped for?"

George followed Lottie's gaze as she tilted her face skyward. A stone angel was perched high on the parapet of the bell tower above them, its weathered wings unfurled. Local legend had it that the angel's mission was to ward off the evil spirits in their midst. Her plump cheeks and pointed chin bore a rather startling resemblance to Lottie's.

Lottie heaved a dreamy sigh. "Then we shall simply have to look heavenward for some divine inspiration."

Laura wondered if it were a sacrilege to be standing in a churchyard dreaming of a man's kisses. Although she managed to smile and nod and squeeze the hands of the villagers who crowded around to congratulate her on her good fortune, all she could think of was a moonlit drawing room and a stranger's intoxicating kisses.

That stranger stood beside her now, the slightest brush of his elbow against her arm making her tingle with awareness. Although she had feigned attentiveness during the rector's sermon, it had been impossible to keep her mind on his words with Nicholas so near. While the rector had been preaching about the virtues of self-control, she had been reliving those delicious moments when she had nearly lost hers.

Betsy Bogworth, the tanner's daughter, whose pronounced overbite and tendency to wiggle her nose made her look like an overgrown rabbit, clutched at Laura's sleeve. "Shame on you for keeping such a secret! Why didn't you tell us you were engaged, you wicked girl?"

"It was actually Mr. Radcliffe's idea to keep our betrothal to ourselves until he was free of his military obligations," Laura replied.

"It was?" Nicholas's innocent expression was at odds with the mischief glittering in his eyes.

Laura's smile tightened. "Of course it was, dear."

Betsy's sister, Alice, a pale wisp of a girl, clasped her hands beneath her chin. "A secret engagement! How thrillingly romantic! How you must have longed for his return!"

"Oh, I did." Laura stole a look at Nicholas, her gaze lingering on his lips. "I kissed him more than you'll ever know."

Alice's flaxen eyebrows shot up. The crowd fell into a sudden silence while Nicholas cleared his throat and scuffed at the ground with the toe of his shoe.

Laura could feel herself turning bright pink. "I mean, I *missed* him more than you'll ever know."

Betsy turned to Nicholas, her nose twitching. "Every eligible man in Arden has tried to win our Laura's heart at one time or another, but failed. How is it that you succeeded when we never even saw you visit the manor to court her?"

Nicholas smiled pleasantly. "I believe I'll let my fiancée answer that question."

Although she didn't dare look at him, Laura could feel his expectant look on her. "The first year of our engagement, his visits to the manor were too short and infrequent to allow for outings into the village. And in the past year, the bulk of our courtship has been conducted through correspondence. It was his letters that truly won my affections. He can be very persuasive with his mouth." Laura gritted her teeth. "I mean, with his *words*."

Her rescue came from a most unlikely place. Halford Tombob was using his cane to battle his way through the mob of well-wishers. The old rascal refused to wear spectacles, but insisted on dangling an enormous quizzing glass from the buttonhole of his waistcoat.

A hush fell over the crowd as he lifted the glass to his eye in one liver-spotted hand and peered up into Nicholas's face like a one-eyed grasshopper. After an awkward moment, he lowered it, and announced with utter conviction, "I know that face."

Chapter 9

*Sometimes I wonder if
you even remember me. . . .*

Laura's heart stopped, then stuttered into an uneven beat. The old man must be mistaken. As far as she knew, Halford Tombob hadn't left Arden since George II had sat on the throne.

"I mean no disrespect, Mr. Tombob," she said, tucking her gloved hand in the crook of Nicholas's arm, "but that's quite impossible. This is my fiancé's first visit to the village."

Tombob's papery brow crinkled in a frown. "Are you quite certain? Why, that's most peculiar. I would have sworn . . ." He shook his woolly, white head. "My mistake, I suppose. Neither my eyesight nor my wits are what they used to be." Still shaking his head, he started to turn away.

"Wait, sir." Despite his respectful tone, Nicholas's command rang with an authority that was impossible to disobey. The old man turned back to find Nicholas peering into *his* face. "Can you tell me why you thought you knew me?"

Tombob planted the tip of his cane firmly in the grass. "You put me in mind of a boy I once knew. Can't remember the lad's name. But he was a generous and good-natured soul—not an ounce of cheekiness in him."

A smile slowly curved Nicholas's lips. "Then the lady must be right. I cannot be that boy."

Both Tombob and the crowd burst into laughter at Nicholas's jest. Laura tugged at his arm, certain her nerves had suffered enough shocks for one day. "Come, Mr. Radcliffe. We really mustn't dally any longer. Cookie will be waiting lunch for us."

When their battered barouche came rolling into the manor's cobbled drive a short while later, it wasn't Cookie but Dower who was waiting for them, fresh from his expedition to London. Since the old man possessed only two expressions—grim and grimmer—it was impossible to tell if he bore good tidings or ill.

Before Nicholas could offer a hand to assist her down, Laura came spilling out of the barouche, nearly shredding her hem in her haste. "Welcome back, Dower. Have you any word on that ram we were thinking of purchasing for our flocks?"

"I might," he said cryptically.

"We've been getting along perfectly well without a new ram." George shot Nicholas a sullen look. "I don't see why we have need of one now."

"Unless we can roast it over a nice hot spit," Lottie concurred sweetly.

"Come, Dower," Laura said, smiling through clenched teeth. "Since it's livestock we'll be discussing, it would probably be best if we conducted our business in the barn."

Before the children could further stir Nicholas's suspicions, she started for the barn, dragging Dower along behind her as fast as his bandy legs would allow. She'd barely gotten the barn door closed and latched before she whirled around to face him. "What have you learned in London, Dower? Is there any word of a missing gentleman?"

"Don't 'urry me, gel. Give me time to catch m'breath."

Despite her impatience, Laura knew there was no rushing Dower when he didn't want to be rushed. Cookie had once nagged him into carrying a freshly baked mince pie to one of their neighbors only to have it arrive a week later with three pieces missing and a moldy crust.

She stewed in silence while he propped one foot on an overturned bucket, drew a pipe from his pocket, lit it, and took a leisurely draw. Just when she thought she might start tearing at her hair or his, he pursed his lips, blew out a mouthful of smoke, and said, "There's a missin' gent, all right."

Laura sank down on a bale of hay, her legs going weak. "Well, that's it, I suppose. We're all going to prison."

Dower took another deep draw on the pipe. "'E went missin' less than a week ago. Started out for one o' them fancy gambling 'ells, but never arrived. 'Is wife's been screamin' foul play ever since."

"Oh." Laura hugged her stomach, feeling as if one of the cows had just kicked her. It seemed that Nicholas wouldn't be needing a wife after all. He already had one.

A leer twisted Dower's thin lips. "Of course, there's some wot say 'e mighta sailed to France with 'is mistress."

Laura's head flew up. "He has a wife *and* a mistress?"

Dower shook his head admiringly, smoke streaming from his nostrils. "You got to 'and it to the bloke. 'Eaven knows I've enough trouble keepin' one woman 'appy, much less two."

Remembering the husky endearments Nicholas had whispered in her ear and the delicious heat of his mouth against her skin, Laura could not quite keep the bitter note from her voice. "I'm sure he knows just what to do to keep a woman *happy*. Such skills come very naturally to some men."

She rose from the hay bale and began to pace between the stalls. It was hardly fair of her to condemn Nicholas's character when her own was so lacking. She ought to be heartsick with guilt, not heartbroken. "His poor wife. How she must be suffering wondering what terrible fate has befallen him!"

Dower nodded his agreement. "I daresay them squallin' brats o' 'ers is more of a trial than a comfort."

Laura halted, then slowly turned to face him. "Brats?"

"Aye. Five of 'em, there are, each more sticky and shrill than the last."

Laura groped behind her for the hay bale, forced to sit again.

Dower drew a crumpled broadside from his pocket and held it out to her. "They been circulatin' these all over town in the 'opes o' findin' out wot 'appened to 'im."

Laura took the broadside from Dower, bracing herself to study a sketch by an artist who couldn't possibly do justice to his subject. Surely not even a master like Reynolds or Gainsborough could have captured the roguish slant of her fiancé's smile or the winning way his eyes crinkled in the bright sunlight.

She smoothed the broadside over her knee to find a pair of small, piggy eyes set deep in fleshy pockets squinting up at her. She leaned closer to the sketch. A bushy set of side whiskers did little to disguise the man's ample jowls. His brow was crowned by a head of black curls so lush as to be almost feminine.

Laura recoiled from the sketch. No artist, not even a blind one, could be *that* inept.

Springing to her feet, she shook the broadside at Dower. "This isn't him! This isn't my Nicholas!"

Dower scratched his head, looking genuinely baffled. "Never said it was, did I? You just asked me if there was a missin' gent."

Laura didn't know whether to kick him or kiss him. She compromised by throwing her arms around his neck. "Why, you wretched, wonderful old man! What would I ever do without you?"

"Steady now, gel. If I want the life choked out o' me, I'll go provoke me wife." Squirming out of her embrace, Dower stabbed the bowl of his pipe at the broadside. "This still don't prove that young gent o' yours ain't goin' to murder us all in our beds in the dark o' night."

A curious flush traveled through Laura's body. She might not know Nicholas's real name, but she did know that if he came to her bed in the dark of night, it wouldn't be with murder on his mind.

But Dower's words succeeded in putting a damper

on her relief. She'd been so overjoyed to learn that her fiancé wasn't a philandering husband and the father of five squalling brats that she'd momentarily forgotten they still hadn't a single clue to his identity.

"You're absolutely right, Dower. You'll simply have to return to London in a few days and make more inquiries. If I'm to be married on the Wednesday before my birthday, we haven't much time." She threw open the barn door, flooding the shadows with sunshine, and stood gazing wistfully up at the second-story window of Lady Eleanor's chamber. "I can't imagine why no one has missed him. If he were mine and I lost him, I'd search day and night until he was safely home again."

"Your cousin has gone missing."

For eleven years, Diana Harlow had waited to hear that voice. Had dreamed of the moment when its owner might stroll through the door of whatever room she happened to be occupying at the time. She had imagined a thousand different variations of her reaction from gracious welcome to aloof dismissal to withering disdain. But she had never dreamed that when the moment finally came, she would be powerless to do anything but continue to stare down at the ledger in front of her on the desk, even as its neat columns and rows of numbers blurred to an indecipherable jumble.

"Your cousin has gone missing," her unannounced guest repeated as he crossed the study and halted before the desk. "Have you any notion of his whereabouts?"

Diana slowly raised her head to find herself looking into the crisp green eyes of Thane DeMille, the marquess of Gillingham and Sterling's most devoted friend. Although time and the self-indulgent excesses expected of any high-living young buck had stamped their mark on his boyish features, his hair was still the same rich russet she remembered. His shoulders and limbs had lost their gangly awkwardness, nicely filling out a gray cutaway coat, a silver-and-burgundy striped waistcoat, and a pair of fawn trousers. He balanced a top hat and walking stick in his elegant hands.

She returned her attention to the ledger, keenly aware of the limp strand of hair that had escaped her chignon and the smudges of ink on her fingers. "My cousin has never made his whereabouts a matter of my concern. Have you made inquiries at all of his usual haunts—Almack's? White's? Newmarket?" She dipped her pen in the inkwell and began to inscribe another neat row of figures. "If he's not to be found in any of those places, I suggest you try the drawing room of the sisters Wilson."

The Wilson sisters were notorious Cyprians, their fondness for wealthy gentlemen of the ton surpassed only by their skills at pleasuring them.

If Thane was shocked that she knew the name of such an establishment, much less was bold enough to mention it in mixed company, he hid it behind a mocking smile. "It just so happens that I spoke with Miss Harriette Wilson only last night. She hasn't seen Sterling since he returned from France."

Diana's pen slipped, turning a zero into a nine. She slowly closed the ledger and peered up at Thane over the top of her spectacles. "I sincerely doubt that there's any great cause for alarm. Like you, my cousin is a man of varied interests and a low tolerance for boredom. He's probably just off indulging one of his many appetites."

Thane's mouth tightened. "I might be inclined to agree with you if it weren't for this."

Striding to the door, he slipped two fingers into his mouth and let out a most ungentlemanly whistle.

Sterling's mastiffs came padding into the room, their enormous heads drooping and their eyes downcast. They bore little resemblance to the magnificent creatures that had trotted into the study at their master's heels only a few short days ago. They milled about the room aimlessly, as if lost without Sterling's voice to guide them. Not even the small white cat napping on the hearth could stir their interest.

"Down, Caliban. Down, Cerberus," Thane commanded.

The dogs spared him little more than a morose glance before wending their way to the window. They nudged aside the brocade draperies and settled back on their hindquarters, pressing their noses to the window as they gazed down upon the fog-shrouded street.

"I don't understand," Diana said, frowning.

Thane threw himself into the leather wing chair opposite the desk.

She had forgotten that about him. He never sat. He always sprawled. "They've been moping about in this manner ever since Sterling disappeared. They won't eat. They won't sleep. They spend half the night whimpering and whining." Scowling, he flicked a brindle hair off of his lapel. "And they shed abominably."

Diana couldn't quite bite back her smile. "Perhaps you're in need of a competent valet, not a duke."

Thane leaned forward, fixing her with a penetrating stare. "Have you ever known Sterling to go anywhere for any length of time without those two beasts at his side? Even the French called them his *chiens de diable*— his devil dogs—and swore they'd been sent to escort his soul to hell if he should fall on the battlefield."

As Diana considered his words, she felt her first tingle of apprehension. She shuffled a stack of papers to occupy her unsteady hands. "Just how long has he been missing?"

"Nearly a week. Thursday morning around ten o'clock he informed one of my grooms that he was going for a ride in Hyde Park. It was the last anyone has seen of him."

"Surely you don't suspect he's been the victim of some sort of foul play?"

"As disagreeable as it may be, I fear we must consider the possibility."

Diana fought her growing panic. Despite their constant quibbling, she adored her roguish cousin as much as he adored her. He might play the devil for the rest of the world, but to her, he would always be the guardian angel who had borne the brunt of her father's displeasure so she wouldn't have to.

"There's no need to fear the worst, is there?" she asked. "He could have been the victim of a kidnapping."

"A likelihood I considered myself. But there have been no threats, no demands for ransom. And besides, if someone were foolhardy enough to abduct your cousin, they'd probably end up paying us to take him back. Why, that scathing tongue of his alone would break the spirit of even the most dastardly of villains."

Diana was too worried to be cheered by his grim humor. "But who would seek to do Sterling harm? Does he have any enemies?"

Thane arched an eyebrow, making her realize just how ridiculous her question was. "Well, let me think," he said, drumming his fingernails on the arm of the chair. "There's the two hapless young fellows he winged in recent duels before they could even get a shot off. Then there's Lord Reginald Danforth, former owner of a charming country estate in Derbyshire that now belongs to your cousin thanks to a winning hand of whist. Oh, and I nearly forgot his passionate dalliance with the lovely Lady Elizabeth Hewitt. To Sterling's credit, he didn't realize the lady in question was married until after their liaison. But I'm afraid her husband didn't appreciate the distinction. He would have called Sterling out himself if he hadn't heard about the earlier duels and feared suffering a similar humiliation."

Sighing bleakly, Diana slipped off her spectacles to rub the bridge of her nose. "Is there anyone in London who wouldn't wish him ill?"

"You and I."

Thane's soft-spoken words stung her. For eleven years, the two of them had been linked only in the minds of the most persistent gossips who had never forgotten the night their engagement—and her heart—had been irrevocably broken. Gazing at him without her spectacles made her feel as if her eyes were as unguarded as her memories.

She slipped them back on with a brisk motion and began to scribble notes on a fresh sheet of stationery. "Then you and I must be the ones to find him. I shall hire a detective while you question all of Sterling's acquaintances. It might be best to keep our inquiries discreet until we have some leads. We wouldn't wish to cause a panic." She glanced up at him. "Does that plan meet with your agreement?"

"I'm simply flattered that you bothered to consult me at all. It's not been a habit of yours in the past."

Although his stinging challenge whipped heat into her cheeks, she refused to be drawn into a duel of words she could not hope to win. "If we are to work together for Sterling's good, it might be best if we forget the past and concentrate on the future—*his* future, to be exact."

"As you wish, my lady." Thane rose, taking up his hat. "I shall call on you tomorrow afternoon so we can discuss our progress." As he started for the door, one of the mastiffs let out a plaintive whine.

Diana grimaced as the animal drooled on one of her father's priceless Turkish rugs. "Aren't you forgetting something, my lord?"

"Hm? Oh, of course." His expression utterly innocent, Thane returned to the chair to tuck the walking stick beneath his arm.

"I meant the dogs," she said icily.

His mocking grin was just as infuriating as she remembered it to be. "Ah, but they're *your* dogs now, my lady. If you require the services of a competent valet, I'd be happy to recommend one." Sketching her a crisp bow, he left her the way he had found her.

Alone.

Chapter 10

Although I don't deserve it,
God has blessed me with a new family. . . .

Laura Fairleigh was a woman of her word.

Nicholas hadn't guessed he would come to rue that particular virtue, but as the days passed and she made good on her vow never to be alone with him, he began to wish she would suffer another lapse in moral judgment. Although his headaches were fading nearly as fast as the lump on his skull, he considered feigning a setback purely in the hope that she might attempt to kiss him back to life.

She had obviously enlisted others to assist her in her mission. If he was so fortunate as to enter the drawing room and find her alone, they would barely have time to exchange the most impersonal of pleasantries before Cookie would come bustling in, trailing a length of white crepe for her young missie's approval or an experimental batch of almond icing for the bride cake that she would beg them both to taste. If they happened to meet on the landing outside their bedchambers, Lottie would materialize like a puckish sprite, waving a short story or poem she'd just written. And he always managed to find Laura sipping her tea alone at the kitchen table at the precise moment George would come banging through the door with an armload of firewood, his cheery whistle making Nicholas want to choke the lad.

If this kept up, he would soon be reduced to brushing past his fiancée on the stairs, trying to steal a whiff of her hair.

She'd done nothing to stir his suspicions since the day she'd rushed off to meet with Dower in the barn. Since he was reasonably certain she wasn't cuckolding him with the grizzled old man, Nicholas had almost succeeded in convincing himself that he simply possessed a mistrustful and jealous nature he'd do well to curb.

He managed to do just that until Thursday afternoon when he saw her start down the lane on foot with a mysterious burden tucked beneath her cloak.

Nicholas watched her go through the lace of the drawing room curtains, torn between instinct and honor.

Dower had set off at dawn with his flocks and Cookie was puttering about in the kitchen, humming beneath her breath. Lottie and George were in the study, quarreling over a noisy game of spillikins.

While George accused Lottie of blowing his jackstraws into a most unmanageable pile when he wasn't looking, Nicholas slipped out the front door of the manor and started after Laura, walking just fast enough to keep the slender, bonneted figure in sight without overtaking her. The day was overcast with a northerly wind and a snap in the air that made it feel more like autumn than summer.

Laura set a brisk pace, which didn't surprise him. In the past few days, he had learned that his betrothed was no delicate flower of womanhood content to dabble in needlework and watercolor. She was just as likely to be found perched on a rickety ladder dusting the crown molding as she was practicing a new piece on the pianoforte. While Cookie reigned over the kitchen with a flour-dusted rolling pin as her scepter, Laura tended both the flower and the herb gardens with an enthusiasm that frequently left her cheeks flushed with exertion and a charming dab of dirt on the tip of her nose.

She had nearly reached the outskirts of the village when she made an abrupt turn toward the church. Nicholas hung back, watching her every move from behind the trunk of a stately old oak. Although he felt like the worst sort of scoundrel, he couldn't make himself turn back. Not when he might discover what secret had cast the shadow of fear in those sparkling brown eyes of hers.

He could only hope he wasn't about to realize his own worst fear. Had some man supplanted him in her affections? And if so, would she be so bold as to rendezvous with him in the village church?

But she ignored the stone steps of the church, passing instead beneath the gabled lych-gate that led into the churchyard. Nicholas followed, but hesitated just outside the gate. Despite Laura's assurances of his devout nature, he still didn't feel quite welcome on hallowed ground.

As Laura disappeared over a grassy knoll, he slipped into the churchyard. A burst of chill wind sent dead leaves whipping around the gravestones in a crackling frenzy. Some of the stones were so old they sat at awkward angles in the ground, their inscriptions half-buried or worn away completely by wind, rain, and time.

He found Laura kneeling between two well-weathered stones on the far side of the cemetery. He halted, watching in silence as she drew her mysterious burden out from beneath her cloak.

It was a great armful of flowers—larkspurs, chrysanthemums, marigolds, irises, lilies—all freshly cut from the garden she tended with her own hands.

As she placed a colorful bouquet at the foot of each stone, arranging the stems with tender care, Nicholas collapsed against a crumbling tomb, feeling like the most contemptible of villains. Laura had come to this place to pay tribute to her parents and he had stalked her as if she were a common criminal. If he had even a shred of decency in his soul, he would creep back to the manor and leave her to grieve in solitude.

But his desire to be near her was stronger than his shame. So he lingered, watching as she turned away from her parents' graves and carried the remaining flowers to a nearby pair of stones. She didn't spare the first marker so much as a glance, but she knelt reverently beside the second. The stone was new, without even a hint of lichen to mar its rough-hewn surface. Although the summer grass hadn't had time to blanket the raw earth, a small alabaster angel kept vigil over the grave, its chubby little hands folded in prayer.

Oddly enough, it wasn't the fresh grave but the angel that sent a shiver through Nicholas's soul. He found himself moving forward without realizing it, inexorably drawn toward that forlorn guardian.

Laura had removed her gloves and begun to tug at the weeds around the edges of the grave. She was so focused upon her task that she didn't even hear him approach.

He didn't stop until he was near enough to read the inscription carved into the stone—an inscription that was both stark and elegant in its simplicity.

Eleanor Harlow, Beloved Mother.

"Who was she?"

As Laura dropped her handful of weeds and turned her head, she was surprised to see Nicholas standing over her, his handsome face closed and still.

She pressed a hand to her thudding heart, despising the guilty conscience that made her so jumpy. "You gave me a terrible fright! I thought you were a ghost."

"Were you expecting one?" he asked, nodding at the grave.

It took Laura a second to divine his meaning, but when she did, she shook her head. "I can't think of anyone less likely to go about haunting someone than Lady Eleanor."

Nicholas reached down and drew her to her feet. Her knees had grown stiff from kneeling and she stumbled against him for a fraction of a moment, leaving no doubt in her mind that he was no ghost, but flesh and blood. Hot blood surging beneath warm, masculine flesh.

"Who was she?" he repeated, gazing down into her eyes.

Dragging both her hand and her look away from him, Laura bent to gather up the remaining flowers. "Most people would call her our guardian. I prefer to think of her as our guardian angel. She was the one who offered my father his living as the rector of Arden." Laying a white lily atop the stone, Laura smiled wistfully. "After our parents died, she took us in and gave the children and me a home."

Nicholas squatted to trace a finger over the dates carved into the granite. "October 14, 1768–February 2, 1815," he read, then frowned up at her. "The things in my room, they belonged to her, didn't they—the sewing box? The Bible? The hairbrush?" He seemed about to say something else, but stopped, his lips pressed tightly together.

Laura touched a hand to his shoulder. "I hope you're not superstitious. I put you in her bedchamber because I wanted you to have the most comfortable accommodations for your recovery. You shouldn't have to worry about any wailing and rattling of chains in the middle of the night. Lady Eleanor wouldn't have been able to bear the thought of disturbing your sleep, much less your peace of mind."

"I don't believe in ghosts," he said, glancing at the weathered stone that would have been a twin to Lady Eleanor's had the grave it marked not been untended and choked with weeds. There was no sign of any flowers having been left on it, either recently or in the past.

"Lady Eleanor's husband," Laura said dryly, answering his unspoken question. "She always said he should have been buried in unconsecrated ground."

"He was a suicide?"

"Of a sort. He drank himself to death. But not before breaking his wife's heart," Laura added softly.

Nicholas's frown deepened. "Did I know her?"

Laura took her time rearranging the flowers—tucking delicate sprigs of sweet william among the hardy marigolds and chrysanthemums. As Cookie had reminded her, one of Lady Eleanor's fondest dreams had been to see Laura wed to a kind and handsome gentleman. She stole a look at the rugged purity of Nicholas's profile. Despite her resolution to lie no more than was necessary, there didn't seem to be any harm in elaborating on what might have been.

"Of course you knew her," she told him firmly. "She doted upon you and took great delight in your visits. She often said that you were like a son to her."

To her dismay, Nicholas's countenance failed to brighten. "The stone reads 'Beloved Mother,'" he pointed out. "What of her own children? Why aren't they here leaving flowers on her grave?"

Laura felt her smile curdle. Fearing that she would reveal more than she meant to, she knelt beside him and began to fan the flowers around the foot of the stone, her motions brisk. "She only had one son, I'm afraid—a repugnant toad of a man who cares nothing for anyone but himself."

His sharp look shifted to her face. "Why, Miss Fairleigh, you're rather *passionate* in your dislike of him, are you not?"

Her fingers tightened, snapping a bloom right off its stem. "On the contrary. I don't dislike him. I loathe him."

Nicholas rescued a handful of the delicate lilies from her murderous grip before she could behead them all. "So tell me—what has this unfortunate fellow done to earn the enmity of such a gentle soul? Kicked a kitten? Made a regular habit of missing Sunday services? Threatened to give Lottie the spanking she so richly deserves?"

"Oh, we've never met. Which is just as well. Because

if we did, I just might give him a tongue-lashing he'd never forget."

"Heaven help him," Nicholas murmured, his gaze lingering on her mouth.

She was too incensed to notice. "It's not just his debauched habits I detest but his colossal indifference toward the woman who gave him life. Lady Eleanor wrote him faithfully every week for years and never once did he bother to send her so much as a perfunctory note. She had to read about his exploits in the scandal sheets, just as we did." Laura yanked up a fat gobbet of weeds and hurled it aside. "As far as I'm concerned, he's a heartless, vile, petty, vindictive wretch."

"Does this mean you won't be inviting him to our wedding?"

"I should say not! Why, I'd just as soon invite Beelzebub himself!"

At the sight of the dimple in his cheek, the tension melted from her shoulders. "You shouldn't tease so, sir," she chided with a half-smile of her own. "It's most unkind."

He gave a mock shudder. "I certainly wouldn't want to incur your wrath. I'm beginning to think this fellow deserves my pity more than my scorn. Surely being cast from your good graces is punishment enough for any man."

As he reached to tuck a feathery strand of hair behind her ear, Laura could no longer tell if he was teasing. She couldn't even quite remember how they'd ended up on the ground, on their knees, so near that if he wanted to kiss her he had only to slip his head beneath the brim of her bonnet and touch those exquisitely skilled lips of his to hers.

Dropping the last of the blooms, she scrambled to her feet. "If you'll excuse me, Mr. Radcliffe, I need to speak with Reverend Tilsbury about a matter of great importance. Please inform Cookie that I'll be back in time for tea." She gathered up her gloves and started for the gate.

"If you don't believe in ghosts," he called after her, rising to his feet, "then what are you so afraid of?"

You.

Half-afraid she had spoken the damning word aloud, Laura hastened from the churchyard, leaving Nicholas standing among the crumbling gravestones, his only companion the alabaster angel who kept vigil over Eleanor Harlow's grave.

When the bells began to toll their melodious invitation on Sunday morning, Nicholas didn't waste time burying his head beneath the pillow. He simply rolled out of bed, ignoring the disgruntled chirp of the small yellow cat who had made a nest of his pillow, and splashed a bracing dash of cold water in his face.

As he ushered George and Laura into the family pew of St. Michael's a short while later and slid in after them, followed by Lottie, he felt nothing more than a sense of mild resignation. He had high hopes of dozing his way through both the sermon and the second reading of the banns, since there weren't to be any surprises to jar him from his nap this week. As the rector mounted the steps to the mahogany pulpit, he settled himself more comfortably into the pew.

"Today," the white-haired man intoned, adjusting his spectacles, "we will examine the wise words of King

Solomon in Proverbs Nineteen—'Tis better to be poor than a liar.'"

George's foot lashed out, kicking Laura soundly in the shin.

She let out a sharp yelp, quickly muffled into her glove, but not before several of the parishioners had turned to glare disapprovingly at them. Frowning, Nicholas shook his head at George, wondering what spirit of mischief had possessed the lad.

Before he could ask Laura if she was all right, Lottie's reticule lurched into his lap and began to gnaw at the edges of his prayer book.

"Sorry," she murmured, retrieving the silk purse with an angelic smile.

Nicholas stretched out his legs and propped his cheek on his open palm, feeling his eyelids growing heavier with each of the rector's droning words. While the sun streaming through the mullioned windows warmed the musty nave, the little man went on and on with some nonsense about liars falling into the devil's clutches.

Nicholas was drifting in and out of a misty dream where he was kissing each freckle on Laura's creamy skin when he heard the man say, "As soon as your new rector is ordained, I will be leaving you."

Good, Nicholas thought uncharitably without bothering to open his eyes. It was a pity he couldn't leave immediately.

"As all of you know, I have been dividing my time between three parishes since Reverend Fairleigh was called home to heaven seven years ago. Although I have grown quite fond of Arden and all of you during this time, I must confess it will be something of a relief to hand over my duties and responsibilities a few months hence. I pray you will join me in welcoming the man who will soon be your new rector to our parish—Mr. Nicholas Radcliffe!"

Nicholas jerked awake, wondering if he was still dreaming. But the only constant between his delicious fantasy and this nightmare was the presence of the woman sitting beside him.

She was staring straight ahead, her profile as brittle as a piece of fine porcelain. Were it not for the uneven rise and fall of her bosom, he would have sworn she wasn't even breathing.

He glared at her until she had no choice but to turn and meet his smoldering gaze.

As she slid her gloved hand into his, a tremulous smile curved her lips. "Welcome to our parish, Mr. Radcliffe."

Chapter 11

*I adore the little ones, but it is
the oldest girl who has stolen my heart. . . .*

They're havin' their first quarrel, they are.
Why, it's enough to break an old woman's heart!"
Cookie whispered, dabbing at her eyes with her apron.

"If he makes her cry, perhaps she'll break the engagement," Lottie said hopefully.

"If he makes her cry, I'll break his neck," George snarled.

Dower scowled. "If they're quarrelin', 'ow come I don't 'ear no shoutin' or cussin'? It ain't a proper quarrel without a bit o' pottery bein' flung."

It was fortunate that their varying heights and Lottie's lack of concern about wearing out the knees of her Sunday stockings made it possible for all four of them to press their ears to the drawing room door at the same time.

"Try the keyhole," Dower suggested.

Wiggling between George's legs, Lottie squinted through the brass opening. "All I can see is the key. I do believe he's taken her prisoner."

Dower began to roll up his sleeves. "That's it, then. Break down the door, George, while I fetch me pitchfork."

"Don't be a ninny, old man," Cookie chided, punching him on the arm. "Young lovers must be left to make up their own quarrels. You might not remember that nasty row we had over that Fleet Street doxy when you was courtin' me, but I bet you ain't ever forgot the cuddle we had afterward."

"Of course I ain't. Why do you think I'm goin' to fetch me pitchfork?"

"Shhhhh," Lottie hissed, flattening her ear against the door. "I think I hear something."

Lottie was mistaken, for inside the drawing room Laura sat on the ottoman in absolute silence, thinking that she'd never actually seen a man too furious to speak. Her father had been a mild-mannered soul who considered displays of temper vulgar and unseemly. She'd once seen him drop an enormous Bible on his foot, breaking two toes, only to roll his eyes heavenward and beg the good Lord's pardon for being so clumsy. She'd never once known him to lift his voice to her mother or any of his children, much less his hand.

Laura watched Nicholas prowl back and forth across the drawing room with wary fascination, the way one might eye a hungry lion pacing its cage in the Royal Zoo. Except at the Royal Zoo, she would have been safely outside the iron bars instead of inside the cage with the lion. The yellow kitten perched on the hearth studied his movements with equal absorption, as if trying to determine which one of them he would gobble up first.

He'd shed his church clothes for the pagan comforts of his lawn shirt and buckskin trousers. Every few steps he would wheel around to glare at her, open his mouth as if to say something, then clamp it shut again, and resume his pacing. After repeating this ritual several times, he was reduced to shaking his head and running a hand through his hair until he looked every bit as wild and dangerous as Dower still believed him to be.

He finally stopped with his back to her, rested his balled fist against the mantel, and said, very softly, "I don't suppose I'm given to swearing, am I?"

Laura shook her head. "Only under extreme duress."

He swung around to face her. "And just what would you consider extreme duress? Would it be waking up naked in a strange bed with no memory of who you were? Would it be suddenly discovering that you're about to become the husband of a woman who swears you've never even had the good sense to kiss her? Or would it be learning, along with the rest of the good folk of Arden, that you're to be the village's new rector?" His voice rose. "Don't you think you might have discussed that little snippet of information with me before sharing it with the town crier?"

"I told you I had to speak to Reverend Tilsbury on a matter of great importance. And what could be more important than our future together?" Laura folded her hands primly in her lap. "I thought you'd be pleased to learn that I'd arranged a living for you. Arden is a small parish, but when you combine the income you'll be receiving from the parishioners with the money the manor earns from its flocks, we should be able to manage quite nicely. We won't be wealthy, but we won't be destitute either."

Nicholas sighed. "I appreciate your practicality, but

what if I don't wish to become a clergyman? Did that thought never occur to you?"

"And why wouldn't you? There's really nothing to it—just marrying, burying, and the occasional baptism. My father studied at home for months, but when he went to take his orders, he was most disappointed in the ease of the examination. The bishop simply asked him if he was the same Edmund Fairleigh who was the son of old Aurelius Fairleigh of Flamstead, then clapped him on the shoulder and took him to see a bawdy play."

"At least I'll have something to look forward to," Nicholas muttered, raking a hand through his hair again.

"I can help you study, you know," Laura told him earnestly. "I'm fluent in both Hebrew and Greek."

"How inspiring. Perhaps *you* should be Arden's new rector."

His jaw taut, he flung open the doors of the secretaire and began to shove aside cracked leather ledgers and scraps of yellowing stationery. A cut-glass decanter Laura had never seen before emerged from the shadows.

As he withdrew the decanter from its hiding place, Laura sat up straighter, thinking it peculiar that he'd known exactly where to find it. Judging from the layer of dust furring the glass, the brandy within must be very well aged indeed.

As he carried the decanter over to the tea cart and found a clean glass, Laura cleared her throat in what she hoped was a delicate manner.

Nicholas jerked the stopper from the mouth of the decanter.

"I hesitate to mention it . . ." she began tentatively.

He splashed a stream of liquor into the glass.

"Especially at such an inopportune moment . . ."

He lifted the glass to his lips, the fierce light in his eyes daring her to continue.

". . . but you never indulge in spirits."

"Bloody hell and damnation!" Nicholas slammed the glass down on the cart, sloshing half the brandy over its beveled rim.

His curse hung in the air between them like a warning roll of thunder. Laura wasn't sure whether to duck or make a run for the door. But then a slow smile began to spread across his features. A smile so sensual it made Laura's toes curl within the pinching confines of her shoes.

"That felt marvelous," he proclaimed. "*Bloody* marvelous!"

Her eyes widened as he raised the glass and tossed back what was left of the brandy. His tongue circled his lips, capturing every stray drop as if it were the sweetest of nectars, while his eyes drifted shut in an expression of pure bliss. When he opened them again, they were glittering with determination. He refilled the glass, then lifted it in a defiant toast before polishing off its contents.

Then he filled the glass a third time and crossed the room to put it into her hands. "Here. You might have need of this."

"But I've never—"

He arched an eyebrow in warning. She subsided and took an obedient sip. The stuff burned a tingling path down her throat that was unnerving, but not unpleasant.

Nicholas retrieved another glass and poured himself more brandy. He draped one arm along the length of the mantel, the glass dangling from his long, elegant fingers. "It has come to my attention, Miss Fairleigh, that every time I've turned around in the past week, you've been telling me what I do and don't fancy. 'Have another one of Cookie's crumpets, Mr. Radcliffe,'" he mimicked. "'You've always loved Cookie's crumpets.' 'Do listen to this poem Lottie wrote. You've never failed to find her sonnets amusing.' 'Why don't you and George play another hand of loo, darling? He does so enjoy your company.'"

His voice rose with each word. "This may come as a shock to your delicate sensibilities, my dear, but your brother can barely stand to be in the same room with me, Lottie is a spoiled brat who couldn't write a decent couplet if Will Shakespeare himself came crawling out of his grave to help her, and Cookie's crumpets are dry enough to choke a camel!"

Laura's horrified gasp was nearly drowned out by a trio of echoing gasps from outside the drawing room door.

Leaving the glass on the mantel, Nicholas strode across the drawing room and flung open the door. The foyer was deserted, but the sound of scampering feet echoed through the manor. Shooting Laura an accusing look, he shut the door with deliberate care and twisted the key in the lock.

She took another sip of the brandy, this one much larger than the last.

He leaned against the door and crossed his arms, continuing as if they'd never been interrupted. "I hate to spoil the sainted image of me you've obviously been cherishing in your heart for the past two years, but spending my afternoons painting watercolors with Lottie bores me to tears and I can't abide those silly card games George seems to be so fond of."

Laura opened her mouth, hoping to stop him before he confessed that he couldn't abide her either.

He held up a hand to stay her. "Now, being a reasonable fellow, I *can* concur that a man's soul might benefit from some spiritual instruction on a Sunday morning." His expression softening, he glanced at the hearth, where the kitten sat grooming her whiskers with sylph-like grace. "I might even be convinced that certain members of the feline species, however much of a nuisance, can possess charms that are difficult to resist."

He moved to kneel beside the ottoman, putting him at eye level with her. "But I cannot and will not be persuaded that I'm not the sort of man who would compromise his fiancée's virtue. Because I can assure you that I've thought of little else since the first moment I laid eyes on you."

Dazed, Laura gulped down the rest of the brandy. Nicholas gently removed the glass from her hand and rested it on the carpet.

"But you always—" she began.

He laid two fingers against the softness of her lips, effectively stilling them. "You've spent the past week telling me what I'm *supposed* to want. Now it's my turn to show you what I *do* want."

As he framed her face in his big, strong hands, she expected him to kiss her mouth. She did not expect him to kiss her eyelids, her temples, the freckled bridge of her nose. His breath fanned her face, as warm and intoxicating as the forbidden sweetness of the port. But as he lowered his lips to hers, the fever that went curling through her veins had nothing to do with the brandy and everything to do with the liquid heat of his tongue tenderly laving her mouth.

Before Laura realized it, she was clutching his shirt-front and meeting each deepening thrust of his tongue with a hungry sweep of her own. She hardly recognized the fierce little creature who clung to him with such abandon. It was as if the prim and proper rector's daughter had disappeared, leaving a shameless wanton in her place.

Perhaps this was the escalating nature of sin her papa had always warned her about. Failing to read your morning psalms led to lying and lying led to abducting strange gentlemen and abducting gentlemen led to kissing and kissing led to lust and lust led to . . . well, she wasn't completely clear on where lust led, but if Nicholas didn't stop nuzzling her ear in that tantalizing manner, she was certainly going to find out.

The seductive rasp of his voice startled her out of her dreamy daze. "Come away with me, Laura."

"What did you say?" She leaned away from him to peer into his face, still clinging to his shirt.

He caught her upper arms in a fierce grip, his eyes as hot as his hands. "Come away with me! Right now. Why should we wait until next week to be married when we can leave for Gretna Green this very afternoon and be sharing a bed before this week is done?"

His words sent a delicious frisson down her spine, half terror and half anticipation. A shaky laugh escaped her. "You left out the part where you make me your wife."

"Simply an oversight, I assure you." He gazed down into her eyes with a curious mixture of tenderness and desperation. "Don't make me wait any longer to make you mine. We've already wasted far too much time."

"You don't know the half of it," Laura muttered, burying her face in his shoulder.

This was a temptation she hadn't anticipated. If she allowed him to sweep her off to Scotland in the heat of the moment for a runaway wedding not bound by the conventions of the English courts, there would be no more worries about forging a false name in the parish register, no more sleepless nights wondering if his memory was going to come flooding back before they took their vows.

But there would also be no more time to send Dower to London. No more time to make sure her fiancé's heart wasn't already pledged to another woman before she claimed it for her own.

Still, she was tempted. Tempted to seize both the man in her arms and the moment and run away to Gretna Green as countless brides before her had done.

They could be sharing a bed before the week was done.

Laura's breath quickened as she envisioned a cozy chamber in a rustic inn. In Gretna Green, such a chamber would be intended for one purpose and one purpose only—seduction. There would be wine and cheese on the table, a fire crackling on the grate to ward off the chill in the damp Scottish air, a downy quilt turned back in invitation on the rough-hewn bedstead. And there would be Nicholas, eager to partake of the first delights of their love.

But he did not love her. She had only tricked him into believing he did. It was that realization more than any other that gave her the strength to shove herself from his arms. She rose and stood with her back to him, hugging back a shiver of shame.

Nicholas followed, catching her gently by the shoulders from behind. "I wanted you to run away *with* me," he said softly, "not *from* me."

"I have no intention of doing either," she replied, thankful he couldn't see her face. "The minute we set out for Scotland together, my reputation would be in ruins."

"I don't mind," he murmured, brushing his lips against her nape in a tingling caress. "As long as I'm the one doing the ruining."

"But it's not only ourselves we have to think of."

His hands slowly fell away from her shoulders. "That's exactly what I'm coming to fear."

Chilled by his abrupt withdrawal, Laura turned to face him. "Don't you see? If we elope, it will break everyone's hearts. Cookie's been working day and night on my dress and on whipping up the perfect batch of almond icing for the bride cake. Dower hasn't set foot in a church since his own wedding, yet he's promised to walk me down the aisle. Lottie has her little heart set on carrying my posy for me. And George"—she forced a smile—"well, if you eloped with his sister, George would feel compelled to call you out, and I simply can't have you shooting my only brother."

Nicholas's reassuring smile didn't quite reach his eyes. "I suppose you're right. You've waited patiently for me for two years. Surely I can do you the same courtesy for two weeks. It was unfair of me to try to cheat you out of the wedding every woman dreams of having." He drew her against his chest, hiding his face from her as he gently stroked her hair. "If you'll give me a chance to redeem myself, I promise I'll see to it that you get everything you deserve."

Laura stood frozen in the warmth of his arms, unable to tell him that was exactly what she feared.

Nicholas spent the next morning prowling the rolling hills surrounding Arden Manor. The sun beamed down from a crisp blue sky, warming his head and shoulders. A buoyant breeze sifted through his hair. He didn't even have to worry about Dower's surly countenance casting a thundercloud over the day. Laura had sent him off to London before dawn to search the livestock markets for another ram.

It was the sort of morning when a man should have no care for the past or the future, only the present. But still Nicholas found himself dwelling on yesterday, reliving the moment when Laura had shoved herself from his arms and stood shivering just out of his reach.

He'd spent most of the night trying to convince himself that he had only himself to blame. He could hardly reproach her for not wanting to be alone with him when he fell upon her like some sort of debauched pirate every time they were. Nor could he blame her for not surrendering to such a foolish, romantic notion as running off to Scotland just so he could take her to bed a few days earlier than scheduled.

She might have refused to run away with him, but that didn't necessarily mean there was something—or someone—she was reluctant to leave behind.

Nicholas tried to shake away the ugly thought. Laura might be able to pretend affection for him, but he couldn't accuse her of feigning the sweet sighs she breathed each time he took her into his arms or the melting softness of her mouth beneath his. He felt himself harden at the memory.

Desperate to distract himself from his licentious thoughts, Nicholas drew a calfskin-bound Greek Testament containing the Gospel of Mark from the pocket of his coat and began to read while he strolled. He had smuggled the book out of the manor's library without Laura's knowledge and was surprised to discover that he was as fluent in Greek as he was in English. He still hadn't agreed to her mad scheme to make a country parson of him, but neither had he completely rejected it. After all, he would require some way to provide a living for his bride and her family. He might have lost his memory, but he hadn't lost his pride.

He became so engrossed in the slim volume that he didn't even realize something had gone whizzing past his nose until it embedded itself in the trunk of the alder he happened to be passing with a resounding *twang*.

He halted and slowly turned his head to find an arrow still vibrating in the smooth bark. Wrenching it from the tree, he glanced around the meadow. Except for a lark trilling a soaring aria from the branches of a nearby hawthorn, it appeared to be deserted.

Or so he thought until he caught a flicker of movement from the corner of his eye.

Something was protruding from behind a faint rise in the land. Something that looked remarkably like a lopsided topknot of golden curls.

Slipping the book back into his pocket, he went

striding across the meadow. Propping one foot on the rise, he leaned over to peer into the hollow beyond.

"Would this, by any chance, belong to you?" he asked its occupant, holding out the arrow.

Lottie slowly emerged from her hiding place, clover in her hair and bow in hand. "It might. I've taken up archery, you know." She shot him a frigid glance. "I find it to be so much more fulfilling than poetry."

Nicholas's lips twitched as her dart hit home. "But far more hazardous for your audience."

"I just took up the sport," she protested. "I'm not a very good shot yet."

"Where's your target?"

"Over there." She gestured vaguely toward a distant clump of trees in the opposite direction of where he had been strolling.

Nicholas lifted one eyebrow. "My, you are a bad shot, aren't you?" He took the bow from her, surprised by how natural it felt in his hands. "Have you any chalk?"

Although her round little face lost none of its contrariness, she began to dig through the pockets of her pinafore. He waited patiently while she sifted through a dozen hair ribbons, an assortment of rocks and twigs, two stale teacakes, and a small brown toad, before finally locating a worn-down stub of chalk.

She watched, trying not to appear interested, as he marched back to the alder and drew four concentric circles on its trunk. He returned to Lottie, knelt behind her, and carefully fitted the bow to her grip.

"Steady," he murmured, guiding her through the motions of nocking the arrow and taking aim.

The arrow took wing, sailing across the meadow to

strike the alder soundly within the boundaries of the innermost circle.

Straightening, Nicholas ruffled her curls and gave her a lazy smile. "Choose something to aim for, Goldilocks, and you'll hit your target every time."

Drawing the book from his pocket, he continued on his way, not realizing that he'd left Lottie at a loss for words for the first time in her young life.

When George entered the kitchen the next day, shaking the rain from an afternoon shower out of his hair, Cookie was nowhere in sight. Instead, he found Lottie standing on a footstool beside the table, beating a batch of almond icing with fierce concentration. Flour smudged her round cheeks and a fluffy gray cat crouched beside the earthenware bowl, pretending disdain.

Watching her pound the hapless ingredients into a stiff froth, George cocked an eyebrow. "Don't know why you've taken up the bow and arrow when you could just whip someone to death with that spoon."

He waited until she'd turned away to retrieve a pinch of cinnamon from a china saucer before swiping his finger around the rim of the bowl.

It was halfway to his mouth when Lottie turned back and cried, "George, no!"

George froze. He looked at her, then back at the bowl, feeling the color drain from his face. He accepted the rag she handed him, wiping every trace of the icing from his skin.

Shooting the door to the dining room a nervous look, he whispered, "What in the devil do you think you're doing? I thought you weren't going to kill him until *after* the wedding."

"I've no intention of killing him," she whispered back. "I'm just going to make him mildly ill. It's the only way I can check my dosages."

"But if he gets sick after he eats this, won't he suspect that you've poisoned him?"

"Of course not. He has no idea we'd wish to do him harm. He'll simply think I'm a dreadful cook." Her face taut with determination, she added another pinch of the stuff George had believed to be cinnamon to the bowl. "The sugar and the almonds together should mask the bitterness of the toadstools."

George swallowed, beginning to feel mildly ill himself. "Are you sure you want to do this?"

Lottie slammed the spoon down, sending the cat careening from the table. "He's left me no choice! Can't you see what he's doing by pretending to be good and kind instead of mean and hateful? How could any girl be expected to resist his soft words and those winning smiles of his?"

George frowned, caught off guard by her vehemence. "We are talking about Laura here, aren't we?"

Ramming the spoon back into the bowl, Lottie resumed her grim battle with the icing. "Of course we're talking about Laura. Do you want things to go back to the way they were before he came or do you want him to steal her away from us the same way he stole my kitten? Because if he does, I can promise you, we'll never get her back."

George might have argued further had he not seen a single teardrop roll off of Lottie's pointed little chin and drip into the bowl. The almonds might hide the taste of the toadstools, but no sugar was sweet enough to mask the bitterness of his sister's tears.

Lottie hesitated in the doorway of the drawing room, observing her quarry. Nicholas was sprawled in a leather wing chair, his stocking feet propped on the ottoman. A fire snapped and crackled on the grate in a cozy counterpoint to the rhythm of the rain beating against the windowpanes. The lamplight cast a rosy hue over the classical beauty of his profile.

He was reading again. One of her father's leather-bound atlases of the Holy Land lay open in his lap. His study was hampered only by the yellow kitten, who insisted upon bouncing from the floor to his lap every time he turned the page, determined to banish the interloper who had usurped its throne. Lottie watched as he scooped up the kitten for the third time and gently set it back on the rug.

Fearful of losing her resolve, Lottie marched into the room, bearing the miniature bride cake on a silver tray as if it were a ceremonial offering.

Nicholas glanced up from his book with a mock shudder of dread. "Oh, no. Please tell me it's not another crumpet. Every time I open my mouth, Cookie pops another one in. Then while I'm trying to choke it down, she pinches my cheek, and says, 'I made a fresh batch just for you, Mr. Nick. I know how you fancy them and I feared the last dozen weren't enough to fill you up.'"

A reluctant smile curved Lottie's lips. "No crumpets, I fear. Cookie went off to the market so I thought I'd try my own hand at making a bride cake."

Nicholas accepted the tray she held out to him, eyeing the lopsided pastry with a dubious eye. "You know, it might be safer for all of us if you'd just go back to writing poetry."

"For once, Mr. Radcliffe," Lottie replied, her smile fading, "you may just be right."

She left him with her offering, turning away a moment too soon to see the kitten go bouncing back into his lap.

Lottie lingered in the kitchen with George for as long as she could stand the suspense, then went creeping back to the drawing room. She briefly closed her eyes before peeping around the doorframe, trying to prepare herself for what she might find.

Nicholas still sat in the chair, his cheek propped on his hand as he flipped to the next page in the atlas. Lottie searched his face for any trace of distress. His eyes were crisp and alert. His skin had lost none of its golden hue.

Perhaps he hadn't yet eaten the cake, she thought, perplexed by his robust good health. But then she spotted the empty tray resting on the floor beside his chair.

And the furry little body draped across the hearth.

Lottie cupped a hand over her mouth, but it was too late to stifle her cry.

Nicholas's head flew up. As tears flooded her eyes, he tossed the book aside and came to his feet. "Lottie, what is it? What in heaven's name is wrong?"

She pointed behind him, her hand trembling. "The cat. You didn't give the cake to the cat, did you?"

"No," came a small voice from the window seat. "He gave it to me."

The kitten lifted its head from its nap just as Laura rose from the window seat, swaying like a willow in the wind. All the color had drained from her face, making her freckles stand out. Nicholas crossed the room in three long strides, catching her in his arms before she could fall to the floor.

Chapter 12

*She has the gentlest of dispositions,
but she's a bit of a dreamer. . . .*

Cookie returned from the market a short while
later to find the manor in total chaos. Lottie was curled
up on the stairs sobbing her little heart out while the
upper floor of the house resounded with masculine
shouting.

"What the devil? . . ." Cookie muttered, dropping
her basket on the floor. She shrugged out of her damp
cape and untied her bonnet. "What is it, child? Why on
earth is everyone carryin' on so?"

Lottie lifted her tear-splotched face from the crook of
her arm. "I didn't mean to do it, I swear I didn't! It's all
his fault! I was only trying to protect her from him!"
Wracked by another sob, she lurched past Cookie,
threw open the front door, and went flying from the
house, disappearing into the rain-drenched yard.

More alarmed than ever, Cookie grabbed the banister and started up the stairs, moving at a pace she
hadn't employed in over twenty years.

She found Nicholas and George standing just outside

the open door of Lady Eleanor's chamber. Nicholas had the boy by the shoulders. "You have to tell me the truth," he was shouting. "What did Lottie put in that cake? I know you're trying to protect your little sister, but if you don't tell me, Laura could die!"

George shook his head. Although his lower lip was trembling, he shouted back at Nicholas with equal vigor. "Lottie would never do anything to hurt Laura! I don't know what you're talking about!"

That was when Cookie saw her young mistress, stretched out on the bed behind them, as pale and still as death.

"What's happened to her?" Cookie demanded, hurrying over to the bed and resting her hand on Laura's clammy forehead. "What's happened to my lamb?"

Nicholas and George followed, their expressions grim. "I'm not entirely certain," Nicholas said, shooting George a dark look. "I suspect she may have been the victim of a malicious prank intended for me."

Remembering Lottie's tearful words, Cookie wheeled on George and snapped, "Run downstairs to the kitchen, lad, and fetch me a kettle of boilin' water and some dried black root from my herb basket. And be quick about it."

His relief painfully obvious, the boy made his escape.

While Cookie rushed about the chamber, gathering a washbasin and clean rags, Nicholas sank down on the edge of the bed. He took Laura's limp hand and brought it to his lips, his eyes never leaving her pallid face. "I can't get her to wake up. Shouldn't we send to London for a doctor?"

"Don't you fret, Mr. Nick," Cookie said. "There's no need to fetch some fancy sawbones who'll do nothin' but slap some leeches on Miss Laura's pretty arms. Why, I've been tendin' to her since she was a mere slip of a girl. Nursed her through a nasty bout of scarlet fever, I did, just after her parents died." Bathing Laura's brow with a damp rag, Cookie shook her head. "Even as a young thing, the girl never did give a care for herself. She was too busy worryin' about that brother and sister of hers." She began to loosen the ribbons at the bodice of Laura's gown, then hesitated, giving Nicholas a pointed look. "Most men aren't of any use in the sickroom. If you'd like, you can wait downstairs."

"No," he said, meeting her steady gaze with a helpless one of his own. "I can't."

Cookie had good reason to be thankful he stayed. When Laura's stomach began to rebel against the purgative tea being spooned down her throat, he was the one who insisted on steadying her head over the washbasin. When she collapsed against the sheets, shivering and spent, he was the one who smoothed the sweat-soaked strands of hair from her face and tucked the chintz coverlet around her. And when she awoke from her exhausted stupor long after dark had fallen, he was the one stretched out in the chair next to the bed.

It took Laura a foggy moment to realize that she wasn't in her own bed. She gazed up at the graceful half-tester, breathing deeply of the clean masculine musk that seemed to surround her, then slowly turned her head to find Nicholas napping in the chair.

Even with his hair hanging loose in his face and smudges of fatigue beneath his eyes, he still looked every inch the prince. If anything, he was more alluring to her now than he had been the day she found him in the wood. Then he had been nothing more than a pretty stranger. Now it wasn't just his fine looks she admired but his intelligence, his keen wit, and those tantalizing flashes of temper and tenderness.

As if sensing her thoughtful gaze, his eyes fluttered open.

"What happened to me?" she asked, surprised by the hoarseness of her voice.

He sat up and leaned over the bed, squeezing her hand. "Let's just say that your sister's culinary skills leave a little to be desired."

"I could have warned you about that," Laura croaked. "Did I ever tell you about the time she baked a dozen worms into a mud pie and served it to Reverend Tilsbury for tea?"

"No," he replied with a crooked smile. "If you had, I might have declined the bride cake she made for me."

Laura groaned as her memory came flooding back. "Oh, I wish *I* had."

"So do I. The next time I catch you coveting my sweets, I'll simply have to find the strength to deny you." He stroked her tousled hair away from her face, his eyes sobering. "Although I have to confess that at the moment, I'm not sure I could deny you anything."

Laura touched a hand to his cheek, wondering how his face could have become so dear to her in so short a time. He was offering her the world while she was denying him his most fundamental right—his own identity. She knew in that moment what she ought to do. She should tell him everything, even if that meant exposing her own deceit. But then he would never again look at her with that beguiling blend of bemusement and tenderness. Never again draw her into his arms or lavish her mouth with his kisses.

Laura turned her face toward the pillow, hiding the tears she could feel welling in her eyes.

Mistaking her sorrow for exhaustion, Nicholas blew out the candle and pressed a tender kiss to her brow. "Sleep, darling. I'll go tell the others you're going to be fine."

"I only wish I was," Laura whispered to the darkness after he was gone.

When Nicholas first slipped into the barn, he thought it was empty. Then he heard a furtive movement from the loft above, as if a small, frightened animal was burrowing deeper into its nest.

He climbed the ladder to the loft and stood peering through the musty gloom, finally locating a glimmer of gold beneath the eaves. Lottie huddled in the hay, her arms wrapped around her knees, her hair hanging in sodden hanks around her face. She stared straight ahead without looking at him, dried tear tracks streaking her cheeks.

"Laura's dead, isn't she?" she said before he could speak. "That's why you've come. To tell me she's dead."

Nicholas leaned against a splintery post. "I came to tell you that your sister is awake."

Lottie's incredulous gaze flew to his face.

He nodded. "She's going to be just fine. She should be up and about by tomorrow morning."

Fresh tears welled up in Lottie's eyes, but before they could cleanse her face of its misery, she dashed them away. "How will I ever face her? She'll never forgive me for what I've done. How could she?"

"She doesn't know she has anything to forgive except a bout of bad cooking. I didn't tell her."

Lottie's tears stopped as abruptly as they'd begun. "Why? Why would you do such a thing?"

He shrugged. "Although I can't seem to remember it, I suspect I was ten once, too. But make no mistake," he added, narrowing his eyes, "it was a nasty little bit of mischief you tried to play on me and I wouldn't suggest you try it again."

Lottie climbed to her feet with a sullen sniff. "The cake wouldn't have done a big brute like you nearly as much harm."

She moved to brush past him on her way to the ladder, but he caught her arm in a firm grip, drawing her around to face him. "I know you don't care for me, Lottie, and I think I can guess why."

He felt a faint tremor run through her small body. "You can?"

He nodded, softening both his voice and his grip. "No matter what you may believe, I have no intention of replacing you in your sister's heart. As long as you desire it, there will always be a place for both you and George in our home."

For a minute she looked torn, as if she would have liked nothing better than to throw her arms around his neck. But instead, she wrenched herself from his grasp and went scrambling down the ladder without another word.

Nicholas had to wander much farther afield to find George. By the time he reached the burned-out ruin at the edge of Arden's property, the rain had stopped completely, leaving a light mist hanging like smoke over the land. He ducked beneath a broken beam to find George exactly where Cookie had said he would—sitting on a collapsed chimney in what must have once been the parlor of the modest rectory. The boy sat gazing up at the sky through the gaping hole that had been the roof.

Nicholas didn't wait for him to assume the worst. "Your sister is awake. She's going to be fine."

"I know that." George spared him a cool, contemptuous glance. "I wouldn't have left her alone with you if I didn't."

Nicholas drew nearer, narrowly avoiding plunging his foot through a rotting board. "This place is dangerous. I'm surprised it wasn't torn down long ago."

"Lady Eleanor and Laura wanted to tear it down, but I wouldn't hear of it. Every time they brought it up, I would throw a tantrum that made Lottie look like a perfect angel." George continued to search the sky, as if hoping to find a single star shining through the clouds. "I was the one who left the lamp burning that night, you know. In all these years, Laura's never once reproached me for it."

Nicholas frowned. "You were only a child. It was an accident. A terrible tragedy."

George picked up a piece of charred rubble and tossed it into the air. "I remember them, you know. My parents."

"Then you're very fortunate," Nicholas said softly, feeling an empty pang in his own chest.

George shook his head. "Sometimes I'm not so sure." Dusting off his hands, he stood, his narrow shoulders slumped. "If you've come to fetch me for my beating, I'll go quietly."

Nicholas put up a hand to stay him. "I don't know whether you did or didn't have anything to do with Lottie's mischief and I don't really need to know. That's not why I'm here."

"Then why *are* you here?" George demanded, no longer making any attempt to hide his belligerence.

"Since it appears your sister is going to live long enough to become my bride next Wednesday morning, I find myself in need of a groomsman. I was hoping you would consider doing me the honor."

George's jaw dropped in surprise. "I can't be a groomsman," he said bitterly. "Haven't you heard? I'm just a boy."

Nicholas shook his head. "The true measure of a man has nothing to do with years and everything to do with how well he looks after those who depend upon him. I've seen how much you do around here—how you chop wood and help Dower tend to the flocks and take care of your sisters. And Laura assures me that a groomsman need have only two qualities—he should be a bachelor and he should be my friend." Nicholas held out his hand. "I like to think you could qualify on both counts."

George stared at Nicholas's outstretched hand as if he'd never seen one before. Although his eyes remained wary, he finally reached out and caught it in a firm grasp, shoulders back and head held high. "If you need someone to stand up with you at the wedding, I suppose I'm your man."

As they picked their way over the rubble, Nicholas draped an arm lightly over the boy's shoulders. "You haven't had any supper, have you? I'm famished.

Maybe we could get Lottie to whip us up something sweet."

Although it took visible effort, George somehow managed to keep a straight face. "That won't be necessary, sir. I do believe Cookie made a fresh batch of crumpets just for you."

As the days passed with no word from Dower, Laura grew increasingly jumpy. The old man had never learned to write, but she'd sent him off with a purseful of coins and instructions to hire someone to pen a note if he discovered anything at all about a missing gentleman that required investigation. In some small shameless corner of her heart, she was hoping he wouldn't return before the wedding. That he would stay gone until Nicholas was bound to her forever—or at least for as long as they both should live.

The wedding preparations continued at a frantic pace, as relentlessly as the ticking of the longcase clock in the foyer. Every time Laura turned around, Cookie was waiting to drape a length of lace over her shoulders or jab another pin into her hip. Although the old woman kept up a cheery stream of chatter, especially when Nicholas was around, Laura knew that Cookie was just as worried about Dower's whereabouts as she was. Even Lottie seemed to have lost her exuberance and had taken to moping listlessly about the house or disappearing for hours at a time.

On Sunday morning, the banns were read for the third and final time. As Reverend Tilsbury asked if anyone knew of any just impediment to the two of them being joined together, Laura sat stiffly at Nicholas's side, terrified she would leap to her feet and shout that the bride was a fraud and a liar. The only thing that stopped her was imagining the look of loathing that would spread across Nicholas's face—a look she endured every night in her tortured dreams.

They were gathered around the dining room table that evening for supper when the jingling of a harness fractured the tense silence. Dropping her spoon in her soup, Laura jumped out of her chair and ran to the window. She was searching for any hint of movement in the shadowy drive when George pointedly cleared his throat.

She slowly turned to find a black-and-white kitten dragging a bell attached to a scarlet ribbon across the floor. As Laura sank back into her seat with a dispirited sigh, Lottie retrieved both bell and kitten, muting the merry tones.

While Cookie emerged from the kitchen with the next course, Nicholas surveyed the circle of their gloomy faces. "I know you've been trying to hide it, but I can tell you're all worried sick about Dower. Would you like me to ride to London and search for him?"

"No!" all four of them shouted in unison.

He leaned back in his chair, plainly nonplussed by their reaction.

Laura dabbed at her mouth with her napkin, hoping he wouldn't notice the trembling of her hands. "I appreciate your offer, dear, but I don't think my nerves could stand the strain. We've only three more days before we're to be married. I can have a wedding without Dower, but I can't very well have one without a bridegroom."

"Don't you fret on our account, Mr. Nick." Although

Cookie was patting his shoulder, she was looking directly at Laura. "That old rascal of mine's probably holed up at some tavern somewhere. He'll come draggin' in here the night before the weddin', reekin' of spirits and beggin' my forgiveness. Just see if he don't!"

Jeremiah Dower sat at a grimy table in a shadowy corner of the Boar's Snout, tossing back his third gin of the night. The tavern was one of the seediest on the waterfront and more than one body had been found floating in the Thames after a night spent partaking of its dubious pleasures. It was whispered that if one of the patrons didn't kill you, the cheap gin would. Or you could stagger upstairs with one of the blowsy whores who haunted the docks and die a slow, festering death of the French pox. Several slumming young cubs had lost their innocence, their purses, and eventually their lives between those plump, accommodating thighs.

Dower's mother had been one of those whores. He'd spent his boyhood scrubbing tobacco stains and emptying slop buckets in a tavern just like this one. After his ma had been strangled by one of her own customers, he'd been only too eager to trade the choking clouds of smoke and drunken shouting for the sweet, pure air of a Hertfordshire morning and Cookie's smile.

It was that smile he was longing to see as he slumped in his chair and surveyed the motley crowd. He'd spent the past week combing the streets and docks for any rumors of a missing gent. He'd even visited Newgate and Bedlam, hoping to hear news of a recent escape. But thus far, his search had yielded nothing and his time was running out.

If he didn't return to Arden by Tuesday night with proof that Miss Laura's mysterious gent was pledged to another, she would go through with the wedding. The young missie had always been sweet natured, but there was no standing in her way once she had her heart set on something. And she definitely had her heart set on that handsome young buck of hers.

Dower scowled. The man might not be a fugitive from the law or an escaped lunatic, but that didn't make him any less dangerous to an innocent girl.

He was about to settle up his tab and take his leave when a lad with a shock of red hair and a mouthful of crooked, yellowing teeth came wending his way through the crowd. He leaned over Dower's table and jerked his thumb toward the back entrance. "There's a bloke out in the alley says 'e wants to talk to you. Says 'e may 'ave somethin' you'd loik to 'ear."

Dower nodded, sending the boy on his way with one of the coins Miss Laura had given him. Not wanting to appear too eager, he took his time polishing off the gin, then wiped his mouth with the back of his hand. As he rose, he took care to shove up the sleeves of his shirt, enjoying the wide-eyed reaction of the whore straddling the lap of a bearded man at the next table. He knew from experience that any cutpurse thinking to rob a frail old man would think again when they saw the thick ropes of muscle that banded his arms.

The fog had come rolling in with the night. As the door fell shut behind him, muffling the drunken din inside the tavern, a man materialized from the shadows. Dower had expected to find some gibbering beggar seeking to earn an easy coin, but it was quickly apparent that this man had no need of his shillings.

He wore a tall felt hat and balanced a marble-headed walking cane in his gloved hands. He had the sort of round, bland face that might be mistaken for a hundred others. "I do hope you'll forgive me for interrupting your evening libations, Mr. . . . ?"

Dower folded his arms over his chest. "Dower. And I ain't no mister."

"Very well, then, *Dower*. I wouldn't have troubled you, but it's come to my attention that you've been making certain inquiries along the waterfront."

"I ain't done no such thing," Dower protested. "I just asked a few questions."

The man had a crocodile's smile. "According to my associates, you've been asking about a tall man with golden hair, well spoken and well formed, who might have gone missing over a fortnight ago."

Dower's nape was beginning to prickle with foreboding. It had been his intention to save Miss Laura from a stranger's clutches, not get her arrested for kidnapping. "Them 'sociates o' yours may not know as much as they think they do."

"Oh, I can assure you that they're very thorough. Which is why I've come to the conclusion that we may be looking for the same man."

Dower's curiosity nearly got the best of him, but something in the man's flat brown eyes put him off his feed. "Sorry, mate," he said. "You've got the wrong bloke. All I'm lookin' for tonight is a bottle o' gin and a willin' bit o' skirt to warm me bed."

"With the reward my employers are offering, you could buy all the gin and whores a man could ever want."

Despite the dank chill in the air, Dower could feel

beads of sweat pop out along his brow. "Just wot makes this fellow you're lookin' for worth so bloody much?"

The man shifted his cane from one hand to the other. "If you'll come with me, I'll show you."

Dower never had taken kindly to bullying. Especially when it came disguised beneath a brittle veneer of cultured speech and polished manners. He bared his teeth in a rusty smile. "I'm afraid I'll 'ave to decline. I got a much better invitation from a little bit o' redheaded fluff at the table next to mine."

He turned, reaching for the tavern door.

"That's a pity, *Mr.* Dower, for I'm afraid I really must insist."

Before Dower could whirl around, the marble head of the cane came down on the back of his skull, sending him spilling to the ground. He barely had time to admire the glossy leather of the man's expensive boots before one of them slammed into his face, plunging him into a pool of darkness.

Chapter 13

*Sometimes she tends to act before she thinks
without counting the cost. . . .*

It should have been the happiest night of Laura's
life.

Tomorrow morning at ten o'clock, she would stand
before the altar of St. Michael's and pledge her heart
and her life to the man she had wanted before she even
knew he existed. He would tenderly take her hand, gaze
deep into her eyes, and vow to keep himself only unto
her for as long as they both should live.

She should have been snuggled beneath her bedclothes, hugging her pillow and dreaming of the day to
come. Instead, she was pacing back and forth across the
bedchamber, nearly frantic with apprehension. She
paused beside Lottie's iron bedstead to smooth a tumbled curl from her sister's cheek, envying her the sleep
of the innocent.

It was a luxury Laura hadn't enjoyed since the day
she found Nicholas in the wood. And if she failed to
heed the prodding of her conscience, it might very well
be a luxury she would never enjoy again. She almost

expected God to force her hand. Expected Him to send Dower galloping down the long curving drive with word that Nicholas already had a fiancée waiting for him back in London.

Even if Dower failed to return before the wedding, she knew it wasn't too late to redeem herself. All she had to do was march across the darkened corridor to Lady Eleanor's bedchamber and confess all, throwing herself on the mercy of a man who would suddenly be a stranger.

But then there would be no sunny wedding morning, no white crepe gown trimmed in Brussels lace, no towering bride cake iced with almond paste. There would be no Cookie beaming at her as she pinned a circlet of roses in her hair, no Lottie to hold her fragrant posy at the altar, and no George to offer his grudging congratulations as he was forced to admit that her plan had been a sound one after all.

And there would be no Nicholas to gently lay his lips against hers, sealing their vows with a kiss.

Laura could feel the tendrils of temptation securing themselves around her heart, as cunning and sinuous as the serpent in the Garden of Eden. Thinking only to escape their hold, she unlatched the window and threw it open, settling herself on the broad wooden sill. The night was warm and windy, thick with the scent of jasmine and honeysuckle. A fat slice of moon brightened the sky, defying the scudding clouds with its brilliance.

It was the sort of night that sang of pagan enchantments, the sort of night that had always quickened Laura's blood and compelled her to throw off the constraints of her safe, tidy life. But now she knew the price of surrendering to those reckless urges.

If she could only return to that moment when she had found Nicholas sleeping in the wood! Perhaps he would have fallen in love with her anyway. She would never know because she'd never given him the chance.

Sighing forlornly, she rested her cheek against the window frame. It was as much of a sin to lie to herself as it was to lie to him. A man like Nicholas probably wouldn't have spared a glance for a humble country girl like her. A girl whose cheeks were sprinkled with freckles because she so rarely bothered to wear her bonnet. A girl whose nails weren't manicured, but were blunt and chipped from digging in the garden dirt. Winning his love would have been as unlikely as Apollo reaching down from the heavens to bestow his favors on a mortal maiden. He might have found her a pleasant enough diversion for a summer's day, but not for a lifetime.

Laura gazed across the rolling lawn to the wood beyond—a wood draped in shadows and secrets. She had been so eager to believe Nicholas had tumbled from the heavens in answer to her prayer that she'd never bothered to explore any of the more rational explanations for his appearance that had been taunting her ever since that day. There had been no trace of hoofprints near the old oak, but it was entirely possible he could have been thrown from the other side of the gorge. Panicked at finding itself riderless in an unfamiliar wood, his mount might have bolted back the way it had come.

Laura tensed, knowing what she must do. She might not be able to return to the moment when she had found him, but she could return to the place. Perhaps there was some clue to his identity that she had missed—an engraved snuffbox, a watch fob, papers that might have spilled from his pockets. She had no choice but to look. She owed him at least that much, even if what she found meant losing him forever.

Laura didn't waste time dressing. She simply donned her shoes and threw a cloak over her nightdress, fearful she would lose her resolve if she lingered for too long. As she slipped from the room, the longcase clock in the foyer began to chime midnight.

It should have been the second happiest night of Nicholas's life.

The happiest night would come on the morrow when he took his bride to bed with the blessing of both the Church and the Crown. Then he would have every right to pluck the pins from Laura's hair until it came tumbling around her face in a sable cloud. Every right to loosen the ribbons at the throat of her nightdress and slip the sleek satin from her creamy shoulders. Every right to ease her back against the feather mattress and cover her softness with the hard, hungry heat of his body.

He should have been sleeping, conserving his strength for the night to come, not prowling the bedchamber like a caged beast. It didn't help that his headache had returned, thudding dully at the front of his skull like a song once heard, but not quite remembered. He rubbed his brow with the flat of his palm, tempted to slip down to the drawing room and retrieve the decanter of brandy.

But dulling his senses would mean dulling his instincts. Which wouldn't be so terrible, he thought with a humorless snort of laughter, if it meant he could go back to fooling himself into believing his bride wasn't harboring some dangerous secret that made her blush and stammer and nearly jump out of her skin every time he entered a room.

Bracing his hands on the dressing table, he leaned down to study his reflection in the mirror. He couldn't blame Laura for being frightened of what he saw there. His hair was wild, his jaw hard. His mouth was drawn into a rigid line, erasing the dimple that usually hovered near his cheek. He didn't look like a man who was to exchange vows with the woman he loved only a few hours hence. He looked like a man contemplating murder.

From somewhere in the house, a clock chimed midnight, each mournful *bong* bringing him closer to the moment when he would stride across the corridor to Laura's bedchamber, kick open the door, and demand the truth from her beautiful, lying lips.

Frustrated beyond bearing, Nicholas slammed his hand down on the dressing table. The bottle of scent perched on its edge went tumbling to the carpet, flooding his every breath with the fragrance of orange blossoms. A needle of pain shot through his skull. Swearing, he staggered to the window and threw it open.

A warm night wind swept through the chamber, its perfumed breath as subtle and beguiling as the scent of a woman's skin. Leaning against the window frame, Nicholas closed his eyes, allowing its gentle fingers to ruffle his hair and soothe both his aching brow and his rioting suspicions.

When he opened them, a slender, cloaked figure was darting across the lawn below, her dark hair streaming behind her.

Nicholas went numb, his blood chilling. He could

think of only one reason a woman might abandon her cozy bed and brave the dangers of the dark on the night before her wedding. He watched her melt into the shadows of the forest through narrowed eyes, thankful for the numbness that deadened both the pain in his head and the pain in his heart.

The ancient trees loomed out of the darkness like the gateway to another time. Their twisted limbs swayed in the wind, beckoning to Nicholas with a lover's grace. He stood at the edge of the wood where he had watched his betrothed disappear, knowing she'd left him with no choice but to follow.

Moonlight silvered the branches overhead, but did little to penetrate the mossy shadows that draped the narrow footpath. The deeper he wandered, the deeper those shadows grew, swelling and darkening until they threatened to consume him. The whisper of the wind through the leaves was broken only by the eerie cry of some small, helpless creature meeting its doom. Although the sound sent a primal shiver of dread through Nicholas's soul, his steps remained sure and fleet. Deep in his heart, he knew he had nothing to fear.

For he was the most dangerous predator roaming the wood on that night.

Laura had never before braved the wood by night.

As she wound her way through the labyrinth of trees, she was dismayed to find her sunny kingdom transformed into a fortress of gloom. She would have sworn she knew every rough-hewn rock and mossy hollow, but the chaotic web of shadows and moonlight rendered even the most recognizable landmarks foreign and forbidding.

The wood no longer seemed the likely home of flitting fairies and giggling sprites but of hulking goblins out hunting a virgin bride for their king.

She pressed on, determined not to let her childish fancies get the best of her. Without the sunny blue sky overhead, the thrill of danger had somehow lost its allure.

Laura passed the same ghostly birch three times before she realized she had been wandering in an ever-narrowing circle. She leaned against the trunk of the tree, struggling to catch both her breath and her bearings. Her errand was beginning to seem like a fool's quest. But even if she didn't find a single clue to Nicholas's true identity, at least she would have the comfort of knowing she had tried when she stood before the altar with him on the morrow.

Knocking a twig from her hair, she set off at a brisk pace, determined to reach the ancient oak where she had first found him. She was leaping over a narrow stream when something behind her let out a shriek that was quickly silenced between the jaws of some more powerful creature. Her foot plunged into the chill water. She glanced over her shoulder, unable to shake the sensation that something just might be pursuing her with equal hunger.

A faint, but unmistakable, crackling in the underbrush reached her ears. She lurched into a run, ducking overhanging branches and dodging tangled roots that sought to snag the hem of her cloak with their bony fingers. She might have gone on running forever if she hadn't stumbled out of the shadows into the very clearing she had been seeking.

The old oak stood sentinel at the edge of the gorge, its broad boughs promising respite for the weary traveler. Moonlight spilled through a break in the foliage just as the sunlight had done on the day she had found Nicholas, weaving an enchantment older than time.

Laura blinked, thinking there could be only one explanation for what she saw. She must have dozed off in the window of her bedchamber, must have dreamed her mad flight through the wood.

For Nicholas stood beneath those sheltering boughs, one foot propped on a gnarled root. The moonlight gilded his hair, cast hollows beneath his regal cheekbones.

She drifted toward him, finding him every bit as irresistible as she had on that hazy summer afternoon.

"There's really no need to hide your disappointment, my dear," he said, his voice both tender and mocking. "I realize you must have been expecting someone else."

His words snapped her out of her daze. She suddenly became aware of the unpleasant way her sodden shoe squelched with each step, the stinging scratches on her arms, the dew-soaked hem of her cloak dragging on the ground behind her.

"I can't imagine what you mean," she said, startled into blurting out the truth. "It's the middle of the night. I wasn't expecting anyone at all."

His face hardened, making him look more like a stranger than ever before. "You can spare me any more of your lies, Laura. I know everything."

Chapter 14

I fear her impetuous nature
might lead her into harm's way. . . .

This wasn't a dream. It was a nightmare.

"Everything? You know everything?" Laura winced when the word ended on a high-pitched squeak.

"Everything," he repeated, taking a carefully measured step toward her. "Surely you didn't think you could fool me forever, did you?"

She took a step backward. "Well, I was rather hoping . . ."

"I have to admit you were very convincing. You're quite the little actress. Have you ever considered taking to the stage?"

"Oh, no." She shook her head passionately. "Lottie was blessed with all the dramatic talent in the family. Although Lady Eleanor would never say an unkind word about my abilities or the lack of them, she always cast me as the back end of a donkey or some other non-speaking role during our Christmas theatricals." Laura sighed. "Now that I think about it, I *feel* rather like the back end of a donkey."

"You're probably wondering how I guessed, aren't you? I suppose it will surprise you to learn that I've had my suspicions all along."

Laura was stunned. "Yet you never breathed a word?"

He drew near enough to touch her, but didn't. "I was hoping I was wrong." A bitter laugh escaped him. "There's really no need for you to torture yourself, darling. In the end, I have only myself to blame."

"How . . . how can you say that?"

"Because I was a damn fool to ever leave you in the first place. It wasn't fair of me to expect a woman with your fire and passion to wait so long for me. I should have married you the first time I laid eyes on you." His words were no less puzzling than the tenderness of his fingers against her cheek or the husky note of regret in his voice. "Will you answer one question for me? I believe you owe me that much."

"Anything," she whispered, mesmerized by the shadow of pain that had darkened his eyes to amber.

"Did you come here tonight to bid your lover farewell or did you plan to continue your assignations after we were wed?"

Laura stared at him, struggling to make sense of his words. "Why, I . . . I . . ."

Nicholas stilled her stammering with his thumb, running it lightly over her trembling lips. "It's a pity the truth doesn't come as easily as a lie to those lovely lips of yours. Perhaps I should have asked you if you were thinking of him every time I took you into my arms." He slipped one arm around her waist, drawing her against him. "Was it his face you saw when you closed your eyes?" Laura's eyes fluttered shut as Nicholas brushed his lips against the feathery softness of her lashes. Those lips followed the curve of her cheek to the corner of her mouth. "Does he make you shiver and sigh with longing every time his lips touch yours?"

It wasn't a sigh but a moan that escaped Laura as Nicholas's mouth took full possession of hers. She didn't shiver, she quaked. If he hadn't wrapped his other arm around her waist, tucking her into the surging power of his body, she might even have swooned. This was not the kiss of a suitor seeking to woo his bride. This was a pirate's kiss—a kiss that gave no quarter and took no prisoners. A kiss more than willing to steal what might not be freely given. His tongue ravished her mouth, thrusting deep with a silky heat that made Laura melt against him. Beyond thought, beyond everything but the exquisite hunger his kiss ignited, she cupped his nape in her palm, urging him even deeper.

"Damn you, woman!" he muttered, burying his mouth in her hair. Although his words were harsh, his arms tightened, binding her even closer to his pounding heart. "How can you kiss me like that when your heart belongs to another?"

His words finally penetrated Laura's besotted brain. As relief washed over her in a warm tide, she shoved against his chest and went stumbling backward, cupping a hand over her mouth too late to contain her ripple of laughter.

Nicholas looked at her darkly. "First you scorn my affections, then you dare to mock me. My compliments, Miss Fairleigh. You're even more heartless than I suspected."

Try as she might, Laura couldn't quite wipe the lopsided grin from her lips or hide the bemused adoration in her eyes. "Why, you foolish man! Is that what you believe? That I came here to rendezvous with a lover?"

"Didn't you?" he demanded, somehow managing to look both dangerous and vulnerable in the moonlight.

Laura shook her head helplessly, taking one step toward him, then another. "Of course not. You should have known such a thing was impossible."

"Why?"

He held himself stiff as she reached up to touch his cheek, her fingertips lingering against the spot where his dimple should be. "Because you're the only man I've ever wanted."

Rising up on tiptoe, she pressed her lips to his. She kissed him as she hadn't had the courage to do that first day in the wood, licking at his mouth with an innocent abandon that melted the last of his defenses. His arms came up, wrapping themselves around her with fierce strength.

Threading a hand through her hair, he tilted her head back so he could gaze deep into her luminous eyes.

"If you didn't come here to meet a lover," he said hoarsely, "then why did you come?"

"For this," she whispered, refusing to profane the moment with a careless lie. "I came for this." Before he could question her further, she seized the front of his shirt and dragged his lips back down to hers, giving him the only answer he needed.

Laura knew in that moment that she had been just as great a fool as he had. It wasn't the wood or the moonlight that had woven the enchantment around her heart; it was this man. She had fallen beneath his spell the moment she had first touched her lips to his. Even as he bewitched her with his mouth, his hands were working their own deft magic, unfastening the frog at the throat of her cloak and easing the garment open.

He drew back to stare down at her, a sharp exhalation escaping him. Whatever he had expected to find beneath the cloak, it plainly wasn't her nightdress.

"You idiot child," he murmured, the chiding words somehow becoming an endearment. "Are you trying to catch your death of a chill?"

"There's little enough danger of that," Laura assured him, shivering beneath the possessive heat of his gaze. "On the contrary, I seem to have contracted a raging fever."

His warm lips grazed the pulse beating madly beneath the fragile skin of her throat. "Then perhaps you should lie down."

If they had been in the drawing room of the manor, she might have offered a halfhearted protest, but here in this pagan wilderness it seemed only natural that her cloak should slip from her shoulders to the bed of leaves behind her. Even more natural that Nicholas should gently lower her into its welcoming folds. As he covered her, his big, strong body blocking out the moonlight, Laura knew that she was no longer flirting with danger but welcoming it with open arms. Prince or goblin king, she would willingly go wherever he wished to take her.

He took her down. Down into a sweet, dark labyrinth of desire where he was her only light. The delicious sprawl of his weight didn't make her feel crushed but cherished as their kisses melted into something richer and more daring. His hand roamed down her side to the ripe curve of her hip and back again, gentling her to his touch until it seemed only fitting that he should cup her breast through the butter-soft linen of her nightdress, brush his thumb across the turgid peak of her nipple.

Laura gasped into his mouth, awakened to a thousand senses she never even knew she possessed. As he teased the throbbing bud between thumb and forefinger, pleasure danced along her nerves, culminating in a rush of liquid sensation at the juncture of her thighs. When she would have clamped them together, his knee was there, nudging those waves of pleasure deep into her womb.

Tangling her fingers in his silky hair, she arched against him, instinctively seeking any relief for the exquisite pressure building within her. He took that as an invitation to settle his hips between her thighs. He was hot, hard, and heavy, the thin sheath of his buckskin trousers barely able to contain him. He rocked against that sensitive cradle in a rhythm older than the ancient oak that sheltered them, all the while lavishing kiss after kiss upon her eager mouth, drinking in her sighs and moans as if they were the most honeyed of nectars.

Between one kiss and the next, Laura's world exploded. It was her cry that echoed through the forest then—a broken wail that seemed to go on and on, just like the rapture cascading through her in shuddering waves.

Nicholas threw back his head, thrilling to its music. Although his memory had failed him, he would have wagered his life that he had never seen anything quite so lovely as Laura in that moment. Her lashes were damp against her flushed cheeks, her lips moist and parted, the skirt of her nightdress pooled between her trembling thighs. In a motion more instinctive than breathing, he slipped one hand beneath that skirt, groaning in both delight and agony as his fingers glided through her damp, silky curls to the melting sweetness beneath. She opened like a flower to his touch, coaxing him to slide his longest finger deep within her.

Laura's eyes flew open. Although they were still dazed with wonder, there could be no mistaking her startled gasp or the quiver of shock that danced through her untried flesh. She was everything she'd claimed to be. She was innocent. She was his.

Or she would be in a few short hours when a minister of God would bless their union and give them dominion over each other's bodies. But Nicholas didn't want to wait for that blessing. He wanted her now.

And she wanted him. There was fear shining in her eyes, but there was trust as well. A trust so tender that he knew she would not stop him if he decided to betray it.

Nicholas was caught off guard by the bubble of amusement that welled up in his chest. As the laughter poured out of him, rich and cleansing, he wrapped both arms around Laura and rolled over until she was the one sprawled on top of him.

Bracing her forearms on his chest, she glared down at him, her expression unmistakably disgruntled. "I'm gratified to know that you find my inexperience so amusing."

"I'm not laughing at you, angel. I'm laughing at myself." He smoothed her hair back from her face, his hand still trembling from its near brush with ecstasy. "It seems you were right about me all along. I'm not the sort of man who would compromise my fiancée. At least not the night before our wedding."

Laura pondered that revelation for a moment, her freckled face losing none of its solemnity. "What about the night *after* our wedding?"

Nicholas grinned. "Then I'll be only too happy to let *you* compromise *me*."

The carriage rocked through the fog-shrouded London streets, its coachman swathed in a woolen muffler and tall black hat. Although the vehicle's passage was marked by curious stares from the drunken stragglers and bleary-eyed women who littered the narrow alleyways, its burgundy curtains were drawn and its imposing doors bore no coat of arms to identify its occupants.

If Diana were to be discovered racing through the night in a closed carriage with the notorious marquess of Gillingham as her only companion, it would do irreparable damage to her staid reputation. She took a rather perverse pleasure in the thought, imagining the pitying looks of the gossipmongers turning to scandalized shock. Let them whisper behind their fans about her for a change!

Smoothing her hair, she stole a resentful look at the man sprawled on the plush velvet squabs opposite her. Despite his indolent posture, he was, as always, impeccably groomed, betraying no sign that he had been dragged from his cozy home in the middle of the night just as she had. The rich fragrance of his bay rum cologne scented the air, making her feel slightly intoxicated.

"You gave my servants quite a fright pounding on the door that way," she said. "I only hope your discovery was worth rousing me from my bed."

Thane crossed his long legs at the ankle. Although

the spacious footwell put him in no danger of touching her, Diana tucked her own feet beneath her skirts. "You have my most profound apologies for disturbing your rest, my lady," he drawled. "When I received word from this detective you had hired, I was also in bed, but not yet asleep."

"Why doesn't that surprise me?" she murmured, keeping her expression carefully bland.

Thane's green eyes narrowed. "I was also alone."

Diana felt herself blush. Averting her eyes from his face, she tugged on her gloves and fastened the satin frog at the throat of her pelisse. "Do you think this Watkins fellow has a genuine lead this time?"

"I hope to God so. If not, we're left with the only other conclusion we've been able to reach in the past fortnight—that your cousin simply vanished into thin air, taking his horse with him."

The carriage made a sharp turn, throwing them both into silence. Diana eased aside the curtain. They were passing a row of abandoned warehouses, each more dilapidated than the last. The carriage finally drew up in front of a forbidding structure with shattered windows that gazed out upon the night like soulless eyes.

The coachman climbed down from his perch and threw open the carriage door. Diana quickly deduced that they couldn't be far from the wharfs. The dank stench of rotting fish was nearly overpowering.

"Wait here for us," Thane commanded the coachman as they climbed down from the carriage.

"Are you sure that's wise, sir?" the man asked, giving the deserted street a nervous glance.

"No, not at all," Thane replied. "But those were the instructions I was given."

As the shadows cast by the hulking ruin swallowed them, Diana shrank against Thane without realizing it, not even thinking to protest when his gloved hand claimed her elbow. He ignored the main door, escorting her instead down a narrow alley that ran between two crumbling brick edifices.

An unassuming wooden door loomed out of the darkness. Thane assailed it with a curt knock. Nothing happened.

"Could it be the wrong address?" Diana asked hopefully, peeping over his shoulder.

Before he could answer, the door began to creak open, its rusty hinges screeching. A vast bear of a man with pointed teeth and greasy side whiskers loomed out of the darkness, a huge bone with bits of meat still clinging to it dangling from his hamlike fist. Diana couldn't help but wonder if it was the thighbone of the last interloper who had dared to disturb his dinner.

To Thane's credit, he didn't even blink. "I'm here to see Watkins. He sent for me."

"This way." Droplets of grease went flying as the fellow jerked the bone toward the shadows behind him.

They emerged from a narrow corridor into a cavernous hall where their every rustle of movement produced an unsettling echo. Abandoning any pretense of pride, Diana clutched at the tail of Thane's coat. Feeling her panicked tug, he reached around and laced his warm fingers through hers.

A pair of lanterns rested on two rotting crates, giving the area between them the ambience of a poorly lit stage. A man slumped against one of those crates, his hands bound behind him. Diana might have thought he was dead had her involuntary cry of dismay not brought his head upright.

He glared at them through the one beady black eye that wasn't swollen shut. Despite the fresh blood trickling from the corner of his gagged mouth and the vivid bruise staining his cheekbone, there was nothing beaten about his posture.

"Lord Gillingham," came a pleasant voice from behind them. "Thank you for replying so promptly to my summons." Mr. Theophilus Watkins emerged from the shadows, his dapper attire spoiled by the flecks of dried blood marring the pristine white of his shirtfront.

Thane wheeled on him. "What's the meaning of this, Watkins? The lady hired you to find her cousin, not rough up some scrawny old man."

The scrawny old man growled deep in his throat, earning a wide-eyed look from Diana.

Watkins's smile faded to a sneer. "Forgive me if I've offended your delicate sensibilities, my lord, but he knows where her cousin is. And he's not talking."

"I don't see how he can with that filthy gag shoved down his throat," Thane retorted.

Watkins shot his captive a feral look. "He has an unfortunate tendency to talk when I'm not asking any questions. I thought perhaps you could make him see reason, you being a gentleman and all. I've told him about the reward, but he doesn't seem to be impressed."

After a brief moment of consideration, Thane snapped, "Unbind him."

"But, my lord, I don't think that would be very—"

"Unbind him," Thane repeated. "Now."

Watkins reluctantly nodded to his hulking hench-man. The man drew out a wicked-looking knife and squatted behind their captive.

As the gag and ropes fell away, Thane said, "Mr. Watkins wasn't lying to you, sir. There's a substantial reward for the information we're looking for."

Rubbing at his chafed wrists, the old man gave Thane a mocking look. "And what would that be, m'lord? Thirty pieces o' silver?"

Before Diana or Thane could react, Watkins drove his booted foot into the man's ribs. "It won't hurt you to show the gentleman and his lady a little respect," he snarled. "But it will hurt you not to."

Appalled at the detective's casual brutality, Diana shoved her way past him and knelt beside the old man. She supported his shoulders while he struggled to catch his breath, then took his grimy hand in her own, heed-less of the damage to her expensive white gloves. She was surprised to feel tears welling up in her eyes, but even more surprised to feel Thane's steadying hand on her shoulder.

"Please, sir," she said. "My cousin has been missing for nearly a month now and I'm frantic with worry. If you know anything at all of his whereabouts, I beg you to tell us." The old man eyed her warily as she dug deep into her reticule, drawing out a miniature of Sterling that had been commissioned on his eighteenth birthday. She held it out to him, her hand trembling. "He's ten years older than this now, but it's a fair likeness."

His stony gaze slowly traveled from the miniature to her face. "Just who is this cousin o' yours, miss?"

"Don't you know?" Taken aback, Diana glanced over her shoulder at the sullen Watkins. "Didn't you tell him?"

The detective awkwardly cleared his throat. "In cases such as this, we try not to divulge our client's identity unless absolutely necessary."

"That way when me bloated corpse washes up in the Thames," the old man said with scathing pleasantness, "I'll be less likely to 'ave told any o' me mates who it was wot tossed me in."

It was Watkins's turn to growl. Ignoring him, Diana said softly, "The man we're looking for, the man who was last seen in London on Thursday, the twelfth of July, is Sterling Harlow, the seventh duke of Devonbrooke."

All the color drained from the old man's gaunt face, making his bruises stand out in stark relief. Although his mouth went slack, his grip on her hand tightened, squeezing painfully.

"Thane!" Diana cried, alarmed by his reaction.

Thane knelt beside her, bracing an arm around the old man's shoulders.

"God in 'eaven," he whispered, clinging to Diana's hand as if it was his only hope. "You've got to 'elp me! We've got to stop 'er before she sells 'er soul to the divil 'isself!"

Chapter 15

I only wish she had a man
such as you to watch over her. . . .

Nicholas awoke to the music of birdsong and bells. He sprang out of bed and threw the window open wide. A patchwork quilt of rolling green meadows dotted with fat, woolly sheep shimmered beneath a dazzling vault of blue. The joyful pealing of the church bells seemed to be calling his name, inviting him to partake in some wondrous celebration. Bracing his hands on the windowsill, he leaned into the sun-warmed breeze, breathing a silent prayer of thanksgiving.

It was the perfect summer day.

It was his wedding day.

He grinned and stretched, flexing his stiff muscles. Although it had been near dawn when he and Laura had slipped into the house, struggling to muffle both their footsteps and their laughter, he didn't feel the least bit weary. She had finally confessed why she'd been wandering around the wood at that unholy hour. She'd been searching for wild rose petals to top the syllabub

Cookie was planning to surprise him with at their wedding breakfast. He shook his head, marveling at the intricate and frequently baffling workings of the female mind.

Leaving the window ajar, he padded to the chair and slipped into his trousers, not giving the dressing table mirror a single glance. He'd been a fool to think he could find himself in its cold, polished surface. If he could be even half the man he saw reflected in Laura's loving eyes, he would be content. It no longer mattered who he had been before losing his memory. All that mattered was who he would be after today—a husband to Laura and a father to her children.

He was reaching for his shirt when a small furry head butted him in the ankle. The yellow kitten twined herself around his leg, her raucous purr making her sound more like a miniature tiger.

Nicholas scooped her up, cradling her plush warmth against his naked chest. "You know I can't resist you, you insatiable little vixen, but I must warn you that this is your last morning to have me all to yourself."

A heavy knock sounded on the door.

"You may come in, Cookie," he called out. "I'm not dressed."

Cookie poked her head in the door, blushing beneath her mobcap. "You ought to be ashamed of yourself, Mr. Nick, teasin' an old woman that way. If I was to barge in here with you wearin' nothin' but that naughty grin of yours, I doubt my poor old heart could stand the shock."

"I'd wager that poor old heart of yours is stronger than you let on. And what's this?" he asked, surveying the neatly folded pile of garments in her arms. "I was expecting a tray of crumpets."

"I haven't spent *all* my time on Miss Laura's gown, you know." She held out her offering to him, ducking her head shyly.

He accepted it, discovering a stylish tailcoat cut from deep Spanish blue broadcloth and a pair of buff-colored trousers.

"Why, Cookie, what have you done?" he murmured, running a hand over her painstaking stitches. "I don't believe I've ever seen a more handsome suit of wedding clothes."

She waved away his praise. "It was just some old fabric I found in the attic. I wanted you to do my girl proud today when you stood up with her in front of all them nosy villagers." She gave his hips a worried glance. "I do hope the trousers'll fit. I had to guess at your size."

Nicholas slowly lifted his head to meet her gaze, blinking innocently.

Blushing anew, she backed toward the door, shaking a finger at him. "Go on with you, you shameless flirt! If you don't mind them wicked thoughts of yours, I'm goin' to run straight to Miss Laura and tell her you can't marry her 'cause you're so besotted with me."

Nicholas threw back his head, laughing aloud. "Then Laura would be wrestling Dower for his pitchfork and I'd be right back where I started." As a shadow passed over Cookie's face, he sobered. "Tell me, has there been any word from him?"

She mustered a brave smile. "Don't you fret about that old heathen of mine. He'll do anythin' to keep from settin' foot in a church. Just you wait and see—

he'll come trottin' over that hill out there as soon as he smells the ham at the weddin' breakfast."

Laura inclined her head, holding her breath as Lottie crowned her with a circlet of woven rosebuds. She straightened, catching her reflection in the standing mirror George had dragged down from the attic. Although the rest of her hair had been gathered in a loose topknot, shimmering ringlets framed her face, coaxed into place with a pair of blistering hot curling tongs and a few impatient tears.

All the pin jabbings she'd endured in the past two weeks had been well worth it. The high-waisted gown fit her to perfection, its puffed cap sleeves trimmed in Brussels lace baring her slender arms. On her feet she wore a pair of delicate kid slippers fastened with ribbons of cream satin.

Laura didn't feel like a bride. She felt like a princess.

"Do pinch some color into my cheeks, won't you, Lottie? And make sure and have some hartshorn at the ready in case I should swoon during the ceremony." Laura hugged herself, trying to still the churning of her stomach. "I never knew it was possible to be so happy and so terrified all at the same time."

"You have every right to be happy," Lottie said firmly, giving Laura's right cheek a stern twist. "In just two days you'll be twenty-one and Arden Manor will be yours forever."

Laura stared down at her little sister as if she'd just sprouted an extra head. Not only had she forgotten about her birthday, she'd nearly forgotten why she had dragged Nicholas back to the manor in the first place.

Since that day, the stakes had climbed much higher. Now she knew that no crumbling pile of bricks, no matter how dear, would be a home without him in it.

She was searching for the words to explain that to Lottie when George appeared in the doorway, his face scarlet with distress. "Laura! Cookie put too much starch in my collar and it's poking me in the ears!"

"Don't turn your head, George," Laura warned. "You'll put your eye out." She turned back to her sister, giving Lottie a brief, but fierce, hug. "I suppose there's no need to explain my happiness to you. Someday you'll understand for yourself."

"And someday *you* will," Lottie whispered, her eyes bleak as she watched a laughing Laura guide George from the room.

All of Arden turned out for Laura's nuptials.

While Betsy and Alice Bogworth dabbed delicately at their eyes, several of Laura's rejected suitors honked loudly into their handkerchiefs. Rumor had it that Tom Dillmore had even bathed for the occasion, although the elderly widow sitting next to him kept her handkerchief pressed firmly over her nose. A gasp went up from the parishioners when Wesley Trumble came marching in, clean-shaven except for the tufts of hair springing from his ears. Even though it was only half past nine in the morning, a drunken Abel Grantham was telling everyone who would listen about the time he had to jump off his donkey and rescue little Laura after she fell into the manger during one of their Christmas theatricals. His son, Tooley, was asleep and snoring with his hands folded over his massive belly before the wedding even started, no doubt conserving his energy for the breakfast to be served at the manor following the nuptials.

Cookie sat all alone in the family pew. Her handsome bonnet was trimmed with feathers plucked from one of the chickens she had slaughtered only that morning. George stood straight and tall at Nicholas's side, looking at least fourteen in his bow-tied cravat and starched collar. Lottie stood beside Laura, gripping her posy of larkspur and lilies so tightly that her knuckles were white.

But Laura only had eyes for Nicholas. Although they were both facing the altar, she kept stealing glances at him from beneath her downcast lashes, noticing things she'd never noticed before—the shallow brackets that lined his mouth even when he wasn't smiling; the way the hair at his neck sought to curl of its own accord; the tiny nick on his throat where he'd cut himself shaving. Last night she had buried her mouth against that throat, tasting his supple skin while his beautiful, deft fingers touched her in places she'd never even dared to touch herself. Yet today he seemed more of a stranger to her than ever before.

Reverend Tilsbury droned on and on from the Book of Common Prayer, his voice barely audible over the humming in her ears.

Until it suddenly deepened, bringing each word into vivid focus. "I require and charge you both, as you will answer at the dreadful Day of Judgment, when the secrets of all hearts shall be disclosed, that if either of you know any reason why you may not be lawfully joined together in matrimony, you do now confess it."

Lottie drew in an audible breath. George tugged at his collar with two fingers.

A bubble of silence seemed to swell around Laura, sucking all the air from her lungs. She stole a panicked glance at Nicholas. He winked at her, his lips curving into a heartening smile. Suddenly, Laura could breathe again.

He was no stranger. He was the man she loved. And if she had to stand before God someday after their life together was done and confess the secret of her heart, she would. Because he was the only secret she'd ever had worth keeping.

Laura held her tongue until it came time to take him for her wedded husband. She did so without faltering, her voice ringing crystal clear through the sunlit nave as she pledged to love, cherish, and obey him for better or worse, for richer or poorer, in sickness and in health, till death did them part.

The reverend held out his prayer book, clearing his throat expectantly. With a start of dismay, Laura realized that Nicholas had no ring to give her. Or so she thought until he drew a narrow circlet of gold from the pocket of his waistcoat and laid it gently on the book.

The priest handed the ring back and Nicholas slid it onto Laura's finger. "I found it in Lady Eleanor's jewel box," he whispered. "If she was as generous as you say she was, I didn't think she'd mind."

Laura gazed down at the lustrous garnet that had once belonged to Lady Eleanor's grandmother, then smiled up at him through a veil of tears. "I think she'd be very pleased indeed."

A beaming Reverend Tilsbury joined their right hands. Holding them aloft, he said in a voice that carried to the far corners of the church, "Those whom God hath joined together, let no man put asunder."

"And a hearty amen to that!" Cookie shouted as the rest of the parishioners broke into thunderous applause.

George emerged from the church with Lottie trailing behind him. While Laura and Nicholas received their first Holy Communion as man and wife, he and his sister joined the others who were waiting in the churchyard to congratulate them.

Drifting toward the shade of an oak tree, George gave his frilled cuffs a practiced flick, just as he'd seen his new brother-in-law do a dozen times. "You know, Lottie, I've been thinking that maybe we were wrong about Nicholas all along. He might not be such a bad fellow after all."

Sullen silence greeted his words.

George sighed. "I know the two of you got off on the wrong foot, but if you could just stop sulking for five minutes, you might be able to see . . ." He turned to find himself addressing thin air. His sister had disappeared.

"Lottie?" He scanned the crowd milling about the churchyard, but her bouncing golden curls were nowhere to be found.

Nicholas and Laura appeared in the doorway of the church, their smiles as dazzling as the morning sunshine. They only made it as far as the first step before they were besieged by a chattering mob of well-wishers. George fought his way through them, finally emerging at Laura's side with his hair mussed and his cravat crooked.

He tugged sharply at her sleeve. "Laura! Have you seen Lottie?"

Still clutching Nicholas's arm, Laura beamed down at him, looking positively dazed with happiness. "Hmmm? Lottie? Yes, of course I saw her. Didn't she look lovely in her new pink frock?"

Before he could explain, she had turned away to greet someone else. Recognizing that he wasn't going to receive any help from that quarter, George dashed back down the steps. Cookie was climbing into the manor's donkey cart, accompanied by several of the village women she'd recruited to help with the breakfast.

As she clucked the horses into motion, George trotted alongside the cart. "Lottie's gone missing, Cookie. Have you seen her?"

Cookie laughed heartily. "Do you really think you'll find your little sister where there's work to be done? If I know my Lottie, she won't pop up till the table's laid with all her favorite sweets."

As she gave the reins a brisk snap, George swung around, his frantic gaze searching the churchyard. Although Lottie was nowhere in sight, he could hear her voice as clearly as if she was whispering in his ear.

In Miss Radcliffe's novels, the villain who seeks to compromise the heroine's virtue always meets with an untimely demise before he can succeed.

After their near disaster with the poison, he had simply assumed that she'd abandoned her wild scheme. But what if he'd been wrong?

He was scanning the shadows beneath the oaks when he caught a glimpse of gold in the bell tower high above. The stone angel perched on the tower's jutting parapet, her unfurled wings reaching for the sky. Directly below, Laura and Nicholas still stood on the steps, the crowd around them finally beginning to thin.

And what will you do if none of these experiments yield the results you had hoped for? he had asked Lottie while they were sitting in the exact spot where Laura and Nicholas now stood.

She had glanced up at the angel and smiled that secret little smile of hers. *Then we shall simply have to look heavenward for some divine inspiration.*

"No," George whispered, his horrified gaze traveling slowly back up to the angel's cherubic face. "Oh, please, God, no."

No one would ever have to know. If he could just reach Lottie before she did something foolish, no one would ever have to know.

That was the litany running through George's mind as he shoved aside old Halford Tombob to reach the door to the bell tower.

The old man shook his cane at him. "In my day, young pups like you had some manners about them!"

There was no time for apologies, no time to allow his eyes to adjust to the shadowy gloom inside the tower. George stumbled his way through the maze of bell ropes, then went flying up the winding stone staircase, his heart racing in his chest.

Until he burst into the tower and saw something that nearly stopped it altogether.

Lottie sat on the ledge behind the angel, digging at the mortar around its base with an iron chisel.

George froze, afraid to take another step.

Lottie's little face was unnaturally composed. She didn't even look up from her task. "You needn't try to stop me. I've worked too hard for this. I've been up here chipping away day after day at this cursed rock while you were practicing tying your cravat in front of the mirror so you wouldn't embarrass his lordship at the altar. If you want to be helpful now, then go back down there and see if you can lure Laura off the steps."

"Put the chisel down, Lottie. You don't want to do this."

"And why not? You have to admit that it's a brilliant plan, worthy of even the most lurid Gothic plot. Everyone will think it was simply a tragic accident. Laura can have Arden Manor. We can have Laura. And everything will go on just as it did before *he* came."

George shook his head. "No, it won't. Nothing would ever be the same again because you would have broken Laura's heart."

"She'll forgive me in time," Lottie insisted, dislodging a large hunk of mortar. "She never could stay mad at me for more than an hour. Remember the time I let Miss Fuzzy birth a litter of kittens on her favorite shawl and she called me a horrid, selfish brat? I cried so hard I couldn't breathe and she was soon apologizing for making me turn blue."

"Your tears won't be enough to fix things this time." George took a step toward his sister before saying softly, "She loves him, Lottie."

Lottie went utterly still, the chisel sliding from her limp hand to clank on the stone floor. When she finally lifted her big blue eyes to George, they were brimming with tears. "I know. So do I."

George barely made it across the tower in time to catch her as she crumpled. She clung to him, sobbing not like the sophisticated young lady she tried so hard to be but like the little girl she was. Her broken wail was muffled into his shoulder. "He called me Goldilocks! He ruffled my hair and called me Goldilocks just as Papa used to do!"

George awkwardly patted her hair. But the words of comfort he started to offer were drowned out by a deafening *bong*.

His entire body began to vibrate.

The bells! he thought, clenching his teeth against a wave of shock. The sexton must be ringing the bells to spread the joyful news of Laura and Nicholas's marriage throughout the countryside. That heavenly chiming created a hellish cacophony inside the bell tower.

Lottie jerked out of his arms with a soundless shriek, clapping her hands over her ears. Before he could grab her, she went reeling backward, stumbling right into the stone angel.

The statue began to rock back and forth. As the last of the mortar binding it to the parapet crumbled to dust, it pitched forward. George lunged for it, but he was too late. He and Lottie could only watch in horror as the angel took flight and went hurtling toward the steps below.

Chapter 16

You've lived long enough now to know that
sometimes people do all the wrong things. . . .

Do you hear bells?" Nicholas shouted as the
tower above them burst into deafening song.

"No bells, darling," Laura shouted back, "just angels singing every time I look into your eyes."

He arched one eyebrow, his expression more devilish
than angelic as he pressed his mouth to her ear, and
murmured, "Tonight I promise to show you a glimpse
of heaven itself."

"Why wait until tonight?" Laura mouthed back at
him. Her tongue darted out to moisten her lips as she
turned her face to his in invitation.

He was about to accept that invitation when a
shadow came plummeting out of the sky, consuming
every drop of sunlight in its path. Laura was still standing with her eyes shut and her dewy lips parted when
Nicholas gave her a violent shove, sending her sliding
down the church steps on her backside.

A tremendous crash sounded, followed by a blinding
cloud of dust and a flurry of gasps, shouts, and cough-

ing. For several minutes, Laura could only lie there in the grass, utterly stunned. Nicholas's kisses had been known to have some startling effects on her, but she'd never had one hurl her down a flight of steps.

Fanning the dust away from her watering eyes, she struggled to her feet. The beautiful gown Cookie had labored over with such care was sullied by grass stains and torn in half a dozen places. Her circlet of rosebuds drooped over one eye. She was vaguely aware of people milling around in the churchyard behind her, their panicked shouts ringing over the unrelenting chiming of the bells, but all she could think of was getting back to Nicholas.

Weaving like a drunken wood sprite, she started up the steps. They were littered with bits of mortar and chunks of stone. She was picking her way over a jagged fragment when a familiar voice shrieked, "Laura!"

Laura jerked around to see Lottie come flying around the corner of the church with George in tow. Lottie's face lit up like a Roman candle when she saw her, but darkened just as quickly. The children both stumbled to a halt, looking at something just behind Laura.

The villagers fell silent. The bells ceased their chiming. The angels stopped singing. Time itself seemed to slow to a crawl as Laura turned. The dust had just begun to clear, revealing a man sprawled like a broken puppet against the church door.

"Nicholas?" Laura whispered.

She dropped to her knees at his side. Except for the blood trickling from a shallow cut on his brow, he looked peaceful enough to be sleeping. Laura blinked, trying to convince herself that the mysterious object lying beside him actually *was* a severed wing. She turned her gaze to the heavens, realizing for the first time what had happened.

When the statue of the angel had come toppling off the parapet, Nicholas had shoved her out of harm's way, taking the brunt of the blow himself.

As the villagers began to creep up the steps behind her, Laura slipped her trembling hand inside Nicholas's waistcoat. His heart beat strong and true against her palm, just as it had that day in the wood.

Relief coursed through her, swelling to joy as his eyes began to flutter open. But the dazed expression in their depths gave her a fresh moment of horror. If a blow to the head could rob him of his memory, was it possible that a second blow could restore it?

Grasping the lapels of his coat, she gave him a gentle shake. "Do you know me, Nicky? Do you know who I am?"

She bit her lip as his eyes struggled to bring her face into focus. She could feel the villagers holding their breath right along with her.

"Of course I know who you are." He reached up to brush a rosebud out of her eye, the dimple in his cheek deepening. "You're my wife."

As Laura threw herself into his arms, laughing through her tears, a cheer went up from the villagers. With her help, Nicholas staggered to his feet, earning another rousing huzzah.

Laura wrapped her arms around his waist, clinging as if she would never let him go. "You gave me the fright of my life! I thought you were done for."

"Don't be silly, pet. A man who can dodge a cannon-ball isn't about to let a mere statue fall on his head." He rubbed at his temple, wincing when his fingertips found the gash. "I ducked beneath the doorframe, but the wing must have struck me a glancing blow." He shot the empty parapet a troubled glance. "What do you think caused it to fall? Could it have been the bells?"

Before Laura could answer, they were borne on a tide of goodwill down the steps and into the church-yard. While Tooley Grantham slapped Nicholas on the back hard enough to make him stumble, Tom Dillmore winked at Laura, and said, "Good thing you came round when you did, mate. I was making ready to offer my condolences to the little widow."

The rest of Laura's rejected beaux followed their lead, gathering around to praise Nicholas for both his bravery and his quick reflexes. They were all too dis-tracted by the joyful chaos to even notice the glossy black town coach that was just drawing up outside the churchyard gates.

Widow Witherspoon dug her bony elbow into Laura's side. "Out of my way, girlie! You've already had your chance to kiss the groom. Now it's mine."

Laura had no choice but to step aside and let the cackling widow press her puckered lips to Nicholas's cheek. She was laughing at his good-natured wince when she saw the coach. Her relief that her bridegroom was alive was still too keen for her to be anything more than mildly curious as a footman garbed in gold livery leapt down from his perch and threw open a door painted with an elaborate coat of arms.

Her eyes widened as two monstrous creatures emerged from the coach's darkened interior. They were far too large to be dogs. They must surely be wolves.

"Look, Mama!" a child shouted. "Look at the bears!"

Alice Bogworth let out a shrill scream and the villagers began to scatter as the beasts came loping into the churchyard, making a beeline for the grassy area in front of the steps. Laura stood paralyzed with fright, unable to run, unable to scream. But the creatures galloped right past her. Leaping as one, they planted their massive paws on Nicholas's chest, knocking him flat.

Instead of ripping out his throat, as Laura had feared, they began to lap at his face with their lolling pink tongues. Nicholas lay in the grass in a dazed heap for a moment, then grimaced and shoved at their mammoth heads. "Good God, would you stop slobbering all over me? I've already had a bath today, thank you very much."

He struggled to his feet, clutching at his head, but the dogs continued to frisk and gambol in circles around him, making escape impossible.

It wasn't until one of them trod soundly on his foot that he threw back his head and roared, "Caliban! Cerberus! Sit!"

Everyone in the churchyard flinched, including Laura. The dogs sat, suddenly as harmless as a pair of bookends.

Nicholas's eyes met Laura's and it was clear from the panic and confusion within them that he was as stunned by his outburst as she had been. But there was no time to compare reactions, for a lady had emerged from the coach and was racing down the path.

Bursting into tears, she threw her arms around Nicholas's neck and began to smother his face with kisses. "Oh, you dear wicked thing, you're alive! You're really alive! I had nearly given up all hope!"

At first Nicholas stood stiffly in her embrace. Then

his arms slowly began to rise. "Diana?" His hand shook as he smoothed her sleek dark hair away from her face. "Is it you? Is it really you?"

Laura turned her face away, no longer able to watch the tender reunion. From her satin half-boots to the swirling ostrich plumes on her hat, this woman was everything Laura would never be—beautiful, elegant, sophisticated. And plainly adored by the man in her arms.

Nicholas had promised her a glimpse of heaven and it seemed that was all she was going to have.

As Lottie slipped her small hand into Laura's, a gentleman with a walking stick tucked under his arm came striding past without sparing either one of them a glance.

Nicholas stared at him blankly for several seconds before recognition dawned in his eyes. "Thane? *Thane?* What in the hell are you doing here?"

The man clapped him on the shoulder, grinning broadly. "I'm charging to your rescue, of course, just as you charged to my rescue so many times on the battlefield. Surely you didn't expect me to sit idly by when I heard you were about to go and get yourself leg-shackled to some silly country chit."

Nicholas blinked and shook his head, as if awakening from some long and fantastical dream. "I can't seem to make any sense of all this." He cradled his brow in his hand. "If I could just get my blasted head to stop pounding . . ."

The woman linked her arm possessively through his. "Don't you worry, Sterling. Everything will start to make sense again once you're back at Devonbrooke Hall where you belong."

Laura would have sworn she'd already endured the worst moment of her life. She was wrong.

That moment came when the man she had just married slowly turned to gaze at her through narrowed eyes. She could almost see the warmth melting from their golden depths, leaving them as cold and calculating as chips of frozen amber. As she realized she had just sold herself, body and soul, to Sterling Harlow, the Devil of Devonbrooke himself, Laura took the only course of action left to her.

She fainted.

Part Two

*The prince of darkness
is a gentleman.*

—William Shakespeare

Chapter 17

. . . for all the right reasons.

Laura sat on the edge of her bed, still wearing her tattered wedding gown and crooked circlet of rosebuds. She was so engrossed in staring at nothing that she didn't even blink when a pink stocking came sailing past her nose, followed by a pair of kid slippers.

All that was visible of Lottie was her round little rump. She was on her knees pawing through the bottom of Laura's wardrobe. Every few seconds, she would toss an item haphazardly over one shoulder to a waiting George, who would catch it and cram it into the brocaded valise sitting open on the other side of the bed.

"I don't know why you're going to all that trouble," Laura said, her voice nearly as flat as her expression. "They won't let me have those things in the gaol."

"You're not going to the gaol," Lottie said fiercely, tossing George a crumpled nightdress. "You're going to run away."

Laura sighed. "I don't know if you've noticed, but there's a rather formidable footman stationed just outside the door. Should I make it past him, which I doubtless wouldn't, I'm sure His Grace would be only too delighted to sic one of his slavering devil dogs on me."

George threw open the window and leaned out, surveying the steep slant of the clay shingles. "We might be able to knot some sheets together and lower you to the ground."

"Now, *that's* a brilliant plan," Laura said dryly. "If I should break my own neck, it would spare him the trouble of doing it."

Lottie sat back on her heels, shooting her brother a frazzled glance.

"He can't keep you under lock and key forever, you know," George insisted.

"And why not? He's a very wealthy and powerful man. He can do whatever he likes with me." Laura couldn't quite hide her involuntary shiver. "Even if I did manage to escape him, where would I go? There's nowhere I could hide where he wouldn't find me."

Lottie sank down on the bed next to Laura, patting her icy hand. "Perhaps it's not too late to throw yourself on his mercy. If you cry very prettily, he might just find it in his heart to forgive you."

Laura slowly turned to look at her sister. "For over six years Lady Eleanor begged for his forgiveness. I can't count the number of times I caught her crying over him. Yet he never spared her so much as a second thought." She went back to gazing at the faded violets on the wallpaper. "I refuse to beg for mercy from a man who has none to give."

"Look on the bright side," Lottie said, leaning her head against Laura's shoulder. "Perhaps he'll forget everything that's happened to him *since* he lost his memory."

Laura studied the delicate garnet ring he had slipped on her finger only an hour ago. "That's what I'm most afraid of," she whispered, resting her dark head against Lottie's golden one.

Sterling Harlow, the seventh duke of Devonbrooke, stood in the drawing room of Arden Manor for the first time in over twenty-one years. He could no longer be sure if it was time or his memory that had betrayed him. He only knew that once the room had been larger and sunnier, the roses embroidered on the settee cushions had been red instead of pink, and his mother's pianoforte hadn't been missing half a leg. Nicholas Radcliffe had never noticed such trifling things, but to Sterling, they were as glaring as the ugly watermark staining the plaster frieze.

He flung open the doors of the secretaire and swept aside the rotting ledgers. The decanter of brandy was exactly where his father had always hidden it. His mother had pretended not to know it was there, even when his father had come staggering up the steps after a long night spent "balancing the books." Books whose columns were devoid of figures because his father had gambled away both his modest inheritance and her dowry at one of the more disreputable gaming hells in Covent Garden.

"Would you care for a drink?" he asked Thane. "I know it's early, but I think a man is entitled to a toast on his wedding day."

"Don't mind if I do," Thane replied, accepting the

glass Sterling offered him. The young marquess was sprawled in the window seat with his booted feet crossed at the ankle.

"It should be well aged. It was my father's," Sterling informed him. "Excellent taste in liquor was his only redeeming quality. He actually preferred port. He was a three-bottle-a-night man."

Thane took a sip. "No wonder you've always had such a fine head for liquor."

You never indulge in spirits.

The echo of those gentle words sliced through Sterling's heart like a knife. His hand tightened around his own glass. It was all he could do to keep from flinging it at the hearth. Instead, he brought it to his lips, tossing back the brandy in a single blistering swallow.

Diana delicately cleared her throat. Taking the hint, Sterling poured her a glass and delivered it to the ottoman where she sat.

Plainly bemused, Thane cocked one eyebrow. "I wasn't aware that ladies indulged in anything stronger than sherry. Should we offer you some snuff as well?"

She smiled sweetly at him over the rim of the glass. "No, thank you. I much prefer a pipe."

While Sterling poured himself another drink, Thane hefted his glass in a toast. "To freedom."

"To freedom," Sterling echoed grimly.

"Freedom," Diana murmured, keeping a wary eye on her cousin as she took a genteel sip of the brandy.

Sterling sank down in the leather wing chair, carelessly sweeping a well-worn Greek Testament onto the floor. He no longer had any interest in reading about forgiveness or redemption.

Thane tilted his head to read the spine, then snorted.

"I still can't believe the chit was going to make a country parson of you. Wait till the lads at White's hear that the infamous Devil of Devonbrooke nearly traded his horns for a halo."

"And you're absolutely sure she had no way of knowing who you were?" Diana asked.

"Not to my knowledge," Sterling replied stiffly.

Diana swirled the brandy around in the glass, a frown creasing her smooth brow. "That's what puzzles me the most about all this. If she wasn't trying to get her greedy little paws on your wealth or your title, then why the elaborate charade?"

Thane leaned forward in the window seat. "According to this Dower fellow, Sterling's mother told the girl that if she wed before her twenty-first birthday, which just happens to be day after tomorrow, the manor would be hers."

"That's impossible," Sterling snapped. "The manor wasn't my mother's to give. By law, two-thirds of my father's property belonged to me the minute my father died. She had no right to offer it to some ambitious foundling."

Thane shrugged. "You know how women are. Leave them to their own devices for too long and they can come up with some very foolish and romantic notions."

Diana cleared her throat again, this time more pointedly.

"*Some* women, that is," Thane amended, struggling to suppress a smile. "This isn't London, you know. It really wouldn't have been that difficult for your mother to find some green clerk willing to draw up an official-looking document containing whatever nonsense she paid him to write. Perhaps she thought you wouldn't care. Your father's been dead for over ten years and you've shown scant interest in claiming your share of his inheritance. Until now, that is."

Gazing at Sterling through puzzled eyes, Diana shook her head. "That still doesn't explain why the girl chose you. And at such grave peril to herself."

"Why don't we ask her?" Thane suggested, bounding to his feet. "I daresay she's had enough time to recover from her brilliantly timed swoon. I'll go fetch her right now."

"No!" Sterling shouted, startling them both.

Thane slowly sank back down.

"I don't want to see her," Sterling added softly. "Not yet."

Thane and Diana exchanged a troubled glance. To escape their scrutiny, Sterling moved to the window on the north wall and drew aside the curtain. Caliban and Cerberus were galloping back and forth through Laura's flower garden, their romp punctuated by joyful barks and flying blooms.

"It should be easy enough to extract yourself from this situation," Diana said gently. "The marriage itself isn't legally binding, of course, given that you signed the parish register under a false name."

"And even a village this size must have a constable," Thane pointed out. "If not, we'll take the conniving little witch to London. The court takes a dim view of kidnapping peers of the realm. She'll be lucky if they don't hang her."

Sterling continued to gaze out the window, silent and still.

"I can make all the necessary arrangements if you

like." It was Thane's turn to clear his throat. "Unless, of course, there are . . . extenuating circumstances."

"He wants to know if you've compromised her," Diana pointed out cheerfully, causing Thane to choke on a mouthful of brandy.

You're not the sort of man who would compromise his fiancée's virtue.

That remembered declaration, delivered with such beguiling earnestness, made Sterling want to ram his fist through the window. He wished to hell he *had* compromised her. Wished he had eased her nightdress up above her waist in that moonlit bower and rutted her like some pagan satyr of old. If he had realized he might never get another chance, he would have done just that and more. Much more.

"I hardly think this is a discussion fit for mixed company," Thane protested when he was done sputtering.

"Oh, for heaven's sake, Thane," Diana said. "You needn't be so condescending. I'm not one of those blushing flibbertigibbets you're so fond of consorting with. Unlike most of your lady friends, I'm even old enough to button my own boots."

"I'm flattered to know you've been studying my habits," he drawled. "Tell me, have you spies in all the London drawing rooms I frequent? Or just the bed-chambers?"

"Ha!" Diana scoffed. "Why would I need spies when your romantic exploits are touted in all the scandal sheets and whispered about behind every fan?"

"Forgive me, my lady," Thane said quietly. "I forgot that you always had more faith in vicious gossip than you did in me."

A tense moment passed before Diana returned her attention to Sterling. "Even if you did compromise her, I don't see that it changes anything."

"At least we're in agreement on that much," Thane said stiffly. "The foolish girl has only herself to blame and she should still have to bear the consequences of her deceit. You may even discover that you're not the first nobleman she's tried to seduce into marriage."

Sterling gave no sign that he had even heard them.

"Oh, Sterling," Diana cried. "You're usually so careful. You haven't gone and gotten her with child, have you?"

You always told me that you only wanted two children—a boy and a girl.

Sterling closed his eyes. He could blot out the mocking beauty of the summer day, but he could do nothing to banish the dulcet sweetness of Laura's voice from his head. Or the vision of the freckle-faced, brown-eyed boy and golden-haired little girl they would never have.

He slowly turned, each movement an exercise in discipline. "As much as I appreciate your concern, I think it best that we discuss this matter no further until the morrow."

Thane started to protest, but Diana obediently rose, smoothing her skirt. "Of course, we'll respect your wishes."

Thane followed her lead, casting the window a glum glance. "I wonder what the odds are of finding some decent food in this uncivilized burg."

Although it came nowhere near his eyes, Sterling smiled for the first time since regaining his memory. "You might try asking the cook for some crumpets. But

I'd stay away from the bride cake if I were you. It tends to leave a bitter taste in the mouth."

Nicholas Radcliffe had once told Laura he didn't believe in ghosts. Which was why it came as such a shock to Sterling Harlow when they began to gather around him, forming from the late afternoon shadows that shrouded the drawing room.

His father materialized first, shoving past him with a bottle in one hand and a top hat in the other. "I'm off to London, boy. If you want to build a silly kite, go find your mother. I've no time for such nonsense."

But his mother was kneeling by the door, tears streaming down her beautiful face. As the ghost of the boy he had once been walked right past her outstretched arms, his small shoulders set in unforgiving lines, she began to fade.

"Mama," Sterling whispered, but it was too late. She was already gone.

He turned around to find old Granville Harlow standing by the hearth, a sneer twisting his thin lips. "I've never believed in coddling a child," the duke said, slapping his walking stick repeatedly across his own palm. "I'll make a man of the lad in no time."

Sterling hurled his half-full glass of brandy at the hearth, vanquishing the old man back to hell where he belonged.

But there was to be no vanquishing the shades that followed. Shades of Laura and the man she had called Nicholas Radcliffe. Radcliffe leaned against the mantel, grinning at Laura like the fool she had made of him.

The two of them shared the window seat, entwined in a tender, yet passionate, embrace. He knelt before the ottoman, framing her lovely face in his hands before touching his lips to hers. She collapsed and he was there to catch her, there to gather her into his arms and hold her against his heart.

Sterling sank down in the leather wing chair, grinding the heels of his hands against his eyes. It seemed that Arden Manor wasn't haunted. He was.

A rumbling purr shattered the silence. Something plush and warm rubbed against his ankle.

"Nellie." His voice broke as he reached blindly down to run his fingers through the heavenly softness of her fur. "Oh, God, Nellie, where have you been all this time?"

But when he opened his eyes, it wasn't Nellie gazing soberly up at him but the small yellow kitten who bore such a striking resemblance to her. He glanced at the door. It had slipped open a mere crack, just enough to grant her entry.

Sterling slowly withdrew his hand. Like everything else at Arden Manor, the kitten was simply an illusion. A taunting reminder of the life he would never have.

"Go on with you," he commanded hoarsely, nudging her with the toe of his boot. "I've no time for your nonsense."

The little cat didn't budge. She simply settled back on her hindquarters and let out a piteous meow, begging to be readmitted into both his lap and his good graces.

Sterling surged to his feet, the last of his control snapping. "I've already told you I can't abide cats!" he shouted. "*Now why don't you leave me the hell alone!*"

The kitten whirled around and darted for the door. Sterling knew instinctively that she wouldn't be coming back.

His hands clenched into fists, he swung toward the hearth, half expecting to hear his great-uncle's mocking laughter. But it seemed the ghosts had all fled as well, leaving him more alone than he'd ever been in his life.

Laura lay on her side in the guttering candlelight, gazing at her sister's empty bed. The all-powerful duke must have decreed that Lottie wasn't to be allowed to share her imprisonment. Shortly after noon, the stony-faced footman had ushered her brother and sister from the chamber, leaving Laura all alone to await a summons that had never come.

She had expected bread and water for supper, but Cookie had sent up a tray laden with all manner of succulent meats and tempting delicacies. Although Laura had rearranged the food so Cookie wouldn't be alarmed when the tray was returned to her, she hadn't been able to choke down a single bite of what was supposed to be her wedding breakfast.

She could only imagine what the villagers must have thought of the morning's debacle. They had probably found it more stirring than any of Lady Eleanor's theatricals, even the one where George's turban caught fire and the sheep ran amok through the village church.

As dark had fallen, she had donned her nightdress and climbed into bed as if it were only one of a thousand other nights. As if she hadn't spent the previous night cradled in the arms of the man she loved—kissing, laughing, sharing their plans for the future. And tasting a tantalizing pleasure that was only a shadow of what they were to have shared tonight.

Laura squeezed her eyes shut against a blinding wave of pain. The only arms wrapped around her tonight were her own, but even they weren't enough to still her shivers of misery. She wished she could cry, but her tears seemed to be frozen into an icy lump lodged deep in her breast. It hurt so much to breathe that she almost wished she could stop.

An eerie hush had hung over the manor all day, as if someone had died and no one dared speak above a whisper. Which made the sudden jingling of a harness and the clop of hooves on the cobbled drive outside Laura's window that much more startling.

She tossed back the bedclothes, flew to the window, and drew aside the drapes. The elegant town coach that had delivered disaster to her wedding was making its way down the lane at a rapid clip, heading toward the village.

Or London.

Laura's wish was granted. Suddenly, she couldn't breathe at all.

Perhaps Sterling Harlow had never summoned her into his exalted presence because he had come to the conclusion that she was beneath both his notice and his contempt. Perhaps he'd simply decided to return to the glittering excitement of the life he led in London and pretend the past three weeks had never happened. Only a breath ago, if someone had asked her what would be the more terrible punishment—facing him tonight or never seeing him again—she wouldn't have been able to say. But as she watched the carriage lamps rock away into the darkness, Laura knew.

She had just managed to drag herself back to bed and draw the feather quilt over her when the bedchamber door came flying open. She sat up with a startled gasp, but this time it wasn't the footman who dared to disturb her privacy. It was the duke of Devonbrooke himself.

He closed the door behind him and leaned against it, folding his arms over his chest as he surveyed her across the sea of rumpled bedclothes. "You needn't look so surprised to see me, darling. Or have you forgotten that it's our wedding night?"

Chapter 18

I swear I never meant to hurt you. . . .

Laura's papa had tried to warn her. If you sold your soul to the devil, it would only be a matter of time before he came to collect. But Papa had never warned her the devil would be so beautiful that she would be tempted to surrender that soul without a fight.

With his lips curved into a mocking smile and his fair hair tumbling around his face, Sterling Harlow looked every inch the fallen angel. His cuffs had been shoved up to reveal muscular forearms dusted with golden hair. His stocking feet and the cravat hanging loose around the throat of his half-unbuttoned shirt only enhanced his disreputable air.

"You may scream if you like," he suggested pleasantly. "My cousin Diana may adore me, but that doesn't mean she'll stand for me accosting a helpless young lady in her bedchamber. If you yell loud enough, Dower might even come running from the barn, pitchfork at the ready."

Laura had no intention of screaming. This was a dance only the two of them could do. "Swooning in front of the Bogworth sisters was humiliating enough. I'm not about to wake the whole household and frighten the children by screeching like some milksop maiden in one of Lottie's novels."

He shrugged. "Suit yourself, then. Just don't forget I gave you the chance."

His eyes flicked lazily downward. When she had sat up so hastily, both the quilt and her nightdress had gone sliding down, baring one creamy shoulder. Struggling to appear casual, she reached for the wrapper draped across the foot of the bed. Sterling got there at the same time she did.

"I don't know why you'd want to bother with that silly old thing," he said, gently tugging it from her hands and tossing it over Lottie's bed. "We've had some of our best conversations while you were in your nightclothes." Although his voice was cool and crisp, his eyes glittered with an unfamiliar fire.

"You've been drinking," Laura observed, settling back against the pillows and smoothing the quilt over her lap.

"Steadily since this morning," he confessed. "Although I was forced to stop a little while ago when I exhausted my father's supply of brandy. Did you know he kept another bottle stashed inside the pianoforte?" Sterling shook his head. "He might have had a tin ear for music, but you have to appreciate his resourcefulness."

"From what I hear, there was precious little else to appreciate about the man."

"Is that what Lady Eleanor told you?" Sterling's voice

was deceptively light. "Ah, yes, dear, saintly Lady Eleanor! I was like a son to her, was I not?"

Laura lowered her eyes, ashamed of her own monstrous cruelty, however unwitting. She would have gladly bitten out her own tongue to take back those careless words.

Sterling frowned at her. "You disappoint me, my dear. I had rather hoped you would throw yourself at me and plead prettily for my forgiveness."

"Would it do any good?" She slanted him a glance from beneath her lashes, halfway hoping he would say yes.

"No," he admitted. "But it would have still proved very entertaining." He leaned one shoulder against the bedpost. "Along with my drinking, I've been doing quite a bit of reading today. Did you know that Lord Hardwick's Act of 1753 made falsifying an entry in a marriage register with evil intent a capital offense?"

"If you're going to have me executed, I wish you'd go ahead and summon the hangman," Laura snapped, frustration making her reckless. "He's bound to be in a better temper than you."

"Killing you wasn't *quite* what I had in mind. But I really shouldn't be so hard on you, should I? After all, you've suffered nearly as great a shock as I have. It must have been quite distressing to learn that you'd just wed 'a repugnant toad of a man who cares nothing for anyone but himself—a heartless, petty, vindictive wretch.'"

"You left off 'vile,'" she reminded him grimly.

"It is rather ironic, isn't it, considering that you weren't even going to invite me to your wedding, that you'd just as soon have invited Beelzebub himself."

Laura briefly closed her eyes as her own words came back to taunt her. "I can't blame you for hating me."

"Good," he said crisply.

"You probably won't believe me, but I did it to protect the children. When you wrote and said you were going to claim Arden Manor for your own, you left me with little choice."

"Did you honestly believe I would cast innocent children into the streets?"

"No. I believed you would cast them into the workhouse."

"Even I'm not that much of a devil. I had every intention of finding Lottie and George homes in some reputable household."

She met his gaze boldly. "And what about me? What was to become of me?"

"As I recall, I was going to marry you off to some fool." Sterling shook his head with a soft, bitter laugh. "And I suppose I've done just that." He came around the bed, his steps as measured as his word. "I really can't blame you for thinking me the devil. You were already well aware of my colossal indifference toward the woman who gave me life, my debauched habits. . . ." He trailed off, leaving those dangerous words hanging in the air between them.

She smelled the heady sweetness of the brandy on his breath before he touched her. Before he sank down on the bed, resting his weight on one knee, and slipped a hand beneath her hair. She stared straight ahead, not responding to the persuasive warmth of his fingers against her nape, but not resisting it, either.

Touching his mouth to her ear, he murmured, "Do

you remember what you promised to give me should we ever come face-to-face?"

"One of Cookie's crumpets?" she ventured.

His lips drifted around to graze the corner of her mouth. "A tongue-lashing I'd never forget."

If he'd been rough with her, if he had taken her mouth with punishing force, Laura might have been able to resist him. But he was far too diabolical for that. Instead, he teased her lips apart with the tip of his tongue, then tenderly claimed them for his own. He might be a devil, but he still kissed like an angel. Unable to resist the devastating sweetness of those silky thrusts, her mouth melted into his, giving him that tongue-lashing she'd promised. He groaned, the deepening ferocity of his kiss giving her a taste of the hurt and hunger raging beneath his iron control. Before she even realized what she was doing, she had risen to her knees and pressed herself against the lean, hard planes of his body.

He tore his mouth away from hers. Breathing hard, he wound one hand through her hair and tugged her head back, forcing her to look him in the eye. "Damn it, Laura, I want the truth! You owe me that much. Why? Why did you choose me? If you didn't know who I was, then it couldn't have been the money and it couldn't have been the title. You obviously had no lack of suitors. If you believed what my mother told you, you could have married any man in Arden and still have inherited this accursed place." Her kiss had stripped the veneer of brittle mockery from his features, leaving them fierce and raw. "*Why me?*"

She gazed up at him, her eyes brimming with both tears and defiance. "Because I wanted you! Because I saw you that day in the wood and I wanted you for myself!"

He went utterly still, not even breathing. Then he shook his head, her own helplessness reflected in his eyes. "No one has ever accused me of not giving a lady what she wanted."

This time when his mouth came down on hers, it was with his full weight behind it. They went tumbling into the bed together, their mouths meshed into a fiery web of delight. As Sterling kicked away the quilt that separated their straining bodies, Laura clung to him, giving free rein to her own hunger. He might not be her Nicholas, but he was no stranger, either. He was her husband. And he had every right to come to her bed, just as she had every right to receive him there, even if it meant wandering in a dark and perilous wood where pleasure could be even more of a danger to her soul than pain.

Laura would have sworn she'd exhausted the last of his patience, that he owed her nothing more than a rough, hasty coupling, but not even his feverish urgency could make him careless with her. The whole time he was tugging up the hem of her nightdress, he was bathing her sensitive throat in hot, damp kisses. Before she could catch her breath, she was naked in his arms. She couldn't say what had become of her nightdress any more than she could say what had become of his shirt. She only knew that she was finally free to press her open mouth to his chest, to run her tongue over the crisp hairs dusting those supple muscles. His golden skin tasted every bit as delectable as it looked, if not more so.

The candle sputtered, then went out, plunging them

into a cocoon of darkness where the only sensation was the rough velvet of his hands against her skin. As he seized her lips again, a wild, sweet madness compelled her to arch against him, to fill those hands with the aching fullness of her breasts.

Still pleasuring her mouth with deep, drugging kisses, he brushed his thumbs back and forth across her nipples until they began to tingle and swell. Just when she thought she couldn't bear another second of that delicious torment, he shifted his kiss from her lips to her right breast, first caressing the rigid bud with the very tip of his tongue, then drawing it into the wet heat of his mouth and sucking hard. Laura clamped her trembling thighs together, stunned by the ripples of sensation between them. It was almost as if he were touching her there.

And then he was.

She gasped as one of his long, tapered fingers went sliding through her damp curls. It didn't take his knee to nudge her thighs apart. All it took was a deft stroke of his fingertip against the throbbing pearl nestled in the crux of those curls. As her thighs went limp, he rolled to the side and trapped one of them beneath his own so that she couldn't have closed herself to him even if she wanted to.

Which she most definitely did not.

He kept her leg pinned beneath his while his hand had its wicked way with her, petting and kneading and stroking until she was panting with blind need.

Sterling had spent most of his life taking pleasure, not giving it. Although he'd certainly earned his reputation as an accomplished lover, he had always measured each kiss and practiced caress against what he would receive in return for his efforts. But with Laura, it was enough to lie beside her in the shadows and watch the flickers of rapture dance over her delicate features, to lavish the creamy skin of her breasts with kisses and absorb each of her sighs as they left her luscious lips.

"Please," she said in a broken whisper, not even sure what she was begging him to give her. "Oh, please . . ."

But Sterling knew. And he was only too willing to oblige.

He reached down to free himself from the agonizing constraints of his trousers. He'd never before had cause to regret his size, but as he slipped between Laura's slender thighs, he knew a moment of genuine trepidation.

Bracing his weight on his elbows, he cupped her face in his hands. "This is going to hurt," he said hoarsely, "but I swear I'm not doing it to punish you. If you don't believe that, then I'll stop right now."

She pondered his words for a minute. "Will it hurt you worse than it hurts me?"

Her words surprised a helpless chuckle from him. "I'm afraid not. But I promise to do whatever I can to make it better for you."

She slowly nodded, her tongue darting out to moisten her lips.

Laura took him at his word, but it was still a shock when he began to lave himself in the copious nectar his skillful touch had coaxed from her body. He was hot and smooth and utterly unyielding, the perfect complement to her melting softness. He slid up and down between those dew-slicked petals, creating an exquisite friction that soon had her writhing and whimpering beneath him, poised on the very brink of madness.

All it took was a nudge to shove her over the edge.

She clung to him as she tumbled head over heels, borne on a quivering tide of rapture. Its waves were still cresting in her womb when he rocked his hips upward once again, this time sliding deep inside of her.

Laura dug her nails into the smooth flesh of his back, biting back a cry.

"We're only halfway home, sweetheart. Take me," he urged, kissing the tears from her cheek. "Take me all the way."

Despite the pain, Laura could not resist such a tender plea. Wrapping her legs around his waist, she buried her face against his throat and arched against him. He pressed forward until every throbbing inch of him was nestled deep within her.

Sterling's memory failed him again. Try as he might, he couldn't recall the face of a single woman he'd ever made love to. There was only Laura—beneath him, around him, bathing him in her tender young body's shuddering grace.

He began to slide in and out of her in slow, deep, sinuous strokes, as if he had all night to devote to that single sacred act. He took her until he couldn't remember a time when he wasn't a part of her, until uncontrollable shivers of delight wracked her inside and out, until she dug her heels into his back and moaned, "Oh, Nicky . . ." in his ear.

Sterling stopped in midstroke. Laura's eyes flew open.

He gazed down at her, his powerful body trembling with the strain of being held in check. "I really wish you wouldn't call me that."

She glared up at him, her breath coming in disgruntled little pants. "What would you prefer I call you? Your Grace?"

For an instant, Sterling feared he might actually smile. "Under these circumstances, I believe 'my lord' will suffice."

He brought his lips down hard on hers, silencing any retort she might have made. His hips resumed their motion, setting a fierce rhythm designed to make them both forget their names.

Too late, Laura realized that she had been wrong. She was going to scream after all. If Sterling hadn't captured her cry in his mouth, it probably would have awakened everyone in the household, if not the whole parish. A guttural groan tore from his own throat as his entire body went as rigid as the part of him still buried deep inside of her.

Still trembling with convulsive aftershocks, Laura clung to him, her breath coming in broken sobs. "Oh . . . oh, my . . ." Before she could stop them, the words echoing through her heart came spilling from her lips. "I'm so very sorry! I was wrong to trick you. I should have told you the truth from the beginning. But I didn't just want you. I loved—"

He pressed two fingers to her lips, shaking his head. "No more lies, Laura. Not here. Not tonight."

She wanted to protest, but something in his face stopped her. Instead, she tangled her hands in his hair and urged his lips back down to hers, telling herself that there would be ample time to convince him of the truth.

A lifetime.

A sharp knock sounded on Laura's bedchamber door the next morning, jolting her from an exhausted slumber. She poked her head out from underneath the quilt, struggling to remember how she'd ended up with her head hanging off the foot of the bed and her feet on the pillows.

When she did, she had to bury her head back under the quilt to smother a naughty giggle. If not for the tenderness lingering between her thighs and the musky aroma clinging to the sheets, she might have thought the entire night was some wild, erotic dream spun from the overwrought imagination of a lonely rector's daughter.

The knock came again, brisk with impatience. Laura's heart quickened with a mixture of anticipation and shyness. It must be Sterling, returning with a tray laden with all of Cookie's most succulent breakfast offerings. Her stomach rumbled, reminding her that she had deprived it of both lunch and supper the previous day.

She scrambled to the head of the bed and artfully arranged the sheet over her breasts before singing out, "Come in!"

It wasn't Sterling who came sweeping through the door but his cousin. Lady Diana Harlow stopped at the foot of the bed and stood peering down her patrician nose at Laura as if she were a particularly nasty bedbug that required a sound squashing. "Forgive me for disturbing you, but His Grace requests your presence in the study."

"Oh, he does, does he?" Laura replied warily, jerking the sheet up to her chin. She was only too aware of the contrast between her own dishabille and the woman's impeccable elegance. Even Diana's dark hair, with its tightly wound chignon and forbidding widow's peak, looked starched.

Diana marched to the window and threw open the drapes. Sunlight came spilling into the room, forcing Laura to shield her bleary eyes with her hand. "Perhaps here in the country you're accustomed to languishing about in bed for half the day, but in London, we prefer to—"

Diana stopped abruptly, her eyes narrowing. Laura could almost see herself through them—lips still rosy from Sterling's kisses, disheveled hair tumbling down her bare back, a whisker burn marking the tender skin of her throat. She had no doubt that she looked exactly like what she was—a woman who had spent the night being thoroughly loved by a man who was a master at it.

Still clutching the sheet, Laura drew herself up, meeting Diana's gaze without flinching. She had many sins to account for, but last night wasn't one of them. "You needn't look so scandalized, my lady. It *was* our wedding night."

Diana's laugh dripped frost. "I hate to be the one to inform you of this, but you're not entitled to a wedding night. You tricked my cousin into signing the parish register under a false name. He has absolutely no obligation to you and no intention of honoring this pathetic sham of a marriage."

"You're lying," Laura said, although a chill began to creep through her heart.

"Unlike you, *Miss* Fairleigh, I don't make a habit of it. I know my cousin can be very charming and persuasive, but you have only yourself to blame if you were fool enough to let him back into your bed after . . ."

Before Laura could correct her unfair assumption that she and Sterling had been lovers all along, Diana trailed off, gazing down at the bed. The quilt had slid halfway onto the floor, baring both the sheets and the rusty stains that marred them.

Diana's disbelieving stare slowly drifted back to Laura's face. Her icy contempt had failed to make Laura blush, but her pity brought a scalding wave of heat to Laura's cheeks.

"God help you both," Diana said softly, shaking her head. "I don't know which one of you is the bigger fool."

If she hadn't spun on her heel and fled the room, Laura could have told her.

Laura descended the steps as if she were marching to the gallows.

She'd donned a dove gray morning dress devoid of ribbons or bows and scrubbed every last trace of Sterling's scent from her skin. Her hair was swept up in a tidy knot that rivaled Lady Diana's. Not a single mutinous tendril had been allowed to escape. She'd even removed the delicate garnet from her finger. No one had to know that she had slipped it onto a silver chain and tucked it deep inside her bodice.

She was surprised to find the foyer deserted. She had halfway expected that Sterling would have gathered her family to witness her disgrace. But she was fiercely thankful that he hadn't. She didn't want George and Lottie to realize that their beloved sister had been had.

In more ways than one.

Sterling no doubt considered it a fitting revenge. She had given him a mock wedding and he had given her a mock wedding night. Now he was free to turn her over to the appropriate authorities, knowing full well the memory of that night would haunt her for as long as she lived. Of course, if he decided to let them hang her, that might not be very long. Her steps faltered briefly, stymied by a wave of self-loathing. No wonder he hadn't wanted to hear her tender declaration of love.

She used her clenched fist to knock firmly on the study door.

"Come in." Even now, when she was fully aware of the treachery it was capable of, that deep, rich voice still sent a ripple of reaction through her. It was too easy to remember the wicked words it had whispered in her ears only a few hours ago, the throaty groans, the breathless exclamations.

Steeling herself against its power, Laura pushed open the door. There wasn't a kitten anywhere in sight, no doubt because the devil dogs were stretched out in front of the hearth, their massive heads cradled on their equally massive paws. As Laura slipped into the room, one of them lifted his head and bared his teeth at her, growling deep in his throat. He looked as if he could be easily placated if she tossed him a side of bacon. Or one of her arms.

The duke's devoted cousin and his gentleman friend perched in a shabby pair of wing chairs in front of the window, looking no less unwelcoming than the dogs. Laura wouldn't have been surprised had Diana bared her teeth and growled as well, but oddly enough, the woman seemed to be avoiding her eyes.

The duke of Devonbrooke himself sat behind the walnut desk, scribbling on a piece of stationery. His cousin must have brought him some of his own clothes from London for he wore a claret-colored coat cut from the finest kerseymere. The frills of his starched white shirt emerged from the deep V of a gray satin waistcoat shot through with silver threads. On the ring finger of his right hand he wore an ostentatious signet ring studded with a blood red ruby. His golden hair, rakishly tousled as was the fashion, looked perfectly capable of absorbing all the sunlight in the room, leaving none for the rest of them. Although she wouldn't have thought it possible, Laura's heart sank even further. This aristocratic stranger bore no resemblance to the wild-eyed, passionate man who had come to her room and her bed last night.

She could see why he had chosen the seldom-used study over the cozy drawing room for her reckoning. It enabled him to keep the desk as a barrier between them. She crossed the faded Turkish rug to stand in front of it, awaiting her sentencing.

"Good morning, Miss Fairleigh." Sterling glanced at the sunbeams slanting through the French windows. "Or should I say 'Good afternoon.'"

Miss Fairleigh. His casual greeting confirmed Laura's worst fears. She wasn't a wife. She was a strumpet. For the first time since the fire, she was almost glad her parents were dead. The shame of her downfall would probably have killed them anyway.

"Good day, Your Grace," she said coolly. "Or would you prefer 'my lord'?"

She must have imagined the faint twitch in his cheek, for he continued to scribble, pausing only long enough to nod toward the straight-backed chair that had been drawn up to the corner of the desk. "Do sit, won't you? I'll be with you in a moment."

She obeyed, thinking what a contrast his brisk words were to the coaxing commands he had given her last night—*Roll over on your stomach, won't you, sweetheart? Again, angel! Don't be shy. One more time just for me; lift your leg just a bit higher . . . oh, God in heaven, that's perfect. . . .*

"We seem to find ourselves in an awkward position."

Laura started, blushing furiously at Sterling's words. Had he read her thoughts? But then she realized she was being ridiculous. He might be all-powerful, but he wasn't all-seeing.

He was, however, leaning back in his chair and surveying her with a speculative gleam in his eye. "Both my cousin and my trusted friend and advisor, the marquess of Gillingham, believe I should leave your fate to the hands of the law."

"Then perhaps you should. From what I know of you, those hands might be more just and merciful than your own."

Thane and Diana exchanged a bemused glance, obviously surprised by her show of spirit, but Sterling didn't even blink. "As much as I value their counsel, I believe I've arrived at a much more . . . um, shall we say . . . *satisfying* solution to the dilemma in which we find ourselves. As you now know only too well, I am the seventh duke of Devonbrooke. Along with the title comes many burdens and responsibilities, not the least of which is to provide an heir so that the line might continue."

Oh, no, Laura thought, her stomach clenching into a knot. He was going to offer her a position as nursemaid to his future children. He was worse than a devil. He was Beelzebub himself.

He leaned forward, fixing his earnest gaze on her face. "Unfortunately, one can't acquire an heir without first acquiring a wife, which is why I was hoping you'd do me the honor of becoming mine."

Chapter 19

I wanted only what was best for you. . . .

Sterling didn't want to hang her. He wanted to marry her.

While Thane and Diana rushed the desk, Laura sat in a blissful daze, struggling to absorb what had just transpired. She and Sterling were going to be married. They were going to live the life she had dreamed of living with Nicholas. There would be long walks at sunset and chocolate in bed every morning.

Thane slammed his palms down on the desk. "Have you gone mad, Sterling? Why should you reward her treachery by making her your duchess?"

Sterling settled back in the chair, a smile playing around his lips. "You may be overestimating my charms. There are some who would argue that I'm no prize. Perhaps being wed to me will be all the punishment she deserves."

Diana shook her head so violently that a stray tendril of hair came tumbling out of her chignon. "I'll never understand you. You won't marry for love, but you'll marry for revenge?"

"Who said anything about revenge? There's no reason I can't be as practical as our Miss Fairleigh here." Sterling shot Laura a cool glance. "I require an heir. She can provide one for me. I told you I was ready to seek a bride before I left Devonbrooke Hall. This way I won't have to go to all the bother of courting one."

Diana lowered her voice to a whisper, but it was still plainly audible to Laura's ears. "If you're seeking to atone for your little indiscretion of last night, there are other, more prudent, ways to do so."

"What indiscretion?" Thane echoed loudly. "Oh, hell, did I miss an indiscretion?"

"You could leave the girl with a nice fat purse," Diana hissed, jabbing an elbow into Thane's ribs. "Or even a monthly allowance if it would soothe your conscience."

Sterling slanted her a chiding look. "Now, Di, you know that I haven't any conscience to soothe."

"That might be what you want the world to believe, but I know better. You made a foolish mistake last night, but that doesn't mean you have to spend the rest of your life doing penance for it. If you married every woman you seduced, Devonbrooke Hall would be overflowing with your brides."

"I hate to admit it, but your cousin is right," Thane said. "And if you are ready to take a bride, you could have your pick of any belle in London. You don't have to settle for some lying little—"

"Thane." Sterling's narrowed eyes were all the warning his friend needed. "As I see it, I owe the girl my name, if nothing else."

"No, thank you." Laura's voice rang like a bell in the sudden silence. Diana and Thane fell back as she rose to stand before the desk, shoulders rigid and head held high. "I'm afraid I shall have to decline your generous proposal, Your Grace. I don't want your name. I don't want to bear your heir. I don't want your fortune. And I most certainly don't want you. As a matter of fact, given your colossal arrogance, I do believe I'd rather be hanged than marry you."

Diana and Thane both gasped. It had obviously never occurred to either of them that a mere country chit would have the audacity to refuse the duke's exalted offer. But Sterling merely lifted an eyebrow.

Although his gaze remained on Laura, he said softly, "Perhaps it would be best if the two of you left us alone."

"I really don't think . . ." Diana began.

". . . that would be very wise," Thane finished.

Sterling began to toy with a letter opener, weaving the blade through his long, aristocratic fingers. "You may wait right outside the door if you like, the better to hear her screams. Or mine."

Still casting apprehensive looks over their shoulders, Thane and Diana filed out, leaving Laura to face Sterling across the dusty expanse of the desk.

He pointed to the chair with the blade of the letter opener. "Please, Miss Fairleigh, do sit."

Feeling a bit like one of his dogs, Laura threw herself back down in the chair. There was no way he could have missed her wince.

"Are you quite all right?" He searched her face with what could easily have been mistaken for genuine concern. "I fear I might have been somewhat . . .

overvigorous in my attentions last night. It was thoughtless of me. I usually handle my brandy with a bit more aplomb."

It was bad enough that their wedding night had already been reduced to a "foolish mistake" and a "little indiscretion." Next he would be telling her that he didn't even remember coming to her bedchamber. That every tender, delicious moment they'd shared had disappeared into some drunken haze.

" *'Thoughtless'* is forgetting someone's birthday," she said stiffly, "not coming to her bed and pretending to be her husband when you knew very well that you weren't."

"If you'd known our marriage was invalid, would you have sent me away?"

Laura lowered her eyes. It wasn't a fair question and they both knew it.

"I'm not blaming you. A man of my station should have a better rein over his emotions. I can assure you it won't happen again." Instead of relief, Laura felt only loss. Sterling tossed aside the letter opener. "At my request, one of my footmen made a little trip to the village church last night."

Baffled by his abrupt shift in topic, Laura frowned. She recalled the coach she had seen rocking away from the manor just before Sterling had burst into her bedchamber. "To what end?"

"In the excitement of my cousin's arrival, I nearly forgot about the angel who came plummeting from the heavens only minutes after we repeated our vows."

Laura shook her head. She would never forget that chilling moment when she had turned and seen him sprawled against the church door. "It was a dreadful accident."

"That's what I was inclined to believe. Until my footman found this in the bell tower." He reached into one of the drawers and drew out an iron object. At first Laura thought it was another letter opener. Then she realized it was a chisel, its thick blade still dusted with mortar. "It seems it wasn't an accident after all but a badly botched murder attempt. So tell me, Miss Fairleigh"—Sterling's golden gaze caressed her face as he leaned back in the chair—"did you want me? Or did you want me dead?"

Although it seemed like a lifetime since she had stood on those church steps in her adoring bridegroom's arms, the minutes went tumbling backward in Laura's mind. She remembered struggling to her feet after the statue's impact, staggering up the stairs, hearing someone shriek her name as Lottie and George had come careening around the corner of the church. She could still see the look on Lottie's face in that moment—guilt-stricken terror mingled with relief. Time went spinning backward even further, all the way back to that moment in the drawing room when she and the children had first learned that Sterling Harlow planned to take possession of their home.

We could murder him. Lottie's cheerful words echoed through Laura's mind, followed by her own careless reply. *It would probably take a silver bullet or a stake through the heart.*

But it was her own heart that had been pierced, not by a stake but by the chisel in Sterling's hands.

She could make him believe she was innocent. She

knew she still had at least that much power over him. After all, if he hadn't shoved her out of harm's way, she would have been the one crushed to death by the statue. But speaking out in her own defense would condemn Lottie and George. And she doubted that even the most benevolent court would look kindly upon an attempt to murder a peer of the realm, even if its perpetrators were barely out of the nursery. What was she supposed to do—blithely become Sterling's duchess while her brother and sister swung from the gibbet or rotted away in Newgate?

Knowing that she was forever sacrificing all hope of future happiness, Laura looked Sterling dead in the eye and said coolly, "I wanted Arden Manor. And I was willing to do whatever it took to get it, even rid myself of an inconvenient bridegroom."

He didn't say a word. He just watched her, his face impassive.

Even though she knew it wouldn't be nearly as effective without a mane of golden curls, Laura tossed her head just as she'd seen Lottie do a hundred times before. Her only hope was to think like her sister. "Lady Eleanor's will stipulated that I *find* a bridegroom. She didn't say anything about *keeping* him. With you out of the way, I knew I could run Arden Manor as I saw fit without some stranger meddling in our affairs. I couldn't very well divorce you. The scandal would have reflected poorly on our good name. So I decided it would be much less of a bother to murder you."

Sterling stroked his jaw, taking great care to cover his mouth. "By dropping an angel on my head."

Laura faked a haughty smile. "It was the only way I

could have it all—the manor and my freedom. Besides, everyone knows that widows have more rights than wives."

Sterling rose without a word and stalked to the door. Throwing it open, he bellowed, "Carlotta!" then calmly returned to his chair behind the desk.

Laura was already babbling before Lottie appeared in the doorway. "I forced Lottie to help me. I threatened to . . . to . . ." She struggled to come up with a vile enough threat. ". . . drown all of her kittens in the well if she didn't. She begged me not to make her hurt you, but I gave her no choice. Why, I . . ." Laura trailed off, staring at her sister.

Lottie's white pinafore was clean and starched, its pockets no longer bulging with kittens or contraband. Even the pink bow binding her topknot of golden curls was perfectly straight.

She marched to the desk, bobbed a genteel curtsy, and said, "Yes, sir?" without even a hint of defiance.

Laura clapped a hand to her mouth. "Oh, Lord, what terrible thing have you done to her?"

Sterling ignored her, choosing to focus the devastating warmth of his smile on her sister. "Lottie, dear, would you mind telling Laura exactly what you told me this morning?"

Lottie shuffled around to face Laura, her big blue eyes downcast. "It was my fault the angel nearly killed you both. I was the one who made it all wiggly so that it fell when the bells started ringing and I bumped into it. I had planned to drop it on Nicholas's . . ." She swallowed hard, shooting Sterling a distressed look.

"It's all right," he said gently. "Go on."

"I mean, on His Grace's head. But then I decided I just couldn't go through with it. Especially after George told me how very much you loved—"

"Thank you, Lottie," Sterling said firmly. "Your honesty is much appreciated. You may go."

Laura waited until her sister had crept from the room before lifting her burning eyes to Sterling's face. "You tricked me!"

"Not a very pleasant feeling, is it?" He rose and moved to the window. He stood with his back to her, the sunlight haloing his tawny hair. "The truth just isn't in you, is it, Laura? You're no different from any other woman. No different from . . ."

"Your mother?" she offered softly. "As I see it, your father didn't give her any more of a choice than you're giving me."

Sterling faced her, his mouth taut. "You're absolutely right. You *should* have a choice. So would you like to become my wife or my mistress? As my mistress, you'd be entitled to a house, a generous allowance—more than enough to care for George and Lottie—a handsome wardrobe, jewels, and a certain amount of social status, however dubious. In exchange, I would expect you to welcome me into your bed whenever I cared to seek its pleasures. Of course, when I did take a bride, I would have to depend upon your discretion. But we've already proved you can keep a secret, haven't we? The choice is yours, Laura, but I'd appreciate it if you'd decide quickly." He swept a distasteful look around the study. "I've wasted enough of my time in this provincial hell as it is."

Infuriated beyond words, Laura rose and started for the door. Her hand was on the knob when he said,

"Before you spurn my offer of marriage, you might want to remember that you could already be carrying my child."

Laura's breath caught in her throat. She touched a hand to her stomach, beset by a most curious sensation—part anger and part yearning.

She slowly turned to face him, shaking her head in wonderment. "You'll go to any lengths to have your way, won't you?"

Sterling lifted one shoulder in a lazy shrug. "What more could you expect from a devil like me?"

Chapter 20

*I pray every day that you will find
a woman to share your life. . . .*

Laura's second wedding bore no resemblance to her first.

A chill rain began to fall shortly after they reached London, making the moonless night seem even darker. Instead of a beaming Reverend Tilsbury, the ceremony was presided over by a grumpy archbishop, who had been dragged out of his bed to produce a special license at the duke's request. She and Sterling were married in the grand drawing room of the archbishop's palace with only Sterling's cousin and the smirking marquess in attendance. Although Diana was forced to use her lace handkerchief to dab a tear from her eye, Laura knew it wasn't a tear of joy, but of dismay.

There was no Lottie to hold Laura's posy, no George to stand proud and tall at her bridegroom's side, no Cookie to offer a hearty "Amen!" when the archbishop pronounced them man and wife.

Laura had sacrificed her pride one last time to ask Sterling if he would allow the children to accompany her to London, but he had refused, telling her, "I can't be looking over my shoulder all the time, waiting for someone to shove me headlong down the stairs of my own house."

So she'd been forced to bid her family farewell in the manor's curving drive with Sterling watching the entire scene, his handsome face revealing nothing.

Dower had stood with his hat crumpled in his hands, his craggy face set in lines of misery. "This is all my doin', missie. I thought to put a halt to the weddin', not see you leg-shackled to the divil for all eternity."

Laura had touched a hand to his bruised cheekbone, still appalled that he had suffered so on her account. "It's not your fault, Dower. I have only myself to blame."

Cookie had been waiting to fold Laura into her arms, her flour-streaked apron smelling of cinnamon and nutmeg. "Don't lose heart, lamb," she had whispered. "Any man who'll choke down a dozen dry crumpets just to spare an old woman's feelings can't be as wicked as they say he is."

Laura had turned to find Lottie and George standing beside the open door of the town coach. Although Lottie's bottom lip was quivering, she managed a tremulous smile. "Everyone knows I'm the Incomparable Beauty of the family. Who would have thought you'd be the one to snare a rich husband?"

"He'd best take good care of you," George had said, shooting Sterling a look that was more wounded than threatening. "If he doesn't, he'll answer to me."

Choking back a sob, Laura had knelt down and opened her arms to them. There simply weren't any words. Thanks to Lady Eleanor's generosity, the three of them had never been separated, not even for a night. Laura had never imagined there would come a time when she couldn't reach out to smooth one of Lottie's curls or rub a smudge of dirt from George's freckled nose.

They had remained locked in a fierce embrace until Laura had drawn away, forcing a brave smile through her tears.

Sterling's expression had never changed, not when he handed her into the plush velvet squabs and not when the coach went rocking past the churchyard where his mother was buried.

". . . if either of you know any reason why you may not be lawfully joined together in matrimony, you do now confess it." The archbishop's nasal whine jerked Laura back to the chilly drawing room.

Sterling's warm breath stirred her hair as he leaned down and whispered, "Is there anything you'd like to share?"

Laura shook her head, her lips pressed tightly together.

When the archbishop held out the prayer book in invitation, Sterling drew the signet ring off his own finger. The priest handed it back and Sterling slipped it onto Laura's finger, his eyes no longer adoring as they'd been in the sunlit nave of St. Michael's but shadowed by wariness. She had to fold her hand into a fist to keep the ring in place. The ruby alone must be worth a king's ransom, but its oppressive weight made it feel like an iron shackle. Sterling didn't know that his mother's garnet still hung between her breasts on a cheap silver chain.

Before Laura even had time to absorb the fact that

she had just been married for the second time in two days, she was bundled back into the coach and whisked off to Devonbrooke Hall. As they ducked through the rain to get from the coach to the entranceway, Laura received only a vague impression of high arched windows and towering stone taking up an entire block of one of the more prestigious squares in the West End.

Someone had sent word that the duke and his bride were to be expected. A groom of the chambers with thinning hair and a faint hump in his back was waiting in the cavernous foyer to greet them, a flickering candelabra balanced in his gloved hand. The candles only seemed to make the gloom more pronounced. Laura could feel the chill radiating from the marble floor through the soles of her slippers.

While a footman emerged from the shadows to relieve her of her damp pelisse and bonnet, the groom intoned, "Good evening, Your Grace."

When Laura remained silent, Diana gave her a nudge. "He's talking to you," she whispered.

Laura glanced behind her only to discover that Sterling had already disappeared into the vast recesses of the house, taking his dogs and the marquess with him. "Oh!" she exclaimed. "And a good evening to you, too, sir." She bobbed an awkward curtsy before remembering that a duchess probably wasn't supposed to curtsy to a servant.

Fortunately, the man was either too polite or too well trained to betray any reaction. "If you would be so kind as to follow me, Your Grace, I'll show you to the duchess's suite. The servants have spent all afternoon preparing it for your comfort."

"How very kind of them," she replied. "But they

really shouldn't have gone to such a bother on my account."

Diana sighed and whisked the candelabra from the manservant's hands. "You may be excused, Addison. I'll show the duchess to her suite."

"Very well, my lady." His bow was directed at Diana, but Laura would have sworn the twinkle in his brown eyes was for her alone.

Diana started up the broad sweeping staircase at a rapid clip, forcing Laura to trot to keep up with her. "You needn't thank the servants for serving you. That's what they collect their wages for. If they don't carry out their duties in a satisfactory manner, they know they'll be—"

"Flogged?" Laura ventured. "Drawn and quartered?"

"Dismissed," Diana retorted, shooting a withering look over her shoulder as they marched down an endless corridor paneled in a dark and ponderous mahogany. "I'm not quite the ogress you believe me to be."

"Nor am I the scheming fortune hunter. You heard your cousin this morning. He all but forced me to marry him."

Diana spun around so fast Laura had to hop back a step or risk having her hair ignited. "And did he force you to bed him as well?" Diana watched a wave of color sweep over her face with visible satisfaction. "I didn't think so. Sterling may have many flaws, but I've never known him to debauch a woman against her will."

Diana swept ahead of her, leaving Laura to follow or risk being lost forever in the dizzying maze of stairs, galleries, and corridors.

The duchess's suite, which consisted of a bedchamber, a sitting room, and a dressing room, was also paneled in mahogany wainscoting and lavished with the same oppressive luxury as the rest of the mansion. A canopied four-poster draped in hangings of crimson velvet dominated the bedchamber. It was at least three times the size of Lady Eleanor's graceful half-tester.

Laura glanced around, searching for a connecting door. "And where would I find the duke's suite?"

"In the west wing."

She hesitated for a moment. "And which wing would this be?"

"The east one."

"Oh." Laura had simply assumed that she and Sterling would be sharing a bedchamber. Her parents always had. She could still remember drifting off to sleep listening to the music of her mother's soft murmur and her father's husky laughter.

As Diana placed the candelabra on a pedestal table, reserving a candle for herself, Laura tentatively asked, "And where do you sleep?"

"The north wing."

With that many wings, Laura was surprised the house didn't take flight. Her face must have reflected her dismay, for Diana let out a beleaguered sigh. "I'll talk to Sterling tomorrow morning about hiring you an abigail to sleep in your dressing room. I can loan you mine until then." She reached over to flick a limp tendril of hair out of Laura's eyes. "She has a flair for hairdressing."

"That won't be necessary," Laura said, drawing on the last scraps of her pride. "I'm quite accustomed to looking after myself."

Once again, there was that disconcerting trace of

pity in Diana's eyes. "If you're going to be married to my cousin, perhaps that's just as well."

Diana drew the door shut behind her. Laura leaned against it, listening to her brisk footsteps fade away.

Sterling had expected the ghosts to pursue him to Devonbrooke Hall, but he hadn't counted on Thane. The marquess's persistent footsteps dogged his strides all the way down the broad marble corridor that led to the library. As a child, the library with its towering shelves and glowering plaster busts had been his only refuge. Between the musty pages of a book of Arthurian lore or a Daniel Defoe novel, he had been able to escape his uncle's withering insults and mercurial temper, if only for a few precious hours. But apparently, there was to be no escaping his well-meaning friend.

"As much as I appreciate you standing up for me at my wedding on such short notice," Sterling informed him, "I won't be requiring your services for the wedding night."

A fire crackled merrily on the hearth, courtesy of the ever-efficient Addison, no doubt. While the dogs padded over to stretch out in front of it, Thane collapsed into a plump armchair. "Are you so sure about that? It appears you handled your last wedding night with less than your usual finesse."

Sterling's laugh held little humor. "You'd think so, wouldn't you, given my bride's reaction to my proposal."

Thane shook his head with reluctant admiration. "I never thought I'd meet a woman bold enough to refuse your suit. And with such dramatic flair! 'I do believe I'd rather be hanged than marry you!' I half expected her to stamp her little foot, and add, 'Unhand me, sirrah!' If this marriage doesn't work out, she has a bright future on the stage. I've always fancied actresses, you know."

Sterling drew a thin cheroot from a satinwood box and lit it. He leaned against the mantel, drawing a welcome ribbon of smoke into his lungs. "I can assure you that she wasn't acting. Her contempt for me was quite genuine."

Thane arched one eyebrow. "More genuine than yours for her, perhaps?"

To avoid answering, Sterling blew out a flawless smoke ring. Now that his memory had returned, he couldn't afford to forget just how well his friend knew him.

"You've gone and gotten yourself into a fine mess, haven't you, Dev?" Thane said softly, the old nickname only making his words more damning.

Sterling shrugged. "You know what the scandal sheets have always said. Cross the Devil of Devonbrooke and there will be hell to pay."

"But at what cost to yourself?"

Sterling flicked what was left of the cheroot into the fire, his anger flaring. "I really don't think you've earned the right to lecture me on the cost of pride."

For a minute, he was afraid he'd gone too far, but Thane only shook his head, smiling ruefully. "We're a fine pair, aren't we? One too stubborn to hang on to a woman and one too stubborn to let her go." He rose and crossed to the door. "If you decide to get married again tomorrow, you know where to find me."

Then he was gone, leaving Sterling all alone with only his ghosts and his pride for company.

Someone had seen to it that the duke's bride would have no lack of creature comforts. A fire burned on the bedchamber grate, its crackling flames dwarfed by a massive chimneypiece carved from pure white marble. A silver tray had been left on the table in the adjoining sitting room. Laura peeked beneath its lid to find an unidentified slab of meat smothered in a rich cream sauce. She quickly replaced it, wishing desperately for some of Cookie's gingerbread, warm from the oven.

She wandered back into the bedchamber. It took her a moment to work up the courage to draw back the heavy bed hangings. She was half-afraid she might find the bleached bones of the last duchess who had occupied this suite. But all she found was a set of neatly turned-back sheets beneath a satin counterpane, a downy nest of pillows, and a diaphanous nightdress and matching wrapper woven from shimmering white silk. Laura held the nightdress up to the firelight, shocked by its transparency. Since her own trunks weren't scheduled to arrive from Arden until tomorrow, she supposed she had no choice but to don it or sleep in her shift.

Finding nothing better to occupy herself, Laura undressed and poured some lavender-scented water from a pitcher into a china washbasin. After she had bathed, scrubbed her teeth, and worked the pins from her hair, she slipped into the nightdress. The sheer fabric caressed her skin but did little to warm it. Despite the fire, an oppressive chill clung to the air, its dampness under-scored by the sheets of rain battering the tall, arched windows. The high-ceilinged chamber would probably be as cold as a tomb in the winter. Shivering, Laura whisked back the hangings and bounded into the bed.

She sank into the feather mattress, feeling positively lost in the vast sea of bedclothes. She wished Lottie were there to scramble into the bed with her, to snuggle close and giggle over the ridiculous extravagance of it all.

But it wouldn't be Lottie joining her tonight. It would be her husband.

Laura sat up abruptly, hugging her knees to her chest. It was her wedding night, and once again she had no idea where her bridegroom was. Was he barricaded downstairs somewhere, fortifying himself with brandy so he could bear the sight of her?

She drew the garnet ring out of her nightdress and held it up to the firelight, remembering the tender look in his eyes when he had slid it onto her finger, a look she would probably never see again. She slipped the silver chain over her head and tucked the ring beneath her pillow for safekeeping. After a moment's thought, she tugged off the duke's ornate signet ring, drew back the bed hangings, and tossed it onto a nearby table. The thing landed with a satisfying *clunk*.

She fell back on the pillows and closed her eyes, her breath escaping in a melancholy sigh. She must have dozed off without realizing it, for when she opened her eyes again, feeling groggy and out of sorts, a clock was just beginning to chime somewhere in the house. Laura counted each mournful *bong* until she reached twelve.

The clock ceased its chiming, leaving behind a hush

so uncanny she might have been the only living soul in the house. Or the world.

Her bridegroom wasn't coming. That whisper of truth echoed through the silence more clearly than any shout.

Laura threw herself to her side, thinking how relieved she ought to be. She wouldn't have to endure the treacherous tenderness of Sterling's caresses. Wouldn't have to wonder if he was mocking her with his whispered endearments, his melting kisses.

But as she lay there, as stiff as a poker, she could feel herself growing angrier and angrier. She remembered how he had ignored his mother's letters for all those years, how Lady Eleanor had struggled to paste on a brave smile each morning when the post came and there was still no word from him. As much as she had loved and admired her guardian, Laura had never quite achieved the dear woman's forbearance. She was rapidly discovering that she could tolerate Sterling's contempt but not his indifference. She would rather he shout at her or shake her than ignore her.

Sitting up, Laura threw back the bedclothes. It might come as a shock to His Exalted Grace, but she had no intention of spending the rest of her life trading insults with his crabby cousin and languishing about in bed, wondering if he was ever going to pay her a visit. If he wouldn't come to her on their wedding night, then by God, she would go to him.

After battling her way through the smothering weight of the bed hangings, Laura dragged the wrapper on over her nightdress and jerked a knot in the sash. She jammed one of the candles into a silver candlestick, and went storming from the chamber, wishing the door wasn't too heavy to slam behind her.

Within five minutes, Laura was so lost she didn't think she would ever find the duchess's suite again, much less the duke's. She had assumed that if she kept veering in the same direction, she would eventually reach the west wing. But the house was a labyrinth of endless corridors, each longer and more confusing than the last. Laura traveled for a very long time without encountering any sign of life at all. Even a mouse would have been a comfort.

She hadn't bothered to ask which floor the duke's suite occupied, but she was hoping all the bedchambers would be on the same floor. That hope was quenched when the corridor she was traveling abruptly deadended in a flight of stairs.

She tried to circle back the way she had come, but ended up on an unfamiliar balcony overlooking what appeared to be a shadowy ballroom large enough to encompass all of Arden Manor, even the gardens. She sighed, wondering what Lottie would do if she found herself in this predicament. Probably sit down in the middle of the floor and start wailing at the top of her lungs until someone came running. Laura was tempted to do just that, but she was afraid no one would hear her or care enough to come running.

A Turkish rug the color of blood ran the length of the balcony, muffling her footsteps to a whisper. Shadows gathered in the corners of the towering ceilings, dwarfing the feeble flicker of her candle. As an impish draft toyed with its flame, Laura cupped a hand around it, her steps faltering.

As she rounded the next corner, a portrait gallery unfurled before her in all of its grim glory. By day, the room was probably just spooky; by night, it was terrifying.

"Don't be silly, Laura," she scolded herself through her chattering teeth. "There's no need to be afraid of a bunch of dead people."

Already ruing her unfortunate choice of words, she forced herself to march forward. She studiously fixed her gaze on the ornately carved double doors at the far end of the gallery, but she could still feel the suspicious eyes of Sterling's ancestors following her every step.

She was so relieved to finally reach the end of the gallery that she didn't see the life-sized portrait hanging over the door until she was almost upon it. As the candlelight danced upward, she recoiled with a startled gasp.

A man was sneering down his long, pinched nose at her, his icy eyes glittering with contempt. As Laura read the brass plaque beneath the portrait, she realized she was gazing up into the sunken face of old Granville Harlow himself. Dressed all in black, he clutched a silver walking stick in one pale hand.

It was difficult to believe such a man could have ever sired a little girl. Laura didn't know whom to pity more—Diana or her mother. Lady Eleanor had rarely spoken of the duke who had adopted her son. Now Laura understood why.

For the first time, she wondered how Sterling must have felt his first night in this drafty mausoleum of a house. Betrayed by his father, torn away from the mother he loved, had he huddled beneath the blankets, shivering in some unfamiliar bed? Or had he wandered these very halls, lost and alone, knowing no one would hear him if he cried?

A brindle mastiff who could very well have been the grandsire of Sterling's dogs sat beside the duke. If including the dog had been the artist's attempt to make his subject appear more approachable, he had failed miserably. The man's spidery fingers were curled around the beast's collar as if he couldn't wait to sic him on the next saucy young upstart who dared to defy him.

A low-pitched growl came out of the darkness behind Laura, lifting every hair on her nape. She had forgotten all about Sterling's devil dogs until that moment. She should have known he would allow them to roam the house by night. How else were they to rip out the throat of any intruder? Or any hapless bride foolish enough to abandon the refuge of her bed?

The growl came again, rumbling with menace. Laura yelped and dropped the candle, plunging the gallery into darkness. She slowly turned, flattening herself against the door. All she could see was the malevolent reddish glow of two pairs of eyes.

"Nice doggies," she whispered, struggling to swallow past the lump of terror in her throat. "Good doggies. You're not hungry, are you? I certainly hope not because I haven't much meat on my bones. Cookie has been trying to fatten me up for years, but hasn't had much success."

The dogs padded closer, so close she could feel their hot, musky breath. Whimpering, Laura turned her face to the side.

She told herself later that she never would have screamed, that she would have surrendered herself to her fate with at least a modicum of dignity if one of the beasts hadn't chosen that moment to ram his big, wet nose soundly into her crotch.

Laura let out an earsplitting shriek. The door behind her was suddenly swept open. She went tumbling into the room, her shriek dying on a startled note. She slowly opened her eyes to find her husband standing over her, arms akimbo.

"My, my," he said, cocking one eyebrow. "Look what the dog dragged in."

Chapter 21

. . . a woman who will love you
as much as I always have.

Laura slowly lifted her head. The savage beasts who had been an inch away from ripping out her intestines were now sitting back on their haunches with their tongues lolling out, just two overgrown puppies with only one goal in life—pleasing their master. A master who was looking none too pleased at the moment.

Sterling reluctantly offered her a hand. Laura took it, allowing him to haul her to her feet and pretending not to notice when he immediately withdrew it.

She brushed an invisible speck of dust from the skirt of her wrapper, still nursing her bruised dignity. "You're lucky you didn't have to step over my eviscerated body on the way to breakfast in the morning. Of course, according to your friend the marquess, you wouldn't have any trouble finding another bride to replace me."

"Ah, but where would I find one so infinitely intriguing?"

Sterling seemed determined to keep a barrier between them, even if it was only the muscular arms folded over his shirtless chest. Remembering the salty-sweet taste of his skin beneath her tongue, Laura felt her mouth go dry. She lowered her eyes, then wished she hadn't. The top two buttons of his trousers were unfastened, revealing a triangle of skin a shade paler than his chest.

Following the direction of her gaze, he abruptly turned away to retrieve two thick slices of pork from his own untouched supper tray. He gave one to each of the dogs, along with an affectionate scratch behind the ears. They went padding back into the gloom of the portrait gallery with their prizes, leaving Sterling to close the door behind them.

"And what would you have given them had they brought you one of my ribs?" Laura asked. "A rack of lamb?"

He leaned against the door. "Contrary to their appearance, they haven't a vicious bone in their bodies. They were much more likely to have licked you to death." Although his provocative words sent a shiver of awareness dancing through Laura's veins, his sulky expression never changed.

To escape it, she turned and studied the chamber. The duke's suite was even more ostentatious than her own. The massive bed was a twin to hers, but draped with hangings of midnight blue velvet that had been gathered at each corner with gold cords. Although Sterling's hair was tousled and his lids heavy, the bedclothes were undisturbed.

"So this is your suite," she murmured, taking in the fire crackling beneath a mantel of black marble, the domed skylight paneled in stained glass, the freestanding columns carved from jasper, the gilded cheval glass perched near the foot of the bed.

"This is my uncle's suite," Sterling said flatly. At her surprised look, he added, "Diana has been the only occupant of Devonbrooke Hall since he died six years ago. I've been off with the army for over a decade. On those occasions when I did visit London, I preferred to stay at Thane's."

She dared a sheepish smile. "I don't suppose you were with the infantry, were you?"

"I was an officer," he informed her gently.

Laura barely resisted the urge to spring to full attention and snap off a salute. "That must be why you're so accustomed to having everyone scramble to obey your every order."

"Everyone but you, of course." He strode to a table and poured a splash of something amber into a glass.

She'd been wrong about the brandy. This appeared to be his first drink of the night. Perhaps he only required fortifying when she was directly in his line of sight.

He swung one leg over a delicate Chippendale chair, straddling it backward, and waved the glass in her direction. "So would you care to explain what you were doing wandering about this musty old tomb in the dead of night?"

Laura sank down on the chaise longue opposite him. The cushions of the single-ended couch were still warm, as if someone had been sleeping on them. "I was lost."

"Then you have my sincere sympathy." He took a sip of the liquor. "I used to get lost in this house all the time as a child. I once ended up in the solarium in the middle of the night, battling an ivy vine to the death. Diana found me the next morning, curled up on the floor sound asleep with the vine still wrapped around my throat."

Although his words didn't betray even a trace of self-pity, the image tugged at Laura's heart. "If your uncle was still alive, I never would have found the courage to leave my room." She shuddered. "The dogs weren't nearly as scary as his portrait."

"It's actually quite a flattering likeness. I've always said he should have paid the artist extra for leaving off the horns and tail and painting him with a walking stick instead of his usual pitchfork."

"I gather the two of you weren't close."

"Oh, we were as close as two human beings locked in mortal combat can be."

"But he's gone. And you're still here. That would make you the victor."

Sterling swirled the brandy around the glass, his eyes distant. "Sometimes I'm not so sure about that." His gaze sharpened, focusing only on her. "You still haven't answered my question. How is it that your wanderings led you here? To my bedchamber."

What was she to tell him? That she was homesick? Lonely? Furious at him for abandoning her on their wedding night?

He cocked his head to the side. "Come now, dear. I can almost see that clever little brain of yours weaving some charming fiction. Why not take a stab at the truth? I'm sure it will become less painful with practice."

She drew herself up, glaring at him. "Very well. I grew tired of waiting for you to come to my bed so I decided to seek out yours."

Fortunately, Sterling had just taken a sip of the liquor so Laura had the satisfaction of watching him choke. He set the glass down on the carpet beside the chair, swiping at his watering eyes. "Do go on. I find your candor quite refreshing."

"Well, it *is* traditional for the bridegroom to pay his bride a visit on their wedding night. Of course, I realize that I'm not being completely fair. Given the unconventional circumstances of our . . . um, courtship, I suppose I have no right to expect a conventional marriage."

"Oh, I think you'll find it very conventional indeed. Especially when compared to those in the social circles in which we'll be traveling."

She frowned at him. "How so?"

He shrugged. "The very nature of marriage itself implies that it's most successful when based on need."

Laura brightened. Now they were getting somewhere. She couldn't think of anything she *needed* more in that moment than his arms around her.

He folded those arms over the back of the chair. "The titled gentleman whose wastrel father has squandered the family fortune weds a wealthy merchant's daughter to fatten his coffers. A young lady with a passion for cards seeks out a gentleman of means so she might continue to indulge her habits. A second or third son woos a young woman of gentle birth who just happens to come equipped with a generous dowry."

Laura's smile faded. "But what about affection? Devotion? Desire?" She bit back the one word she was aching to say.

Sterling shook his head, his expression gentle, almost pitying. "Most of the ladies and gentlemen of my acquaintance prefer to seek those pleasures outside the bounds of matrimony."

Laura sat in silence for a moment before rising and moving to stand before the hearth. She gazed into the hypnotic flames, weighing her words with great care. "So you married me simply because you had need of an heir and I was in a position to provide one for you. And now that you've done your duty, it only remains to be seen if I've done mine."

"I suppose that's a fair way of putting it."

Even before she started to turn around, Laura was tugging at the sash of her wrapper. As she faced him, the garment slipped from her shoulders, drifting down to pool on the heated marble of the hearth.

Sterling went rigid, the flames leaping in his eyes. Laura could almost see herself reflected there. Could almost see the firelight melting the silk of her nightdress into a shimmering veil that only served to accentuate her long, slender legs, the rosy pout of her nipples, the elusive shadow at the juncture of her thighs.

She glided toward him. She'd had little experience at playing the temptress, but she wasn't playing now. She was dead serious. "Since you've yet to determine if your efforts have met with success, my lord, there are some, even in your own social circle, who might accuse you of being less than diligent."

As she approached, Sterling came to his feet, his wariness the only barrier left between them. "What do you think you're doing, Laura?"

"My duty," she whispered, twining one hand around his throat and coaxing his lips down to hers.

Their breath mingled for a tantalizing heartbeat before Sterling let out a hoarse groan. Then there were no barriers between them at all. There was only his tongue plundering the sweetness of her mouth, his arms wrapped tightly around her, his body molding itself to her every curve and hollow as if he'd spent most of his lifetime memorizing them. As Laura felt him rubbing up against the softness of her belly, she knew why he'd taken such care to keep her at arm's length. Why he'd insisted she be put in a suite at the other end of the world. His heart might never forgive her for deceiving him, but his body was only too eager to offer her pardon.

And anything else she was willing to accept.

Although she was the one who should have been doing penance, it was Sterling who dropped to his knees at her feet. Laura's head fell back as the searing heat of his mouth molded the silk of the nightdress to her nipple. He licked at the sensitive bud, then blew gently against the clinging silk. As he shifted his exquisite attentions to her other breast, pleasure pulsed like liquid velvet along her nerve endings, making her knees go weak. But he was there to catch her. There to cup the softness of her rump in his strong hands. He lowered his mouth yet again, this time pressing it to the dusky triangle beneath the silk in a kiss that was both shocking and irresistible. His tongue tasted her through the damp fabric and she cried out his name in a voice she hardly recognized as her own.

Laura clung to his shoulders as he lifted her and carried her over to the bed. She expected him to follow her down, but instead he reached beneath the nightdress and dragged her hips to the very edge of the bed. He slowly pushed up the silk, leaving her utterly exposed to him, utterly vulnerable. But instead of being embarrassed or frightened, Laura was exhilarated. He was her husband, and there was nothing forbidden or sinful about the things he wanted to do to her. Or the things she wanted him to do.

He didn't look like a devil but a pagan god standing between her legs in the firelight, his glittering eyes heavy lidded with desire. She was only too willing to offer herself as a sacrifice on his altar of pleasure. But as he dropped back to his knees and pressed that beautiful mouth of his to the gossamer curls between her thighs, now unveiled, she realized with a shiver of raw delight that she was the altar and it was her pleasure he sought. And he knew just where to find it.

Laura arched off the bed as scorching tongues of flame licked her higher and higher. He might be a devil, but his skillful mouth was giving her a taste of heaven itself. She writhed and whimpered and tugged at his hair until a particularly diabolical flick of his tongue sent her soaring into paradise. Instead of trying to muffle her wail, he made it go on and on by thrusting two of his long, aristocratic fingers deep inside of her.

As he rose to his feet, Laura could only gaze up at him in wonder, limp and sated, yet still panting with desire. She surprised them both by being the first to reach for the buttons that had yet to be undone on his trousers. His tensile weight sprang free from its honey gold nest of curls, astonishing her anew.

"I know it was dark in my room last night, but you can't mean? . . ." She shook her head, blinking up at him in disbelief. "Surely I couldn't have . . . I didn't . . ."

"You most certainly did. Quite ably, I might add." He sucked in a jerky breath through gritted teeth as her fingers danced along his length. "But if you don't believe me, I suppose there's only one way to prove it to you."

Prove it he did, cupping her bottom in his hands and lifting her so that they could both watch every fulsome inch of him disappear inside of her. Laura gasped as he filled her to the brim, the lingering tenderness from last night making her exquisitely sensitive to his every motion. She could already feel her heart beginning to shudder in time with the primitive pulse that beat where their bodies were joined. Modesty demanded that she close her eyes, but she could not look away from his beautiful face, now taut with hunger and gilded by a sheen of sweat.

His powerful body was trembling with need, yet he held it in check, gazing deep into her eyes. "Who am I?"

"My husband," she whispered helplessly, reaching up to stroke his chest.

He slid all the way out of her, then all the way back in, so deep she knew he would always be a part of her.

"Who am I, Laura? Who are you giving yourself to? Who's taking you?" A fierce urgency was reflected in his face, as if everything he was and everything he would ever be hinged on her answer.

"Sterling," she sobbed, calling him by his Christian name for the first time in their acquaintance. She turned her face to the side, tears spilling from her eyes. "Oh, Sterling . . ."

Her fingernails scored the satin counterpane as he began to stroke hard and deep, wild and tender, urging her toward a place where only he could take her. By the time she reached it, they were both half-mad with pleasure. As a pulsing tide of rapture swept over her, obliterating everything in its path, Sterling stiffened and threw back his head with a roar, spilling his nectar deep into the chalice of her womb.

Sterling lay on his side with his head propped on one hand, watching his wife sleep and wondering how it was possible for a woman to look so innocent and yet so wanton at the same time. She sprawled on her stomach on top of the rumpled sheets, her cheek pressed to the pillow, her hands curled into loose fists on each side of her head. He had covered her with the counterpane to shield her from the chill, but the sleek satin had ridden down, baring the graceful curve of her back and the soft swell of one creamy buttock.

He could hardly blame her for succumbing to exhaustion. She'd had little enough sleep in the past two nights. He'd seen to that.

He shook his head, still marveling that she had been bold enough to seek him out. She might be a cunning little liar out of bed, but she was utterly devoid of artifice in it. And unlike so many of the more experienced women of his acquaintance, she made no secret of the fact that her passion was only for him.

Whoever the hell he was.

Sterling rolled off the bed and dragged on his trousers. He poured a generous splash of brandy into a glass, but not even its heat could completely sear the taste of her from his mouth.

From the first moment he had set foot in this house over twenty-one years ago, Sterling Harlow had known exactly who he was and exactly what was expected of him. Until Laura Fairleigh had come along with a passel of lies and half-truths, shattering every illusion he'd ever held about himself. Now he felt even more of a stranger in his own skin than he had at Arden Manor as a man with no memory.

When he had first learned of Laura's treachery, he had believed he could simply go back to being the man he had been before she had melted the icy wall of detachment around his heart. But that man would have never been fool enough to let her back into his arms. Or his bed.

Nor would he have forced her to stay by his side simply because he couldn't bear to let her go. Perhaps Diana had been right. Perhaps it wasn't expediency that had prompted his proposal but some twisted desire for revenge. But that didn't explain the aching tenderness in his touch as he leaned over the bed to brush a stray lock of hair from Laura's cheek.

Sterling wanted nothing more than to slide his hand beneath the counterpane and stroke her to purring delight once again. Instead, he gathered her into his arms, counterpane and all, and started for the door.

"Mmmm," she murmured, looping her arms trustingly around his neck without even bothering to open her eyes. "Where are you taking me?"

"To bed," he whispered, burying his lips in the lavender-scented softness of her hair.

Since Laura could apparently find no argument with that, she simply snuggled deeper into his arms, resting her cheek against his chest.

Laura awoke just as she had the previous morning— alone in her own bed without so much as a stitch of clothing.

She sat up, clutching the sheet to her breasts and wondering if she was losing her mind. Scrambling to her knees, she poked her head through the bed hangings. Although a few sunbeams had braved the forbidding grandeur of the mullioned windows, the duchess's suite wasn't much cozier than it had been during the rainstorm.

She sank back on her heels, doubting her own senses. Had her nocturnal encounter with her husband been one long, delectable dream? She closed her eyes and was immediately beset by an image of herself and Sterling kneeling in a nest of midnight blue satin in front of a gilded cheval glass. He had wrapped his arms around her from behind, urging her to watch the mirror, to see how very beautiful she was. He had gently cupped her breast while his other hand drifted down the creamy plane of her belly. Laura had watched his long, elegant fingers dip into her, mesmerized by the contrast between his questing strength and her yielding softness.

She wasn't beautiful. They were beautiful together.

Then, when he had tenderly kissed her throat and entered her from behind . . .

Laura gasped, her eyes flying open. Her imagination had always been fruitful, but not *that* fruitful.

She peeped beneath the sheet. Aside from the pronounced absence of her nightdress, there were other, far more subtle, signs of Sterling's possession—the delicious languor in her muscles, the rosy tenderness of her nipples, a faint whisker burn on the inside of her thigh.

Laura sighed as other images drifted through her mind, each more provocative than the last. After last night, no one could accuse the duke of Devonbrooke of not being diligent in his duties. If she wasn't already carrying his heir, it certainly wasn't for lack of effort on his part. Or hers, she thought, feeling her cheeks heat as she recalled her own boldness.

Perhaps she should be grateful she hadn't awakened in Sterling's arms. She might have stammered and blushed and blurted out all manner of unseemly confessions. This way, before she faced him, she would have a chance to clothe herself in the dignity befitting a duchess.

Wrapping the sheet around her, Laura slipped from the bed. But her regal demeanor was spoiled when one of her feet became tangled in the bed hangings. She was hopping up and down on the other foot, trying to free herself, when a knock sounded on the door.

Before she could dive back into the bed, the door swung open and a maidservant strode briskly into the room. "Good morning, Your Grace. Lady Diana sent me to inform you that your trunks have arrived from Arden Manor." She froze, spotting Laura. Laura had to give the woman credit. She didn't even bat an eye to find her new mistress standing on one foot, garbed in nothing but a rumpled bedsheet. "And not a moment too soon, I can see."

After several conflicting sets of directions provided by well-meaning chambermaids, three wrong turns, and twenty minutes spent wandering through a warren of interconnecting rooms, Laura finally found the dining room. Her husband sat at the head of a table at least eighteen feet long, firmly entrenched behind a copy of the *Morning Post*. Diana sat near the middle of the table, sipping tea from a delicate Wedgwood cup. The only other place setting was laid at the foot of the table. Laura was seriously considering ignoring it and taking a seat closer to Sterling when an underfootman appeared out of nowhere to whisk out the chair for her.

She sat, thanking him with a wan smile. While he moved to the sideboard to fill a plate for her, she gazed down the gleaming expanse of mahogany, feeling quite invisible.

"Good morning," she said loudly, barely resisting the urge to cup her hands around her mouth and shout *Halloo!* as George doubtlessly would have done.

Diana murmured something noncommittal.

Sterling flipped to the next page of the paper without looking up. "Good morning, Laura. I trust you rested well."

So that was the way it was to be, was it? Laura smiled sweetly. "Oh, very well. As a matter of fact, I can't remember the last time I had such a deeply satisfying sleep."

Her plate slipped from the underfootman's gloved hand, landing in front of her on the table with a ringing crash. Diana choked on her tea, then dabbed at her lips with her napkin.

While the servant beat a hasty retreat, Sterling slowly lowered the paper, giving Laura a look that should have melted the charming little rosettes of butter on her plate.

Folding the newspaper into a neat square and tucking it beneath his arm, he rose to his feet. "I'm delighted that you found your accommodations to your liking. Now, if you ladies will be so kind as to excuse me . . ."

"Are you off to Hyde Park to ride with Thane?"

Diana asked, devoting all of her attention to spreading marmalade on a piece of toast.

Sterling shook his head. "I plan to spend the day in the study reviewing our properties and accounts. I've shirked my responsibilities for far too long already." He patted Diana's shoulder. "Now that I'm back to stay, there'll be no need for you to trouble yourself with those dull ledgers and boring columns of numbers any longer. Why don't you take Laura shopping for a proper trousseau?"

Although she offered him her cheek for a dutiful peck, Diana didn't look any happier at being dismissed than Laura felt.

Laura waited until he was almost to the door before asking, "Haven't you a kiss for your bride, darling?"

He turned on his heel, his mouth taut. As he leaned down to kiss her cheek, she tilted her face so that his lips grazed the corner of her mouth instead.

She heard his indrawn breath, saw his tawny lashes sweep down to veil his glittering eyes. But when he straightened, his demeanor was as formal as ever. "Good day, my lady."

When he was gone, Diana set down her teacup. "He doesn't like to be toyed with, you know. You're playing a dangerous game."

Laura dug into a slice of warm plum cake, surprised to discover that she was suddenly ravenous. "I'm well aware of that. But I'm hoping its rewards will far outweigh its risks."

Chapter 22

I hope you'll spoil her as I wish
I could have spoiled you....

The Devil of Devonbrooke had taken a bride. By early afternoon, when Diana and Laura began to make the rounds of the Oxford Street and Bond Street shops, all of London was abuzz with the news. It was difficult to say who was more heartbroken—the besotted belles or the ambitious mamas who had hoped to land one of the most wealthy and eligible bachelors of the *haut ton* for their little darlings.

As Diana ushered Laura into an exclusive linen-draper's shop festooned with a dazzling array of silks and muslins and thronged with female shoppers waiting to place their own orders, the flurry of conversation died to a pronounced hush. Laura received several pointed looks, a few of them openly hostile.

One of the mercers rushed over, tutting and clucking in dismay over the pale yellow muslin gown that had seemed perfectly serviceable when Laura had donned it that morning. Before Laura could explain that she didn't speak Italian, the tiny, dark-haired woman swept her away to a curtained alcove to be poked and measured and prodded with a ruthlessness Cookie would have admired.

After several minutes spent enduring the indignity of having two strangers argue over the dubious merits of her bosom in fluent Italian, Laura was left to her own devices while the mercers went in search of a fresh paper of pins with which to torture her. She was standing on a low stool, shivering in her shift, when she became aware of two women conversing on the other side of the curtain. They, unfortunately, *were* speaking English.

The first voice was soft, but ripe with venom. "Can you believe he married some penniless country chit with no dowry and no title? Rumor even has it that she's a . . ." Laura leaned closer to the curtain, straining to hear the woman's sibilant whisper.

"No! You can't be serious! A rector's daughter?" The second woman's titter of laughter would have been no more disbelieving had Sterling wed a charwoman. "Is there any chance it could have been a love match?"

The first woman sniffed. "None whatsoever. I heard they were caught in a compromising situation and he was forced to marry her against his will."

Laura closed her eyes, the woman's words striking a raw nerve.

"From what I hear, he's not the sort of man who can be forced to do anything he doesn't truly want to do."

"That may be so in most circumstances, but when a man's honor is at stake, he will go to any lengths to defend it, even marry beneath him."

"Perhaps the girl just requires a bit of polish."

"He can polish all he wants, but he'll still end up with a lump of coal, not a diamond of the first water."

The woman's voice deepened to a throaty purr. "She hasn't a hope of satisfying him. Have you forgotten that I know firsthand just how demanding he can be in bed? He'll tire of the silly little commoner soon enough . . . if he hasn't already. And when he does, I'll be there. She may have won his name, but she'll never win his heart."

Laura was an outraged breath away from charging through the curtain and showing the treacherous vixen just how common she could be, when there was a sudden rustling of skirts in the next alcove.

"Why, Lady Diana," crooned the woman who had been scheming to bed Laura's husband. "I didn't realize you frequented this shop. It's such a pleasure to finally meet you. Your cousin and I are very dear friends."

"Indeed?" Laura didn't have to imagine the icy look Diana raked over the two women. The temperature in her own alcove dropped with such haste she half expected to see her breath. "He's never spoken of you. Although I do seem to recall a fond mention of your husband. And how is Lord Hewitt these days? In full vigor, I hope."

The fawning tone disappeared from the woman's voice, leaving it as frosty as Diana's. "My Bertram has been spending a great deal of time at our country house."

"I can't say that I blame him." When the second woman gasped, Diana smoothly added, "The summer heat, you know. Now, if you'll be so kind as to excuse me, I must continue in search of my cousin's new bride. He sent me to help her select a proper trousseau. The dear man is quite ashamed of himself for insisting they marry in such haste, but he couldn't bear to be apart from her for another day. He adores her, you know, and is determined that she will lack for nothing as long as he's around to spoil her."

Unexpected tears of both gratitude and longing stung the back of Laura's eyelids. Once, in another lifetime, Diana's words might have been true.

When Laura emerged from the alcove a short while later, she found her unlikely champion sitting stiffly in a straight-backed chair, perusing the latest fashion plates in *La Belle Assemblée* with a jaded eye.

"I heard what you said to those women," Laura said softly. "I really should thank you."

Diana snapped shut the periodical and rose, her pointed chin set at a defiant angle. "I didn't do it for you. I did it for me. Empty-headed beauties like Elizabeth Hewitt have been sneering down their noses at me for years just because I didn't have the misfortune to marry some gouty old sot who cares less for his wife than his prize spaniels."

"If you're referring to Lord Hewitt, his spaniels are probably more loyal than his wife."

Diana didn't exactly smile at her, but her eyes did betray a faint sparkle. "I suppose you're right. You can hardly fault the man for preferring bitches of the four-legged variety."

The rest of the afternoon passed in a dizzying whirl for Laura. As she and Diana darted from milliner to perfumier to shoemaker along the broad flagstone pavement of Oxford Street, she couldn't help but think how much Lottie would have enjoyed such an expedition. Although Diana showed no interest in purchasing so much as a single trinket for herself, she insisted that

Laura be outfitted with the finest of everything—an array of bonnets trimmed in fruit, feathers, and flowers; hand-painted fans; cut-glass scent bottles; cashmere shawls; kid gloves and silk stockings; ruffled parasols; perfumed soaps; pastel slippers and not one but two pairs of smart little nankeen half-boots; silver filigree combs and coronets; pearl-studded bandeaus; even a rather shocking pair of long drawers, which an enthusiastic silk mercer assured her were becoming all the rage in London salons. All of the goods were to be delivered to Devonbrooke Hall at the shopkeepers' earliest convenience.

By the time they emerged from a charming little shop that sold nothing but lace, Laura's poor head was aching from trying to keep track of all their purchases. If her calculations were correct, they had spent more in one day than Arden Manor would earn in a year.

As they strolled toward the waiting town coach, nursing bags of warm pistachios they'd bought from a vendor, a lamplighter melted out of the falling dusk to light the streetlamps. Their soft glow fell upon the shop windows, making the goods displayed within look even more tempting.

As they passed a brightly decorated toy shop, Laura halted, a soft cry of delight escaping her.

A china doll festooned in ruffles and lace sat in the window, her plump cheeks painted with a rosy blush. From her topknot of golden curls to her snub nose to her miniature kid slippers, the doll was the very image of Lottie.

Diana peered through the window. "What is it?"

"I was just thinking how very much my little sister

would fancy that doll," Laura replied, pressing her fingers to the glass without realizing it.

Diana shrugged. "So purchase it for her."

Laura tucked her hands back into her new swansdown muff. "I couldn't possibly presume upon the duke's generosity any more than I already have. He's been far too extravagant."

Diana gave her an odd look. "Sterling hasn't a stingy bone in his body. He may begrudge you his forgiveness, but not his purse. If you can't have one, you might as well make do with the other." Diana touched her own fingers to the glass, her expression curiously wistful. "It was one of the few lessons my father taught me."

When Laura marched out of the toy store nearly an hour later, her arms were laden with gifts for her brother and sister, including a skipping rope for Lottie and three shiny new decks of cards for George. She had refused to have her treasures delivered to the hall, not wanting to trust them to any hands but her own. Diana waited patiently while she ducked into a haberdashery to buy a pair of soft leather riding gloves to warm Dower's aching hands on cold winter nights. She'd already decided to send Cookie one of the bonnets trimmed with ostrich plumes that she had chosen for herself.

As they approached the town coach, Diana came to a sudden halt, sending Laura crashing into her back. While one of the footmen leapt down from his perch to rescue their packages, Laura peeped over Diana's shoulder to find the marquess of Gillingham lounging against a lamppost, top hat in hand and shiny walking stick tucked beneath his arm.

He straightened, sweeping them a graceful bow. "Your Grace, Lady Diana. I saw the coach when I was coming out of my tailor's and thought I'd linger to bid you a good evening."

"And a good evening to you, my lord." Diana crisply brushed past him, allowing the footman to hand her into the coach. "Now that my cousin has been safely returned from his little adventure, I don't suppose we'll be seeing much of you anymore."

"On the contrary," Thane drawled, neatly jostling aside the footman to hand Laura into the coach himself. "With the duke back in residence at Devonbrooke Hall to stay, I plan to make a regular nuisance of myself."

"That shouldn't be too much of a challenge for you." Diana stared straight ahead while the footman secured the door. "I'm sure my cousin will be only too delighted to receive you."

Thane gazed up at her profile, smoothing his hat brim between forefinger and thumb. "What about you, Diana?" he asked softly. "Would you be delighted to receive me?"

Before she could answer him, the coach lurched into motion.

"Insufferable man," Diana muttered, jerking off her gloves and slapping them into her lap.

Intrigued as much by the hectic patches of color in Diana's cheeks as by that rare display of passion, Laura leaned out the window to find Thane still staring after them, hat in hands.

When they arrived back at Devonbrooke Hall, Addison was waiting for them in the foyer. "His Grace wishes to see you in the study," he informed Laura, handing her pelisse and muff to a footman.

Laura's heart leapt. Perhaps Sterling was finally willing to stop pretending last night had never happened, willing to admit that it was impossible for a man to take a woman so thoroughly, yet give nothing of himself in return. She smoothed her hair and started for the nearest corridor, hoping her pathetic eagerness didn't show.

Addison politely cleared his throat. "That way, Your Grace," he said, pointing in the opposite direction. "Seventh door on the left, just after the marble fountain."

She wheeled around, giving him a grateful smile.

Laura slipped into the study to find Sterling sitting behind a mahogany monster of a desk, surrounded by several towering stacks of ledgers and papers. She was relieved to find his dogs nowhere in sight. Despite his assurance that they were gentle giants, she still suspected them of harboring a secret desire to gnaw off one of her feet and bury it in the solarium.

Sterling had carelessly discarded his coat across a nearby stool, leaving him in a rumpled waistcoat and rolled-up shirtsleeves. Laura studied his unguarded face in the lamplight, thinking how very little she really knew of him. He wasn't a creature of her own invention but a complicated man molded by influences both cruel and kind. She only wished that could make her want him less instead of more.

Although she would have sworn she didn't make a sound, he suddenly looked up to catch her watching him. The pleasant mask she was coming to hate slid neatly into place. "So you're back from your shopping expedition, are you? I trust you found everything you needed?"

"Not everything," Laura said cryptically, gliding over to sit in the leather wing chair in front of the desk.

"Well, perhaps this will help to assuage your disappointment." Sterling leaned over the desk, handing her a folded piece of parchment. "Happy birthday."

Laura blinked at him, caught completely off guard.

"Surely you didn't think I'd forget, did you?"

"To be honest, I'm the one who forgot. I certainly didn't expect you to remember." She shyly lowered her eyes. "Or to get me a gift."

"Go on," he said, nodding toward the paper. "Open it."

She slowly unfolded the official-looking document and scanned the elegant script, not completely sure what she was looking at.

"It's the deed to Arden Manor," Sterling explained. "I found it yesterday morning when I was sifting through the papers in my father's study. I summoned a solicitor today while you were gone and had the house and lands entailed to your name. You'll never again have to worry about George and Lottie not having a roof over their heads. No one can ever take it away from you, not even my heirs."

His heirs. Laura continued to gaze blindly down at the paper, refusing to look up as long as there was any danger of him seeing her cry.

"I thought you'd be pleased," he said softly. "Would you have preferred a pair of emerald earbobs? A diamond necklace?"

Laura's fingernails dug into the paper. "No, thank you, my lord. You've been entirely too generous as it is."

He shrugged. "Nonsense. There are those who might even say you've earned it."

Laura jerked her head up. She glared at him disbelievingly, images tumbling through her mind of the past two nights she'd spent in his arms. In his bed.

"With your resourcefulness, of course," he added, the glint in his eye telling her that he knew exactly what she was thinking. "You did take a tremendous amount of risk for a run-down old manor house."

"A run-down old manor house you were only too eager to claim for yourself. Or have you forgotten what brought you back to Arden Manor in the first place? It certainly wasn't to pay your last respects to your mother."

Sterling leaned back in the chair, his polite mask showing signs of strain. "My mother is none of your concern."

Laura stood, crumpling the deed in her fist. "She certainly wasn't any of *your* concern, either. If she had been, you wouldn't have let her die without your forgiveness. But since it seems I'm to share her fate, I suppose it's only fitting that I inherit her house as well. Even if I do have to spend the rest of my life *earning* it." She strode to the door, then turned on her heel. "Oh, and I ran into one of your very dear friends today—a Lady Hewitt. She made it clear that she would be only too delighted to welcome you back into her bed after you become bored with me."

Although it took every ounce of strength in Laura's slender body, she still managed to slam the study door hard enough to rattle the candle sconces on each side of it.

"Not much chance of that, is there?" Sterling murmured, shaking his head ruefully as he listened to her angry footsteps fade away.

Laura lay flat on her back in her bed, glaring up at the canopy. Last night, she'd been angry. Tonight, she was livid. Her husband could play the benevolent nobleman all he liked, but she had recognized his gift for what it was—yet another reproach. A mocking reminder that no moldy old pile of bricks could compensate her for what her lies had cost them both.

Somewhere deep in the heart of the house, a clock chimed twelve times, heralding the end of her birthday.

Laura threw herself to her side. The clock could chime thirteen times and she still wouldn't go to him. Not that she could even find the west wing again. She supposed he'd be only too relieved if she took a tumble down a flight of stairs and broke her neck. She could just see him standing over her grave, his handsome face set in lines of mock grief as he accepted the sympathetic murmurs of Lady Hewitt.

He might not even be willing to wait for her untimely demise. What if she marched over to the west wing right now only to find his bed cold and empty? Perhaps he'd already gone to seek out his former mistress. Perhaps they had spent the evening sipping champagne and laughing together over his misfortune at being tricked into marriage by a penniless rector's daughter who couldn't possibly hope to satisfy his *demands* in bed. Perhaps at this very minute, he was tangled in the woman's silk bedsheets, doing to her voluptuous body all of those sweet, wicked things he had done to Laura's only last night.

Groaning, Laura dragged the counterpane over her head to blot out the image.

Which was exactly how Sterling found her when he parted the bed hangings and sat down on the bed next to her.

Chapter 23

. . . and that she will prove worthy
of your devotion.

Laura sat up, shaking her tousled hair out of her eyes. "What are *you* doing here?"

Sterling rested his pewter candlestick on a small shelf that jutted out from the headboard, creating a cozy nest of light. "I didn't want to be accused of being derelict in my duties as a husband. I doubt my debauched reputation could withstand the blow."

She seemed to consider his words for a minute, then flopped to her back. "If your only aim is to get an heir on me, then you might as well dispense with the niceties and get on with it."

"The niceties?" Sterling echoed, fascinated by this new mood of hers.

"You know—the kissing . . . the touching." She waved a disdainful hand at him. "All of that silly bother."

"So you don't want me to kiss you?"

"I don't really see the point, do you?"

Sterling kept his expression deliberately innocent. "Not anywhere?"

He was near enough to see her convulsive swallow, hear the faint catch in her breath. She tossed back the bedclothes and lay staring up at the canopy. "Just cover me up when you're finished. There's a distinct chill in the air."

There most certainly was. But it had nothing to do with the ever-present drafts wafting through the cavernous old house and everything to do with his bride's sulky expression and rigid posture. She looked as if she were waiting for the apothecary to pull an abscessed tooth. Sterling had to bite the inside of his cheek to keep from smiling.

"I'll have to lift your nightdress," he warned her. "That won't be too much of a bother, will it?"

She heaved a long-suffering sigh and turned her face away from him. "I suppose there's no getting around it."

Her eyes fluttered shut as he ran his warm hands up her long, silky legs, easing the nightdress up past her hips. His own breath caught. She looked like an angel in the candlelight—all silky dark curls and pale freckled skin.

"And it will probably make things easier for both of us if I touch you just . . . here."

Her lips parted in a soundless gasp. Sterling bit back a groan of his own. Although he'd done nothing to deserve such an indulgence, she was as ready for him as he was for her. He shrugged out of his satin dressing gown, thankful he hadn't bothered to don his trousers before making the long, lonely trek to her room.

"If it's too much of a nuisance for you to put your

arms around me, it might be best if I held your hands just so." He gently laced his fingers through hers, bringing her hands up to rest on each side of her head until they were palm to palm.

She clutched at his hands as he slid over her and into her in one smooth motion. Sterling clenched his eyes shut against a savage rush of sensation. He'd never dreamed any woman could be so silky-sweet, so hot, so tight. As he began to move within her, she gloved him as if she'd been fashioned just for him. *Only* for him.

When he opened his eyes, she was gazing up at him through her lashes, her lips parted and her luminous eyes glazed with desire.

"Are you sure you don't want me to kiss you?" he whispered in a voice thick with passion.

Her tongue darted out to moisten her lips. "Well, perhaps just once . . ."

Sterling kissed her once, a single kiss that went on and on, its deep and primitive rhythms keeping time with the hypnotic tempo of his hips and each thundering beat of his heart. He didn't ever want it to end, not the loving and not the kiss. But his body couldn't be staved off forever. Determined to show Laura just what he could accomplish even without the *niceties,* he deliberately angled his hips so that each downward stroke brought him into contact with that priceless pearl nestled at the crux of her nether curls.

He felt her coming apart beneath him, knew he had no choice but to follow. As he collapsed on top of her, gasping for breath, the last thing he expected to hear was her small, determined voice in his ear. "You've done what you came for. You can go now."

He slowly lifted his head.

Laura was staring at a spot just over his right shoulder, trying to pretend that her luscious body wasn't still quaking in reaction to the earth-shattering pleasure they had just shared.

"Am I being dismissed?"

"No, you're being excused. Job well done and all that rot."

A part of Sterling wanted nothing more than to gather her into his arms and hold her until dawn came creeping into the chamber. But he'd surrendered that right when he'd outlined the conditions of their marriage in such dispassionate terms. Silently cursing his own lack of foresight, he gently tugged down her nightdress and tucked the counterpane around her before donning his dressing gown and taking up the candle.

He slipped out of the bed, counted to ten, then poked his head back through the bed hangings. Laura lay on her back, eyes closed and arms outflung. Her sullen expression had melted to one of breathless, disbelieving rapture.

Sterling cleared his throat, causing her to sit up so fast she hit her head on the headboard. She rubbed her head, glaring up at him through a tumbled lock of hair. "I thought you'd gone."

He leaned against the bedpost. "I've been thinking that perhaps we shouldn't be so quick to dispense with the niceties. Upon further consideration, they're rather . . . nice."

Laura toyed with the ribbon at the throat of her nightdress. "Well, if you think it will make your task less burdensome . . ."

"Oh, I think it will make both of our tasks less burdensome. Why don't I show you?"

Her eyes widened as he slipped back out of his dressing gown and back into her bed.

Sterling Harlow might have the face of an angel, but by night he was a devil, stealing Laura's soul even as he scorned her heart. Although he had professed a fondness for the niceties, the things he did to Laura's eager young body when he slipped between her sheets each night weren't nice at all but deliciously naughty. Some of them were even downright wicked.

Laura took to languishing in bed every morning until ten or eleven, trying to put off the moment when she would have to face the remote stranger who bore no resemblance to the hot-blooded man who had coaxed her to shuddering delight only a few hours before. The more heated their couplings, the more cool and distant he became, until even his cousin grew frustrated with his aloof manner and noncommittal murmurs.

After he had excused himself from dinner one night to barricade himself back in the study, Diana tossed her napkin into her plate. "What was he like?" she demanded, turning her fierce gaze on Laura.

Laura froze, a forkful of curried salmon halfway to her mouth. "Who?"

"This Nicholas of yours. What was he like? What manner of man was he?"

Laura lowered her fork, her lips softening in a wistful smile. "He was kind and tender with a rather dry wit. He was a little suspicious in nature. But I suppose I can't really blame him for that," she admitted, dabbing at her lips with her napkin. "He had a bit of a temper as well. You should have seen him when he found out I'd arranged for him to be the new rector of the parish without consulting him first. He couldn't even speak for the longest time. He just kept shaking his head at me and running his hand through his hair, all the while turning redder and redder until I thought he was going to explode."

Diana abandoned her chair and slid into the one next to Laura. "Oh, do tell. Did he throw a proper tantrum? I always wished he would when my father was caning him, but he was far too proud. He would take the beating and I would cry."

For a minute, Laura thought she was going to. But instead she found herself reaching for Diana's hand and gently squeezing it. "If you wanted to see a proper tantrum, you should have been there the first time he met my little sister. Lottie let her kittens loose in his bed and he thought they were rats."

"That doesn't surprise me one bit. I've had my Snowball shut up in the north wing ever since he returned. Sterling never has been able to abide cats. He's just like my father in that respect."

"Ha! You should ask him about the kitten that used to follow him all over the farm. I actually caught him kissing its little pink nose and tucking it into the pocket of his coat one morning when he thought no one was looking. And you should have seen the two of them all curled up asleep in the . . ." Realizing that the underfootman standing at attention by the sideboard was craning his neck to hear their conversation, Laura leaned over to whisper in Diana's ear, eliciting a throaty burst of laughter.

The endless columns of numbers that had been copied in Diana's tidy hand were beginning to blur before Sterling's exhausted eyes when he heard a sound he'd never before heard within the thick stone walls of Devonbrooke Hall—musical peals of feminine laughter. He slowly stood, letting the ledger fall shut.

The sound was as irresistible as a siren's song. He followed it all the way back to the door of the dining room. His wife and his cousin were sitting with their heads together, laughing and whispering as if they'd been friends for years.

As his gaze traced Laura's lovely profile, he felt a peculiar ache low in his chest. He hadn't heard her laugh like that since they had stood on the steps of St. Michael's that sun-drenched morning an eternity ago.

He might have stood there watching her forever if the underfootman standing by the sideboard hadn't pointedly cleared his throat. Laura and Diana whipped their heads around, their smiles fading and their eyes growing wary.

"Forgive me for interrupting," he said stiffly. "I left the *Times*." He tucked the newspaper beneath his arm and strode back to the study, feeling more like an intruder in his own house than ever before.

A few days later on a chill and rainy afternoon, Sterling was headed for the study to spend more interminable hours reviewing his apparently infinite number of properties when he heard a most curious sound behind him.

Dead silence.

He halted, cocking his head to the side. There was no panting, no toenails clicking on the marble, no jostling for position.

He slowly turned.

No dogs.

Caliban and Cerberus had been his constant companions ever since he'd returned from Arden. They even napped patiently outside of Laura's door each night until their master emerged in the wee hours of the morning, flushed and sated. They were the only ones who knew that he never returned to his own cold, empty bed but spent what was left of the night smoking in the solarium, waiting for the sun to come up.

Sterling tucked two fingers in his mouth and let out the low-pitched whistle that never failed to bring the mastiffs trotting to his side. His only answer was a hollow echo.

He frowned. Perhaps Addison had simply neglected to tell him that he'd ordered one of the underfootmen to take them for a walk in the park.

As he neared the library, he noted that the door was half-ajar. He leaned against the doorjamb, rendered speechless by the sight that greeted him.

Laura sat on the hearth rug with Cerberus stretched out beside her. Caliban lay with his head in her lap, his big brown eyes pools of slavish devotion. She was absently fondling his ears, not the least bit concerned that he was drooling all over the pale blue silk of her skirt. Sterling could only imagine what his old enemies the French would say if they could see his devil dogs brought to heel by nothing more than a woman's touch. But he knew only too well the power of those hands against his own flesh.

He shook his head ruefully. First his cousin, now his dogs. Was she to leave him nothing?

He was about to turn away, but her melancholy sigh rooted his feet to the floor. Although an open book was propped on her knee, she was gazing into the fire, her expression pensive. Sterling studied her, noticing changes that had eluded him in the velvety shadows of her bed. The sun-kissed bloom was fading from her cheeks. Her rich brown eyes no longer sparkled but were shadowed by loneliness.

She had risked everything, including her heart, to keep her home and her family intact. Yet he'd torn her away from the both of them, not allowing her so much as a backward glance.

Sterling's uncle had ordered all manner of exotic blooms for the solarium, but they rarely flourished because they needed warmth and sunlight, two things the cold, drafty hall could never provide. In the end the blooms had always died, leaving only Sterling to mourn them.

He must have made some small sound, for Cerberus lifted his head to give him a quizzical look. Touching a finger to his lips, Sterling slowly backed out of the room.

He strode to the study, infused with a genuine sense of purpose for the first time in days. After he'd finished penning a rather lengthy note, he rang for Addison.

The manservant seemed to materialize out of thin air, just as he always did. "You rang, Your Grace?"

Sterling handed him the missive. "I need you to see that the marquess of Gillingham receives this message right away."

"Very well, Your Grace. Will there be anything else?"

Sterling settled back in his chair, smiling in spite of

himself. "You might want to give the servants a generous bonus. I'm afraid they're about to earn it."

By the end of her second week at Devonbrooke Hall,
Laura was so desperate for company that she found
herself wandering the portrait gallery in the west wing,
searching the faces of Sterling's dead relations for any
hint of a resemblance. She amused herself by naming
the more colorful of them and making up stories about
their lives. She'd decided that the smirking fellow in the
doublet and pleated ruff was Percival the Pert, beloved
confidant of the very first duchess of Devonbrooke. The
ruddy-faced, red-bearded warrior draped in chain mail
was none other than Sir Boris the Bloody, defender of
the wrongfully condemned. And the buxom vixen with
the defiant glare? Why, she must be Mad Mary Harlow,
who had murdered her unfeeling husband after she
caught him in bed with his married mistress, an acid-
tongued wench who just happened to be named
Elizabeth.

Laura sighed and made another circuit of the gallery.
Even the portrait of old Granville Harlow had lost its
power to terrorize. She would almost rather encounter
the ghost of the former duke than the present one.

She leaned closer to the wall to examine a small portrait she'd nearly overlooked. It was a stiff, unsmiling
likeness of a fair-haired boy, no more than eleven or
twelve. His back was ramrod straight and his eyes
gazed out upon the world with a guarded cynicism jar-
ring in one so young.

Laura touched her fingertip to his cheek, but could
find no hint of the dimple she loved. There was no need

to employ her imagination. She already knew his story. He had been abandoned by those he loved the most. He had been given into the clutches of a despotic old man determined to mold him in his likeness. And he had been betrayed by the woman he had trusted with his heart. Laura slowly lowered her hand. Could she blame him for not believing in happy endings?

She was turning away from the portrait, head bowed, when a savage barking shattered the silence. The sound was accompanied by raised voices, a blistering stream of profanity delivered in a Cockney accent so thick as to be mercifully indecipherable, and a shrill shrieking.

Laura jerked her head up. Thinking that she must surely be losing her mind, she snatched up the hem of her skirts and took off at a dead run.

She'd almost reached the top of the main staircase when Diana emerged from the north wing, her usually impeccably styled hair dressed on only one side. "What on earth is that dreadful cacophony? It sounds as if someone was torturing a cat!"

Instead of answering, Laura flew past her and down the stairs. She didn't wait for the startled footman to sweep open the front door but wrenched the knob from his grasp and flung it open herself.

"Laura!"

While Addison struggled to restrain the lunging mastiffs, his face going purple from the effort, a golden-haired moppet launched herself into Laura's arms. The gingham-draped basket hooked over her arm might have looked totally innocent were it not for the number of colorful, swishing tails hanging over the sides and the frenzied reaction of the dogs.

"Lottie! Oh, Lottie, is it really you?" While Addison handed the dogs off to two burly footmen, Laura buried her face in her sister's curls, breathing deeply of their baby-fresh scent.

"Of course it's her," said someone just behind Lottie. "Do you know anyone else who would make such a god-awful racket just because one of those nice doggies mistook her basket of kittens for a picnic lunch?"

Laura lifted her head to discover her brother lounging against the door of the handsome carriage parked in front of the hall, his cravat tied in a flawless knot. "Why, George Fairleigh," she exclaimed, "I do believe you've grown an inch just since I last saw you!"

"Half an inch," he admitted. Although he squirmed and rolled his eyes, he still allowed her to throw her arms around him and give him a hearty kiss. "Mind the whiskers," he warned her. "I may have only two, but they're quite bristly."

"If you ask me, which no one ever does," someone growled, "I still think we should hie our arses back to Arden. Your sister is a lady now—far too fine for the likes of us."

Laura whirled around to find Dower standing behind her, his brow furrowed in a mock scowl. "Come here, you crusty old curmudgeon," she said, "and give this fine lady a kiss." While he pecked her on the cheek, she squeezed his gnarled hands, pleased to see that his bruises had nearly faded.

Cookie was just being handed down from the carriage by none other than the marquess of Gillingham himself. The ostrich plumes adorning her new bonnet waved majestically in the breeze. As Laura buried her face in Cookie's ample shoulder, her throat closed, squeezing off any words of welcome she might have offered.

"There now, lamb," Cookie crooned, stroking her hair. "Cookie's here now. Everything'll be all right."

Even though Laura knew they weren't true, Cookie's words still gave her the courage to swallow the lump in her throat. She surveyed the circle of their beaming faces. "I don't understand. Why aren't you all in Arden? What are you doing here in London?"

Cookie simpered up at the marquess. "Why, your husband sent this handsome young gent here to fetch us, he did."

Thane brought her hand to his lips. "It was my pleasure. It's not every day I get to travel with a woman who can wring a chicken's neck with her bare hands."

Cookie tittered and gave his cheek a pinch. "If I was a few years younger, you'd find out that's not all I can do with them."

Dower rolled his eyes. "Don't mind 'er. She's a shameless flirt."

"So is he," Diana murmured, earning a loaded look from Thane.

Laura was still reeling with shock. "Sterling sent for you? But why on earth didn't he tell me?"

"Because he wanted it to be a surprise." As her husband's rich voice poured over her, Laura turned to find him leaning against one of the portico columns. "And judging from your expression, I'd say he was successful."

It was all Laura could do to keep from flinging herself into *his* arms. But they remained folded over his chest, a formidable barrier to anything but the most reserved expressions of gratitude.

"Thank you, Your Grace," she said softly. "There are really no words to express my appreciation for your kindness."

There might be no words. But there were feather-soft caresses and deep, soul-stirring kisses. And it was those she promised him with her ardent gaze.

Lottie tugged impatiently at her hand. "You must show me your bed—the one that looks like a sultan's tent. You described it so well in your letters that I can almost picture it. Can I sleep with you the whole time we're here, Laura? Can I? Oh, please say I can!"

Every eye, except for the ever-discreet Addison's, turned to the duke.

Sterling cleared his throat awkwardly, a most endearing flush creeping up his jaw. "That won't be necessary. I've arranged for you and your brother to have your own suite with your own beds that look like sultans' tents."

Before Lottie could launch into a full-blown whine, Cookie drew a linen-wrapped package from her bag and offered it to Sterling. "I made a fresh batch of crumpets just for you, m'lord."

"How very . . . thoughtful of you," Sterling replied, a hint of his old twinkle in his eye.

"I've something for you, too!" Lottie began to fish around in her own basket.

"Please tell me it's not a bride cake," he murmured.

She shot him a reproachful look, then hefted her find triumphantly into the air.

It was the yellow kitten. The one who had tagged after his every step at Arden Manor.

As she held the squirming creature out to Sterling, his face went utterly still. "Thank you, Carlotta," he said stiffly, making no move to take the cat. "I'm sure Addison would be more than delighted to find appropriate accommodations for all of your pets."

He turned on his heel and marched back into the house. After a moment, they heard the sound of a distant door slamming.

Her expression crestfallen, Lottie tucked the kitten back into the basket. "I don't understand. I thought he'd be pleased."

Laura gave her sister's shoulders a squeeze, exchanging a troubled look with Diana. "It's not you, Pumpkin. It's just a bit more difficult to please him these days than it used to be."

Laura didn't tell her little sister that she was beginning to fear it might just be impossible.

After Addison had ushered their rambunctious party of guests into the foyer, Diana and Thane were left facing each other.

"It was a great kindness you did for my cousin," she said. "You've always been more of a brother to him than a friend."

"Just as you've always been more of a sister than a cousin."

Diana laughed awkwardly. "I suppose that would make us siblings of a sort."

The last thing Diana expected Thane to do was touch her hair. She had forgotten how ridiculous she must look, rushing out with it only half-dressed. But instead of tucking the loose strands behind her ear, he reached around and gently tugged at the pins on the other side, sending the silky dark tendrils tumbling around her face.

His voice was nearly as smoky as his green eyes.

"I've thought of you many ways in the past eleven years, my lady, but *never* as a sister."

Then right there in front of the footmen, the carriage driver, and God Himself, he grazed her lips with a kiss no one could have mistaken for brotherly.

Diana stood there, utterly dazed, while he climbed back into his carriage. As the vehicle rolled into motion, he leaned out the window and tipped his hat to her, the wicked sparkle returning to his eyes. "Don't mind me. I'm a shameless flirt."

Chapter 24

I still see your face in my dreams. . . .

His mother was calling him.

Sterling sat bolt upright in the bed, trembling all over. He threw back the blankets and slid to the floor. It felt like ice beneath his bare feet as he padded across the chamber and wrestled open the heavy door.

Darkness seemed to rush toward him, but he held his ground, clenching his jaw against a shudder of fear. As the sound came again—plaintive and sweet—hope soared in his heart. His mother wasn't just calling him. She was calling him to come home.

He started down the long corridor at a trot, following the music of her voice. But as the corridor unfurled before him, he became aware of another sound, this one coming out of the shadows behind him. He froze, plastering himself to the wall.

At first he could hear nothing but the harsh rasp of his own breathing. But then it came again—a sound he'd heard a thousand times before, a sound that sent a chill skittering like a spider down his spine.

It was the rhythmic tap of his uncle's walking stick.

Sterling shoved himself away from the wall, breaking into a sprint. But no matter how fast he ran, the relentless tap-tapping kept pace with him, swelling until it nearly drowned out the echo of his mother's voice. If only his legs were longer, he might be able to reach her before his uncle caught him. If only the corridor would stop unraveling beneath his feet with each step he took. If only . . .

A bony hand shot out of the darkness behind him, closing around his throat.

Sterling sat bolt upright on the chaise, trembling all over.

During his decade in the army, he'd been mercifully free of the nightmares that had plagued him throughout his boyhood. But they'd been crouching in the shadowy corners of Devonbrooke Hall all along, just waiting for him to return.

He swung his legs to the floor and dropped his head into his hands. He still couldn't bring himself to sleep in his uncle's bed. It felt too much like a tomb. He was half-afraid that if he sank down into the feather mattress, he might not be able to claw his way back up.

He glanced at the mantel clock. He'd only meant to steal a brief nap before going to Laura's chamber, but it was nearly one o'clock in the morning. He rose, jerking a knot in the sash of his dressing gown. If Laura was already asleep, he vowed to himself as he strode toward her chamber, he would simply slip into her bed, draw her solid warmth against him, and bury his face in her sweet-smelling hair until the bitter aftertaste of the nightmare had dissipated. He wouldn't even kiss that sensitive spot behind her ear that made her press her rump against him or cup the creamy softness of her breasts in his hands. He shook his head helplessly. The hell he wouldn't.

Sterling eased open Laura's door to find Caliban and Cerberus stretched out on the rug at the foot of her bed like a pair of snoring guardian angels.

"Traitors," he muttered, leaning down to rub their heads.

The exhausted dogs had spent all afternoon chasing Lottie's kittens around the hall until a fluffy gray spitfire had wheeled around and taken a swipe at Caliban's nose. They'd spent the rest of the evening whining and cowering under the kitchen stairs.

Sterling's pulse quickened with anticipation as he parted the bed hangings, only to slow to a dull thud when he saw the golden head nestled next to Laura's dark one.

His wife had obviously been waiting for him. Her eyes were bright and unclouded by sleep. "Lottie had a bad dream," she whispered, giving him an apologetic look. "I couldn't very well send her away, could I?"

Sterling gazed down at the child nestled in her arms, at the half-dozen kittens drowsing among the bed-clothes in cozy abandon, and felt a keen stab of envy.

"Of course not," he murmured, reaching down to stroke Lottie's hair. He stuffed his balled fists in the pockets of his dressing gown to keep from doing the same thing to Laura's. "She's in good hands. I trust you'll be able to keep her monsters at bay for the rest of the night."

As Sterling headed for the solarium, drawing a che-root from his pocket, he only wished she could do the same for his.

* * *

Devonbrooke Hall resounded with merriment.

If the dogs weren't bounding through the house in a good-natured romp with one of the kittens, then Lottie was sailing down the banister, squealing at the top of her lungs while George slid across the floor of the foyer in his stocking feet. A beaming Addison proclaimed that both the marble and the mahogany had never been so well polished, and gave several of the maidservants an extra day off.

Cookie swept through the kitchens like a fresh Hertfordshire breeze, brandishing a rolling pin at the haughty French chef when he attempted to order her off his turf. When she fed one of his rich cream sauces to the cats, the tiny man quit in a huff, storming through the dining room and spewing Gallic curses with a flair that impressed even Dower. Cookie simply rescued the apron he had hurled at her head and set about making a fresh batch of gingerbread.

The only person who seemed to be immune to the cheerful chaos that had descended upon the house was its master. Sterling rarely emerged from the paneled gloom of the study, even choosing to take most of his meals there since Laura's family had commandeered the dining room table for their card games and boisterous meals.

He was working at his desk late one evening by the light of a single lamp when his cousin came marching in.

"How remiss of me," he said dryly. "I must not have heard you knock."

As usual, Diana didn't mince words. "You've been wed for nearly a month now, yet you've made no effort whatsoever to introduce your bride to society."

Sterling made a vague gesture with his pen, then resumed scribbling a note to one of his stewards in Lancashire. "Most of the families are visiting the seaside or are away at their country houses right now. Perhaps when they return in September—"

"She thinks you're ashamed of her."

Sterling's head flew up. "Ashamed of her? Where would she get such a ridiculous notion?"

"There have been certain *rumors* about the unusual circumstances of your marriage, which you've done nothing to quash."

"Elizabeth . . . " he breathed, raking a hand through his hair. "Damn that woman and her venomous tongue."

"Unfortunately, shortly after she arrived in London, Laura was privy to a rather malicious conversation detailing her various shortcomings."

"Shortcomings?" Sterling surged to his feet. "She doesn't have any bloody shortcomings! She's lovely and generous and loyal and funny and far too clever for my good. Why, any man would be lucky to have her for a wife!"

Diana arched one sleek eyebrow.

Sterling sank back down in the chair, avoiding her eyes. He supposed Elizabeth wasn't solely to blame for Laura's misconception. After all, he was the one guilty of seeking out her bed in secret each night, treating her more like a mistress than a wife.

He tapped his pen against the leather blotter. "How much time do you need to plan a ball?"

"With Addison's help, a week and a half," Diana said firmly, as if she'd already anticipated his question.

"Then you'd best get started." As she turned toward

the door, he added, "Oh, and do make sure that Lady Hewitt receives an invitation."

Diana gave him a feline smile. "With pleasure."

Sterling was reviewing Diana's meticulously prepared guest list on the morning of the ball when Addison poked his head into the study, his nostrils pinched as if he'd been subjected to an unpleasant odor. "There's a man to see you, sir. A Mr. Theophilus Watkins."

The manservant had proven himself to be an impeccable judge of character over the years. It was one of the reasons Sterling had trusted him to look after Diana all the years he was away.

"Very well," Sterling said warily. "Send him in."

Addison ushered in a well-dressed man, but instead of leaving the two of them alone, as was his usual custom, he moved to stand at rigid attention behind Sterling's right shoulder.

The stranger offered Sterling a dapper bow. "Theophilus Watkins, Your Grace, at your humble service."

Despite his words, there was nothing humble about the man's demeanor or his hungry smile. Sterling's eyes were drawn to the marble-headed walking cane in the man's gloved hands. He handled it more like a weapon than a fashion accessory.

"How may I be of service to you, Mr. Watkins?"

Watkins settled himself into a chair without being asked. "You may not be aware of it, Your Grace, but I've already been of service to you. It was my fine detective work that got you rescued from those greedy ruffians who abducted you. If not for me, you might still be in their clutches."

Sterling stared at him for a long moment without blinking. If not for this man, he might be happily wed to a woman he adored. He might be living at Arden Manor in blissful ignorance of his own identity with no boring ledgers to keep and no properties to review. He might be happy.

Suddenly, Sterling was as enraged as he'd been since finding out Laura had deceived him. He wanted to slam this man against the wall, wanted to press his forearm to the wretch's throat and watch his smug face turn purple.

He cleared his own throat and shuffled some papers from one pile to another. "My cousin left me with the impression that you'd already been compensated for your efforts."

"Oh, I was. And quite fairly, I assure you. But I thought you might want to throw in a little something extra for my trouble." He caressed the marble head of his cane. "Since it was *your* hide that I saved."

Sterling tapped his lips thoughtfully. "You know—I believe I might have just the thing."

He crooked a finger at Addison. Addison leaned down and Sterling whispered something in his ear that made the manservant's eyes widen. As he dutifully marched from the room, Watkins settled back in the chair, propping his cane against its arm and grinning like a crocodile. He was obviously expecting Sterling to provide him with a nice fat purse.

The two men exchanged small talk about the weather until Sterling heard footsteps approaching the study.

He leaned forward, smiling pleasantly. "I'm only too aware of your *fine detective work*, Mr. Watkins. You were the one who beat my wife's devoted manservant to a bloody pulp, weren't you? Or did you hire some bloodthirsty thug to do your dirty work for you?"

Watkins's smile faded. Addison swept open the door and Dower came strolling in.

"Dower, Mr. Watkins here was just leaving," Sterling said briskly. "I was wondering if I could presume upon you to escort him out."

Dower shoved up his shirtsleeves, revealing the thick ropes of muscle that corded his upper arms. "It'd be me pleasure, m'lord."

"You might want to take him out the back way," Sterling instructed. "There's no need to upset the ladies."

Dower snapped off a smart salute, then hauled a sputtering Watkins out of his chair without giving him time to retrieve his cane.

"Damn you, Devonbrooke! You've no right to treat me this way! I know all about your kind. You think you're so high and mighty, but I've heard about that wife o' yours, I have," he snarled, his crumbling diction betraying his East End roots. "You're probably not the first bloke she tricked into her bed, just the only one stupid enough to marry the little slut."

Before he even knew he was going to do it, Sterling had vaulted over the desk and slammed his fist into Watkins's face. The man slumped in Dower's arms, out cold.

"Aw, 'ell," Dower whined. "Why'd you 'ave to go and spoil all me fun?"

"Sorry." Sterling rubbed his raw knuckles, not feeling the least bit repentant. He retrieved Watkins's cane, snapped it in two over his knee, and thrust the pieces down the front of the man's coat. "Just leave him in the alley with the rest of the garbage, won't you?"

"Aye, guv'nor." Dower began to drag Watkins toward the door, making no effort to support his bobbing head, not even when it rammed into the doorframe. "Although that's too kind a fate for the likes of 'im."

"I couldn't agree more," Sterling murmured.

Haunted by the man's cruel words, he wondered if it wouldn't be too kind a fate for him as well.

Chapter 25

*And I wish those dreams
could go on forever. . . .*

"**Lady Hewitt was right,**" Laura wailed. "You can polish me all you like, but I'll never be anything more than a lump of coal!"

As she turned away from the mirror and collapsed across Diana's bed, flinging one arm dramatically over her brow, Diana and her abigail exchanged an exasperated look.

"Don't be silly, Laura," Diana snapped. "You're simply suffering from a case of nerves. Why, you're going to be the loveliest woman at the ball."

Laura sat up. "Why? Did you forget to invite anyone else?"

Even Diana had to admit that no one would have mistaken the young duchess for a diamond of the first water at that moment. She wore a ratty old dressing gown stained with numerous splotches of tea. Her hair was wrapped in curling papers that stuck out from her head at all angles and her face was smeared with a thick layer of Gowland's Lotion, the miracle cream that was guaranteed to bleach away even the most disfiguring of freckles.

Diana gently wiped a smudge of the stuff from the tip of Laura's nose. "You may look a fright now, but by the time Celeste here is through with you, you'll be the toast of London."

Laura's countenance brightened. "Toast? I'm so ravenous I could eat a whole loaf of bread. Could we ring for Cookie to bring up some toast?"

"Perhaps later," Diana promised. "But right now we need to concentrate on getting you dressed."

"Why? So your cousin can parade me in front of all of London? So all the lords and ladies can sneer down their noses at the penniless country chit who tricked him into marriage? I knew he was determined to have his revenge on me, but even for him, this is too diabolical. I should have married Wesley Trumble or Tom Dillmore. They might have been hairy and smelly, but they weren't mean." She flopped back down on the bed. "Your cousin is a devil. I hate him!"

"Of course you do," Diana crooned, frantically gesturing to Celeste to fetch the duchess's silk stockings while she was distracted.

Before the maid could begin to roll them over Laura's ankles, she sat up again, her sullen scowl replaced by an expression of abject misery. "I shouldn't blame him, you know. God wouldn't be punishing me if I hadn't been so wicked. I was the one who mistook my will for His, the one who coveted, the one who lied, the one who . . ."

That somber soliloquy of Laura's sins might have gone on for days had Lottie not come barging into the bedchamber, carrying a plate laden with sweets.

It hadn't taken Laura's sister long to figure out that the north wing was one of the best-kept secrets of Devonbrooke Hall. Diana had created a cozy haven there for herself, a world away from the chilly marble and oppressive mahogany of the rest of the hall. The floral-chintz-draped walls and fitted carpeting provided the perfect backdrop for the fluffy white cat who reclined on an overstuffed ottoman in front of the hearth like a sultan's most cherished wife.

As was her custom, Lottie was already talking when she entered. "Oh, Laura, you should see all the treats Cookie has prepared for tonight! There are sweetmeats and gingerbread and ices and a syllabub decorated with sugared violets and the most enchanting little heart-shaped French cakes soaked in rum. She gave me some of each to taste and Sterling said that even though I was too young to dance, I could stay up all night if I was so inclined."

Laura's gaze was locked on Lottie's plate. Her tongue darted out to lick her lips. "I'm starving. Give me some of that."

Lottie picked an unfortunate moment to turn truculent. "No, it's mine!" She hugged the plate close to her breast. "Go get your own."

Laura rose from the bed, her eyes narrowing dangerously. "Give it to me now, you greedy little brat, or I'll smack you, I will."

Lottie's mouth fell open. "You most certainly will not! You've never smacked me. Not even when I needed it."

"Well, there's always a first time, isn't there?" Laura snatched the plate out of her grasp.

Lottie's plump lower lip began to quiver. "You're a mean old duchess, you are, and I'm going to tell

Cookie!" She ran from the room, slamming the door behind her.

"Celeste, why don't you go see if the laundress is done pressing Her Grace's gown?" Diana suggested softly, watching in horrified fascination as Laura began to cram pastries into her mouth, one right after the other.

As the maid obeyed, Diana circled Laura, unable to look away.

"Oh, Lottie was right!" Laura exclaimed, rolling her eyes in rapture. "These French cakes are exquisite." She polished off the last of them, then licked the crumbs from her lips, grimacing when she got a bit of the lotion as well.

"Good Lord." Diana sank down on the ottoman, nearly crushing a startled Snowball. "You're with child, aren't you?"

As the disgruntled cat darted under the bed, Laura slowly sank back down on it, her own bottom lip beginning to tremble.

"How long have you known?" Diana asked gently.

A single tear spilled from Laura's eye, tracing a crooked path through the lotion. "I've suspected for nearly a week now, but I wasn't sure until this morning when I tossed up my breakfast in my washbasin and bit poor Addison's head off for no reason at all. I thought the dear man was going to burst into tears."

"This couldn't have come as a complete shock to you, could it? Especially given my cousin's nightly visits to your bedchamber."

Laura's eyes widened. "How did you know?"

"This may be a large house, but I'm not blind. Or deaf."

The lotion couldn't stop Laura's ears from blushing a fiery pink. "Well, you needn't avail yourself of any romantic notions. He was just doing his duty."

"And with unflagging enthusiasm, I might add," Diana said dryly. "Have you told him?"

Laura shook her head. "Why should I? Once I've given him his precious heir, he'll just shuffle me off to one of his properties, preferably in Wales or Scotland, and forget I ever existed."

"That might be more difficult for him than you realize."

Laura watched warily as Diana sank down on the bed next to her.

"When my cousin first came to Devonbrooke Hall, my father delivered on everything he had promised. Sterling might have been deprived of affection, but he lacked for no luxury." Even now, Diana could still feel the old sting of envy. "There were toys of every imaginable sort, a fat Shetland pony, the finest of tutors. Yet every night, I'd find him sitting in the window seat of the nursery, gazing out into the darkness. Although he would never admit it, he was waiting for his mother. Somewhere in some forgotten corner of his heart, he still believed she might come for him."

Laura drew in a ragged breath. "When did he stop believing?"

"Ah, but there's the rub. I'm not so sure he ever did." Diana took Laura's hand in hers. "You have to be stronger than she was, Laura. You can't afford to give him up without a fight."

"But what if I lose?" Laura whispered.

Diana gave Laura's hand a fierce squeeze. "Then

you'll simply have to sweep up the pieces of your broken heart and go on, just as I have."

As the duchess of Devonbrooke appeared at the top of the marble staircase that spilled down from the gallery, a feverish murmur swept through the ballroom.

The cream of London's aristocracy had gathered beneath the glittering chandeliers to witness her debut into their exalted society. Upon receiving their invitations, many of them had rushed back from their country houses, crowding the narrow lanes with their barouches and town coaches. There had been no grand entertainments at the hall since the last duchess had died, and they were nearly as eager for a look at the fabled house as they were for a glimpse of the Devil of Devonbrooke's notorious young bride.

As it turned out, they were not to be disappointed by either.

The ballroom was vast enough to spare them the heat and crush of most such gatherings. The floor gleamed beneath their feet, the delicate scent of waxed cedar mingling with the perfumes of the ladies. Wall lights fashioned from pink wax complemented the mellow glow of the chandeliers.

But they both paled before the radiance of the woman standing at the top of the stairs.

The rich brown velvet of her hair had been swept atop her head in a gentle swirl, anchored by a pearl-studded coronet. A handful of curls had been allowed to escape, accenting her luminous eyes and arched sable brows. Freckles dusted her cheeks like shimmering flecks of gold. By the following evening, both matron and belle would be painstakingly trying to duplicate the effect by powdering their skin with gilt.

Her slender figure was well served by a high-waisted gown of white sarcenet draped with a gauze overskirt of the iciest teal. Both her puffed sleeves and her hem were edged with alternating ribbons of satin and lace. Her pale throat was unadorned except for a slim silver chain that disappeared into the low-cut bodice of her gown and led to much speculation as to what fantastically extravagant gem she might be hiding.

Sterling was standing near one of the French windows, sipping champagne and conversing with Thane, when the low-pitched murmur began to swell.

He turned to find his wife standing on the stairs.

The first time he laid eyes on Laura Fairleigh, Sterling had decided she was no beauty. He had been wrong. Her grace went far beyond mere prettiness. The hint of defiance in her unflinching gaze and uptilted chin only made her that much more beguiling to him.

Thane nudged him. "You all right, Dev? You look as if someone just punched you in the chest."

"It's not my chest I'm worried about." Handing Thane his champagne flute, Sterling began to wend his way through the crowd.

Although there was really no need, since Laura had already captured the attention of every eye in the ballroom, Addison dutifully stepped forward to announce her. "Her Grace, the duchess of Devonbrooke."

As Laura began to descend the stairs beneath the assessing eyes of society's finest, she had only one thought—she was thankful that trains had gone out of vogue so she didn't have to worry about tripping over hers and rolling the rest of the way down the steps.

Her feet didn't falter until she saw her husband standing at the bottom of the stairs, waiting for her. His honey gold hair cut a dazzling contrast to his black tailcoat and the starched white frills of his shirt. Although his eyes were somber, that elusive dimple of his flirted with his cheek.

"It's traditional for the ball to be opened by the guest of honor," he murmured, extending a hand.

Slipping her gloved hand into his, Laura allowed him to lead her to the center of the floor. Recognizing their cue, the musicians launched into a tinkling minuet.

Laura had never considered the minuet to be a particularly passionate dance, but each time she and Sterling came face-to-face and lightly clasped hands, the look in his eye made her heart beat faster. They danced as they should have at their own wedding breakfast, their measured motions no less tender or erotic than the dance they'd done in her bed only last night. By the time the last delicate note sounded, Laura was as breathless as if they'd been dancing a reel.

The hearty applause had yet to die out when an auburn-haired beauty whose ample breasts were threatening to spill from her low-cut bodice came rushing over. "Your Grace," she purred, sinking into a deep curtsy that only increased that danger.

"Why, Lady Hewitt, isn't it? I trust your husband is well." Sterling scanned the crowd, most of whom were watching their exchange with rapt interest. The guests nearest them were in danger of straining their necks in their transparent attempts to eavesdrop. "Did he accompany you tonight?"

"I'm afraid my Bertie is laid up with a rather nasty

case of the gout." She made a pretty moue. "I suppose that's one of the hazards of marrying a man *much* older than oneself. I'm frequently left to look after my own needs."

"Such a pity. I was rather looking forward to making his acquaintance. Have you met my wife?"

Lady Hewitt spared Laura a cool nod. "How do you do, Your Grace. I've heard much about you. All of London is a-twitter with talk of your *whirlwind courtship*." She imbued the words with as much malice as she dared.

"That doesn't surprise me." Sterling gave the woman a devilish wink. "The very height of scandal, wasn't it?"

She looked somewhat taken aback that he would admit such a thing. Her pale hand fluttered nervously about her throat. "I'm sure you can understand how such talk gets started. After all, you have been something of a recluse since your return."

"That's because I can't bear to drag myself away from my beloved's side." Sterling slipped a possessive arm around Laura's waist. He smiled fondly down at her, his eyes twinkling with mischief. "As soon as I laid eyes on my Laura here, I knew I had to have her. Why, it was almost as if we'd been betrothed for years, wasn't it, dearest?"

"Um . . . uh . . ." Laura had forgotten how devastating the full force of Sterling's charm could be. She might have gone on stammering indefinitely if he hadn't given her a sound pinch. "Oh! Yes, it was quite extraordinary. Why, at our very first meeting, we found ourselves discussing our future together."

"Just how did the two of you meet? Given your

disparate . . . *circumstances*"—Lady Hewitt flared her patrician nostrils—"I'm assuming it must have been pure chance."

Sterling chuckled. "Some might call it chance, but I call it fate. I owe it all to a skittish mare. After I was thrown, Laura was the first to stumble across me. I must confess that I found myself quite at her mercy."

Although she continued to beam up at him, Laura placed her foot on top of his and pressed firmly on his instep. "I don't recall hearing any complaints at the time."

"On the contrary. The happiest day of my life was when she agreed to marry me."

Laura batted her eyelashes at him. "And how was I to resist such an eloquent and romantic proposal?"

His eyes narrowed ever so slightly. "It's no wonder we've set the gossips' tongues to wagging, is it, darling? Who would have thought the dastardly Devil of Devonbrooke would end up surrendering his heart to such an angel?" Bringing Laura's hand to his lips, he bestowed a tender kiss upon it.

The women who had been eavesdropping on their conversation didn't bother to hide their sighs of envy. When one of their husbands dared to roll his eyes, his wife smacked him on the arm with her fan.

Lady Hewitt's mouth pursed as if she had eaten something exceedingly bitter. "If you'll excuse me, I do believe I've promised the next dance to the marquess of Gillingham."

"Heaven help him," Sterling murmured, watching her flounce away.

Laura could no longer hold in her laughter. "And

heaven help you for spouting such drivel. Why, it was enough to make Lord Byron himself blush!"

"On the contrary, he was standing just over your left shoulder during the entire exchange, frantically scribbling down notes."

"No! Why, Lottie will expire from envy!" Laura spun around, hoping to catch a glimpse of the dashing poet.

Sterling rested his warm hands on her bare shoulders and brought his mouth close to her ear. "I can assure you that before this night is done, no one in London, including Lord Byron, will doubt that the duke of Devonbrooke adores his wife."

His cryptic words sent a shiver of longing through Laura's soul, but before she could question them, the musicians launched into a rollicking Scottish reel that made further conversation impossible.

Thane ducked through the dancers, desperately trying to elude one woman and find another. Lady Elizabeth Hewitt had been stalking him for the past hour, pursuing him with chilling relentlessness. Since Sterling had thrown her over, she had obviously decided to seek consolation in the bed of his dearest friend. Only a few weeks ago, bedding one of Sterling's castoffs might not have been such an unthinkable proposition, but now the woman's throaty titter and incessant preening made Thane shudder.

He much preferred tall, willowy women who were so confident in their timeless elegance that they didn't find it necessary to follow the fickle tide of fashion. Thane sighed. Although he'd combed every corner of the ballroom, he had yet to find such a woman.

What he did find was Lady Hewitt heading his way again, her bosom jutting forward like the prow of some mighty ship. Biting back a groan, he ducked behind a footman's tray of empty champagne flutes. He was seriously considering making his escape through one of the tall French windows when he caught a flicker of movement on the gallery above.

Lady Diana Harlow stood with her elbows propped on the gallery rail, her chin resting in the cup of her palms. Thane shook his head. She might disdain the shallow gaiety of the festivities, but he should have known she'd want to keep a close watch on her cousin and his bride.

But she wasn't watching Sterling and Laura. She was watching him.

Their eyes met over the sea of dancers. She straightened, her wistful expression replaced by one of alarm. As she turned to flee, Thane started up the stairs, his long legs easily clearing two of them at a time.

She'd just reached the mouth of the corridor leading to the north wing when he made it to the top of the stairs. "Running away from the ball, are you? I thought that was Cinderella's role."

Chapter 26

*But even the sweetest of dreams
must come to an end. . . .*

Diana halted, then slowly turned, smoothing the rich burgundy of her skirts. "I never thought it quite fair that the fairy godmother didn't enjoy the same privileges as her protégée."

Thane moved toward her. "Aren't you tired of running, Diana? I know I am. I've been running for eleven years now and it hasn't gotten me anywhere I wanted to be."

A mocking smile touched her lips. "And just where do you want to be, my lord?"

"In your heart. In your arms." As the shimmering strains of a waltz wafted up from the ballroom below, he took another step toward her. "In your bed."

Diana turned away from him, but not before he saw her stern mask crumble. "How dare you insult me so? Why, one word from me and my cousin will be compelled to call you out."

"Let him," Thane said grimly. "I'd rather die on the dueling field tomorrow than spend the rest of my days only half-alive. Which is how I feel whenever I'm not with you."

Diana turned back to him, blinking furiously. "Well, that's just your wretched luck, isn't it? Because you're the one who squandered the last eleven years of our lives, not me."

"That's not true and you damn well know it. You were the one who broke off our engagement. You were the one who chose to believe an ugly morsel of gossip instead of the man you professed to love." He shook his head. "I still can't believe you thought I'd throw you over for some brainless chit like Cynthia Markham."

"I saw you!" she shouted. "I saw the two of you together that night at Lady Oakley's party! I saw you holding her in your arms! I saw you kissing her just as you always kissed me!"

Thane felt the blood drain from his face. "Oh, God," he whispered. "I never knew."

"Aren't you going to deny it? Aren't you going to tell me that *she* kissed *you*? Who knows? After all these years, I might just be lonely and desperate enough to believe you!"

Thane closed his eyes, buffeted by the secret shame that had kept him from defending himself to her for all these years. A lifetime of regrets flashed before them— the tender moments they might have shared, the children they might have had. But when he opened them again, he knew this was the only moment that mattered.

"I'm not going to lie to you. I did kiss her."

"Why?" Diana whispered, the tears spilling from her beautiful eyes breaking his heart all over again. "Why would you do such a thing?"

Thane drew a handkerchief from his breast pocket and handed it to her. "Because I was young and foolish and alone in a moonlit garden with a pretty young thing who was looking at me as if I hung the moon. Because I was going to be married in less than a fortnight. Because I was half out of my mind with loving you, but terrified of the depth of my feelings." He shook he head helplessly. "The moment my lips touched hers, I knew it was a mistake."

Diana crumpled the handkerchief in her fist. "Georgiana and Blanche came to me the next day and told me you were planning to marry Cynthia instead of me. And, of course, I believed them. How could I not? I'd seen the evidence with my own eyes. You left me no choice but to break our engagement before you did. How else was I to spare my pride?"

Thane cupped Diana's chin in his hands, forcing her to look him in the eye. "You might have seen me kissing Cynthia Markham in the garden that night, but you didn't linger long enough to see me push her away. You never heard me tell her that my life and my heart were already promised to another." He caressed her trembling lower lip with his thumb. "To you."

She clutched his wrist, revealing just how badly she wanted to believe him. "But why didn't you come to me? If you'd have only explained . . ."

"God knows I should have. I should have hurled rocks at your windows and broken down your door. I should have shouted my love for you from every rooftop in London until you had no choice but to listen. But I was little more than a lad myself then and your lack of faith in me dealt my pride a terrible blow." He lowered his eyes. "And I suppose I was ashamed knowing that there was even the tiniest morsel of truth in that cruel gossip."

Diana searched his face, tears continuing to trickle down her cheeks. "It seems that pride and time have made fools of the both of us."

Thane wrapped his arms around her, holding her as he'd longed to do for so many years. "I'm much older and wiser now. I say to hell with pride. And as for time, well, I've no intention of wasting another precious second of it."

Making good on that pledge, he brought his lips down tenderly on hers, making sure she would never again have reason to doubt him.

It was well after midnight when the last guest departed Devonbrooke Hall. Both the ball and the formal supper that had followed had been proclaimed a smashing success. The highlight of the entertainment had come when the countess of Rockingham had peeked beneath the lid of a serving dish only to discover a plump black kitten nibbling at the chicken beneath. Believing it to be an enormous rat, the buxom dowager had screamed and fainted dead away.

As was his habit, their dashing host had set every tongue in London to wagging. But this time it wasn't the duke's philandering, his gambling, or his dueling that had captured their imaginations. It was his touching devotion to his lovely young bride.

Although it was hardly the fashion to dance the night away with one's spouse, he refused to be coaxed away from her side. Between dances, he introduced her to each of their guests in turn, regaling his rapt audience with the dramatic story of their first meeting and subsequent courtship. During supper he offered a toast in her honor that was so tender, so very eloquent that even the jaded Lord Byron was seen to be dabbing a tear from his eye. Poor Lady Hewitt became so overcome with emotion that she could barely speak and had to depart shortly thereafter.

As the musicians packed away their instruments and the footmen doused the candles in the chandeliers one by one, Laura wandered through the ballroom. She wished the ball could have gone on all night. Or forever. Forever would be too short a time to spend basking in the warmth of Sterling's eyes, the heat of his touch. A wistful sigh escaped her. For a few precious hours, it was almost as if she had her Nicholas back.

Someone behind her cleared his throat. Laura turned to find Sterling standing in the gathering shadows, a sleeping Lottie in his arms.

"I found her curled up beneath the dessert table, fast asleep," he said softly.

Laura crossed to them. Correcting the awkward angle of one of Lottie's arms, she whispered, "The poor thing will be devastated. She was determined to stay up all night."

"She probably just succumbed to a surfeit of treats. George said she was complaining earlier of an aching tummy. I'm sure she'll be fine in the morning."

As he turned away, gently cradling Lottie's head against his shoulder, Laura was struck by a rush of unbearable tenderness. Would he carry their own children just so? Would he tuck them into their beds and kiss their rosy cheeks before leaving them to their dreams each night?

Laura had no way of knowing if he would. But she had to give him the chance. Her hand brushed her stomach. Not just for his sake, or even her own, but for the sake of their unborn child.

"Sterling," she said, lifting her chin high.

"Yes?" he replied, turning in the doorway.

"After you tuck Lottie in, may I have a word with you in the study?"

Wariness darkened his eyes for the first time that night, giving Laura a pang of regret. But she couldn't afford to waver. If she waited until he came to her bedchamber to try to talk to him, there would be no words.

"Very well. I'll be back shortly."

Laura slipped into the study to wait for him. She hadn't breached Sterling's sanctuary since the evening they'd quarreled over her birthday gift. The fireplace was dark and cold so she lit the lamp sitting on the corner of the desk. She sank down in the wing chair in front of the desk, tapping her slippered feet impatiently.

The moments seemed to crawl by. She finally rose and made a restless circuit of the room. The lamp was doing little to banish the oppressive gloom.

"Perhaps he has some candles tucked away somewhere," she muttered.

She poked around on the bookshelves, but failed to locate anything but two candle stubs and an empty tinderbox. She would simply have to brave the monstrous desk. She intended to perch on the very edge of Sterling's chair, but instead found herself sinking deep into the seductive comfort of its burnished leather.

So this was how it felt to be duke, she thought, surveying the room from an entirely new perspective.

Perhaps when Sterling came in, she should make *him*

sit on the other side of the desk. Then she could lean back in the chair, tuck a cheroot in the corner of her mouth, and explain that she'd had quite enough of his brooding and he was simply going to have to forgive her for being such a ninny.

Laughing softly at her own foolishness, Laura began to search through the desk drawers. Soon the bottom left-hand drawer was her only remaining hope. She tugged on its mahogany knob, but the drawer stuck, as if it hadn't been opened for a while. Gritting her teeth, Laura gave it a mighty yank.

The drawer slid free from its moorings, filling the air with the unmistakable fragrance of orange blossoms.

Chapter 27

I pray that someday you will find it
in your heart to forgive me. . . .

When Sterling pushed open the study door, he found Laura standing behind the desk, clutching a fistful of papers to her breast.

Alarmed by the tears streaming down her cheeks, he started toward her. "What is it, Laura? Did someone say something cruel to you tonight? Because if they did, I swear I'll—"

Before he could reach for her, she slapped the papers against his chest. "You never opened them," she said, her voice low and fierce. "You never read a single word."

As Sterling gazed into her anguished eyes, a killing frost began to creep through his heart. He didn't have to examine the papers to realize what they were. He could smell them.

He gently, but firmly, removed his mother's letters from Laura's grasp and dropped them back into the drawer, pushing it shut with his foot. "She had nothing to say that I cared to hear."

"How can you know that when you refused to listen?" Before Sterling could stop her, Laura had yanked open the drawer again and began to pull out handfuls of his mother's letters. She tossed them on the desk until they were piled so high they started to spill over onto the floor. "Every week for the last six years of her life, this woman poured out her heart to you. The very *least* you could do was listen."

Sterling could feel his temper rising. "I don't wish to discuss this with you, Laura. Not now and not ever."

"Well, that's just too bad, isn't it? Because I'm not some unwanted piece of correspondence you can stuff into a drawer. You can't make me disappear just by ignoring me. If you could, I would have vanished the minute we set foot in this accursed house." Laura tore open one of the letters, her hands shaking violently. "'My dearest son,'" she read.

"Stop it, Laura. You don't want to do this."

She shot him a defiant look. "'Winter is coming and the days are growing shorter, but I begin and end each one of them with thoughts of you. I think of how you might be passing these brittle autumn days and wonder if you are happy.'"

Sterling propped his hip on the edge of the desk and folded his arms over his chest. "If my happiness was of such import to her, I don't think she would have been so eager to sell me to the highest bidder."

Laura broke the seal on another letter. "'My dearest Sterling, I dreamed of you again last night, not as the boy I remember but as a man whose handsome countenance and fine character made my heart thrill with pride.'"

He snorted. "My, that was a dream, wasn't it? Had

she encountered the reality, she would have been keenly disappointed."

Ignoring him, Laura unfolded another letter. "'My darling son,'" she read. "'Please forgive my atrocious penmanship. The laudanum I'm taking to dull the pain seems to befuddle the hand as well as the mind.'"

Sterling straightened. "Don't, Laura," he said softly. "I'm warning you . . ."

Although fresh tears began to trickle down her cheeks, her voice remained ruthlessly steady. "'Don't waste any of your pity on me. It is not such a terrible thing that I should die, only that I should die without seeing your precious face one last time.'"

"Damn it to hell, woman, you haven't the right!" Sterling snatched the letter from her hands, crumpled it into a ball, and hurled it into the fireplace. "She wasn't your mother. She was mine!"

Laura pointed a trembling finger at the hearth. "And those were her last words to you. Are you certain you want to just throw them away as if they were so much garbage?"

"And why not? That's what she did to me, wasn't it?"

"What about your father? I've never been able to understand why you blame her and not him."

"Because she was the one who was supposed to love me!" Sterling roared.

They stared at each other for a long moment, both trembling and breathing hard. Then Sterling strode to the window and stood gazing out at the night, appalled by his lapse of control.

When he spoke again, his voice was crisp and cool. "My father barely tolerated my company. He would have sold me to a band of passing Gypsies for thirty pieces of silver if it would have bought him a bottle of fresh port or another hour at the gaming tables." Sterling slowly turned to face Laura. "He might have been the one who sold me, but she was the one who let him. I can't understand it. And I can't forgive her for something I can't understand."

Laura scooped up a handful of the letters and held them out to him, her expression pleading. "But don't you see? These might help you understand. If you read them, then perhaps you'll be able to comprehend how powerless your father made her feel, how he convinced her that your uncle could give you a future that she never could. Then after the deed was done and she realized it had all been a terrible mistake, your father refused to let her have any contact with you. He tore up the letters she wrote to you before she could post them. He persuaded her that you were better off without her, that she no longer had a place in your life. It took her years to find the courage to write you again."

"My father has been dead for over ten years now. Yet in all that time, she never once tried to see me."

"Would you have received her?" Laura asked, lifting her chin.

"I don't know," he admitted.

"Neither did she. And I don't think she could have borne it if you had turned her away." Laura drew nearer to him. "Even if she had tried to stop your father from letting Granville Harlow adopt you, what power did she have? She had no legal power. She had no moral authority. She was only a woman trapped in a man's world—a world created by men just like you and your father."

"I'm not like my father," Sterling bit off.

Laura drew in a deep breath. "You may be right. According to Diana, you're growing more and more like your uncle every day."

Sterling sank down against the windowsill, letting out a bitter snort of laughter. *"Et tu, Brute?"*

"Your mother made a terrible mistake, Sterling. And she spent the rest of her life paying for it."

"Did she? Or did I?" He raked a hand through his hair. "I've yet to tell another living soul this, but do you know the one thing she did that I'll never forgive?"

Laura shook her head.

"After I realized what she and my father had done and I was getting ready to walk out the door with my uncle that day, she knelt down and held out her arms to me. It was the last time I would ever see her, yet I walked right past her without so much as a word." Although Laura stood only a hand's length from him now, Sterling gazed down at the carpet, refusing to look at her. "I have relived that moment in a thousand dreams, but they always end the same. I walk past her open arms, then I wake up to the sound of her crying." He lifted his head, meeting Laura's eyes squarely. "That's the one thing I will never forgive. *Never.*"

"But who is it you can't forgive, Sterling? Her?" Laura reached up to touch his cheek. "Or yourself?"

He caught her wrist and gently drew her hand away from his face. "I don't really see that it makes any difference."

Leaving her standing there, he returned to the desk and began to rake the letters back into the drawer.

Laura watched him, her face pale and set. "Have you ever asked yourself why you kept your mother's letters if you never intended to read them?"

Steling didn't answer her. He simply scooped up the letters that had fallen to the floor and tossed them carelessly on top of the others.

"The Devil of Devonbrooke might not be able to forgive her," Laura said, "but I'll wager Nicholas Radcliffe could."

"There is no Nicholas Radcliffe. He was nothing but a figment of your imagination."

"Are you so sure about that? Perhaps he was the man you might have become if you had grown up at Arden Manor, confident in your mother's love. Perhaps he was the man you could still be if you could only find some small crumb of mercy in your heart—for her, for yourself." Laura swallowed, fresh tears welling in her eyes. "For me?"

Although Sterling knew instinctively that it was the last time she would swallow her pride and plead for his forgiveness, the last time she would cry for him, he dropped the last of the letters into the drawer and firmly shut it.

Laura closed her eyes. When she opened them again, they were dry. "You broke your mother's heart," she said softly. "I'm not going to let you break mine."

After she was gone, Sterling swung his chair around, no longer able to bear the sight of the door she had just walked out of. His glance fell on the one letter he had missed, the letter lying crumpled and all alone on the fireplace grate.

He ought to light a fire, he thought savagely. Ought to toss the whole lot of them into the flames and watch them burn. Biting off an oath, he reached into the fireplace and plucked the letter from the cold ashes.

He slid open the drawer, determined to seal it away

with the others. But something stayed his hand. It might have been an elusive whiff of orange blossoms or the shock of seeing the deterioration of his mother's gently looping script in the last days of her life.

Sterling's own hands trembled as he slowly uncrumpled the letter, smoothing it on the blotter before him. It was dated January 28, 1815—only five days before his mother had died.

> *My darling son,*
> *Please forgive my atrocious penmanship. The laudanum I'm taking to dull the pain seems to befuddle the hand as well as the mind. Don't waste any of your pity on me. It is not such a terrible thing that I should die, only that I should die without seeing your precious face one last time.*
>
> *My Maker and I made our peace long ago, so I have no fear for my future. I consider myself blessed among women because I had the privilege of being your mother, if only for a few short years.*

His mother's voice was so clear she might have been standing just over his shoulder. Sterling pinched the bridge of his nose, thankful that his uncle had caned all the tears out of him long ago.

> *We never said a proper good-bye and I have no intention of saying one now. Although I have been deprived of your sweet company for much of this life, it is my hope that I can watch over*

*you from heaven. That I can send sunshine to
warm you on a cold winter's day and pass my
unseen hand over your brow when you are weary
and the day is long.*

*Wherever this life may take you, know that I
will follow. And if I can't, then I will send one of
God's angels in my stead.*

Sterling laughed in spite of himself. "You sent me an
angel, all right, Mama. An avenging one."

*As much as it is within my power, I will see to
it that you never walk alone. Not in this life, nor
in the next. My hands may be shaking, but my
heart is steady and it is with that heart that I
make this final promise to you—a promise I will
endeavor to keep through all eternity.*

*Ever your loving mother,
Eleanor Harlow*

Sterling traced his fingertip over her palsied signa-
ture. It was ever so slightly smeared, as if a tear had
fallen, then been hastily blotted away.

"You tried to keep your promise, didn't you?" he
whispered.

Laura had been wrong. He hadn't broken his
mother's heart after all. In the end, her heart had been
strong and true enough to survive all the cruel disap-
pointments of her life—even his indifference.

He gently folded the letter and set it aside. Drawing
in a shaky breath, he reached down and slowly slid
open the drawer. After a moment's hesitation, he chose

a letter from the top of the stack, broke the wax seal, settled back in his chair, and began to read.

When the duke of Devonbrooke came barreling out of the study the next morning, he plowed right over a freckled young maidservant. She tumbled to her backside, letting out a startled shriek and dropping the mop she'd been carrying.

"Oh, Yer Grace, I'm ever so sorry! I didn't know you was in there."

She was struggling to scramble to her feet when he caught her by the arm and hauled her upright. "No need for apologies, dear. I'm the clumsy oaf, not you." He thrust the mop back into her hand and continued on his way, glancing over his shoulder to find her staring after him, her eyes as round as saucers.

Sterling supposed he couldn't blame her. Although he was still garbed in his formal attire from the night before, it was much the worse for wear. His cravat hung loose around his neck and he'd abandoned his tailcoat altogether. He'd raked his fingers through his hair, but that had only made the unruly strands wilder than ever. But he was sure the most unsettling thing about him was his grin. A grin he couldn't quite suppress, no matter how hard he tried. After watching him mope around for weeks, a somber scowl his only expression, was it any wonder the poor girl thought he had lost his wits?

Although it was nearly midmorning, the foyer was deserted and the hall was unnaturally quiet, much as it had been when his uncle still lived. Sterling didn't realize how accustomed he'd grown to the cheerful chaos of Lottie and George quarreling, Dower swearing, and

Cookie singing as she bustled about the kitchens. They must all still be tucked away in their beds, he decided, sleeping off the aftereffects of the ball.

He was halfway up the stairs when he heard Addison's crisp footfalls on the marble floor below. "Your Grace!" the manservant called out, his voice resounding with an uncommon urgency. "I must have a word with you."

"Sorry, Addison. I haven't a minute to spare. I've wasted enough precious time already."

"But, my lord, I—"

"Later," Sterling sang over his shoulder as he strode across the balcony, heading for the east wing.

A snippet from one of his mother's letters echoed through his mind:

My little Laura grows more lovely every day, yet still I find myself fretting over her future. I fear she will not be content with mere affection as long as she hungers for that all-consuming passion which most women dream of, but never find.

Sterling was surprised to find the dogs milling restlessly about in the corridor outside of Laura's door. As he approached, Caliban began to whine while Cerberus lifted his massive foot to paw at the door.

"What is it, lads?" he asked, bewildered by their behavior. "I wouldn't blame her for locking me out, but you're hardly deserving of such a fate."

Sterling tested the knob, only to discover that the door wasn't locked at all. As he pushed it open, the dogs brushed past him and began to circle the room, sniffing at everything they could reach.

As Sterling gazed around the barren chamber in mute disbelief, he was tempted to do the same. It seemed that her scent was all that remained of Laura. The room had been stripped of everything else that had belonged to her, leaving no sign that it had ever been occupied at all.

Except for the folded piece of stationery that rested in the middle of the satin counterpane.

As Sterling reluctantly unfolded it, he was reminded of the first time he had seen his wife's bold handwriting when she had written to inform him of his mother's passing. Although he hadn't admitted it, even then he had found her voice impossible to resist.

> *Dear Sterling,*
> *I have no way of knowing if you'll ever read this or if you'll simply shut it away in the desk drawer where you keep your heart.*
> *There can be no denying that I wronged you. Although I might be willing to continue to pay for my sins for the rest of my life, I don't think it's fair to ask my unborn child to share in that penance.*

As the chamber began to spin, Sterling decided he ought to sit down. But he missed the edge of the bed and ended up sitting heavily on the floor. He leaned his head against the bed, sucking in a deep breath before continuing.

> *It seems we are both to be commended for having done our duty. Since your attentions will no longer be necessary, I have decided to retire to Arden Manor for the duration of my confinement. Being that your sole reason for*

*marrying me was to acquire an heir, I'm assuming
a daughter will be of little interest to you.*

A daughter, he thought, dazedly running a hand over
his mouth. A dark-haired, freckle-faced child who would
bound into his arms and fling her chubby little arms
around his neck. A bright-eyed dreamer still innocent
enough to believe a sleeping prince could be roused with
nothing more than a kiss.

> *I must warn you that should our child be a
> son, I will not allow him to grow up in that
> mausoleum of a house with a cold, unfeeling ogre
> for a father. He will be raised right here at Arden
> Manor where he can be surrounded by sunshine
> and kittens. He will have his irrepressible aunt
> Lottie to adore him and his devoted uncle George
> to teach him how to cheat at whist. Cookie will
> stuff him full of hot cross buns and when he is
> old enough, Dower will teach him how to swear
> like a man.*
> *I will call him Nicholas and I will raise him to
> be the man you might have been had the world
> and your uncle not poisoned your soul.*
> *And no one, not even you, will ever take him
> away from me.*

"That's my girl," Sterling murmured, surprised to
feel moisture on his cheeks.

> *Please do not blame Diana or the servants for
> not alerting you to our departure. As I'm sure
> you know, Dower can be very resourceful when*

he has to be. Despite our differences, I shall
continue to be . . .

> *Your devoted wife,*
> *Laura*

Sterling pressed the letter to his lips. "If I have anything to say about it, you most certainly will be."

He scrambled to his feet and charged out the door, already bellowing for his cousin.

Chapter 28

*But even if that day should never come,
know that I will always love you. . . .*

As Sterling approached the north wing, a most remarkable sound slowed his long, impatient strides. He pressed his ear to the door of Diana's suite, beginning to wonder if lack of sleep wasn't scrambling his senses. But no, there it was again.

Diana was giggling. His staid cousin, whose smile was as rare and precious as a rose blooming in winter, was actually *giggling*. Then came an even more shocking sound—the low, husky murmur of a man's voice.

Sterling was too stunned to think. He simply lifted his foot and kicked open the door.

Diana sprang up in the bed and snatched the sheet to her breasts, her dark hair tumbling loose around her pale shoulders. "How remiss of me," she said with acid politeness. "I must not have heard you knock."

Next to her in the bed, a wild-eyed Thane appeared to be torn between ducking beneath the blankets or making a leap for the window. "Are you armed?"

"Not at the moment," Sterling bit off. "Although I

can ring for Addison to bring me my pistol if you feel it's necessary."

Thane raised a placating hand. "Let's not be so hasty. There's no need to call me out. I can assure you that my intentions toward your cousin are entirely honorable."

Sterling took in the garments scattered all over the floor, the rumpled bedclothes, the telltale flush on his cousin's cheeks. "Yes, I can certainly see that."

"I've been trying to talk him into eloping to Gretna Green," Diana admitted, settling back on the pillows with a feline smile.

"And I won't hear of it!" Thane was so outraged, he seemed to forget all about Sterling. "After all the years you've made me wait, you owe me a proper wedding. I want every gossip and scandalmonger in London to see what a beautiful bride you make."

"But I don't think I can wait another day to become your wife."

As the two of them rubbed noses, all but cooing at one another, Sterling rolled his eyes. "Laura's gone. She's left me."

Thane and Diana exchanged a knowing look.

"I can hardly blame her," Diana said.

Thane shrugged. "It was only a matter of time, wasn't it?"

Exasperated by their lack of alarm, he added, "She's carrying my child."

Diana tilted her head to the side. "Is that why you want her back?"

"No," Sterling snapped, his heart too full to manage anything else.

Diana waved her hands at him. "Then why are you wasting time talking to us? Go after her! Go!"

Sterling winked at his cousin before turning a threatening glower on his best friend. "I suggest the two of you elope, Thane. Because if you're not married by the time I get back, I'm afraid I'll be forced to shoot you."

As he dragged the door shut on its loose hinges, the last thing he saw was Diana's triumphant smile.

Sterling Harlow was going home.

The hedgerows and fences flew past, their glossy leaves and weathered stones gilded by the light of the setting sun. The blue sky was slowly melting into shades of pink and gold, edged with a deepening ribbon of purple.

As the day waned, summer seemed to follow. But Sterling drove his mount through the pockets of chill air so quickly he hardly felt them. He had no reason to fear the coming autumn. He planned to spend it toasting his toes in front of the hearth in the cozy drawing room of Arden Manor, watching his beautiful young wife's belly grow.

If she would have him.

Before he could find out, he had one more stop he had to make.

By the time Sterling reached the churchyard of St. Michael's, the shadows of twilight were falling fast. He looped his horse's reins over the cemetery gate and picked his way through the leaning stones until he reached his mother's grave.

Although Laura couldn't have been home for more

than a few hours, a bouquet of fresh orange blossoms had been tenderly laid at the foot of his mother's stone. Sterling dropped to one knee and brought them to his nose, breathing deeply of their familiar fragrance.

The alabaster angel who stood guard over the grave watched him with knowing eyes. Laying aside the flowers, Sterling gently traced the inscription on the stone with his fingertip.

Eleanor Harlow, Beloved Mother.

He bowed his head, free at last to grieve not only for the years they'd lost to his father's greed and duplicity but also for the years his own pride had cost them. He remembered kneeling in the church at Laura's side, pretending to pray even though he knew no one was listening. Now he knew someone was listening, yet there were no words to express what he so desperately needed to say. So he simply knelt there, his spirit in turmoil and his heart bereft.

Until an invisible hand passed over his brow, stirring his hair even though there was no breeze.

Sterling gasped as a tremendous sense of peace flooded him, filling all the empty places in his heart. When he lifted his head, it seemed no less of a miracle that Laura was standing a few feet away beneath the shadowy branches of an old oak.

He slowly came to his feet. "How did you know I'd come?"

"I didn't," she replied softly.

He nodded toward the gravestone. "I read her letters, you know."

"*All* of them?"

"All three hundred and sixteen."

"She was a very dutiful correspondent."

"That she was." Sterling thrust his hands in his pockets. "She thought I'd lived long enough to learn an important lesson. But I hadn't. Not until now."

"And what lesson was that?" Laura asked, her eyes wary.

"That sometimes people do all the wrong things for all the right reasons."

Laura wasn't quite able to hide the bitterness in her voice. "Is that why you came here? To tell me you've graciously decided to forgive me?"

"No. I came here to beg *you* to forgive *me*."

She shook her head, utterly disbelieving. "For what?"

Sterling moved toward her, no longer able to resist the temptation. "For having too much pride and too little sense. For lying about my reasons for marrying you. For pretending all I wanted from you was an heir, when the truth was I couldn't bear to let you walk out of my life. For making you my wife, but treating you like my mistress." As tears welled in her beautiful brown eyes, he cupped her face in his hands. "For not being willing to admit that your ridiculous little charade was the best thing that ever happened to me and probably saved not only my life but my soul as well." He brushed his lips against her downy cheek, wishing he could kiss away every tear he'd ever made her cry, every tear she would cry for the rest of her life. "But most of all, for not having the courage to tell you how very much I love you."

When she pulled away from him, it was all Sterling could do not to groan aloud. He gazed at her unyielding back, balling his hands into fists to keep from reaching for her again. "If you can't find it in your heart to forgive me, I won't blame you. I know I don't deserve it."

She turned to face him. "You once told me there was one thing you'd never forgive." Before he realized what she was going to do, she opened her arms to him just as his mother had done so long ago.

Without so much as a heartbeat of hesitation, Sterling went into them, gathering her tightly against him and burying his face in the softness of her hair. "Oh, God, Laura, I don't think I could have waited another moment to see you, to touch you. When I saw you standing there, it was like a miracle." He shook his head. "If you hadn't come here to leave the flowers . . ."

"Flowers?" Laura echoed, plainly puzzled. She leaned away from him, still clinging to his arms. "I didn't bring any flowers. I came to wait for you. I thought *you* brought the flowers."

They stared at each other for a stunned moment, then slowly turned as one to look at the bouquet lying on his mother's grave. A warm wind suddenly whipped through the churchyard, sending the delicate blossoms dancing through the air.

Sterling laughed aloud as he swept Laura up in his arms and spun her around in a dizzying circle. "She kept her promise, didn't she? She swore that I would never walk alone."

Laura smiled down at him through her joyful tears. "And you never will, my darling. Because I'll always be here to love you."

As the heavenly fragrance of the orange blossoms wafted all around them, their lips met in a kiss neither one of them would ever forget.

Epilogue

At four years of age, Nicholas Harlow, the future duke of Devonbrooke, could be quite the little devil. Especially when his will was being thwarted by his five-year-old sister. The two of them stood glaring at each other in the yard of the manor, his freckled nose nearly touching her snub one.

"You have to do whatever I say," he proclaimed, raking his dark mane out of his eyes, " 'cause I'm Papa's hair and I'm going to be the duke someday."

Ellie planted her hands on her hips, tossing her golden curls. "Papa's already the duke and Mama doesn't do everything he says. Besides, you might be Papa's hair, but I'm the Incomparable Beauty of the family. Aunt Lottie says so!"

As she stuck her little pink tongue out at him, he stomped his foot and let loose with a blistering stream of profanity. Fortunately, no one could understand him because he'd picked up Dower's Cockney accent along with the naughty words.

"Eleanor! Nicky!"

At the sound of their mama's voice, they both whirled around to find their parents sitting on the back stoop, having witnessed the entire exchange.

Their papa blinked at them, looking as innocent as the plump yellow cat drowsing on the flagstones at his feet. "Cookie just made a fresh batch of crumpets."

The children exchanged an alarmed look, then went sprinting in the opposite direction of the house.

"That was cruel!" Laura said, swatting Sterling on the arm. "Now *you'll* have to eat them."

His wicked grin faded. "Oh. I hadn't thought of that."

Laura sighed with delight as she watched their children romp across the sunlit meadow, two roly-poly mastiff puppies nipping at their heels. "They're just what you always wanted, aren't they? A boy and a girl."

"That's what Nicholas Radcliffe wanted. I wanted half a dozen babes myself." He leered at her. "To begin with."

She gave his hair a teasing tug. "If that's so, my lord, then you'd best be more diligent in your duties."

He drew her into his lap, tenderly nuzzling her throat. "If I were any more diligent, we'd have a dozen babes by now."

Laura twined her arms around his neck. "That would be quite a feat since we've only been married for ⌐six years." She shook her head. "It's hard to believe George will be starting his first year at Cambridge in the fall. And now that Lottie has reached the exalted age of sixteen, she's counting the days until that London season you promised her."

Sterling shuddered. "I dread the thought of unleashing her on those poor helpless cubs. It wouldn't be such a terrifying proposition if the mischievous little hoyden hadn't turned out to be an Incomparable Beauty after all."

"You'll simply have to find her a husband to keep her out of trouble."

"Don't worry," he assured her solemnly. "You'll be the first to know if I find any unsuspecting prospects lying unconscious in the old oak wood."

Laughing, Laura made a halfhearted effort to squirm out of his grip. "You are such a devil!"

"That's what they tell me." Sterling caressed her cheek, the teasing look in his eyes softening to one of helpless wonder. "But that still doesn't explain why God chose to bless me with my very own angel and my own little corner of heaven right here in Hertfordshire."

As he touched his lips to hers in a fierce, yet tender, kiss, the yellow cat butted her head against their entwined ankles, purring madly.

Laura rested her head against Sterling's shoulder. "Your mother once told me that all of Lottie's kittens were descended from a single mama cat. Did you know that?"

"Yes," Sterling said softly, his throat tightening as he reached down to bury his fingers in the cat's plush fur. "I think perhaps I did."

About the Author

USA Today and *Publishers Weekly* bestselling author Teresa Medeiros was recently chosen one of the Top Ten Favorite Romance Authors by *Affaire de Coeur* magazine and won the *Romantic Times* Reviewer's Choice Award for Best Historical Love and Laughter. A former Army brat and a registered nurse, she wrote her first novel at the age of twenty-one and has since gone on to win the hearts of critics and readers alike. The author of thirteen novels, Teresa makes her home in Kentucky with her husband and two cats. Readers can visit her website at www.teresamedeiros.com.

Teresa Medeiros

A Kiss to Remember	___58185-6	$6.50/$9.99 in Canada
The Bride and the Beast	___58183-X	$6.50/$9.99
Charming the Prince	___57502-3	$5.99/$8.99
Lady of Conquest	___58114-7	$6.50/$9.99
Nobody's Darling	___57501-5	$6.50/$9.99
Touch of Enchantment	___57500-7	$6.50/$9.99
Breath of Magic	___56334-3	$5.99/$7.99
Fairest of Them All	___56333-5	$6.50/$9.99
Thief of Hearts	___56332-7	$5.99/$7.99
A Whisper of Roses	___29408-3	$6.50/$9.99
Once an Angel	___29409-1	$6.50/$9.99
Heather and Velvet	___29407-5	$6.50/$9.99
Shadows and Lace	___57623-2	$6.50/$9.99

Please enclose check or money order only, no cash or CODs. Shipping & handling costs: $5.50 U.S. mail, $7.50 UPS. New York and Tennessee residents must remit applicable sales tax. Canadian residents must remit applicable GST and provincial taxes. Please allow 4 – 6 weeks for delivery. All orders are subject to availability. This offer subject to change without notice. Please call 1-800-726-0600 for further information.

Bantam Dell Publishing Group, Inc.
Attn: Customer Service
400 Hahn Road
Westminster, MD 21157

TOTAL AMT	$_____
SHIPPING & HANDLING	$_____
SALES TAX (NY, TN)	$_____
TOTAL ENCLOSED	$_____

Name _____

Address _____

City/State/Zip _____

Daytime Phone (_____) _____